The reviewers are raving about *DAYS OF ATONEMENT*

"His best work to date ... It's so good that you'll see it on the 'Best of 91' prize ballots. You may well see it in the winner's circle."

— *Analog*

"Rousing, vintage Williams!"

— *Kirkus Reviews*

"Williams' longest, most densely realized and successful book to date."

— *Washington Post Book World*

"Williams has written one of the most arresting depictions of a character in recent times."

— *Locus*

"A tightly plotted, hugely complex, but ultimately very satisfying novel."

— *Interzone*

"Williams' most ambitious novel to date combines mystery, hard science, character study, and setting with impressive success ... In overall technical excellence, this proves to be the best book by an increasingly skilled author. It is also an above average portrait of scientists at work. Highly Recommended."

— *Booklist*

Tor books by Walter Jon Williams

Ambassador of Progress
Angel Station
Aristoi (forthcoming)
The Crown Jewels
Elegy for Angels and Dogs
Facets
Hardwired
House of Shards
Knight Moves
Voice of the Whirlwind

DAYS OF ATONEMENT

WALTER JON WILLIAMS

A TOM DOHERTY ASSOCIATES BOOK
NEW YORK

DAYS OF ATONEMENT

Copyright © 1992 by Walter Jon Williams

Cover art by Martin Andrews

A Tor Book
Published by Tom Doherty Associates, Inc.
49 West 24th Street
New York, N.Y. 10010

ISBN: 0-812-50180-2
Library of Congress Catalog Card Number: 90-49029

First edition: February 1991
First mass market printing: January 1992

Printed in the United States of America

0 9 8 7 6 5 4 3 2 1

TO MY PARENTS,
Eva Williams and Walter Ulysses Williams,
I dedicate this story of
a mythical land called New Mexico.

I would like to acknowledge
DETECTIVE DAMON FAY,
Albuquerque Police Department,
and DOUG BEASON,
for their enormous technical assistance.
I am also indebted to Howard Waldrop
for the Straight Poop on exploding gophers.
All credit for accuracy and accomplishment
should be given to them.
Mistakes and blunders, as usual, are mine.

DAYS OF ATONEMENT

ONE

The mayor's secretary was on the phone. "I thought I'd better let you know," she said, "that the last three hundred sixty miners got their pink slips today."

Loren Hawn considered this information for a moment as he watched the flicker of the slow ceiling fan reflected in the bright gold surface of his boxing trophies. In the silence the cool plastic phone made distant ticking sounds in his ear.

"Thanks, Eileen," he said finally. "Does Ed know?"

"The mayor's known for three days."

Anger began a slow simmer in Loren's belly. "God damn, Eileen," he said.

"I would've told you," apologetically, "but he would have known it was me."

"Not your fault, Eileen."

A picture of Eileen flashed suddenly, intensely, into Loren's mind: a smooth-faced, dark-haired woman, her head thrown back, sweat dotting her upper lip. Passion glowing through half-slitted eyes.

An old picture. Years before, when Loren's wife was going through one of her failed pregnancies, Loren had cheated with Eileen.

Years ago, though the memory still glowed in his mind. Guilt coiled about his nerves. So did arousal.

Get thee behind me, he thought.

"See you at church tomorrow?" Eileen said.

"It's a Friday, and the bars will be open late tonight. I'll try to make it, but don't depend on me."

"Sorry, Loren."

Loren scowled at the BUY AMERICAN sign on the opposite wall. THE JOB YOU SAVE, it said in smaller type, MIGHT BE YOUR OWN.

No shit, he thought.

"Does that Republican son of a bitch Edward Trujillo know you're calling me?" he asked.

Eileen laughed. "He hasn't got a clue, Loren."

"Thank you. I hope I see you tomorrow morning."

"Bye."

Loren considered slamming the phone back into its cradle, but it was made of cheap Singapore plastic and probably would have shattered, so he placed it carefully and then, with some deliberation, smashed the walnut desktop with his big fist. Then he stood, adjusted his gun, and walked out of his office.

His secretary's desk was empty, its surface covered with a light film of dust and a growing pile of unanswered mail. She was on vacation and the city budget didn't encompass the hiring of a substitute. Loren was answering only essential mail and went to one of Judge Denver's clerks for his typing.

Wanted posters fluttered in the gentle wind of another overhead fan. The face of a young girl no older than seventeen gazed sadly out at him. WANTED, the poster said, FOR ECO-TERRORISM.

Jesus, Loren thought, he hated the new century.

He knocked on the warped wooden door frame of the assistant chief's office.

"Hey. Pachuco. Qué paso?"

Cipriano Dominguez had his booted feet up on his desk. A window was open to the breeze and the low hum of midafternoon traffic. He looked up from a dog-eared western novel and smiled with big yellow teeth.

"Just improving my mind, jefe. What do you need?"

"They're closing the pit."

"Shit." The smile went away fast. Cipriano closed his book and took his feet off the desk. He put the book on the overflowing shelf behind him.

Cipriano was one of those people who would happily read anything. Thrillers, history, melodrama, biography, westerns, any book that crossed his path. Loren had once found him reading a college-level text on economics—Cipriano hadn't understood any of it, but had read it with the same pleasure he would have got from Agatha Christie.

"Call upstairs and tell the sheriff so he can tell the county guys," Loren said. "Then call the night shift and let them know they're going on at six. I'll get on the radio and let the day shift know they'll be working till after midnight."

"How about the swing shift?"

"They'll figure it out when they come on at four-thirty."

"Okay, Chief." Cipriano reached for the phone.

Loren went out to the front desk and the police radio. The department had once had civilian dispatchers, but there had been cutbacks, and now the desk man had to handle all the calls himself.

Loren told his two patrolling officers that they'd be working an extra shift, then he went downstairs to let Ed Ross, the jailer, know that maybe he'd want to bring in some extra personnel. He went upstairs, then decided he was too angry to sit at his desk for the rest of the day. He walked across the yellowing white tile hallway and boomed out through the glass doors, passed between the copper deco griffins guarding the entrance and then crossed West Plaza to the old town square.

Once—he'd seen the pictures—the plaza had had a neat little white gingerbread bandstand on it, and on Friday and Saturday nights bands from various organizations, the Knights of Columbus or the Mine Workers or the high school, would put on concerts there. The custom had ended during the Depression, when the WPA knocked down the bandstand and put up the white granite Federal Building, the same white federal granite they'd put up everywhere, just as the high school the WPA erected at the same time was the same red brick building they'd built across the entire republic.

There were pieces of the old plaza left, sagging brick sidewalks that had once radiated from the bandstand, and a small Stonehenge of monuments, once scattered across the plaza but now collected in one area opposite Central Avenue. The grass around them was brown now, brown with the drought that had afflicted the area all summer and the three summers previous and had raised fire danger to an extreme high.

Despite the drought, October sang in the air with a pure, cool effervescence, the first tang of autumn. Loren thought of band-tailed pigeon clustering on the high plains south of town, the feel of his shotgun in his hand, dogs rollicking and sniffing up ahead.

He thought of pissed-off miners clustering in bars. Maybe if he was going to be up late tonight, he should go home and take a nap.

Above his head the town's art-deco clock struck one.

An old brass memorial plaque sat at his feet, fixed to a chunk of green copper ore. NEAR THIS SPOT STOOD THE ORIGINAL VILLAGE OF EL PUEBLO DE NUESTRA SEÑORA DE ATOCHA, DESTROYED IN 1824 BY AN ARMY OF SAVAGE REDSKINS. Below, in smaller letters, were the words *Women's Historical Society, 1924*. The anniversary of a bloodbath.

The Apaches had set a range fire, Loren knew, that threatened the copper diggings. When the menfolk ran out to save the wooden mine buildings, the Apaches swarmed over the adobe wall of the town and killed or enslaved every woman and child. The disheartened men, staggered by the scope of their loss, had mostly returned to Mexico. Except, history recorded, for those who went mad, and lived in the wilderness like bears.

Latter-day Indians had objected, Loren knew, to the characterization of "savage redskins." The objections hadn't made much of an impression—the past was still too much of a weight here. Who else but a savage would cut the throats of children in their cradles?

That had been the town's first destruction, but not its last. Long after the Apache wars had been won, in the 1920s, Atocha had been destroyed again, when the copper pit engulfed the town. Atocha had been rebuilt twelve miles to the west, and all the old nineteenth-century town that Loren had seen in photographs, all the neat brick Victorian buildings with their pillars and stained glass, gables and towers and widow's walks, the little identical side-by-side houses that the early Mormon polygamists had built for their wives . . . all had been destroyed.

The city of Atocha had always changed its face when necessary. That was the way it had survived.

The new town, built in the 1920s, was meant to be a wonder, a showplace of modernity. All the buildings fronting the central plaza were faced in art deco, a streamlined assembly of winged radiators and bulbous Flash Gordon cupolas, Bel Geddes speed lines and gondolas from soaring Raymond Leowy zeppelins. Even the Catholic church was streamlined, and the Church of the Apostles of Elohim and the Nazarene, right next to it, was even more extreme, with a pair of bell towers that looked like bottle-nosed rockets about to launch. Atocha, the designers implied, was not afraid of the twentieth century, of the World of Tomorrow. Things could only improve.

It was all shabby now, the polished steel fading into rust, the black and white tile cracking. But how, Loren wondered, could the city resurrect itself a third time? It had survived the Apaches, it had somehow survived the Anaconda, but the Big Strike and the twenty-first century were another matter.

Anger and frustration simmered in his heart. He wasn't doing anyone any good standing here. He decided to go home for a nap.

He was heading for the spread-winged griffins when a chocolate-colored Blazer pulled into one of the parking spaces in front of the building. Loren felt a sour taste in his mouth. This was all he needed.

Two young men in baggy gray suits and dark knit ties got out of the jeep. Both wore gold-rimmed Ray-Bans. One fed the meter while the other waited for Loren to cross the street.

"Excuse me, sir." The man's fair hair was arranged in a flattop haircut. A fringe around the top had been bleached a lighter shade, providing a halo effect. He was thick-necked and well muscled and stood an inch taller than Loren's six feet two. He looked like a Mormon missionary turned professional assassin.

The current look, Loren thought, in company goons.

"Yes?" Loren said.

The man looked at a piece of paper. "Do you know Assistant Chief Dominguez's office? We're here for orientation."

"Ah." A slow smile crept across Loren's features. Maybe this would be fun. "Inside," he said, "past the desk. Corridor on your right, first door on the left."

"Thank you, sir." The man started up the steps.

"Check your guns at the desk," Loren said.

The man hesitated on the top step, then went on. His partner finished with the parking meter, nodded to Loren as he passed, then bounced up the stairs.

Loren noticed the second man's shoes. They were black and had a military shine. As they went by, Loren could see blue sky reflected in the heels. Blue sky, the solemn griffin, Loren's own distorted face with a scowl plain to see.

Loren waited a moment, then went back in the building. The man at the desk, Al Sanchez, was looking at a pair of heavy automatics. Both had custom walnut grips.

"Nice," he said. "Nine-millimeter."

"Berettas?"

Sanchez picked up a gun and squinted at it through dark-rimmed spectacles. "Tanfoglio, it says."

Loren picked one up, sighted it on the picture of the mayor behind the desk. Bang, he thought. "Nice balance." He put the gun down. "Don't see why they don't buy American, though."

Sanchez grinned up at him. "Wanna bet whether they were wearing *anything* made in this country?"

Loren thought about it. Chinese silk suits; Italian shoes, belts, guns; Indian underwear. "Maybe their ties?"

"Maybe. But I bet they're English."

Sanchez put the guns in a drawer. Loren moved down to the corridor. Cipriano had left his door slightly ajar.

"Ames, Iowa, sir." Loren recognized the voice of the man with the flattop.

"You're from Iowa." Cipriano's voice. "And your partner's from North Carolina. Guess you don't have many Spanish people there, huh?"

"No, sir."

"And you've been in town how long?"

"Two days."

Loren grinned. He noticed that Cipriano had cranked his Spanish accent way up. Normally it was almost undetectable.

"Well," Cipriano said, "that's what this orientation is about. So you know how to deal with the local Spanish people." Cipriano cleared his

6

throat. "There are only two things you gotta remember. Two sentences. And you'll get along fine."

"Yes, sir."

"Repeat after me: *Out of the Tchevy, Pedro.*"

There was a moment of surprised silence.

"I said repeat!"

"Out of the Chevy, Pedro." The chorus was a little uneven.

"Not Chevy, it's Tchevy. Let's get the accent right."

"Tchevy."

"From the top."

"Out of the Tchevy, Pedro."

Cipriano barked like a Marine D.I. "Say it like you mean it!"

"OUT OF THE TCHEVY, PEDRO!" In perfect chorus.

"That's good." Cipriano's voice was warm. "That'll get the attention of any Spanish guy you need to talk to. Now here's the other sentence: *Comprende jail, asshole.*"

"Comprende jail, asshole!"

"Like you mean it!"

"COMPRENDE JAIL, ASSHOLE!"

Trying not to laugh out loud, Loren ambled back to the front desk. Sanchez looked at him. "No offense, Chief," he said, "but white people sure are stupid."

"But they're *so* well brought up."

"When I was in the Air Force," Sanchez said, "they kept me busy for a whole day wandering around the base trying to get the sergeant a left-handed monkey wrench."

"And you say *white* people are stupid?"

"Too bad ATL will only let us have these guys for an hour." Sanchez turned meditative. "Those sons of bitches. They think Spanish people are retarded or something, need special treatment. Shit."

Cipriano's voice echoed from his office. "And we're all *Spanish*, okay? Or Hispanic. Latinos are from Cuba or Puerto Rico or someplace. Chicanos are from California. But we're the pure-blooded descendants of Castilian conquerors, and *don't you ever forget it!*"

Cipriano was laying it on a little thick today. Loren hitched up his gun belt. "I'm ten-seven outta here. Gonna rest up for tonight."

"You can rest easy, Chief." Grinning. "Now the ATL guys are here."

Loren left the building, got in his Fury cruiser, and drove down West Plaza to Central. He turned right, then turned left again at the big LDS church, which had its own monument, an obelisk of Utah granite, marking the resettlement of Atocha in the 1870s by Mormons sent at the command of Brigham Young. They had established a small farming community along the Rio Seco in the face of the Apache terror, intended as a way station in case the Saints' simmering disagreements with the federal government forced them to evacuate to Mexico. Before long, the Mormons had been submerged by miners brought in by the silver and gold strikes, but they were still a powerful presence.

Estes Street was shaded by old Japanese elms, a contrasting green that looked startling among the dusty brown New Mexico hills. The trees' shadows cast glowing, shifting patterns on the worn, patched cement of the street. Too many of the houses had old FOR SALE signs sitting on overgrown lawns. Loren drove past the gray-white Church of Christ—a converted private home— and then, a block later, into his own driveway. The old rusting carport, with its trellises of fading morning glorys, was empty. Loren parked to one side of the wide drive, leaving room for Debra's Taurus in the carport. His yard was mostly bare southwestern earth, with native grasses, yuccas growing against the side of the house, and a decorative ocotillo. A rush of happiness welled up in him.

Querencia. That was the Spanish word: home-for-the-heart. The place where he could rest.

The house smelled of the morning's breakfast bacon. Loren opened a window, then headed for the bedroom and took off his gun belt and shoes. He hung the gun belt on a prong of his gun rack, next to his Heym shotgun and Russian hunting rifle, and then stretched out on the bed.

He was very good at falling asleep on command.

When he woke he knew that things had changed, that Debra had come from her part-time job at the library—she would have gone full-time after the girls left grade school, but the town couldn't afford full-time librarians. She had quietly started work in the kitchen. He rose from the bed and padded in stocking feet through the living room. He paused in the kitchen door.

Debra was a strong-boned woman almost six feet tall. She was efficiently chopping up celery for turkey stuffing, hampered slightly by straight straw-colored bangs that hung in her eyes.

At the sight of her a rush of tenderness sailed through Loren. At some point in his mid-twenties it had occurred to him, with something of the force of revelation, that Debra was the woman for him, that the tall, hunch-shouldered girl two grades behind him in high school who had gone away to college and returned a straight-backed schoolteacher was the person with whom he wanted to spend his life. After two years of more or less relentless pursuit, she'd finally agreed.

He'd had a reputation for wildness to live down before she capitulated, and live it down he somehow did, for Debra's sake. Not without backsliding—the memory of the times he'd cheated on her went through him in a weak-kneed, giddy wave, warmed by the blazing image of Eileen—but since the birth of their elder daughter, Loren's commitment had stayed firm, absolutely firm, without a single fling with the wife of a colleague, without a visit to Connie Duvauchelle's that wasn't in the line of Loren's business.

Perhaps it was Katrina's birth that had saved the marriage. She had come late—Debra was thirty-six—after a long series of miscarriages and a newly developed operation that had made it possible for Debra to carry to term.

But now the marriage was solid. Perfect. And so were his daughters.

A steel wall of protectiveness fell about his mind. There was so much that could go wrong here—in his job he saw that more than anyone. He would guard his marriage, his daughters, his community. He would help make Atocha a *nice place*.

He promised himself that every day.

"Didn't expect to see you." Debra hadn't turned to Loren, just stared severely at the celery through rimless schoolmarm spectacles.

"I'm resting up for tonight. They laid off everyone at the Atocha pit."

Debra paused on her chopping. She put her knife aside and wiped her hands on her apron. "I should call Linda."

Linda was married to Debra's brother, who was a miner. Debra reached for the telephone.

"If I see him tonight," Loren said, "I'll send him home."

Debra looked at him, one hand on the phone. "Will I see *you?*"

"Probably not."

She turned toward the fridge. "Let me make you a sandwich."

"I can get something at the Sunshine."

"Just in case."

The refrigerator door had a poster on it with a view of the round blue Earth from space. Large white letters commanded him to GUARD THE PLANET! One of his daughters had put it up.

Debra got out an elk steak left over from dinner last night. Loren had shot the elk the previous autumn with his Russian military-surplus rifle.

"Mrs. Trujillo called. She was hoping Kelly could baby-sit tomorrow night."

"No."

She looked baffled. "Why not, Loren?"

"Because she can't."

"She baby-sits for everyone else."

Loren spoke through clenched teeth. "Not for the mayor. Never."

"It would help you at City Hall."

"I don't need that kind of help."

Debra turned back to the elk steak. With precise, economical moves, she began slicing it.

"This isn't just political, is it? I wish you'd explain. I never know what to tell Kelly."

He sighed. "It wouldn't be a good idea."

She made two sandwiches in silence and wrapped them in a Baggie, then put the Baggie and an orange in a paper sack along with a can of grape soda. Loren put on his shoes and gun, then carried the sack to the Fury and backed out of the driveway. He opened the can of soda and drove one-handed as he drank. A towheaded kid on a bicycle, one of the Adams sisters, was flinging copies of the *Copper Country Weekly* onto front lawns. Loren waved at the girl as he passed, and in answer she stared at him as if he were a stranger.

Somehow that nettled him. He pressed the accelerator and the Fury's engine grumbled as it took him down the street at thirty past the limit.

He wondered about the headline on the *Weekly*. Probably some kind of puff piece on economic development from the mayor's office. The mayor had undoubtedly kept the one important piece of news from the paper as well as from everyone else.

By the time the paper came out next week, the headline would be optimistic again. ATOCHA RIDES THE STORM, something like that. Edward Trujillo would come up with some way to turn the mine closure into a blessing in disguise. He was good at that.

West Plaza was one-way, so to get back to his parking place Loren stayed on Estes as he crossed Central, then put on the turn signal to go right, past the Methodist church, onto Railroad.

In the wink of an eye the sleek silver maglev train moved across his path and then was gone, leaving only the lingering impression of the gray and red ATL logo burned onto Loren's retinas. The station was only a quarter mile away, but the maglev was already going at least eighty, moving in total silence with its rubber wheels a precise four centimeters above the rails.

Probably no one was aboard. The computer-operated train kept its schedule whether there were passengers or not.

The future has arrived, Loren thought. A train with no passengers shuttling over a twenty-five-mile length of track at two hundred miles per hour.

Loren made his turn, passing the old Spanish-style Santa Fe passenger depot. A chocolate-colored Blazer with its ATL issue of two young Anglo men in Ray-Bans drove past heading the other way, then made an illegal U-turn and fell into place behind Loren.

Practicing their tailing skills. What idiots.

Loren watched them in his rear view mirror and considered, then dismissed, pulling them over and handing them a ticket.

Serve them right if he did, though.

He passed the Southern Baptist Assembly and turned right onto West Plaza. The deco Chamber of Commerce, topped by a kind of fan-shaped stylized winged radiator, was followed by the deco City-County Building, with its restored clock tower and the old-fashioned big receiver dish for the LAWSAT. Loren pulled into his parking space. The ATL jeep cruised past, its passengers carefully not looking at him. Loren got out of the car and walked through the police entrance.

Edward Trujillo, the mayor, stood on the yellowing white tile of the foyer talking to Cipriano Dominguez. Al Sanchez was off somewhere; the front desk was unoccupied. Trujillo was a short man, his back longer than his legs. He had carefully styled hair and a practiced sunny manner. He wore a beige jacket and a turquoise and silver string tie.

It didn't pay to look too formal in a place like Atocha.

Trujillo gave Loren a smile white as a movie star's. He shook hands. "I came down to see you, Loren. I was wondering where you were."

"I was at home taking a nap."

The shadow of a frown crossed Trujillo's face. "I expect to find city officials in their offices during daylight hours."

"Normally I would be, but I'll have to be up late tonight, dragging drunken, unemployed miners to jail. You know. The ones you've known about for days but didn't tell me about."

Trujillo reddened. Loren could see an amused but well-behaved gleam in Cipriano's eyes.

"I was going to tell you this afternoon."

"Right. After half my men had got my permission to go off hunting this weekend, or got extra leave for the Days of Atonement. There could be a riot on the City Line and I couldn't do anything about it."

Trujillo mentally processed the consequences of a riot on the Line, then dismissed them. Out of his jurisdiction.

"I was told in confidence," he said, "so that I could make preparations."

"What preparations are those? A press release maybe? If I didn't have a few sources in Riga Brothers myself"—protecting Eileen—"I wouldn't be able to keep the peace tonight."

"I have to consider all manner of consequences—"

"God damn it, Ed, so do I!"

Loren glared at Trujillo for a moment, anger burning in his throat. Trujillo cleared his throat and took a half-step back.

"I can see that you're upset. Maybe if I were police chief I'd feel the same. But I was told in confidence, and I had a lot of preparations to make. Our whole city is going to be changed by this. We've got to be ready with alternatives."

Loren looked at Trujillo in amazement. "Alternatives? *What* alternatives? There aren't any goddamned alternatives!"

"There are always alternatives, Loren. You just have to know how to find them."

Trujillo bounced away in apparent good cheer. Loren looked at Cipriano.

"He's awful happy, considering his town's tax base just went to hell again."

Cipriano shrugged. "Shit, Chief. Atocha's always been a company town. The way I figure it, all that's happened is that the company's changed."

Loren snorted. "ATL? It has not exactly come to my attention that Advanced Technology Laboratories fucking *wants* this town."

Cipriano chewed on that one for a moment. Loren started walking for his office, then hesitated. He turned back to Cipriano.

"Pachuco, have you ever wondered why William Patience lets you make idiots out of his new men?"

The assistant chief grinned. "'Cause he's a good sport, jefe?"

"Patience never struck me as much of a sport."

"Me, either. You're right, there. Maybe he does it for the same reason Sanchez's sergeant sent him off for a left-handed monkey wrench. Some kind of initiation thing."

Loren nodded. "Maybe. But I think they can do their own initiations without our help."

"Okay, jefe. I give up. What's your theory?"

"'Cause they don't give a shit what we do," Loren said. "We're a bunch of small-town rubes, and nothing we do matters. So they let us make fools out of them because it keeps us amused, and back in their burb they can sneer at us for being hicks."

Cipriano seemed offended for a moment, then dubious. "I dunno, Chief."

"That's my working hypothesis, anyway."

"I dunno."

"For what it's worth."

Loren went into his office and sat in his leather chair and stared at the pale green walls. Distorted images of the ceiling fan rotated slowly in the gold surface of his old boxing trophies. His framed Certificate of Achievement from the American Association of Police Chiefs needed dusting.

He remembered that he'd left his sandwiches in the hot car.

Sanchez knocked, then entered. "Got a message from the DEA on the LAWSAT receiver," he said. "There's supposed to be a shipment of drugs coming up from Mexico today or tomorrow."

"Great. Just what we need."

"White late-model Chevrolet camper pickup, U-Haul trailer, two Mexican nationals. Supposed to be keeping to the back roads."

"That's us," Loren sighed. "Back roads our specialty."

"Armed and dangerous."

"Natch. Three UZIs per Mexican. What's supposed to be in the trailer?"

Sanchez looked at the printout. "All designer stuff. Riptide, black lightning, love beads."

"Whatever happened to potoguaya?" Loren wondered, then sighed. "Put it out on the radio."

Sanchez grinned. "I'll get the word out."

Loren's stomach growled. He thought about his sandwiches. Maybe he'd just eat the orange.

He looked down at his desk calendar. *Yom Kippur*, it said over today's date. (*Begins at sunset.*) Loren had put a little red tick mark against each of the seven days following. Jews had one Day of Atonement, but as a result of a church meeting in 1831 Loren was compelled to acknowledge seven.

That meeting took place in Palmyra, New York, where a thirty-one-year-old Pennsylvanian, Samuel Catton, had gone to hear the preaching of Joseph Smith. (Mormon historians claimed that Catton had briefly been appointed apostle in the Church of Christ, as the LDS was then known, but Catton's followers denied it.) At that meeting, Catton found himself sitting next to a quiet, eagle-eyed, smooth-faced gentleman in gray broadcloth, a man who led him away from the teachings of the false prophet Smith and took him on a tour of the universe. He was known to Catton's followers as the Master in Gray, though Joseph Smith later identified him simply as Satan. Among the *Authorized Revelations* written by Samuel Catton were the commandments to return to the Jewish sabbath and other holy days, though with a few improvements.

Catton was preferred over Smith by those who thought their prophets should be grave and serious. Smith laughed and joked, and stripped off his coat and wrestled any challenger; he married around fifty women, including some already married to his closest friends, and got together with those same friends for nights of drinking beer and wine—Catton did none of these things, nor was ever accused of them. As a consequence of his rectitude the Jewish Day of Atonement was multiplied by a factor of seven: the Holy Church of the Apostles of Elohim and the Nazarene contemplated their sins for a whole week.

Anything worth doing, the Apostles figured, was worth doing right.

Loren, looking at the week of red tick marks spreading out before him, decided to go to the car and get his sandwiches. Might as well enjoy a sensual indulgence while it was still possible.

T W O

THE 41 CHURCHES OF ATOCHA WELCOME YOU. The sign stood between Atocha proper and the long strip of bars and clubs just over the city-county line. The forty-one churches in question had kept the city of Atocha dry since 1919, but the county allowed liquor sales by the drink—package sales were still illegal—and the miles of dusty, hilly road between Atocha and the copper pit were lined with places where miners could drink away their paychecks before they ever got them home. The city and county, by long-standing agreement, had always shared responsibility for policing the Line—the sheriff's posse was spread too thin to be effective here.

Loren pulled off the road at an open gate and followed a half-mile dirt driveway. Behind an eight-foot-high Cyclone fence was a house trailer with a sliding glass window in it. Loren waited in line behind an old blue GMC pickup that had a bumper sticker that read REDUCE WELFARE COSTS. WORK FOR A LIVING. The driver, a woman in a checked shirt and kerchief, bought two six-packs of Coors, and then Loren pulled up to the window.

"Hi, Loren."

"Hi, Maddy."

"What can I get for you?"

Maddy Dominguez was a round-faced, white-haired woman

married to one of Cipriano's cousins. She ran the City Line's largest bootlegging operation.

"They've closed the Atocha pit," Loren said.

Maddy's grin turned sour. "God damn," Maddy said. "Sallie's going to have to move in with me again." Sallie was her younger son.

"I want you to close up for the weekend," Loren said. "I'm gonna have enough trouble policing the bars." ·

Maddy looked dubious. "I don't know if I want to do that, Loren. The weekend's when I do most of my business."

"I need you to close, Maddy. Rubén's closing. So is Kevin."

"What about Connie Duvauchelle?"

"People don't go to Connie's to get drunk."

"Rubén and Kevin don't do my volume. I'd like to oblige, Loren, but if Sallie's going to be needing help, I've got to keep open."

Loren let his gaze settle on her. "I'm not asking, Maddy."

Her reply was immediate and angry. "Dammit, Loren. What am I paying you for?"

Loren was out of the Fury in an instant, big hands closing on the window frame, his head and shoulders thrusting through. Maddy jumped back, eyes wide in fright. Through his anger Loren saw she was dressed in a red housecoat and blue carpet slippers.

"I just saw you make an illegal beverage sale," Loren said. The flimsy aluminum window frame bent under his weight as he leaned inward. "I can arrest you for that. And after what I've seen with my own two eyes, I've got grounds to kick down your door, search your place, and confiscate your stock."

Maddy's fear turned to outrage. "My stock's worth fifteen grand!"

"Then if you want to keep it you'd better close down till Monday, hadn't you?" Loren said. "That's my working hypothesis, anyway."

"Okay." Quickly. "I'll close."

Loren stared at her for a long moment, then turned away. "See you in church," he said. He returned to his car and drove down the dirt drive. He waited by the gate till he saw Maddy, in her housecoat and an oversize pair of cowboy boots, clumping down the dusty drive to close the gate.

A convoy of trucks went past, full of fire fighters wearing hard hats and carrying saws and spades. Many of them were Apache. Another fire in the national forest, Loren thought. There had been dozens of them in this year of drought.

Some timber companies, he'd heard, were blaming eco-terrorists. Several of the fires had started in areas where lumbering was authorized, and the companies claimed the monkeywrenchers were burning as much of the wood as possible before it could be harvested.

Loren didn't think he quite believed it. He had been living in a company town too long to entirely believe what a company was going to say about its opposition.

He pulled onto the highway and headed toward the pit. Bleached white tailings piles occupied the whole of the eastern horizon. The day shift would be ending in about ten minutes. Loren figured the miners wouldn't get juiced enough to start any trouble for at least an hour after that. Then he'd be busy till the bars closed at two.

He'd eaten a sandwich and the orange, but he was still hungry.

He decided he didn't want to see the pit. It would be too depressing. He pulled into the driveway for the UFO landing field that had been built out on the Figueracion Ranch in '99, backed onto the highway heading west, and went back into town. Maybe he'd get something to eat at the Sunshine.

Just past the sign from the forty-one churches was a big Riga Brothers billboard that showed a cheerful guy in a flannel shirt and a hard hat tossing the motorists a cheery salute. THIS IS COPPER COUNTRY! the sign said.

Not anymore, Loren thought.

His anger simmered on.

He remembered the first time he realized how Atocha County really worked. He'd heard about it, of course, all his life, the supposed payoffs from Connie Duvauchelle and what the newspapers called "the liquor interests," the network of complicated obligations, the graft . . . The police department and sheriff's office were a steady job with good health and retirement plans, but (perhaps as a consequence) they were also some of the last political patronage jobs in the county—no civil service tests, no background checks, and only Democrats need apply.

Loren was a Democrat. His father was an official of the miners' union, which counted, and his parents always showed up at precinct meetings, which counted even more.

Within a week of his arrival, the shine not yet off his seven-pointed APD star, the chief sent him to Luis Figueracion's office for a package.

The Figueracion Ranch was the largest in the county, and half of it was later sold to ATL at about three times its real value—the price, everyone knew, of doing business in Atocha County. The head of the Figueracion clan had been chief patrón of the county for as long as there had *been* a county, the dispenser of favors and political office—if business needed doing, it was often as not a Figueracion who saw it was done.

Figueracion's office was a musty old storefront next to a fruit and vegetable stand, its flaking tin walls decorated with yellowing election posters for every Democratic presidential candidate from FDR on. There were also pictures of the teenage Luis shaking hands with Roosevelt himself. Loren didn't see Figueracion himself that first trip—it was one of his clerks, another cousin of Cipriano Dominguez, who handed him the unsealed manila envelope.

Loren looked into the envelope on his way back to the station and found it full of crisp new money.

He remembered the wave of surprise that went through him, that this was how it was done. He wasn't surprised that there was money wandering from hand to hand in this way—a lifetime of rumor had prepared him for that—but what astonished him was that he had actually been made the chief's bagman with less than a week on the job.

But that had been Chief Odell's way, to get a young officer in on the corruption as soon as possible and thereby assure his own safety. With the entire department on the take, all of them had a stake in keeping things as they were. And that was—qué no?—the job of the police department in the first place.

Later that day, Loren found an unmarked white envelope in his locker. In it was a ten-dollar bill, his share.

The take, he discovered, had been settled at some point in the 1930s and never revised. It ran from ten dollars each week for the patrolmen all the way to twenty-five dollars for the chief. Probably in the thirties it had been a lot of money, but by the time Loren joined, all it amounted to was pocket change. There were other benefits available, money that could arrive from Figueracion's office in the event of a medical catastrophe, or interest-free loans to be paid back out of the weekly take; when Loren, with a sergeant's weekly supplement of fifteen dollars, got married and bought a house, he had been able to afford a substantial down payment courtesy of the Democratic chairman, and was left out of the graft tree till he paid it off.

Still, the chief purpose of the money was symbolic. Those who broke the law had to pay, pay one way or another. The weekly cash transaction demonstrated that the lawbreakers knew they had done wrong and were willing to atone.

Atonement was something Loren believed in.

Loren told himself that the graft also built morale and comradeship among the police. They had a secret they shared among themselves—a bond, even if it was a bond that consisted of a shared sin.

Sometimes, however, the lawbreakers forgot what the money meant, thought it actually bought the law instead of simply permitting a grudging toleration of their activities. One of the reasons Loren admired Connie Duvauchelle was that she had done business in the county for over fifty years and had never once stepped out of bounds, never had to be reminded who was really in charge. Maddy had made a tactless remark, and it had been Loren's job to make her regret it.

He hadn't really been angry, he thought. He'd just been pretending. Just to show her who was boss.

Still, it was usually the boss that paid the employees. An uncomfortable thought.

One Loren was determined to ignore.

There was a five-ton truck outside the Sunshine filled with sawn-off elk antlers. The antlers were in their velvet stage, covered with soft-furred flesh and spots of blood.

It was not a sight to improve Loren's temper.

Loren opened the avocado-green deco door and walked to the

counter along lineoleum worn in spots to the wood floor underneath. Two Korean vampires in suits and ties sat at a back booth talking to Sam Torrey, the man who ran the elk ranch south of town. Loren looked for blood spots and saw flecks on one white collar. Sitting at the counter was Len Armistead, a barrel-chested, bearded man who ran a service station on the west side, and two garrulous old codgers, Bob Sandoval and Mark Byrne, retired miners living on their Riga Brothers pensions. Both wore checked shirts, gimme caps perched back on thinning white hair, and had probably been boozing since noon.

Loren sat next to Armistead. Coover, the Sunshine's owner, poured Loren a cup of coffee without being asked. Loren looked at the coffee and saw it had oily scum riding on top.

The local groundwater was awful, filtered as it was through a couple centuries' worth of mine tailings. Most people had water filters or bought bottled water.

Coover felt free to serve it to his customers.

Loren looked at Armistead's plate and saw the last of chicken fried steak with cream gravy. It had been Friday's special for as long as he could remember.

"How is it?" he asked.

Armistead frowned at his plate. "'Bout what I expected," he said.

Loren looked at Coover. "I'll have the special." He looked over his shoulder at the Koreans. "And some blood for the vampires."

Coover smiled thinly and wrote the order down on his pad.

Sam Torrey's elk ranch was one of the county's few successful new businesses. Torrey had discovered that traditional Chinese and Korean medicine prescribed powdered elk horn to return potency to aging males. Newly grown autumn velvet antlers were particularly useful, supposedly because they were loaded with hormones. Some Chinese and Koreans went so far as to fly to New Mexico to drink the blood that gouted from the elks' spongy skulls after the horns were sawn off—supposedly the hormone-enriched blood was better than the powdered horns themselves.

The local chapter of the Eco-Alliance was up in arms about the country selling off its natural resources in order to cater to some bizarre Asian obsession with virility. Hunters like Loren weren't wild about it, either, and also didn't think much of the game ranch's other purpose, which was to provide hunting trophies—at eleven thousand dollars for the larger racks of antlers—to any sorry, incompetent, well-heeled hunter who could stomach the notion of walking into a pen and shooting a helpless tame animal.

Loren looked at the Koreans again. Maybe they'd be testing their newfound potency at Connie Duvauchelle's tonight.

"You gonna get an elk this year?" he asked Armistead.

"Got my permit." Armistead dabbed cream gravy from his mustache. "Gonna go out with Pooley and get him a bear tomorrow."

He pronounced it *b'ar*. Of course.

"Everybody in this town's got a bear but him," Armistead went on. "He's feelin' left out." Pooley was his nephew.

"Good luck," Loren said.

"He figures to make a rug out of it."

"It'll cost him a couple thousand, if he wants the head and all."

"I think he'll settle for the hide." Armistead looked at his coffee, screwed up his face, then put the coffee down. "How 'bout you?"

"I've got my permit, too."

"Still gonna use that fancy Russian gun?"

"The Dragunov? Yeah. I like it. The Russians do good with small arms."

The Dragunov had been Loren's extravagance of the previous year. The Russians had begun to sell surplus military equipment in the West, and the Dragunov SVD was supposed to be the world's best sniper rifle. He'd replaced the Russian PSO-1 4x military scope with better optics by Fujinon, and last autumn had shot an elk dead at six hundred yards.

"It's a good gun," he said.

Armistead rose from his stool and pulled his gimme cap down over his eyes. "Reckon I'd better push on."

"See you later."

"See you."

Loren looked out through the spotted plate-glass window. His stomach rumbled. The Sunshine had the world's worst food, but it was on Central across from the town plaza, and from the counter Loren could keep an eye on what was happening at police headquarters. And Coover was a honcho in the Democratic Party—there was that to consider, too.

"It's because that part of the country was too poor to afford regular churches," said Byrne, one of the old-timers farther down the counter. He held a hand-rolled cigarette between two yellowed fingers. "That's why the Apostles and the Mormons both sprang up there."

"Yeah."

"They had all kinds of stuff going on up there. Joseph Smith's granduncle started a religion, you know that?"

"Nope."

Loren, listening to this, asked the Lord for patience. Byrne, who had a colossal shrew for a wife, spent a lot of his time in the town library, and had absorbed tons of facts that he was happy to show off to anyone close enough to be victimized, and do so with an aggression he plainly borrowed from his wife.

"Religion was sort of the family business, I guess. And Samuel Catton, who started the Apostles, nobody even knew who his father was. But they both made good. They both figured out that the way to start a new religion was to preach to all the poor people that none of the other religions wanted."

"Jesus did that."

"Exactly my point!" Byrne was gleeful. "Poor people want religion as much as anybody. And if you get enough of them putting their pennies in the collection plate, you can live pretty damn well. That's why there are all these American churches trying so hard for converts in South America, and so on."

"And that Joseph Smith had a lotta wives, too."

"You get poor people hoping, you can do anything you want with them. Look at Jim Jones, who killed all those people in Surinam."

"Guinea."

"Guyana. That's the place."

"Guinea."

Loren decided he'd had enough. He put down his cup and looked at Byrne. "What about God?" he said.

Byrne seemed surprised. "What about him?"

"What if God decides to start a new religion? Suppose God decides that all the other religions are on the wrong path, and that they're neglecting the people, and he *tells* someone to start a new ministry?"

Byrne grinned with tobacco-stained teeth. He was having a good time. "Well, Chief." He began rolling a new cigarette. "I figure if God tells someone to start a new religion, why don't he tell a bunch of other people to believe in it?"

"What if he *does?*" Loren argued. "Samuel Catton was the leader of the Apostles, but he didn't go it alone. He had twelve deacons who received the revelation right along with him."

"A revelation that included support for the Anti-Masons and opposition to the Bank of the United States, right?"

Coover appeared with Loren's steak. He gave an irritated glance at Byrne and Sandoval. "Don't you have anything better to do than argue about people's religion?" he demanded.

"I'm not arguing about nothing, Coov. I'm talking about historical fact. You can go down to the library and read it yourself."

"The Masons were committing murders and smashing printing presses, and the bank was oppressing the people," Loren said.

Byrne lit his cigarette and puffed. "Well, there ain't no Bank of the United States no more, not since the Apostles helped elect Andy Jackson. And the Masons aren't doing much of anything these days but putting on silly hats and getting drunk down at the Shrine Temple. I'm a 32nd-degree Scottish rite myself, and if we were conspiring to oppress people anymore, I'd know about it. So why don't you disband your religion and let people get drunk in the city limits instead of having to go west, hey?"

"Go west" was Atocha dialect for going past the city limits for a bottle.

"The ministry is ongoing," Loren said, "supported by the force of continuing revelation."

"What I wanna know," said Bob Sandoval, "is which of these revelations we're supposed to believe in." He wasn't wearing his upper plate and his words were slurred by more than alcohol. "God told one thing to Joseph Smith and something else to Sam Catton, so which one do we believe in?"

"They both agreed on the subject of the Masons," Byrne said.

Loren looked over one shoulder to make sure that no Mormons had come in while they were talking. None were in sight. "I don't say anything about the LDS," said Loren, "but my working hypothesis is that I wouldn't choose a religion whose founder went and got himself lynched."

"Like Jesus Christ?" Byrne asked.

Loren was speechless. Sandoval laughed at his expression.

"I don't wanna say anything about you guys or the Mormons," he said, "but I'm a Catholic, and we say you're both cults."

Loren glared at him. "You don't want me to tell you what my religion says about the Pope."

"Loren," said Coover, "that nice steak of yours is getting cold."

"One of the great minds of the sixteenth century," Loren said.

Sandoval looked offended. Byrne turned to him. "I'm a Lutheran," he said. "Am I a cultist, too?"

"You're okay, ése," Sandoval said. "You're just a heretic."

He and Byrne cackled. Byrne took a flask out of his pocket and added whiskey to their coffee cups.

"Eat your steak, Loren," said Coover. He turned to the two old men. "Can't you talk about politics like everyone else?"

"Sure," Byrne said. His eyes were bright. "When are Luis Figueracion and the rest of you Democrats gonna do something right for a change and get somebody elected?"

"Now, Mark," said Coover.

Loren looked at the congealing gravy that concealed the overdone breaded meat and reconstituted potatoes. Watery pale green peas from out of a can floated randomly on the surface. He jabbed a fork into the steak with a vicious gesture, then picked up his knife and started to saw. His appetite was long gone.

"Nobody even knows what the Democrats stand for," Sandoval said. "Letting those fucking Japanese and wetback Chilote assholes steal our work, maybe."

"You know we tried to keep foreign copper out," Coover said.

"I don't hear nothing but words, ése."

Loren's jaws worked at tough, overdone meat and scorched breading. He'd listened to these kinds of conversation all his life and could gratefully spend his remaining years without hearing another one. A couple drunken old geezers, he thought, telling God and everybody else what to do. American copper production was dying because it couldn't compete with the combination of South American peon labor and efficient West German industrial smelters, and there wasn't much a local Democratic Party chairman could do about it.

Sandoval and Byrne jabbered on.

Taxpayers, Loren thought. Voters.

He took a forkful of thick, dry reconstituted potatoes and looked at them and tried to smile, the way a public official should.

It was lucky, he figured, that his job was an appointed one.

For most of Loren's life the western horizon had stayed bright long after sunset. The lights of the Atocha pit burned through the night hours as the miners worked their late shifts, and the neon signs of the City Line burned right along with them. When the wind was easterly you could hear a continual moaning, like ten thousand distant flute players all holding the same low note, the sound of all the giant trucks rolling out of the pit on tires twelve feet high. Now the pit was dark and silent and the Line was on fire.

The first call came at six-thirty, when two female ten-eighteens, meaning drunks, went after each other in the parking lot of the Geronimo, a classic 1950s roadhouse featuring a neon Indian in a Plains warbonnet that the real Geronimo wouldn't have been caught dead in. The two women battled it out while their husbands staggered around beerily and then got into a fight themselves over the best way of putting a stop to it.

The Line was no stranger to violence. Loren remembered midnight smokers after he'd joined the force: a bar—since burned down—called the Ringside, with a small boxing ring in the back room, where Loren and some other cops would each be paid $150 for squaring off against some hard-timer furloughed from the state penitentiary for the one event.

The ring was only fifteen feet across, too small to give the fighters much maneuvering room, and Loren hated it—he was a boxer, not a brawler, and the close confines gave the advantage to the latter. In the Army his style had been distance-oriented, snapping out with his long left arm to keep his opponents at a distance, then going in with the right when they got impatient or tired and tried to charge him. He'd developed a way of twisting his punches at the moment of impact, ripping open his enemies' faces with the gloves, spraying blood into the delighted front row of the audience . . . he had liked that, found a brutal, joyous satisfaction in the way he could cut up an opponent and keep himself safe. The satisfaction lasted until his second title defense, when he ran into the hammerhand right of a nineteen-year-old private from Detroit, and went down for the count in the forty-first second of round one.

There was no satisfaction to be had in the small ring in the old Atocha bar. He hated the advantage it gave to the tattooed, muscular cons with the wispy prison mustaches who came into the ring smiling around their mouthpieces because they'd finally got a chance to hurt a cop and get away with it. His first fight was a one-and-a-half-round slugfest, a hateful, vicious fight, the two windmilling each other at close range until Loren got lucky and flattened his opponent with an instinctive right cross that only God could have foreseen. Because he hated it, hated the little ring and the smell of beer, hated every second of sweating, bruising, merciless combat, Loren spent hours at the Ringside working on footwork, on sidestepping and feinting and bobbing, anything to duck those heavyweight bruisers with their head-down charges and short, sharp flurries to the body that were often as not followed by an elbow to the teeth or a head butt to the face. He didn't want to quit—the Ringside faithful were usually members of the Atocha establishment and Democratic Party faithful from outside the county, and Loren wanted to use the smokers to gain himself a name among people who could help him later. Loren's footwork got far better than it had been in his prime. And hate fueled his punches, hate for the big shots at ringside and the con-boss fighters with their gold teeth and scarred faces.

Because of the hatred, he'd never lost. And at some point in each fight he always transcended the hatred, found it turning to joy—a mean-spirited joy, perhaps, but joy nonetheless. And he found, suddenly, that he knew things, knew what the other fighter was going to do before he did it, knew, even if his eyes were swollen shut or if he was blinded by sweat or blood, just where his opponents were and how they were standing. And just how to take advantage of it, how to put them off balance and destroy them. Just as if he'd developed radar in his hands.

Of course he fought dirty when the occasion demanded it, butting, using elbows, stomping on a con's lead foot to hold him in place for the straight right . . . The politicos loved a dirty fight, screamed in pleasure when someone went down out of a clinch after taking an elbow to the jaw. If the cons fought dirty, it was to be expected; if the police did likewise, it was only poetic justice.

Loren remembered a head butt from his last opponent, a left-handed B&E specialist who drove his forehead with stunning impact against Loren's nose . . . Loren, blind with pain and half stunned, stumbled back trying to shake off the reeling dizziness, battling the feeling that he was going to vomit at any second, knowing the B&E man was driving in to follow up. Loren couldn't see the enemy but knew he was out there, knew somehow that he could sidestep to the right and unload with a straight power right hand over the man's thrusting left.

Loren hit so hard he broke one of his own knuckles. The B&E man dropped to the canvas like a sack of peat and was still unconscious when they carried him away. Loren remembered leaning against the referee as the ref held his hand up in victory, trying to stay on his feet, blinking blood out of his eyes, and gazing down, through some miraculous gap in the crowd, into the back row of the audience, and saw there a state senator from Bernalillo County being given a blowjob by a redheaded exotic dancer he'd brought with him from Albuquerque.

That was Loren's last fight. He knew he had apprehended a clear stream of serious truth, and he didn't want to do any of this anymore. He'd made sergeant and finished paying his dues, and it was pretty clear that Debra wouldn't marry him until he gave up this kind of wildness.

He had been happier than hell when the Ringside burned down, and he could write an end to the whole damn sorry chapter.

But fights on the Line went on, just less sanctioned ones.

The next was at the Atom Lounge, whose neon sign featured a rocket with a tail of red flame, when a hard-ass retiree and his newly unemployed son tried to take the place apart on general principles. Before any officers could show up, the bouncers had handled everything but the arrests.

And so on through the night. Until, shortly after ten, the word went out that George Gileno had just walked into the Doc Holliday Saloon and demanded a drink.

Loren turned on the lights and hit the Yelp button on the siren.

Adrenaline was already doing a dance in his body. His Fury roared along the gently winding road. This one was going to be a nightmare.

George Gileno was probably the world's largest Apache. He'd torn up Holliday's before, and now the place refused to serve him. This apparently furnished him with further reasons to smash up the bar.

Loren's cruiser was the third into the parking lot. He grabbed his baton and ran for the door.

The place was rustic in a studied way, with rough wood paneling and old bits of buggy harness and rusting mining equipment on the walls. Standing in the middle of the barroom, Gileno towered over the crowd that surrounded him. A triumphant grin was spread across his dark, bloodied face. Two yelling officers, Begley and Esposito, hung on to Gileno's arms while a third, Ron Quantrill, belabored the neckless Gileno from behind with his baton.

The giant Apache looked like Frankenstein's monster beset by peasants.

Loren shouted as he tried to drive through the crowd. The Apache swung his stocky body left and right as he tried to brush Begley and Esposito off against pieces of furniture. Chairs and tables tumbled. A pitcher of beer exploded like a grenade. Long-haired members of a bar band stood warily on the bandstand, watching solemnly from under the brims of straw cowboy hats and gimme caps, ready to protect their instruments and amps if the fight lunged their way.

Gileno swung completely around, driving five-foot-four-inch Eloy Esposito's head into the side of the bar. Esposito's eyes glazed over and he slumped to the floor, but somehow managed to hang on to the big man's arm. A chrome-legged stool staggered, then fell. Quantrill backed up, raising his baton defensively. Behind him, Loren saw another officer lying stunned on the floor.

Loren broke free of the crowd and charged. The smell of spilled beer hit him in the face. The neckless monster's broad back, up close, seemed daunting as the side of a mountain.

Loren smashed the back of Gileno's left knee with a backhand swing of the baton, then kicked at the other knee. Gileno went down with Loren on his back trying to get his baton under the man's chin and maybe cut off his air. Quantrill rushed forward, baton thrusting into Gileno's midsection like a spear. Loren's baton slipped under Gileno's chin.

Gileno ducked his head.

Loren's arms jerked forward and the world swung around him in a giddy wheel. Something hit him hard and the wind went out of him. He stared up into Gileno's delighted brown eyes, and the first wave of real terror roared through him.

Gileno had pulled Loren over his back by his neck and shoulder muscles alone, accomplished by effortless strength something a judo player studied for months to learn. Loren smashed up at Gileno's face with his baton, but he didn't have room enough to really swing and the baton rebounded as if Gileno's skull were made of steel. Helpless fear balled in Loren's throat. Gileno heaved himself up to his feet, Begley and Esposito still hanging on to him, and Loren rolled away. Spilled Cheetos crunched under him.

Gileno swung his body around, smashed Eloy Esposito into the bar again. This time Eloy crumpled. Quantrill swung again, but Gileno caught Quantrill's baton in one hand, twisted it out of his grip, then tried to use it upside Begley's head. Begley caught the blow on his forearm, but had to let Gileno go. A laugh rumbled out of George Gileno as he realized he was free. He scaled the baton away into a corner. The officers near him shrank back.

Loren got to his feet and tried to think what to do. Maybe they should just give the Apache a bottle and let him drink himself unconscious.

Two more officers, a man and a woman, burst through the crowd, stared for a moment with wide eyes, then charged, their batons held horizontally in front of them. Gileno swung to face them, left foot forward in a boxer's stance.

The hell with this, Loren thought.

He lurched forward and hit Gileno with his shoulder above the right hip just as the two other officers slammed into him higher up. There was a crack that seemed to transmit itself to Loren right through his bones. Everybody went down in a tangle of limbs and obscenities.

Loren rolled clear and rose, breathing hard, his head swimming. He'd lost his baton somewhere. The other two officers were already on their feet, batons poised. George Gileno was trying to rise, but couldn't seem to get his legs to work. He watched, catching his breath, while four officers sat on Gileno's arms and managed to wrestle his wrists together long enough to put a pair of handcuffs on them. The Apache's wrists were so thick the cuffs barely reached around them. People began drifting back into the room, setting tables and chairs upright.

The band kicked off Bo Diddley's "I'm a Man." They were a blues band really, but if you wanted to earn money playing music in Atocha, you played C&W and fed your blues jones by trying to sneak in the odd Chuck Berry tune when nobody was paying attention.

Apparently the fight had inspired them to throw caution to the winds.

"Call an ambulance from County," Loren said. "We don't want to move him."

"Damn," someone said. "You clipped him. No wonder you can't do that in football." Loren recognized the voice of the saloon's manager, Evander Fell.

Loren turned and glared at him. "What the hell did you *want* me to do with him? Let him go on busting up my men?"

Fell looked startled. He raised his hands. "Hey, Loren, I didn't—"

"Or maybe you'd just want me to shoot him? Because that's what it would come to if I couldn't have put him down that way."

"I wasn't criticizing!"

"It sure as hell sounded that way to me, Evander." Loren pointed a finger at him. Adrenaline raised waves of heat in his body. "Let me tell you something," he said. "I've been a police officer for over twenty years, and I haven't drawn a weapon against one of my neighbors yet. Not in twenty years, and I'm not going to start now, and neither are any of my men."

Fell was turning bright crimson.

"Let me tell you what to do, Evander," Loren said. "How many times has he busted up your place?"

"This is the sixth time."

"So go to Judge Denver and get Gileno served with a restraining order. Then the next time he comes in, *you* can shoot him. Okay?"

"I didn't mean—"

Loren ignored him and stalked away toward where one of his officers was being carefully set on his feet by Begley and Esposito. "How you doin', Buchinsky?"

Buchinsky's eyes widened as he rubbed the back of his neck. The front of his uniform shirt was torn open, revealing the gray underwear worn by devout Mormons, with the little stitches over the nipples and navel.

"Got knocked into a table, Chief," Buchinsky breathed. "Went out for a while."

"You could be whiplashed or something. Get yourself checked out at County." He turned to Eloy Esposito. "Drive him down to the hospital. Get yourself looked at, too."

Esposito shook his head. "Don't need to, Chief. I just got my chimes rung for a minute. I'm okay now."

"This is the kind of thing the city pays insurance premiums for. Let the city get its money's worth, okay?"

"Okay." Reluctantly.

"After you take Buchinsky home, take the rest of the night off. You guys all did good. It's not your fault that King Kong decided to start a riot in our town." He looked behind him. The citizens had settled into their tables for drinks, studiously ignoring the handcuffed giant lying in the middle of the floor. A few diehard dancers were swinging to Bo Diddley. Gileno was still trying to get his legs to work properly. Loren turned back to his men. "Begley, you'll ride with Quantrill for the rest of the night." He looked down at his uniform and brushed absently at the patches of spilled beer and powdered cheese curls. "I'm going home to change."

Loren found his baton and went out into the parking lot and sucked October air into his lungs. A lovely autumn coolness invaded his being. He could almost smell the band-tailed pigeon and the dusky grouse waiting out on the national forest north of town. He'd have to give himself some comp time next week and head out with his shotgun.

The ambulance from the County arrived, and Loren nodded hello to the two parameds as they carried in their stretcher. "Can't have a western town without a saloon brawl now and again, can you?" one said.

"Guess not."

"And at Doc Holliday's, too."

"Yeah."

Evander Fell's place was supposed to be a kind of spiritual descendant of a place the real Doc Holliday had owned briefly in the

1880s, at least till he emptied a pair of pistols at his business partner during a drunken argument. He missed, at close range, with all twelve bullets; and the pious citizens of Atocha, no longer impressed by his death-dealing reputation, promptly rode him out of town on a rail.

It was enough, Loren thought, to make a man nostalgic for traditional forms of law enforcement. Now the only way a bad man got run out of town was if he lost his job at the pit.

Inside the bar, the band caved in to popular prejudice and started on an Ernest Tubb tune. Bright neon, orange and blue and green, burned westward along the Line to the darkened copper pit. For how long? he wondered. A lot of these businesses were barely surviving as it was. With the mine closed, not just the bars but a lot of Central Avenue businesses were in jeopardy.

And that meant bad times for Loren. More cutbacks on his force, and more nasty police work for those who remained. Financial desperation led to a gradual erosion of all civilization. There would be more frustrated, unemployed, angry people getting drunk, getting loaded, getting themselves in accidents or fights. More cases of jobless men going after their wives or children or parents with fists or belts or baseball bats, more wives trying to carve up girlfriends, more guys in pickup trucks shooting up streetlights or traffic signs or each other. All totaled up in police radio codes: ten-thirty-two, a fight; ten-eighteen, a drunk; ten-fifteen, family fight. Codes designed as if to suppress how sad and sordid it all was.

Serve and protect, Loren thought. His job. He thought of his family, his two daughters, and resolve began to stiffen his weariness.

All he wanted was for his town to be a nice place.

From down the neon strip came a chocolate-brown Blazer. It slowed when it saw the collection of emergency vehicles. Loren caught a glimpse of young eyes, a brush cut, a neat suit. At least they didn't wear their Ray-Bans at night.

The Blazer speeded up, heading into town. Apparently ATL Security had concluded there were no foreign spies in Doc Holliday's parking lot. Just another Friday night among the working class. Hardly the sort of thing the lab would concern itself with.

The locals, perhaps, could be trusted to do a few things on their own.

* * *

Debra's Taurus was in the old vine-covered carport. Loren parked behind it and walked through the front door. Debra was watching television with their younger daughter, Kelly. Sitting next to Kelly was a friend from high school whose parents had loaded her with the unfortunate name of Skywalker Fortune.

Loren winced at the title music he heard coming from the box. *Cybercops*, last year's hit series, based on *Cybercops*, the motion picture. Impossibly hip and styled police—hundred-dollar hair clips, three-thousand-dollar jackets—doing unlikely and largely illegal things with high technology. Sixteen-ounce tumblers now available at Burger King.

Loren hated television police shows. He hated television police with implant cyberware worse than anything.

Kelly looked up and giggled. "Been in a food fight, Daddy?"

"Exactly that," Loren said.

"You smell like a wino," Kelly said.

Kelly was fourteen. She wore a plaid shirt with the long tails worn outside of her roll-cuffed Jordache jeans. The shirt was open to reveal a GUARD THE EARTH! T-shirt. There were pink foam-plastic Reeboks on her feet. Loren believed she was the only child he'd ever known who looked good in braces.

Skywalker was a couple years older, a quiet girl with long black hair who was a friend of both of Loren's children. She wore baggy light blue denim pants and an ECO-ALLIANCE T-shirt. Her parents worked for ATL in some scientific capacity, one of the few ATL families who chose to live in town instead of their little self-created suburb. She used words like "syzygy" and "advolution" in conversation, but otherwise seemed a fairly normal girl, a member of the drill team with Katrina and the chorus with Kelly.

Loren went to his room and yanked off his tie. It was the kind sold to law enforcement people, with the velcro tabs in back so that it would come free if someone grabbed it in a fight. Loren took off his gun and ID, then began to empty his pockets.

Debra quietly came into the room and closed the door. "Anyone I know?" she said.

"George Gileno."

"At Holliday's again?"

"He never goes into any other bar. Just Holliday's. It's weird."

She touched his shoulder. "Are you okay?"

"I just got rolled around in the Cheetos some." Loren stood on one leg and pulled off a boot.

"Any wives I should call?"

Loren stood on the other leg, hands gripping the remaining boot, and thought for a moment. "Chuck Buchinsky got knocked around a bit. I sent him to the E-room, but I don't think he was hurt too bad."

"I'll call Karen, then."

Loren pulled off the boot and began unbuttoning his trousers. "Don't get her alarmed. You know what she's like. It's probably nothing."

"It may be *something*."

Loren pulled off his pants. "I won't say it isn't. But Karen's excitable—try not to get her too worked up." He considered for a moment. "Why don't I call the E-room and find out how he's doing? Then you can call Karen."

"Fine. Just don't leave it too long."

Debra went to the closet and took out a clean uniform. "I can get Jerry tomorrow morning," she said. "Let you sleep a little later."

"You don't have to."

"It's okay. Katrina and Kelly can finish making breakfast."

He thought for a moment. "Where is Katrina, anyway?"

"Out with Buddy."

Loren grunted. He wadded up his shirt and tossed it into the hamper. He changed, buckled on his gun, and kissed Debra. Then he walked into the living room on his way to the phone in the kitchen.

"Daddy?" Kelly bounced up from the couch and followed Loren into the kitchen. Skywalker reached over to press the Pause control on the remote. "Mrs. Trujillo called and wanted me to baby-sit."

"No." Loren reached for the phone.

"Why not? She'll pay three dollars an hour."

"No."

"I told her I'd have to ask you."

Loren looked at her. "Why make me the heavy? Why couldn't you find some excuse?"

Kelly looked exasperated. "Daddy. You *are* the heavy."

"Thanks." Loren looked at the phone and pressed the button on the DialComp that would trigger a memory function that called the

E-Room. While rapid-fire tones sounded in his ear, he turned to Kelly. "Tell her you've got to do something for church."

"On a Saturday night?"

"They're Episcopalian. They don't know anything about when we do our church stuff."

"God." She made it two syllables, *Gah-ahd*. "Whoever heard of a Trujillo from Taco Town being an Episcopalian?"

Loren opened his mouth to reprimand Kelly both for taking the Lord's name in vain and for using offensive phrases like "Taco Town," but the nurse at the emergency room answered and Loren had to deal with business for a while.

"Thanks," he said. He hung up the phone and looked at Debra. "Karen's already there, having a fit probably. Buchinsky's still in X ray."

Some of the tension left Debra's face. "Glad I don't have to make any phone calls."

"I think you better. To Mrs. Trujillo."

Debra looked fierce. "Damm it, Loren!"

He started heading for the door. He didn't want to deal with this. "Make up something. I don't care what."

Debra followed him. "I wish you'd tell us what this is all about."

"Can't. Sorry." He considered kissing her goodbye but concluded she wasn't in the mood, and furthermore neither was he. He'd just had a fight with the world's meanest Apache, and even his own family wasn't going to cut him any slack. "I'll be back around three," he said. "Don't wait up."

"Bye, Mr. Hawn," Skywalker said as he left.

There was piñon smoke in the air and a background hum of resentment in Loren's heart. Loren backed the Fury out of the driveway, then listened carefully to the police radio as he drove back to Central. There weren't any calls. Maybe the night's violence had peaked. Maybe all the troublemakers would realize they couldn't top George Gileno if they tried.

As Loren pulled up to the stop sign on Central, a jacked-up Charger roared by in the westbound lane dragging little animal corpses on a line, and Loren knew his brief fling with optimism was over.

Loren pulled the Charger over into the high school parking lot, under the HOME OF THE MINERS sign. The rear bumper featured a profusion of weathered bumper stickers, one saying PARTY ANIMAL, another that advertised Coors, and one with the Playboy rabbit symbol.

Assholes, Loren thought, always advertise.

Also attached to the rear bumper was a length of barbed wire with eight dead cats strung on it. Some of the cats had collars and tags, and all had been shot. Sickness warred with anger in Loren's belly as he approached the driver's door, his flashlight in his hand. He'd been dealing with this kind of small-town crap for far too long.

Loren was not surprised that the driver was A.J. Dunlop, the seventeen-year-old scion of one of Atocha's best-known white-trash families. Loren had been arresting various members of the Dunlop clan all his professional career, and before that he'd had frequent occasion to knock A.J.'s dad around the high school yard with his fists.

A.J.'s passenger was another seventeen-year-old, Len Bonniwell, for whom Loren still had hopes.

"Hi, A.J.," Loren said. He shined the flashlight into A.J.'s eyes. "You're busted, you little piece of shit."

A.J. grinned up at him, his eyes narrow in the light of the flash. He wore a dusty green gimme cap with the brim turned back over his neck and a black heavy-metal T-shirt that featured an animated corpse armed with a kitchen knife.

"Read me my rights, cocksucker," he said.

Loren turned the flashlight beam into the car and saw the pair of opened Budweiser talls sitting in Bonniwell's lap, the half-empty fifth of Early Times lying on the back seat next to the .22 target rifle that had killed the cats. The area in front of the back seat was full of crumpled fast-food cartons, empty bourbon miniatures, and crushed beer cans.

"Out of the car, both of you," Loren said. "Let's see you walk a straight line, A.J."

"Fuck this," A.J. said. He reached for the glove compartment. "I've got something here that'll take care of you."

A sudden onslaught of terror ignited a thermite rage in Loren's chest. He dropped his flashlight, lunged into the car window, dragged A.J. out through the window frame with his big hands, set the terrified boy on his feet, then popped him a left in the nose. The skinny kid went back, cap falling off his head, and then bounced forward off the car. Loren's right cross caught him on the rebound and put him down; and then Loren was jumping up onto the Charger's hood, trying to get to Len Bonniwell before Bonniwell got to whatever was in the glove box.

Bonniwell was half out of the car, eyes wide, as Loren jumped down off the car hood. Loren couldn't see if he had anything in his hands. He kicked the door with all his strength and the swinging door caught the boy in the crotch. Bonniwell's breath went out of him. The door rebounded and Loren danced around it. He grabbed Bonniwell's ears and yanked the kid's head down as he brought up a knee into the boy's face.

Bright halogen light blinded Loren just at the instant he heard the crunch of the boy's breaking nose. Bonniwell spilled to the surface of the parking lot like the contents of a torn sack. Loren blinked, blinded, breathing hard, his pulse hammering in his ears. Running feet crunched on gravel.

"Is there a problem, sir?"

The speaker was a thick-necked man in a jacket, the lights haloing him from behind. Loren dragged cool air into his lungs. ATL goons, he thought, oh, boy.

"Kids made a move on me," Loren said. "They had a gun."

The man seemed to reserve judgment. "I saw you hit that little skinny one and figured *someone* for sure needed help."

Loren looked down at Bonniwell. The boy didn't have anything in his hands. He shaded his eyes against the glare and looked into the open door. A can of beer was slowly draining itself on the fake fur cover of the front passenger seat. "Can you turn off your lights?" he asked.

"Jack." The man called back over his shoulder. "Cut the lights, will you? Everything's okay."

Bonniwell moaned and tried to sit up. His face was webbed with blood and mucus. The stranger knelt by him, gently touched the boy's face. "You likely got yourself a broken nose, bud," he said.

The halogen lights winked off. Loren blinked to clear his vision. He reached for the glove box and opened it.

There was only junk inside. That, some loose change, and a couple crumpled twenty-dollar bills.

A.J. had been reaching for a bribe.

Bile rose in Loren's throat as he picked the bills up. "Shit," he said. He threw the twenties down in the pool of beer on the passenger seat.

The other ATL man got out of the jeep and moved forward. "Let me look at the other one," he said.

"Stupid," Loren said. Adrenaline-fear whirled through his mind. "Real stupid."

He walked around the Charger. Jack, the other ATL man, was kneeling by A.J. Dunlop.

"Broken jaw here, Elton," he said.

Loren stood above the sprawled boy. A stiletto of guilt stabbed him to the heart. "Stupid," he said.

Jack stood up. "You want us to call an ambulance?"

"Didn't think I'd hit him that hard."

"You outweigh him by how much? Eighty pounds?"

Guilt did a dance through Loren's blood. He looked down at his hands. His knuckles were scraped and bleeding. "I thought he was going for a gun."

Jack's face was without expression. "Better call that ambulance, Elton," he said.

Elton started walking back to his Blazer. Loren wondered what stories they were going to tell when they went back to their little suburb, how they'd tell their boss, William Patience, that they'd seen the police chief, the big ex-boxer, beating up a couple of kids in the high school parking lot. *Said* they'd tried to pull a gun.

A residue of anger crackled through him. What the hell was he feeling bad about? He was just doing his job.

"Put them in the back of my car," he said. He pulled a pair of handcuffs from his belt and cuffed A.J.'s hands behind him.

"Are you sure about this?" Jack said. "This kid's out like a light."

"He'll wake up. And when he wakes up, I want him in restraints." He looked in the direction of Len Bonniwell, who had risen groggily to his feet, hands over his bloody face. "The other one won't be any trouble. You got any wire cutters?"

It turned out they had. The ATL men watched in silence as Loren cut the barbed wire off the Charger's bumper, then put the dead cats in the back seat of his car next to Len Bonniwell. He put the .22 in the front seat, along with the beer cans, the bottle of Early Times, and the two soaked twenties. By that time A.J. was awake, and Loren, with Elton helping, hoisted him into the Fury's back seat next to the dead cats.

"This is weird stuff, man," Jack said under his breath. He was talking to Elton.

"Small-town Saturday night," Loren said, and wondered why he felt compelled to explain any of this. "Bored white trash looking for something to do. You shoot a cat with a .22, he jumps about eight feet in the air and then runs half a block before he knows he's dead. Some people think it's entertaining."

Elton and Jack looked at him, then at each other.

"Beats what kids get up to in big cities these days," Loren said.

"We'll follow you to the hospital," said Elton.

"You don't have to. And thanks for helping."

A studied shrug. "We might as well."

Loren knew why they were following him—they were afraid Loren would inflict further damage on his prisoners if he wasn't supervised. Resentment hummed through him at the thought.

Still. If he'd seen what they had, maybe he wouldn't have acted any different.

And maybe they were right, anyway.

"Mack. I get you up?"

"Yeah, you did. Who is this?" Len Bonniwell's father sounded as if he were getting an early start on Saturday morning's hangover. Loren knew he'd been laid off just that afternoon.

Loren identified himself. "I thought I'd better let you know that I just arrested your kid."

"Aw, shit."

"He was shooting cats with A.J. Dunlop. Then they resisted when I tried to arrest them."

"Jesus, Loren."

"You're going to have to come in tomorrow and bail him out."

Mack Bonniwell gave a heavy sigh. Loren gazed at his desk calendar, at the little red tick marks that represented the Days of Atonement.

"Can you go bail, Mack? I know you got laid off."

"Guess I'll have to."

"Tell you what I'll do. I'll send a note to Judge Denver to go easy."

Another sigh. "Thanks, Loren. I know the kid doesn't deserve it, but—"

"Just don't let him keep running around with the Dunlop boy, okay? That whole family's bad news, lived in Picketwire forever. A.J.'ll get Len in trouble surer than anything."

"I'll try, Loren." Doubtfully. "But I don't know how I can—"

"And ground his ass till he pays off the fine."

"Yeah. I'll do that. Thanks again."

"See you in church."

"Yeah. See you then."

Loren hung up and looked at the red tick marks on his calendar again and tried to fight off the restless tension he felt gnawing at him. The Lord was testing his servants.

He'd booked the boys for resisting rather than attempted bribery. You didn't break jaws and noses for bribery. Resistance, particularly if the resistance was complicated by the presence of a firearm, would make the visits to the E-room look a lot more understandable.

He looked down at his desk. On top was a form he hadn't noticed before, the printout of a LAWSAT report. The alert for the white Chevy van and its cargo of drugs had been called off.

Well. At least there was one little something he didn't have to worry about anymore.

There was a hasty knock on his door, then Sanchez bustled in before Loren could answer.

"Call just came, Chief. Two guys with shotguns just held up the Copper Country."

Loren rose from his seat and ran out to the Fury.

The Lord was testing his servants pretty damn good tonight.

T H R E E

"They even robbed the table," Cipriano said. "I can't fucking believe it."

Police and a couple of the sheriff's posse, wearing flak vests, with Remington 870 shotguns propped on hips, were cluttering the Copper Country's back hall. If the two robbers were stupid enough to return to the scene of the crime, they'd be dead meat.

"Hey!" Loren yelled. "Everybody but the witnesses get out of here!"

Cipriano Dominguez rightly concluded that this command did not include him. He let the officers and bystanders file out, then led Loren down the back hall with its cheap paneling, then through a door marked with a cardboard sign that said EMPLOYEES ONLY in fading red letters.

A wide poker table sat like a bright green mesa beneath a circular imitation-Tiffany lamp. The last hand still lay where the players—mostly graying cowboys, along with a few miners tossing away their last paychecks—had thrown down their cards. The place smelled like a century's consumption of cigarette smoke, and there were honest-to-God brass spittoons on the floor for those who dipped snuff.

Loren saw a possible diamond flush and turned over the hole card. Two of clubs, no help.

"Okay," he said. "How much was on the table?"

"A few hundred."

"More'n that."

"Five, six hundred, anyway."

Loren watched while the cowboys argued about that for a while. Taken all together they were the laziest men Loren knew, boozy, shiftless, and rarely employed. The ranches in the neighborhood knew them all too well and had started to supply themselves with wetback Mexican vaqueros who worked a lot harder and spent a lot less time romancing waitresses in places like the Copper Country. The local cowboys lived chiefly off women; their girlfriends, most of them waitresses here at the Copper Country, provided them with the principal part of their gambling money in the form of tips. There should be a bumper sticker, Loren thought: REAL COWBOYS DON'T WORK, THEY LIVE OFF WAITRESSES.

Still, there seemed no lack of waitresses to support these cowboys, real or not. And Loren could never figure out how men who worked so little and drank so much still had those slim hips that looked so good on a dance floor. Loren considered it unjust that he probably got a lot more regular physical activity than these guys and still carried twenty too many pounds.

"Okay," he said, after the argument rattled around for a while. "I guess it doesn't much matter. Who saw the perpetrators first?"

"Bill Forsythe," Cipriano said, before the cowboys could start arguing about it again.

Forsythe was the man who had owned the Copper Country and its illegal, perpetual poker game for the last twelve years, having taken over both from the previous owner.

"Where's he?" Loren asked.

"In his office."

Forsythe's office was a small room walled in the same cheap paneling he'd used on his back hall. The empty safe stood open behind his desk. He was a gangly man, with wavy iron-colored hair. He wore a western shirt with pearl buttons. He normally augmented this with a silver and turquoise squash-blossom necklace and a big matching bracelet on his left wrist, but the stickup men had taken them. He kept rubbing his wrist as if he missed the bracelet.

He'd spent most of the evening playing poker, occasionally leaving the table to check on the bar, make a phone call, or transfer money from the cash registers to the safe. After last call at one-thirty he'd left the game to go to the bar and collect the excess cash receipts. He'd gone down the back hall to his office to put the receipts in the safe till Monday morning. Two men in ski masks were waiting for him. One of them had a sawed-off shotgun.

"Was the other armed?" Loren asked.

"I only had eyes for that sawed-off," Forsythe said. "I didn't notice if the other guy was packing when he came in, but he is now." He cleared his throat. "I had a .38 Chief's Special in the safe, just in case this kind of thing happened, but when I saw that shotgun I knew I didn't want to use it." He seemed mildly embarrassed by the fact he hadn't turned Clint Eastwood in the clutch.

"Very smart," Cipriano said.

"Yeah," Loren said. "If you'd resisted, we would've had to scrape you up with a shovel."

Forsythe's eyes got bigger. Any trace of embarrassment vanished.

After taking the night's receipts and the other contents of the safe, the robbers had marched Forsythe to the back room and stolen the poker bank. "Even took the dimes and quarters," he said.

"Description? Start with the guy with the weapon."

"He looked like King Kong with that goddamn gun."

"Sure it wasn't Mighty Joe Young?"

Forsythe looked blank. People in shock, Loren thought, never understand when you tried to make a joke.

"Forget it," he said. "Let's start with his shirt. Just close your eyes and think for a minute. What kind of shirt did he have on?"

After twenty minutes Loren had a good description. Two young Hispanic men, aged eighteen to twenty-five, an inch or two shorter than average, dressed in work boots, blue jeans, dark blue or black zipped nylon jackets. The man with the shotgun had long black hair that stuck out of the bottom of the ski mask. He was the only one who had talked, and he had a light Spanish accent. The other guy had the tails of a red plaid shirt hanging below the waist of his jacket. Loren told Cipriano to get the descriptions out immediately, and use the LAWSAT antenna to get them out to New Mexico and Arizona state police.

"It's not much to go on, jefe," Cipriano said. "That description could fit maybe a couple hundred people living in this county."

"Put it out, anyway. We might get lucky." Cipriano turned to leave. "Wait a minute," Loren said. "I just thought. Call Connie Duvauchelle and see if she's got these two guys celebrating in her parlor."

"Good idea."

Cipriano left the room, and Loren turned to Forsythe. "I got one important question," he said. "Was the door to the poker room open when you went down the hall?"

Forsythe shook his head. "No. They marched me right to the door and told me to go inside."

"So they knew it was there."

Forsythe did not seem to comprehend the significance of this. "Anyone you've had to fire recently?" Loren asked. "Any bad blood between you and any of your employees?"

"Hell, Loren. Everyone in the county knows that game is back there anymore. It doesn't have to be someone who worked for me."

"Answer the question, Bill."

Forsythe thought for a moment. "Business is good. I fired one guy for stealing three months ago, but it wasn't him held me up."

"Why not?"

"Because Robbie Cisneros is almost as tall as you are."

Loren scratched his jaw. "Yeah, I know him. I arrested him a couple times for drunk and disorderly. How much did he steal?"

"A lot of tip money, I think. He was a bus boy so he could just grab the money from the tables when no one was looking. But I only caught him with about twenty bucks. It seemed easier just to kick his ass out of here."

"Always prosecute," Loren said. "Even if it's for pocket money. Never let them get away with anything. Because for every theft you catch them at, they've committed a hundred more."

"Robbie didn't hold me up." Insistently. "He was taller."

"Have you had a fight with anyone lately? Anyone complain the poker game is rigged?"

"Rigged!" Forsythe was indignant. "We don't even have a dealer!"

"Yeah, okay. I was just asking."

"And the *players* are too damn dumb to cheat one another." Now that he was safe and his shock wearing off, all Forsythe's fear and adrenaline was beginning to come out as belligerence. In a minute, Loren figured, he'd start yelling at the police for not protecting him properly. "Nobody's complained!" Forsythe said. "Nobody! Those good ole boys have been losing all their girlfriends' tips to me for years, and nobody's ever said a word about it."

"Fine. Any of the regulars not around tonight?"

Forsythe gave a few names. Loren knew them all and knew they didn't fit the description of the robbers.

Cipriano came back and reported that he'd sent the LAWSAT alert and that Connie Duvauchelle had reported no suspects in her vicinity. So much for that.

Loren decided to leave before Forsythe's growing anger got annoying. He thanked the man and went down the hall to the table. Maybe the ole boys had remembered something.

The ole boys contradicted one another at every turn and it took over an hour to get their stories straight. No details of any significance were added except that they heard a car pull out of the back parking lot just after the robbery.

"Did anyone hear it start?" Loren asked.

A few said yes, a few no. That left the possibility of a third robber sitting in the back with the engine running. Loren grew unhappier by the minute at the implications of all this. He and Cipriano left the poker room and closed the door behind them. The EMPLOYEES ONLY sign came loose at one corner and flopped down at an angle.

"It's folks from around here, jefe," Cipriano said. "There's too much local knowledge for it to be anything else."

"Yeah." Loren found himself getting unhappier still.

"Maybe it's that Cisneros kid, after all. Maybe he was the driver."

"Could be."

"I'll go down to Las Animas and cruise by his folks' place on the way home. See if his van is there."

"Okay. Do that."

"I can talk to his parents tomorrow. But I don't think they'll give me nothing. They're harder cases than he is."

All the bars were closed. If anyone was getting drunk and belligerent now, Loren figured he didn't have to be awake for it. He thanked everybody for their cooperation, told Sanchez on the desk to send himself and everyone but the regular shift home, and drove home himself.

The house smelled of popcorn. There was a half-eaten bowl sitting on the coffee table in front of the TV, and Loren ate a couple handfuls quietly, in the dark, before walking into the kitchen for a glass of water. The water cooler was empty and he had to use the stuff from the tap. Wincing at the mineral taste, he finished his water, then took off his shoes and gun belt and padded into the bedroom.

Debra's breathing pattern changed as he entered the room—without quite waking up, she was reassuring herself of his continued health and well-being—and then her breathing normalized. He undressed and slid into the bed beside her and thought about what had just happened out on the City Line.

Some citizen or citizens of Atocha, it was fairly clear, had used his knowledge of the town to conspire to rob one of the town's most venerable, if illegal, institutions. Growing resentment bubbled in Loren's mind. The town—*his* town—and its way of life were threatened, not just from acts of God like the pit closing and the advent of ATL, but by treachery on the part of its own inhabitants. They were disloyal, Loren thought, betraying the town. Undermining its foundation. Threatening its way of life.

He had to find the assholes, whoever they were. Make an example of them.

He thought about the twenty-first century and what it was bringing. Chevy pickups full of designer drugs and automatic weapons. Imported gunmen holding up bars. People not standing up for their neighbors or institutions or what was right. Incomprehensible and threatening technologies like all the Star Wars weaponry erupting through the sky over the ATL compound.

Once, he thought, the future had been a special place. Full of wonder gadgets and streamlined design, like the deco façades on the buildings downtown. The World of Tomorrow. The future had been a place, like Oz, where all sorts of delightful things seemed possible.

Then somehow, he thought, the bad guys had occupied the future. They were sitting up there, like Apaches in a western film, occupying the high ground. And the good guys had no choice but to ride into the next century under their guns.

"What's wrong?" Debra was sitting up in bed, her eyes fixed on him. He looked at her in surprise.

"What do you mean?"

"You were grinding your teeth loud enough to wake the dead. What happened?"

Loren had to think for a moment about what had started his train of thought. "Copper Country got held up. Including that poker game that Bill Forsythe runs in the back."

"And that means someone from around here did it."

"Yeah." Loren wasn't surprised at her acuity; Debra had always been quick to pick up on these things. She propped her head up on one hand and regarded him.

"Any idea who?"

"Not really, no. A couple Spanish kids did the holdup. They maybe had a third man as a driver."

"And nobody's seen the two guys."

"Right. They probably got out of town before the description ever went out."

"Or they're hiding out with their friend."

"Maybe."

There was silence for a moment, filled only by the ticking of the Little Ben alarm clock on the night table. Loren sighed. "Nothing I can do about it now."

"I can make you some hot milk."

"No. Thank you. I can get to sleep."

"Watch that grinding."

"Okay. I'll try to remember."

She kissed his cheek and buried herself in the covers. Loren closed his eyes, tried to deepen his breathing. Bits of the day floated across his vision, superimposed in meaningless juxtaposition: Gileno looming over the crowd at Holliday's, the deco griffins at the City-County Building staring with blind white eyes, Len Bonniwell's sprawled body limned in the halogen light of the ATL jeep, Bill Forsythe rubbing the wrist that had worn his stolen turquoise bracelet . . .

Out of this, somehow, he put it all together. He knew who had done the holdup, and when he realized that he knew, he wasn't surprised.

He looked at the fluorescent hands of the Little Ben. It was five-thirty.

Time to get up, anyway.

Loren had finished his shower and was starting his shave when Debra appeared puffy-eyed in the doorway. Energy hummed happily in his mind. He gave her a cheery smile. "Go to sleep for another hour," he said. "I might as well get Jerry, since I'm up, anyway."

Debra blinked at him sleepily, then without a word turned and headed back to bed.

Loren finished shaving, then dressed in a blue wool blazer, white shirt, red linen tie, and gray slacks. He unlocked the gun rack and took out the short-barreled .38 Chief's Special, clipped the holster to his belt on the left side, under the jacket, then went out to the driveway and got in the police cruiser.

He headed north along Estes, through the town center and across the maglev tracks, down the steep hillside, lined with willows, that marked where the Rio Seco cut through town. Estes Street cut right through the bottom of the dry river, with a steel pole stuck in the riverbed nearby. The pole was painted with depth markers so people would know whether they could safely get across in case of flood. On the opposite bank was the ramshackle neighborhood called Picketwire, all cinder block and rusty tin roofs and old cars sitting on blocks in sandy front yards.

True to every small-town stereotype, in Atocha there was a right side of the tracks on which to be born. Picketwire was on the wrong side.

Loren turned right and drove past the residence of A.J. Dunlop's father—no fewer than four cars sat on blocks in the front yard—then west along the barren ridge that overlooked the south side of the Rio Seco. He went down another slope, then up another rise, into another neighborhood. This one was called Las Animas on the town plots, but Taco Town by snotty Anglo kids like Loren's daughter Kelly.

Las Animas was still on the wrong side of the AT&SF tracks, and looked more or less like Picketwire, the same rusty tin roofs rising up the side of a treeless ridge, the same junked autos gathering graffiti as they sat in the sun. Maybe there was a higher percentage of adobe used in construction, but the main difference was not architectural, but racial.

No one had ever drawn any lines, and there had never been any formal segregation, no racial laws, no Jim Crow. There had always been exceptions, intermarriages—many of the town's founding aristocracy, in fact, had created Spanish/Anglo marriages, Anglo businessmen marrying Spanish women to have access to the Hispanic market, after which the children chose their ethnic identification for themselves. Informal segregation was simply a fact—Las Animas was for the poor Spanish, Picketwire for the poor Anglos, both being named after the same evocatively named Colorado river, El Rio de las Animas Perdidas en Purgatorio, the River of Lost Souls in Purgatory, Picketwire being an Anglo corruption of Purgatoire, which was itself a French version of Purgatorio. Loren had never been clear concerning how neighborhoods in a southwestern New Mexico town had been named after a Colorado river, but then the other districts were oddly named, too. Loren's neighborhood, Rose Hill—few roses, not much of a hill—was for the better class of Anglo; and it was mirrored by Port Royal—no port, no royalty—where Cipriano and the better-off Hispanics lived. The city's tiny handful of black people clustered around the African Baptist Church in an informal no-man's-land north of Picketwire. Nothing concerning this arrangement had ever been said; nothing ever needed saying.

Power in the town had been divided up in the same quiet way. The police chief was always Anglo; the assistant Hispanic. The president of the city council was always Spanish, and the chairman of the county's Democratic Party organization had been a member of the Figueracion family for over a hundred years. The mayor had always been Anglo, at least till Edward Trujillo created a minor political earthquake first by running, then by getting himself elected, not simply the first Hispanic mayor ever, but the first Republican since the 1890s.

Unseen boundaries were coming down. It made Loren nervous.

Loren drove into Las Animas, then slowly down the cracked surface of Cedar Street. He passed a little adobe chapel, its windows and doors painted blue to symbolize devotion to the Virgin. A miniature house of worship built on someone's front lawn, marking the meeting place of a few families who had come from northern Mexico to work in the mines during the Depression. Ostensibly Catholics—Bob Sandoval would have called them heretics—they belonged to some small divergent sect that had gotten thrown out of Spain in the 1600s. Another of Atocha's forty-one Welcoming Churches.

Parked right where he thought it would be was a little dusty car with Texas plates. Loren took down the plate number, used the Computer-Aided Dispatch Keyboard to check the license number, then drove home. He walked through the living room to the kitchen phone and told the DialComp to call Cipriano.

Debra was loading the coffeemaker with water from the water cooler that she'd loaded with a fresh bottle. She brushed straight blond hair out of her face and looked at Loren with narrowed eyes, squinting without her glasses.

"Where's Jerry?" she said.

Loren gave a laugh. "I got distracted by police work. I'll get him in a minute."

She nodded. "Got it figured out?" she said.

"I think so."

The line went four rings before it answered with a single word.

"Dominguez." Cipriano's voice was full of sleep.

Loren grinned into the phone. "Y andale, bubba," he said.

There was a long moment of silence. "I hope this is good, jefe. It's six in the fucking morning."

"I figured out who popped the Copper Country. But I've got to go to church at seven o'clock and I can't keep on top of it."

"Let me get a pencil." There was another moment of silence. "Okay, jefe. Shoot." Each word sounded like a groan.

"Remember your cousin Félix?"

Another moment of silence. "My cousin by marriage. You're saying he robbed the Copper Country?"

"Naw. But remember when we had to bust his daughter's wedding reception because some asshole called Rose's mother a fat old bruja and got punched in the nose by the old lady's bad-ass nephew Anthony from Laredo?"

"He's from Harlingen. But okay."

"So who did we have to drag off to the jail because they kept trying to slug it out even though they were too drunk to stand up?"

"Anthony. And his two boys. And Rose's mother, because she tried to kick Eloy Esposito when he was hauling Anthony away."

"She really *is* an evil old bruja, you know? But who else?"

"Ahhh." Cipriano was beginning to sound as if he was awake. "Robbie Cisneros."

"Yeah. So if you go drive by Félix's place you'll see a car with Texas plates out front. Because my working hypothesis is that Robbie and Anthony's two boys got to be good buddies in our drunk tank, and that yesterday the two boys from Harlingen drove up here to stick up the Copper Country with Robbie as their driver."

"God damn. I'm impressed, jefe." Cipriano sounded as if he had finally come awake.

"The car is there. I've run the number on the C. A. D. and it has a Harlingen address. I need somebody to watch the car, okay?"

"I'll check it out."

Loren put the phone back in its cradle. The smell of coffee began to rise in the room. Debra peered at him nearsightedly. "When did you work all that out?" she said.

"When I was grinding my teeth." He grinned and backed out of the room, heading for his brother's place.

Loren's brother, Jerry, had been living for the last ten years or so in an automobile graveyard east of town, where the owner allowed him to live in an old trailer in exchange for looking after the place and doing some free-lance auto repair. A ruddy tinge crept across the horizon as Loren drove the Fury out of town on Route 82, the red horizon calibrated by a marching succession of silhouetted black power poles. The automated maglev train, off to Loren's right, winked redly as it soared airborne over its pathway of rusting steel.

A bulky adobe structure appeared on the left: the Earth Church, Atocha's forty-second, a religion for those who found spirituality in environmental activism. The doctrine itself was, to Loren, an offensive, not-quite-settled mixture of revived paganism, political radicalism, and bits borrowed from Christianity and Daoism—the "Earth gospel was evolving," to quote the official literature. Evolving, Loren figured, to the point where it could extract the maximum contributions from the gullible.

Churches, Loren thought, were about eternal things, not about contemporary politics. Loren knew all he needed to know about politics, and he knew he wanted to keep them as far away from his own faith as possible.

In the church parking lot Loren saw a pair of elderly Apaches, in traditional garb, climbing out of an old jeep. This morning's guest shamans, Loren figured. White people who, strangely, had no use for Native Americans as *people* nevertheless seemed to need them as spiritual entities—yuppies who would look with a certain well-bred trepidation upon an Apache and his large family moving into the neighborhood would nevertheless happily participate in a ceremony in which the same Apache, in a shamanistic capacity, blessed them with pollen and urged them to respect Mother Earth. Indians, in this respect, were treated as both inferior and superior—superior in terms of spiritual resonance, inferior in every other way. You didn't want them next door, you wanted them safely up on a mountain somewhere, talking to spirits on your behalf.

Indians, according to Anglo myth, were more spiritual, "closer to the Earth." It never occurred to the whites that the reason the Indians were so close to the Earth was that they were poor, and that they had been kept in poverty and on reservations by vicious and stupid policies set up and tolerated by the same white folks who had become so respectful of their spiritual condition.

Loren remembered that, some years before, running water and flush toilets had been introduced into the Taos Pueblo. There had actually been opposition to the move on the part of Anglos who were horrified by the desecration of a historical and sacred site. That was the problem with the whole view of Indians as our spiritual superiors, Loren thought: people forgot that these superior, spiritual beings were actually people who needed to take a crap now and again.

Almost directly across the highway was a contrasting point of view in the form of a rugged monument of stones with a bronze-green plaque. ON THIS SPOT ON JULY 21, 1884, SIX MEN OF H

TROOP, 9TH U.S. CAVALRY, WERE KILLED BY RED SAV-
AGES.

The history didn't let you forget.

The junkyard was on a hill, visible for miles in all directions. It was
surrounded by a ten-foot-high fence, chain link in back, painted wood
in front. The wooden fence had been painted with a Hamm's beer ad,
a bright pastoral view of evergreens and lakes, rioting green grass,
stately white-tailed deer, a glowing sylvan Minnesota scene as far
removed from the reality of dry, alkaline New Mexico as from the
moon.

Loren pulled onto a dirt side road that led to the yard's side
entrance. German shepherds paralleled him, barking cheerfully. He
parked in front of the gate, let the dogs lick his hand for a while—they
were so starved for company that they were utterly useless in their role
as guard dogs—and then Loren let himself in. The dogs jumped
around him in chaotic joy.

Jerry's trailer was an old Airstream sitting on rotting tires flat for
twenty years. Strings of rust drooled from its rivet heads. It was
surrounded by the decayed rubble of twentieth-century transportation
systems: cars, trucks, buses, even a sagging row of electric streetcars
that had been pulled out of Atocha in the 1940s. Loren banged on the
door, then opened it and stepped into the darkness. He couldn't see
anything at all. A male voice speaking Russian gobbled at him from
the back of the trailer. His foot hit something solid. He groped for the
light switch and flipped it.

The trailer was full of stuff that Jerry had collected over the last ten
years, most of it malfunctioning apparatus. In the dim light of the
sixty-watt overhead bulb Loren could see several typewriters, a pair of
old Osborne computers, an ancient stainless-steel Waring blender, a
couple toasters, an IBM PC keyboard with several keys missing, and
some mismatched tire hubs, gears from a manual transmission, all
interleaved with piles of paperback books, magazines, old newspapers,
a huge backlist of *National Geographic* . . .

The stuff rose to the rounded ceiling on all sides, giving off a faint
odor of dust, decaying pulp, and machine oil. Loren tried not to let
any of it touch his clothing. The voice in Russian continued. Loren
recognized a few words: *Cuba, Castro.*

"That you, Loren? I'm getting dressed!"

Jerry's voice came from the back of the trailer, over piles of stuff. Though the trailer was less than twenty feet long, there was no obvious way from one end to the next. Loren knew there was a tunnel, however, created when Jerry had laid some planks between the built-in dinette and the sink, then piled more of his kibble on top.

There was a scurrying sound. Preceded by a strong scent of Mennen's Skin Bracer, Jerry appeared in the tunnel entrance. Loren stepped back to give him room. Jerry stood up. He was carrying a small pink cardboard box and wore a yellowed white shirt, a pair of pleated brown slacks, and old brown cowboy boots. Jerry rose and brushed off his knees, then opened the box and offered it to Loren.

"Chocolate-covered doughnut?"

Loren eyed the box and wondered how old the doughnuts were. "No, thanks," he said. "Debra's cooking."

"Right. I'll have just one, then."

The Russian voice babbled on. Jerry stuck a doughnut in his mouth, then jammed the box carefully between an old upright office typewriter and a bunch of crumbling science-fiction magazines tied up with twine. Loren wondered how long the box would stay there. Years, maybe. He left the trailer and Jerry followed. Delighted dogs swirled around them as they walked to the gate. Jerry reached into his pants pocket and pulled out a string tie, then put the tie around his collar.

"Learning to speak Russian from the shortwave?" Loren asked.

Jerry removed the doughnut from his mouth. "I just like to listen to the sounds. And Radio Moscow has the most amazing music. Like from another planet."

You're the one from another planet, Loren wanted to say, but he never actually managed to say it. It would have been pointless, anyway.

"I can listen to Russian Top Forty," Jerry added, "because the radio's based on transistors, and they're based on the holes between things."

Loren looked at his brother. "Holes?" he said. He knew what was coming.

Jerry, the Useless Fact Machine.

"Yeah. Holes. See, there are atoms, right? And atoms are protons and electrons. Electrons move, and that's electricity. But when electrons move, they leave big holes behind. And that's what transistors are based on."

Loren peered at his brother across the roof of his car. "Based on holes?" he said.

"Yeah. See, when the electrons move off, new electrons appear out of nowhere to fill the holes. I can't remember what they do then, I just remember reading about it."

Loren opened the car door. "The holes are in your head, Jerry."

Jerry resembled his younger brother, the same strong build, the same broad cheekbones and curly dark hair, but there was something undefined about him. *Unfocused*, Loren thought. As if you were looking at him through a pane of glass smeared by fingerprints.

He hadn't always been that way—growing up he was a healthy Atocha kid, popular, outgoing, a member of the high school basketball and football teams. And then the draft got him, and when he came back from overseas something had changed him.

Whatever happened, Loren knew, it wasn't war. The Vietnam War was going on at the time, but Jerry was sent to Europe instead, to Germany. He was a tank crewman in the 9th Armored Division, like Elvis Presley. And by the time Jerry came back, something had gone out of him—he'd become vague, lost focus—and he bounced around Atocha aimlessly until one of the deacons at Loren's church, as a favor to Loren, gave him the Airstream to live in.

Loren got in the car and started the engine. Jerry sat in the passenger seat, then reached to touch the walnut stock of the Remington shotgun propped in the rack between the two front seats.

"Duck season opens next Friday," Loren said. "I'm planning on taking the day off. You wanna go?"

"Sure."

"Right after church."

Jerry gave a sigh. "We'll miss half the morning."

"Jerry," Loren said. "The church got you a place to live. *And* a whole bunch of jobs that you tossed away."

"Did I ever ask the church for anything?"

"*I* did."

"Did I ever ask you to ask?"

There was silence. Loren backed the Fury onto the dirt road, then turned back to town.

"You've got to hang on to the things that are important," Loren said. "You've got family, you've got a faith that wants you. A whole town you grew up with. You can't just let it all slip away."

Jerry brushed doughnut crumbs off his shirtfront. Beneath the strong after-shave he had an odd smell, part auto grease, part dust, as if he were a bit of disused machinery sitting on the shelf for a long time, another item in his pile of kibble.

"I don't know why you're always complaining," Jerry said. "I'm still here, aren't I?"

"Yeah. You're still here."

"I'm going to church like you want me, and I'm going hunting with you on Friday."

"Yeah."

"So what's your problem, Loren?"

Loren didn't answer, using the necessity of stopping at the end of the dirt road and turning onto Route 82 as an excuse.

The Fury raced on in silence, a good ten miles above the limit. Ahead of them were lines of sandy ridges painted bloodred by sunrise, the valleys between them all deep purple shadow. The terrain, Loren thought suddenly, looked like the weathered, wrinkled skin of an old Apache woman. Dry and aged and filled with reality. He found himself struck by the insight as the car coasted over a ridge.

"Holy fuck!"

Loren slammed on the brakes. The Fury lunged for the narrow shoulder, into the entrance to the Earth Church parking lot. A pair of old pickups, both heavily laden with what seemed to be a ton of old furniture crowned by mattresses and box springs, one trying to pass the other on a rise, did a slow-motion dance of inept avoidance and managed to miss the cruiser by inches. As Loren weaved past he glanced directly into the dark, unsurprised eyes of a small boy, the child riding in the bed of one of the pickups surrounded by stacks of household goods.

Loren brought his car to a stop, heart flailing in his chest. He reached for the siren button, then hesitated.

Breakfast was waiting. Church was waiting.

The hell with it. New Mexico had long been the worst state in the U.S. for auto accident statistics—by a considerable margin—and it was time to make at least a little change.

Both drivers were, in fact, clearly drunk. Loren cited them and called for a patrolman to come up from town and haul them to jail. The little kid jumped out of the truck and followed Loren around, yelling curses in Spanish that he probably assumed Loren didn't understand. His favorite word was "chota," which any southwestern cop understood as being an uncomplimentary reference to the law enforcement profession. Loren looked down at the boy. "Cállate la boca, chivito!" he said, and the kid shut up in a hurry.

Jerry gave a laugh as Loren got back in the car. "New Mexico drivers," he said. "Nothing like 'em."

"Worst in the world," Loren said. "And these were drunk, too."

"You know," Jerry said, "I wonder if there's some kind of bacteria in New Mexico, in the soil and in the air. A little bug that transmits incompetence. And everyone who lives here gets it sooner or later."

Loren grinned. "You may have something there."

"It's the Third World here. Drivers who can't drive, teachers who can't teach, administrators who can't sign their names, politicians who only get elected because the voters are as stupid and bigoted and inept as they are. An aboriginal population that gets shat on by everybody. Nothing sensible ever prospers, everything ambitious turns to farce. Pathetic. It's the land of mañana. And it's been that way forever, and nothing's gonna change it."

Loren gave his brother a surprised look. Jerry's bizarre speculations were hardly ever serious; this last seemed heartfelt.

"Maybe not, Jer," he said. "But maybe it's just the way we do things."

"The way we don't do things, you mean."

There was a wink of red on Loren's left. He turned to see the red sun gleaming on the silver body of the maglev train returning from the ATL facility to town, a sign of the latest attempt to transform the country, to inject, as with a hypodermic, a new century into the land where the germ of incompetence had for so long thrived.

F O U R

The Church of the Apostles of Elohim and the Nazarene was Atocha's largest church. The Apostles, unlike the Saints and the Holy Romans, had been imported specially in the 1880s, when Riga Brothers began their copper operation. The gold and silver miners already living here were too unreliable—they'd work long enough to get a grubstake, then go off prospecting. Riga Brothers, whose board chairman was an Apostle, proposed importing entire families of coreligionists from upstate New York and northern Pennsylvania— stable family people, the kind you could count on to form a community. Maybe five hundred families had answered the call, singing hymns as they rode to Atocha on the train.

But like all populist religions, the Apostles were prone to schism.

In the plaza across the street from the deco church was a small group of people clustered around a gray-haired man standing on a wooden box. The box was sky-blue, and on each side was painted a carefully detailed pyramid above which hovered a gold-glowing eye.

"I have the answer!" the man shouted. "I have *seen!*"

"Oh, hell," Loren said as he got out of his car.

The man on the box was named Alfred Roberts, and he was a former mayor of the town and a former member of the Apostle congregation. When his brother was convicted of stealing highway funds, and after his own trial ended in a hung jury, he lost his job to Trujillo; and since then he'd been disbarred, split from the Apostles, and set himself up as a prophet, living off welfare and the earnings of his tiny band of converts.

"As the Lord spake to Samuel Catton," he shouted, "and so he has spaken unto me!"

Spaken? Loren wondered. He and his family moved rapidly up the sidewalk, their eyes turned away. The whole scene was too embarrassing.

"Listen!" said Roberts's wife, Amy, "and ye shall be saved!"

Loren remembered dating Amy for over a year, just after he came back from Korea. She'd left him for Roberts, he'd figured, because a successful contractor had a lot better prospects than a rookie cop.

Look at her now, he thought.

The people around him were his family and disciples, and were draped in blankets against the October morning chill, an Old Testament touch that, against the plaza's deco background, made them seem more demented even than their ravings. Amy Roberts carried a sign that said HEAR THE TRUTH. Others carried books and pamphlets. A vacant-eyed teenage girl, visibly pregnant, with bad skin and her hair frizzed up above her ears, carried another sign that said THE CHURCH REFORMED. No one knew precisely who she was or where she had come from; she was only seen rarely, cashing her checks from the Aid to Mothers with Dependent Children program. Rumor had it she was Roberts's "bound concubine."

All false prophets, Loren figured, tended toward harems. One of the signs by which you knew them.

"The church is *corrupt!*" Roberts screamed. His fist thudded repeatedly against his chest. "Its doctrine is *perverted!* Mine* is the true road to heaven!"

Another kind of asshole, Loren thought, another kind of advertisement.

"Get a job!" yelled one cheerful churchgoer.

"*I am the one and true prophet!*"

"Get thee behind me, welfare!"

"*Follow me to salvation!*"

"Give the taxpayers a break!"

Loren reached the top of the church steps, then hesitated. Official duty seemed to be interrupting him a lot this morning.

"Go on in," he said to Debra, and turned around. He crossed West Plaza and walked up to his former boss. His skin crawled as he neared the man on his box—he remembered Roberts as a pleasant, hand-shaking, inoffensive member of the establishment, and the transformation to Old Testament lunatic gave Loren a case of the certified creeps.

Roberts's eyes twinkled as he beamed down from his perch. His cheeks and nose were rosy from drink or the cold. His flock watched Loren with silent, suspicious eyes. "Loren!" Roberts said. "Long time, no see! Hast thou seen the light, my son?" Loren could smell whiskey on his breath.

"If you don't shut up, Al," Loren said, "I'm going to bust you."

Roberts raised a hand, but his voice was still cheerful. "Thou canst not halt this new preaching. Thou couldst as well stand against the wind, or the tide."

"Let's see your permit, then."

Roberts frowned down at him. "Thou art wearing the seven-pointed Star of Babylon on thy breast. Does this mean that thou hast given thy heart to the Evil One?"

Loren sighed. Some fundamentalist looney had started the Star of Babylon business a few years ago, and he hadn't heard the end of it since.

"What it means," he said, "is that the sheriff's department has six-pointed stars, and we wanted to look different. Now, how about the permit?"

"The Lord's servant," loftily, "does not need—"

"You can stand here all you like," Loren said, "and you can offer your literature, but if you start shouting and creating a disturbance, I'm going to pop you."

Roberts thought for a long moment, then resolution entered his face. He drew his blanket tighter about him and straightened, staring at the church.

"I shall stand mute," he said.

"Fine. That's all I ask."

As Loren turned to go back to the church, he heard Roberts's soft voice.

"Miracles happen every day."

A miracle, Loren figured, the guy could stand up.

"Before I begin today's message," said Pastor Rickey, "I would like to remind everyone that the Calamity Fund is running low on supplies of food and clothing. Let the lucky among us share our bounty with our neighbors."

Rickey looked up. "Today is the day in which we begin a week of contemplation and meditation upon our sins," he said. His Susquehanna accent made the word "our" sound like "ower."

Loren sat in his pew and scowled at the hymnal sitting in the rack in front of him. He had heard this opening sermon, or something very like it, once a year for every year of his life, and his mind was occupied with other matters.

Cipriano had called in the middle of breakfast to tell him that while staking out the Texas car, a battered old Geo, that was sitting in front of his cousin Félix's house, he'd seen Félix himself walking out of the house, wearing his bathrobe and picking up his Albuquerque newspaper. Cipriano stopped to ask, like any friendly relation, if Félix had had any company. Félix's relations from Harlingen had indeed stayed for two nights, but just that morning Robbie Cisneros had picked them up to go hunting, something Félix thought was just fine because, to tell the truth, he never much cared for Anthony and his horrible family, anyway.

Cipriano had then cruised by the Cisneros place, but Robbie's van was indeed gone. Loren told him to get out a LAWSAT alert to the New Mexico and Arizona state police, and also to start calling motels throughout the area, just in case Robbie & Co. checked in somewhere for a riotous weekend of spending their money away from inquisitive relatives. Since the Texans had left their car behind, Loren didn't think they'd gone far.

Loren figured they'd used the out-of-state car for the robbery itself, then planned to drive the strangers around in a vehicle driven by a local man.

Strange to think of a little-bitty Geo used as a getaway car, though. Loren doubted there was evidence enough for a warrant. Everything was purely circumstantial. If some state cop stopped them and bungled the search, the whole case could be lost.

Dammit, anyway! he thought. Some local had betrayed the town, and done so right in the middle of the worst crisis Atocha had faced since the Apaches destroyed the original settlement.

"You're grinding your teeth again," whispered Debra. Loren's mind snapped back to the present.

"Sorry," he said.

"We have before us a week devoted to the Seven Deadly Sins, which are above all other sins," said Pastor Rickey. "Why are these particular sins thought of as deadly? Why is gluttony a Deadly Sin and not, for example, simony?"

"What's simony?" whispered Katrina, more or less simultaneously with at least fifty other hushed voices. Katrina was Loren's older daughter, seventeen and blond, something of a tomboy. Beneath a pale pink headscarf, she looked uncharacteristically demure.

"Hush," said Loren. Not that he knew the answer, anyway.

"The selling of church offices," said Jerry. Loren looked at him. Jerry blinked back in total innocence. "I don't make this up, you know," he said.

"The Deadly Sins," Pastor Rickey went on, "are so called because indulgence in these sins leads without fail to further sin as a consequence. Gluttony, aside from overeating, also includes drunkenness and the use of drugs, and alcohol and drugs can lead to violence, to adultery, to anger, to theft.

"And of the Deadly Sins, pride is considered primary, because pride was the sin of Lucifer and led to war in Heaven. So on the first day of the Days of Atonement, we consider pride."

Pastor Rickey was young, just over thirty, but he looked older. Balding and prematurely gray, with a lined, weathered horse face, Rickey had spent years in the Peace Corps and working in soup kitchens for the needy before going to Catton College in Pennsylvania and the ministry. He brought a kind of restraint and intellectuality to his sermons that Loren wasn't certain he quite liked. The previous pastor, an old Pennsylvania Dutchman named Baumgarten, would have jumped up and down, waved his arms, poured sweat by the bucketful, and got to the subject of Hell long before this.

Not that Loren particularly enjoyed the contemplation of Hell. But since the Reverend Samuel Catton had been taken on a tour of Hell and various other parts of the cosmos by the Master in Gray who had dictated the *Authorized Revelations*, the existence of the Land of Fire was a necessary part of the faith, and Loren sometimes wondered why Rickey never seemed to mention it.

"The pride of Lucifer is one thing," the pastor said. "We can all see it for what it is, and we can condemn it. But even if we had the inclination, none of us can raise an army against Heaven. The sin of pride nevertheless exists in our community, and it is this kind of pure domestic pride I propose to examine this morning."

Loren gnawed his lower lip and wondered how Cipriano was faring.

"Pride is a particularly difficult sin to understand, because it is a perversion of something good," the pastor said, enriching the word *perversion* with his grand and rolling *r*'s. "Pride is a grace as well as a sin." *Grace* was heavy on the *r*, too; the pastor was willing to invest glory as well as sin by his dialect. "Your soul naturally desires pride—pride in yourself, in your family, your community and country. But the *sin* of pride is pride carried beyond its natural limits. The *sin* of pride is pride carried to the point where it *turns away from God*!"

Loren glanced up. A rare light was burning in Rickey's eyes. Maybe the man had finally taken fire.

"When you take proper pride in yourself, your community, and so on, that is because you *recognize God in all these things*." Rickey waved an arm. "You are taking pride in the majesty of God's creation! It is the *reflection of God* in which you take pride. Pride becomes an act of worship.

"But when your pride becomes a sin, it is because you have ceased to recognize God in these things, in yourself and your country and so on, and have begun to see in them a reflection of *yourself*! Pride has ceased to be worship, and begun to be an exercise in ego."

This last thought rolled through Loren, leaving a surprised feeling behind. He had never thought about it this way. Pastor Baumgarten had never analyzed sins in this fashion, just relied mainly on Samuel Catton's description of the personified Deadly Sins in the *Supplementary Revelations*, Pride with the diamond-encrusted gold and ivory neck brace that kept his chin aloft, Wrath with his hair aflame and his double-bitted axe that cut through friend and enemy alike, and so on.

Maybe there was a point to this fellow, after all.

"And when you see things only as bits of yourself, then you lose the sense of how they exist as their own unique and individual reflection of God. You start thinking of them as things you can toy with, to manipulate as you wish. You start thinking of your neighbors as people that you can save or condemn all on your own, instead of leaving that job up to God. You start thinking of your community as something you can arrange to your liking, and your country as something that exists to do your bidding throughout the world.

"And that is where the sin of pride enters daily life. You think of things as objects to be rearranged—not for their own good, although that's what you tell people, but in order to satisfy your own pride. You put yourself in debt in order to have a bigger car than your neighbor. That car has become an ornament to your pride. You break up with your girlfriend not because she isn't a fine person, but because she isn't pretty enough, or fashionable enough—she isn't a good enough ornament for *you*. You break your daughter's engagement, say, because her boyfriend doesn't come with enough dollars, or in some other way isn't good enough—not for her, but for you, because he wouldn't be a fine enough ornament to have around you. Your community becomes something you rearrange to suit yourself, so you join civic improvement organizations or run for office or join committees, and all because the way your neighbors are running their lives isn't good enough for you, you have to interfere and improve them."

Loren found himself becoming indignant. He turned to Debra and whispered. "Is he saying I'm not supposed to care about my neighbors and family?"

"Hush."

"We're *supposed* to care about our neighbors. That's what being an Apostle is all about. It's my *job* to care about my neighbors. They *pay* me for it."

Debra's look was fierce. "You're supposed to be humble when you do it, that's what he's saying."

"Try knocking down George Gileno with humility sometime."

"Everyone's looking at us."

"I don't think this college boy knows anything about the real world."

"The answer is God!" the college boy was saying. "We must trust in the wisdom and mercy of the Lord! We are fallen, and we must beg the Lord for understanding and for the knowledge of our own actions!"

"What a wimp," said Loren.

Debra pinched him hard on the hand.

Loren thought about the robbery for the rest of the service.

When Loren came out of the church with his family, he saw that the Roberts family had left and taken their box with them. In their place was a huddle of young Apaches surrounding an older man in a flannel shirt, who was pointing from place to place on the plaza with a stick.

Loren saw that every so often. He'd have to ask someday what it meant.

Cipriano was standing by his patrol car parked in the church loading zone. Loren saw the deputy chief and at once his mind seemed to leap into high gear. He almost ran down the steps to Cipriano's car, feeling an eagerness he could almost taste.

"What's up?"

Cipriano smiled with his big yellow teeth. "I found them, jefe. They're in El Pinto."

"El Pinto?" Loren gave it some thought and came up with little that made any sense. "Why El Pinto?" he asked. "It's just a goddamn crossroads ghost town. That's not where I'd go to spend my ill-gotten gains, that's for sure."

"They're in one of those cabins that Joaquín Fernandez owns up there. By that little trout pond."

"Huh. Thought he'd closed those cabins years ago."

"Guess he'll still rent if he gets a customer."

Loren looked at his family, who were clustered on the sidewalk just out of earshot, waiting for him to finish his business. "Have you talked to the sheriff?" he asked. "We'll need a liaison."

"He's going himself."

Loren was startled. "Shorty?"

"Election coming up, jefe. And the robbery was on his turf—technically, anyway."

"Yeah. Okay."

"There's still the problem of a warrant. We got no cause."

"Let me talk to Debra for a minute."

He stepped back to where his family was waiting for him. He could detect the well-concealed tension in Debra's posture, see the way the girls kept exchanging glances. It was one of those moments, known to every cop, when duty called and the family became aware, at least on some level, of the possibility of violence, of injury. He'd never known a policeman's family not to betray the strain in these little ways, even in a small town like Atocha.

"Looks like we found the guys we were looking for," he said.

"Good," said Debra.

"Why don't you take the car back home? Don't hold lunch for me."

Debra looked up at him. Loren could see his reflection in her wraparounds. "Take your vest," she said.

Loren blinked. "Yeah," he said. "Okay."

"I love you."

A sudden wave of pride almost took his breath away. Presumably it was the nonsinful kind, but if it was he didn't much care. Debra was perfect. He'd never been more certain of his marriage, his place in the town.

"I love you all," he said. "But don't worry. They're just some lightweight scumbags."

Scumbags with a sawed-off. No one said the words, but the presence, the weight of the unseen weapon, seemed oppressive on Loren's heart.

Loren went to the trunk and opened it. A few years ago the federal government had supplied personal armor for rural police departments, supposedly to give them some protection against drug dealers armed with AKMs. Loren took out the black kevlar flak jacket with the laminated steel and ceramic inserts, the spare shotgun, and the blue helmet he was supposed to wear when directing traffic. Churchgoers looked at him curiously as he carried the gear to Cipriano's cruiser and threw it all in the back. He got in the car.

"Let's go to the Sunshine," Loren said. "Deal with that warrant problem."

Cipriano drove around three sides of the plaza and parked in front of the café. Loren got out and walked through the avocado-green door into the Sunshine. He gave a half-wave to Coover behind the counter and went to the pay phone by the men's room door. A couple decades' phone numbers were jotted on the yellow flowered wallpaper. Two Korean businessmen, not the ones he'd seen the day before, sat drinking coffee. A plastic jar of elk blood was on the table between them. Mark Byrne, dressed exactly as he had been yesterday, grinned at him over his cup of coffee. He hadn't bothered to shave or comb his hair this morning.

"Hey," Coover said. "You can use the phone in my office."

"No problem," Loren said. He put a coin in the telephone and dialed the police number.

"Atocha Police Department." Loren recognized Eloy Esposito's voice.

"How's the neck, Eloy?"

"They got me in some goddamn brace, Chief. Gotta wear it for a month at least. Even in bed."

"Stay on the desk, then."

"Buncha bullshit."

"How's Buchinsky doing?"

"Mild concussion. Doctor said he can't work till Monday. Karen's giving him a raft of shit about it. She keeps telling him about how she could get him a job driving truck in Albuquerque."

"Think she'll ever get him to do it?"

"She keeps at him long enough."

That was too bad, Loren thought. Buchinsky was a good officer. It was just a pity that all police wives couldn't be like Debra.

Eloy's voice was cheerful. "So what do you need, Chief?"

"You got me mixed up with someone else," Loren said. "This is an anonymous call."

"Huh?"

"I'm not the police chief. I'm an informant calling with a tip."

"You're not the chief? This is a tip?"

"Yeah."

"I don't understand."

"Will you listen for a minute, Eloy?"

"If this is a tip, I'm supposed to get your name."

"Jesus Christ, Eloy!" Loren said. "How small-town can you get? It can't be an anonymous tip if I give you my name, now, can it?"

"I guess not." Doubtfully.

"Here's the tip. The guys who held up the Copper Country are in El Pinto, in one of Joaquín Fernandez's cabins. There are three of them, and they're armed and dangerous. You got that?"

"Armed and dangerous. Got it, Chief."

"I'm not the chief. But if I were you, I'd call the chief and tell him."

"Right. But I'm supposed to get your name and phone number."

Loren hung up, trying through his exasperation to decide whether having his head jammed into Doc Holliday's bar had scrambled Eloy's brains or whether the man was just having some kind of weird fun with him.

He started heading for the door. Coover, misinterpreting his presence, already had a cup of coffee waiting for him on the counter.

"Hey, Chief," said Byrne, waving a cigarette at him. "I wanna report a suspicious character. There was a guy with a turban in here a while ago eating breakfast. Probably a terrorist."

Probably another blood-drinker, Loren thought. He looked at Byrne. "So where's Sandoval? Gone to the library to look up some more facts he can embarrass people with?"

"Naw. He's gone west so we can get drunk." Byrne puffed on his cigarette. "Great anonymous tip, by the way. Anyone asks, I'll say I didn't recognize you."

"Shut up," Loren said.

Loren stalked out through the green deco door, his good mood gone. Now he just wanted to get to El Pinto, break down the door of whatever cabin the robbers were in, and get it all over with.

He got in Cipriano's car. "Courthouse," he said.

Cipriano waited in the car while Loren went in to meet the sheriff outside Judge Denver's Saturday morning district court session, an institution that existed primarily to process all the Friday drunks out of the jail to make room for Saturday night's crowd.

Eusebio Lazoya, the sheriff, was an elderly, somewhat frail man all of six feet four inches tall. He'd been known as "Shorty," of course, all his life. He was a pillar of the local Democratic Party machine and had been sheriff for as long as Loren could remember.

Shorty was a terrible police officer, with an appallingly bad memory for procedure—he had lost, tainted, or inadvertently damaged the evidence from several important investigations in his early days as sheriff—and his attitude toward his work had been thoroughly summed up by his failure to arrive at the robbery scene the previous night. He'd quite early realized that he would never make a career as a crimebuster, and allowed his underlings, and sometimes Loren's department, to handle the occasional puzzling investigation that came along.

Nevertheless Loren had learned to respect him as an administrator and politician. Despite his early blunders, Shorty had been unopposed in the last three elections. Everyone knew him. His reelection posters just said SHORTY in big red letters; everyone knew who the signs meant to advertise. But despite his personal job security, the cuts in county services that followed the progressive closing of the Atocha pit had sliced his department in half, and now he leaned on the city police more than ever.

Loren figured that Shorty was smelling news cameras, as the sheriff was dressed in the cream-colored western-cut suit that he only wore for public appearances, and had a broad-brimmed white Stetson perched on his wide, hairy ears. As Loren walked closer he saw that Shorty's dignified little white mustache had been freshly waxed.

"Hey, Loren," Shorty said, grinning. "Qué paso, hombre?"

Loren shook his hand. "I'd say we got a solution to the current crime wave."

"You got grounds for a warrant?"

"Somebody just phoned in an anonymous tip."

Shorty gave a little laugh as dry as an alkaline wash. "I like them lucky little anonymous tips, cousin. Let's get our warrant. Piedra movediza no cría lama."

Loren hesitated for a moment while he mentally translated. Moving rocks, right. He nodded. "Let's stop gathering lama, then."

"Yeah. There's a ball game on TV this afternoon I want to catch."

Loren and Shorty filed into the courtroom. The room was occupied primarily by the bruised warriors that Loren and his crew had hauled in the night before. Broad-shouldered George Gileno bulked huge in a wheelchair, almost blocking the aisle. Len

Bonniwell, a bright metal splint taped to his broken nose, sat next to his father and about as far away from A.J. Dunlop as the room permitted. Loren felt Dunlop's sullen eyes on him and grinned. He wouldn't be getting any more lip from A.J. as long as the boy's jaw was wired shut.

The town's assistant district attorney, Sheila Lowrey, was in the midst of a long speech asking for the judge to throw the book at a defiant drunk named Anderson who'd been picked up on DWI for the fourth time this year. Lowrey was a short, fierce-eyed young woman who wore a gray suit with padded shoulders. She had large tortoiseshell spectacles that she rarely wore but used as a prop, waving them by an earpiece like an orchestra leader slicing air with his baton. Small-town D.A. staffs were becoming dominated by recent female law-school graduates, who could get ahead a lot faster in small towns desperate for legal talent than in the established male power structure of the big cities. So far as Loren could tell, Lowrey was a pretty good A.D.A., but she hadn't been in town long enough to understand the foundation of kinship, religious, and political networks that lay beneath Atocha society, or to realize that Judge Denver wasn't going to allow one of his cousins, who also happened to be a loyal precinct worker, to have a DWI conviction on his record.

This was going to take a while. Loren parked himself on a bench. Shorty joined him.

Something huge moved in Loren's peripheral vision. Loren looked over his shoulder to see George Gileno pushing his wheelchair toward him. Gileno parked himself next to Shorty and leaned over Shorty's lap to whisper to Loren.

"Hey. Chief." Gileno spoke through split lips in a voice that was surprisingly light and gentle. His face was a mass of contusions and bits of white tape. Both eyes were black and two of his fingers were taped together. Loren leaned toward him.

"How's the back?"

"Sprained. I could walk but I'm gonna try to get sympathy."

"Good luck." Gileno had been in front of Denver every time he'd busted up Doc Holliday's, and Denver didn't like Indians to begin with.

"What is it," Loren asked, "that you've got against Holliday's, anyway?"

"I don't know, man."

"Why not someplace else?"

Gileno looked stubborn. "Holliday's is as good a place as any."

Loren shook his head. "Do me a favor, George. Wait till I retire before you get drunk in this town again."

"I wasn't drunk. I was *trying* to get drunk and they wouldn't serve me."

"Stay out of Holliday's, George."

"I lost my job along with everyone else. I don't think I'm gonna be visiting town very often anymore." He looked hopeful for a minute. "Can you do me a favor, Chief?"

"Maybe."

"I'd like to do my time in the jail here. Not back on the reservation."

Loren scratched his neck. "I don't know if I can help you, George. The municipality has an agreement with the reservation authorities. Apaches do time on the rez, white folks in Atocha."

"You know what the reservation cops are like. Man, I'd rather do a hitch in the Marines."

"I can't help you. Not when the jail's budget is bound to get chopped again."

Gileno gazed unhappily into a future filled with bullet-headed Apache cops and jailers.

"Sorry," Loren said.

"Hey," Shorty said. His little mustache twitched in a slow, wicked grin. "Listen up. Here come the punch line."

Sheila Lowrey had been winding up her speech while Gileno was trying to slide out of reservation stir. Judge Denver, looking stern, summoned the defendant Anderson to stand before him.

"I don't believe in those breath tests, anyway," Denver said. He banged his gavel. "Case dismissed."

Anderson turned to shake hands with his public defender, another cousin. Sheila's eyes bugged from her head, and Loren clamped down hard on his mirth. An angry flush began to creep upward from Sheila's collar. Loren had a feeling she might say something rash. He stood up.

"My apologies for interrupting, Your Honor," he said. "I was wondering if the sheriff and I might beg some of your time in the matter of a warrant."

"Say what you've got to say," said the judge.

"Could we do this in chambers, Your Honor? This is a matter involving some confidentiality."

"Ten-minute recess," said Denver.

He banged his gavel and headed toward his chambers. Loren dropped a sympathetic hand on Lowrey's padded shoulder as he followed.

"Facts of life, Sheila. Sorry."

Lowrey looked ready to hit somebody. "I'll get the son of a bitch someday," she said. Loren wasn't sure whether she meant the DWI or Denver.

"I wouldn't go home this afternoon," Loren said. "I'm gonna have some work for you."

"God dammit. I was gonna change my oil filter this afternoon."

"You're a lawyer, Sheila. You can afford to have a filling station do that."

"Bullshit. You know what I get paid. And you know what?" She waved her spectacles like a sword. "*It isn't enough to put up with this crap!*"

"You'll get used to it."

Loren walked away feeling a sincere sympathy for whoever was up next. Denver was going to have to reestablish his law-and-order credentials by being hard on somebody, and Lowrey was ready to exsanguinate the next defendant with her very own teeth.

It took only a few minutes to secure the warrant, about as fast as it took for Denver to get a typist to process it. YOU ARE HEREBY COMMANDED, it said in big, reassuring letters, *to search forthwith* (check one) **XX** *the place described in the Affidavit.*

Loren liked the word "commanded."

Denver didn't question the anonymous call, nor did he balk when Loren used the "armed and dangerous" part of the tip to ask for a no-knock provision. Loren tucked the warrant into his breast pocket, shook the judge's hand, and used the judge's private exit from his chambers, happy in the knowledge that he could break down any doors he needed to.

Cipriano, anticipating the warrant, had in the meantime got a knock-knock from police stores. The knock-knock was a six-inch-diameter piece of lead pipe three feet long, filled with concrete and equipped with handles. It was used for breaking down doors. Someone had put little happy-face stickers on both ends.

Loren drove out to El Pinto with Cipriano, and two more officers followed in another cruiser. Shorty and a sheriff's deputy followed in one of the four-wheel-drive Broncos the sheriff's department used to negotiate the county's horrid back roads.

The drive to El Pinto took them west on 81, then north on State 103, past the little bedroom community of Vista Linda that had been built chiefly to house ATL employees. Tract homes sat atop barren brown earth, surrounded by breast-high concrete-block fences and empty acres of yucca, prickly pear, and ocotillo. Solar collectors stood in black, quiet rows on the roofs. On the town's north side was a shopping mall, its parking lot crowded with cars, another blow to downtown Atocha business.

"Those people," said Loren, "sure like their privacy. Build on those big lots, then wall themselves off."

Even though laid-off miners selling out had dropped real estate values into the basement, few newcomers ever chose to live in the old town. Loren had been told that they felt that Atocha houses were too little and were set on lots that were too small. If you lived in one, you might actually be forced by proximity to *pay attention to your family and neighbors*, an idea that the ATL people seemed to find uncomfortable.

Cipriano lit a cigarette with the car's lighter as he drove. "They're from the big city," he said. "They don't know how to be neighborly. In a city your neighbor'll kill you soon as look at you. They spend their days trying to avoid talking to their neighbors."

"Those little cinder-block fences are gonna keep them safe, huh?"

"They got zoning laws to keep out the riffraff, ése."

"Riffraff. That's the community they're living in."

"Yeah."

"Those guys." Loren found himself getting angry. "They wouldn't know a community if it bit them. They don't have a clue. They're all goddamn *commuters*." Even Pastor Rickey was like that, he thought, with all his talk about not caring for your community anymore.

"You said it, Chief."

"Just shuttling in and out." Loren found himself enjoying the commuter analogy. He wanted to expand on it for a while. "Getting their tickets punched," he said. "Riding on their goddamn friction-free railway."

"With briefcases of money."

"Yeah." Loren's buoyant mood began to slide. "With lots of money that they all keep to themselves." That was the foreign competition, he thought, that had taught them that. ATL was owned by a consortium of high-tech concerns, diffusing both the risk and the new technology. All of them were presumably making tens of millions on the new superconductors. Their new-style company town featured housing subsidized Japanese-style through a corporate-owned credit union. The money was kept in the family, spent in the shopping mall, where all you got with your purchase was a financial transaction and a phony smile rather than an interaction with a real neighbor. An attempt, Loren thought, to create a common corporate culture rather than a community based on shared values.

All these decades trying to stay out of the grip of the Anaconda, Loren thought, and we get paid with this.

"We sort of started the feud, Chief, if you think about it," Cipriano said. "We voted not to let their development incorporate with the town."

"Why should our mill rates go up so they can put in their sewers and water? We already *had* sewers and water. If they wanted to live in their own little town instead of moving in with us, why should we pay for it?"

"Maybe ATL thought that was unfriendly of us."

"Maybe ATL wanted to fuck us over. They're trying to cut smart deals with us, just like our ancestors did to the Indians. And before we know it, we're stuck out on the rez like poor George Gileno."

Cipriano pitched his cigarette out the window. Being compared to Gileno had not pleased him.

"You're going to start a fire doing that," Loren said.

"We're being followed," said Cipriano. "One of those jeeps."

"God damn it. We're in marked cars, fer chrissakes."

"Maybe you should call up Bill Patience and have him tell his people to stop following us around."

"Maybe I should call up Patience and tell him to ram one of his fancy Italian pistols up his fucking ass."

They crossed a bridge over the wandering Rio Seco. A shining concrete overpass rose ahead of them, marking where the maglev train crossed the road. Vista Linda faded away behind Loren's right shoulder. On the left was the entrance to the Advanced Technology Laboratories, well marked, with a stoplight. The stoplight was green. Past the entrance, Highway 103 deteriorated into a patched, potholed, shoulderless two-lane blacktop. Off to the left, ATL was visible only as a long shining ribbon of twelve-foot-high chain link fence beyond which were the long mounds that covered the accelerators and a few barely visible low, earth-colored buildings.

Sometimes at night, when they were running their experiments, you could see them firing up into the sky, bright thundering lightnings reaching for the vacuum.

Shooting at Heaven, Loren thought. You had to live in hope that Heaven didn't start shooting back.

One of Shorty's reelection posters sailed past, its one-word message riddled by someone's .22. Tall mountains, huge slabs of eroded igneous rock, loomed closer, high clouds casting shadows on the bright green like oil spots on a lawn. Loren could count three columns of smoke rising from the mountains, forest fires started by lightning or careless campers. Fire-fighting helicopters reflected bright sunlight as they hovered over the source of the smoke. In another few weeks, Loren thought, he and Jerry would climb one of those steep ridges and shoot a deer or two.

If the fires spared any of the timber and wildlife.

A suppressed excitement began to hum in his mind at the thought of what was waiting for him. He tried to picture Robbie Cisneros staring down the twelve gauges of his shotgun. The thought was entirely satisfying.

El Pinto was an old silver boom town settled in the 1890s, buried in a lightless narrow canyon, surrounded by towering igneous formations. There was nothing left of the original settlement, which had burned down eighty years ago—the town couldn't survive as a quaint tourist village—and even the new town had seen better days. There were probably more personal computers and satellite receivers in a ten-mile radius than there were flush toilets. The current village consisted of the ruins of an old red brick filling station burned down twenty years before in yet another fire, a new cinder-block filling station across the road from the old one, a combination general store and post office, a tavern, a Tastee-Freez, and, a little north in a side canyon, Joaquín Fernandez's bait shop and cabins.

Fernandez was half Apache and maybe eighty years old. For years he'd been a guide, showing strangers how to track mountain lion, elk, and bear, renting cabins to his customers, and earning a small amount by placer mining on his little creek. He'd given up guiding, but fisherman who didn't want to go home empty-handed could catch meal-fed trout on his little stocked pond for a dollar per catch.

The roadside sign—EL PINTO CABINS VACANCY—hadn't been repainted in years. Fernandez's shambling house and bait shop was near the road. The cabins were a quarter mile down the canyon, screened from the highway by a clump of willows.

Cipriano pulled the cruiser up on the overgrown lawn in front of the bait shop, keeping between it and the cabins. A dead century plant and a big white old-fashioned receiver dish cast a shadow on the car's hood. The other lawmen joined Cipriano on the lawn. Loren got out of the car and stepped onto the worn wooden porch, pulled aside the battered screen door that said WE HAVE WATER DOGS, and stepped inside. Out of the corner of his eye he saw the ATL jeep drive past on the patched old two-lane.

The sound from the ice machine almost drowned out the report of a football game coming from one of the back rooms. Old bags of potato chips stood on shelves next to racks of dusty canned food. "Hey, Joaquín." Loren pushed into the back room.

Galvanized tanks full of live bait bubbled on all sides. Big black salamanders with huge branching gills on either side of their goggle eyes—"water dogs"—seethed in the frothing water. The Longhorns were down 14–3 on the live satellite feed from Austin.

Fernandez was tilted back in an overstuffed chair, eyes closed, mouth open. His pants were unbuttoned. A cold shudder went through Loren at the thought the old man was dead. But then Fernandez opened his black eyes and gave Loren a sharp, birdlike look.

"Pretty damn nice clothes if you're going fishing," he said.

"You got some people staying in your cabins?" Loren asked.

"Three young guys? Robbie Cisneros and his two cousins from Texas?"

"First customers I've had in four weeks." Fernandez stood up and buttoned up his pants. "I got some coming in later today, and that makes a good season anymore."

"Go ahead and sit down," Loren said. "Robbie and his punk cousins held up a bar in Atocha last night, and I've got a warrant to go in and get them." He took the warrant out of his pocket. "You want to read it?"

Fernandez patted the pockets of his flannel shirt. "Ain't got my reading glasses, Loren. I'll take your word on it."

"What cabin are they in?"

"Number nine. The one that's painted kinda pink. You want the key?"

"I guess. What kind of door is it?"

"It's just a door. You ain't gonna bust it down, are you?"

"Might have to. They've got a sawed-off."

"Jesus howdy." Fernandez seemed impressed. "Hell, Loren," he said. "Bust the son of a bitch down. I'll get it fixed."

"Thanks."

Fernandez shambled into the back and came out with a key hanging on an old twisted piece of wire, the kind that came on loaves of bread. There was a piece of tape on the key that had once had the cabin number on it but had since faded completely.

"I'll get my thirty-ought-six and go with you," Fernandez said.

Loren put a hand on the old man's arm. "No way, Joaquín. You stay here till it's over."

"I'm a good shot," Fernandez complained. "With my scope I can shoot a sparrow in the eye no sweat."

"Sit down, Joaquín." Loren guided him back to his chair. "Listen to the game. This won't take but a minute."

Anticipation chanted a vengeful chorus in Loren's mind. He took off his blazer as he left the store, folded it carefully, and put it on the front seat of the car. Cipriano stood wordlessly on the other side of the car, chewing on a long brown stem of grass. Loren opened the back door and took out his flak jacket, then buckled it on. Fire-fighting helicopters throbbed in the distance.

"What's the plan, Chief?" Cipriano asked.

"We go in and knock the door down before they figure out we're here."

"I take it you're going in first?"

Loren buckled on the helmet and lowered the faceplate. He felt as if his blood were singing a Wagner aria. "Fuckin' A," he said.

"Hey," Shorty called from his Bronco. "What's happening?"

"Follow us," Loren said.

"That's your plan?"

Loren skinned his lips back from his teeth. "That's the plan."

"You might consult, you know. That's what I'm here for."

"Shit, Shorty. We're wasting time. Anything else, we'll have to call in a negotiating team from Albu-fucking-querque or something."

Shorty waved his hand. "Yeah, okay. It's your funeral, cousin."

Cipriano got his vest out of the car trunk and buckled it on. Loren jacked a shell into the chamber of his shotgun and got in the car. Cipriano slid behind the wheel and gunned the Fury's engine.

Blood wailed in Loren's ears. "Fast and quiet," he said. "Number nine. It's painted pink."

The Fury spat gravel as it spun in a short turn, then dove down the two-rut drive. Dying willows shot past them. Towers of eroded igneous rock, a miniature Grand Canyon, eclipsed the sun. There was a blue glimpse of the trout pond sitting in its meadow, the wooden structures of Joaquín's placer mine, and then cabins started flashing past.

"There's the van. Number four. Right here."

The cabin was a square frame building plastered over and painted to look like adobe. There was a tiny front porch with a peaked roof on it that made it look like an ancient one-room school.

The Fury skidded to a halt like a baseball player sliding into home. Loren's door was already open, his foot ready to take the first step onto the brown soil.

He lunged out of the car, his shotgun at port arms. The door was a flimsy frame thing, he saw, and he wouldn't need the knock-knock. The second step took him onto the porch, and at the third he turned his body and drove his shoulder into the door.

There was a shriek of wood and the frame tore away. Loren spilled into the room, took a cross-step, recovered his balance, brought the shotgun down. A five-foot white sliver of the door frame clattered to the floor.

"Hi, Robbie," said Loren. What he was actually supposed to say was something like "Police! Open!" and say it before he actually smashed the door down. It seemed pointless now. Blood sang in his ears like a swarm of angry bees.

Three young men had been half lying on pieces of furniture in the front room. They were all dressed in tank tops and rolled-up blue jeans. One of them, a stranger, was wearing a green pachuco handkerchief low over his eyes and had a little goatee. There were prison tattoos on his forearms, and he wore Bill Forsythe's turquoise bracelet. All three were sitting up now, staring at the shotgun with glazed eyes.

There was a bong on the scarred old coffee table. A green mound of marijuana sat on an opened newspaper next to it. Sharing the table with the dope was the sawed-off, several piles of dirty bills, and a bunch of Riga Brothers paychecks.

Cipriano ran through the door, followed by another pair of cops.

Robbie and his friends seemed too stoned to react. Loren nevertheless advanced cautiously, reached down, picked up the sawed-off. He pushed the lever that opened the breech with his big thumb and broke the action. He read the inscriptions on the base of the shells. Double-ought buck.

"Serious kind of fishing equipment," he said. "Now, everybody get up slowly and put your hands on top of your head."

Shorty and his deputy came in while the suspects were being handcuffed. Loren's heart was turning over like a smooth turbine. His body felt light, almost weightless. He knew he was invincible, that anything was possible.

Shorty reached into a pocket, took out his six-pointed sheriff's badge, and put it on his perfect white lapel.

"You guys are under arrest," he said, as if for the cameras.

Loren looked at Robbie Cisneros. "Too bad one of you decided to resist."

He grabbed Robbie by his hair and pulled him across the room. "Something you forgot, Robbie," he said, hustling the boy into the bathroom. "Nothing happens in my town without my say-so. And when you decided to invite a couple of strangers to come into *my town* and point a sawed-off full of double-ought in *my neighbors' faces* and steal a bunch of laid-off miners' paychecks, *you didn't ask my permission first."*

He pushed and Robbie crashed over into the old claw-foot bathtub, unable to keep his head from slamming into the tile because his hands were cuffed behind his back. Loren raised his shotgun butt over the boy's body. Robbie looked up with a dazed lack of comprehension.

In his mind Loren saw his daughters, their eyes hard with need, veins pitted with addiction.

Not here, he thought.

"I am the sword and the arm of the Lord," Loren said.

Some time thereafter Loren felt a hand on his arm. He shrugged it off and brought the shotgun down again. The hand came back, more insistent this time.

"That's enough, cousin." Shorty's voice.

Loren looked down at the bloody, whimpering mess in the bathtub and took a long breath. Sweat was pouring down his face inside his helmet. Vertigo eddied through him. He rocked on his feet.

"Time to get some air," Shorty said.

Loren turned and brushed past Shorty and stepped past the other officers and the wide-eyed suspects and out onto the porch. He unbuckled the chin strap of his helmet and pulled it off, then put down his shotgun and laid the helmet next to it. A breeze that carried the scent of piñon cooled the sweat on his face. He unbuckled the vest and dropped it, then stepped to Cipriano's car, got the keys out of the ignition, and opened the trunk. He took out the LAWSAT kit, put it on the roof of the car, and opened it. The antenna was about the size and general shape of an attaché case. Loren took it out and laid it on the roof, then took the antenna lead and jacked it into the C.A.D. keyboard in the Fury. He leaned over the car's keyboard, pressed a function key, and looked at the car's little liquid-crystal display.

ESTABLISHING SATELLITE UPLINK, it said. Then, SATELLITE UPLINK ESTABLISHED.

Loren entered his user number and password and told the

LAWSAT computer in Washington to cancel the alert for Robbie and his pickup. OK, the display said. Loren logged off and leaned his head back against the rest. Cipriano walked over to the car door and leaned down to look at Loren.

"I think maybe I'll go hunting," Loren said. "I don't have any dogs and I'm not dressed for it, but what the hell. The pigeon won't care how I'm dressed."

"You gotta work on that temper of yours, jefe," Cipriano said.

"Fuck that. It needed doing."

"You can't get away with that kind of shit anymore, man."

Loren pulled the antenna jack out of the computer. "It's my town, Cipriano," he said.

He got out of the car and packed the LAWSAT kit and put it back in the trunk. He put on his blue blazer and went back into the cabin. He could hear the shower running as somebody cleaned up the mess. The money was still lying on the table. He reached down and picked up a couple twenties.

"For Joaquín," he said, just in case anyone wondered. "So he can get his door fixed."

Robbie Cisneros, limping, eyes swollen shut, was marched to the back seat of the second cruiser, and the two Texans were put into the sheriff's Bronco. Cipriano and Loren followed the other two cars to the bait shop, then pulled into the parking space out back and went in the rear, through the screen door into Fernandez's kitchen.

Fernandez shambled toward them out of the front. Behind him Loren could see a pair of ATL security people, one a stranger, the other one of the men who had been at Cipriano's lecture the previous day, the guy with the halo of bleached hair around his flattop.

"Everything go okay?" Fernandez asked.

Loren gave him the twenties. "For your door," he said.

Fernandez gave a grin. Loren looked up into the Ray-Bans of the two security men. "Buying some bait?" he said.

"Potato chips," one said.

The sound of a starter grinding came from the front. Fernandez looked over his shoulder. "Glad my other customers didn't show up till it was over. Hate to scare off the only ones I got."

"Hunters?" Loren asked.

"I dunno, Loren. Maybe. They didn't say."

The world seemed to slow down for a moment. The starter ground on. Loren drifted through the door into the little store and looked out the window.

Fernandez's other customers were two dark-skinned men in a cream-colored Chevrolet pickup with a small camper shell. They were towing a little homemade trailer.

"Lookit that," Loren said. Now Loren knew why Robbie and his buddies had come to a nowhere place like El Pinto to celebrate their stickup.

They were waiting for someone to come and sell them something.

Cipriano came up and looked out the window and gave a whistle. The ATL guys followed, sensing something significant.

Loren mentally reviewed the search-and-seizure laws. He didn't need a warrant for something he had an active LAWSAT tip on, and in any case the Supreme Court had pretty much abolished the Fourth Amendment for drug dealers, anyway.

The pickup's engine finally caught. Loren pushed open the screen door with one hand while he withdrew his pistol with the other. Cipriano was right behind him.

"Uhh," said one of the ATL men, trying to decide how to react.

Aware that the security men were watching his technique, Loren stuck the Chief's Special through the open window and put the barrel under the astonished driver's left ear. Cipriano ran around the other side, his own pistol out.

Loren looked at Cipriano's face through the cab of the pickup.

"Out of the Tchevy, Pedro," he said.

The expression on Cipriano's face was like a sunrise.

F I V E

Loren told the press to meet him at Fernandez's at five o'clock, while there was still enough light to roll tape and enough time to make the feed for the ten o'clock news. He'd just made the largest drug haul in Atocha County history, and more capsules of black lightning were confiscated than at any time in the history of the state. The new drug, one of the variants on red kryptonite that had been showing up in the last few months, had only been declared illegal six days before, and a bust this big was news.

He knew if he put the news on the LAWSAT, DEA or Customs or some other freebooting agency would try to claim the arrest for themselves, so he decided to let them hear about it on television.

He didn't tell the mayor, either. The less credit Trujillo was able to claim for his administration, the better.

The conference itself went well, even though Trujillo did eventually hear the news from somebody and arrived at the last minute. Loren, wearing a fresh uniform and his photogenic flak jacket, drank grape soda with Shorty in Joaquín's store while the reporters made their mike tests. Shorty, still in his western suit, star, and Stetson, cracked jokes with the local CBS stringer, an old crony of his. Loren had decided, in view of the election and party solidarity, to allow the sheriff's department partial credit for the drug bust.

Cipriano arrived in his uniform. Loren saw he had a new haircut. Cipriano stood in front of the mike stand and stiffly related the events of the afternoon. He mentioned that Loren was first through the door, and subsequent follow-up questions allowed him to give answers that made Loren seem a hero. Still cameras began clicking.

Loren got his picture taken brandishing the Ingram Mac-11 that the smugglers had been carrying under the front seat of the pickup, a tiny gun that looked like a toy in Loren's big hand but that would still rock and roll to the tune of twelve hundred rounds per minute. When Loren passed out pictures of the suspects and the crime scenes, Trujillo took the opportunity to offer formal congratulations and handshakes, made an impromptu speech about the various things his mayoral administration was doing to combat drug abuse, and handed out lapel buttons that said DESIGNER JEANS, NOT DRUGS.

Loren looked at his button for a long, hard moment. He put it in his pocket.

Assholes always advertise.

Afterward, while the television people started packing up cameras and microphones, Trujillo came back to shake Loren's hand again. "You should have let my office know you were setting this up, Loren," he said.

"Didn't we?" Loren looked at Cipriano and tried to imitate surprise. "I'm sure I told somebody to do that."

"Something of this magnitude, we should have the whole administration here. It's important to present a united front against the drug menace."

"I'm sorry, Ed. I'll try and find out how we screwed up." Loren cleared his throat. "Ed, I'm going to have to ask for a special voucher for funds to send the drugs up to Albuquerque. We don't have secure facilities for this big a haul here in town."

Trujillo blinked. "What do you mean?"

"The evidence, Ed. Normally I'd just put it in our safe, but this is a whole camper pickup and a trailer full of black lightning and love beads and kryptonite. Right now we've got it all in the city garage under guard, but we can't have it stay there."

Trujillo's look was doubtful. "Can't we destroy it?"

"It's *evidence*, Ed. We'll destroy it after the trial, but—"

"I mean just destroy most of it. Keep enough to convict the felons."

"There's this whole principle called the chain of evidence. We can't mess with it, otherwise a good attorney could get the whole trailerful suppressed. Sorry, Ed, but I'm gonna have to ask for special funds."

"I don't know." Reluctantly.

Loren looked at him. "You just made a big speech about all your administration is doing to fight drugs, Ed, and you won't give me a lousy pay voucher?"

"Can't we get the county to pay for some of it? They're sharing a credit."

"That's your department. But they've got even less money than the city."

"It's just that you've been running up a lot of unanticipated expenses recently. And then there's all the overtime your people pulled last night."

"And will pull tonight. Tonight might even be worse than last night, because people have had all damn day to get drunk and belligerent."

"Okay." Trujillo looked pained.

"Just think how much worse it would be if they weren't just sucking up booze, if they had a whole big supply of kryptonite to chug down with their Coors."

"I guess it's inevitable. If you want good publicity, you have to pay for it."

"What a weasel!" Loren said later, as Cipriano drove him back to the office. "We bust some scumbags who were going to peddle that designer shit in our town, and all he thinks about is the publicity."

"And the extra expense," Cipriano said. He scratched the back of his neck where hair clippings were irritating him.

"Yeah. That kind of stuff burns my ass."

Long shadows crossed the road ahead of them. It would be dark in another hour. "Makes you nostalgic, you know?"

"The last mayor might have seen visions and had relations who were thieves, but at least he was solid about some things. He wasn't a weasel."

"Yeah. And if Roberts hadn't appropriated them highway funds for his brother's company, we wouldn't have Little Eddie to deal with."

"Little Eddie. I like that."

"People in this town have been stealing federal funds for fifty years. And all of a sudden the voters realized they were taxpayers, too, and it was their money, after all, and got offended."

"Took 'em long enough."

"Roberts just happened to be mayor when the rules changed right out from under him."

Loren pulled off his velcro tie and loosened his blue uniform shirt collar. For some reason, despite all the activity and lack of sleep over the last twenty-four hours, he wasn't tired at all. The elation that had possessed him during the drug bust wasn't about to fade away, not yet.

"You know," he said, "I remember going down to that old adobe by the tracks and buying paper bags of Mexican potoguaya from old man Martinez. Everybody from the high school used to smoke it and drink mescal out of smuggled mason jars that had the worm in the bottom, and there wasn't any harm in it that I could see."

"You used to do that?" Cipriano seemed surprised. He slowed to make the turn onto 81. "I bought pot from Daddy Martinez, too."

"And now look at what's happening with drugs. Dealers with Mac-11s. People cooking up new stuff in labs. A brand-new substance every week. Murders. Brain damage. Gene damage." He shivered. "Foreign governments run by the dealers."

"It's a new century."

"It's not happening in this town," Loren said. He thought about people like Robbie Cisneros selling stuff to his daughters. Katrina sailing on something like black lightning, eyes hard and inward and unreachable. "Not if I have anything to say about it," Loren said. He reached down and picked up the Mac-11. The setting sun gleamed a dull red on the blackened surface. Twelve hundred rounds per minute, he thought. A man could pack that in a gun so small no one would ever see he was carrying it.

"Jesus, jefe," said Cipriano. "What did I do?"

"Huh?" Loren stared at him.

"For a second there you looked like you were gonna blow me away."

"Oh. Sorry." He put the gun down. "I was just thinking about dealers in this town. Shit, I'd even run in Martinez if he were still alive."

"You better start being more careful, jefe. Those two Mexican dudes could have been in the room with Robbie when you busted down that door, and that gun would have made a cheeseburger out of you. A flak jacket isn't gonna stop a whole magazine full of nine-millimeter rounds."

"Not if they never reached it. Not if they were surprised."

"Still." Cipriano scratched his neck again. The Fury slowed as it entered town.

"I knew the sawed-off was there. That's a lot more dangerous a weapon. Shotguns kill a *lot* more people than automatics."

"Jefe," patiently, "*I* sure wouldn't take chances like that. That's what young, unmarried guys are for."

Loren thought about that for a moment, thought about charging through the door into a spray of 9mm rounds. Debra's face when she heard. Katrina and Kelly standing by the coffin.

"You're right," he said. "I shouldn't do this kind of stuff."

"You're the chief. Let the Indians do the work anymore." Scratching.

Loren grinned. "Still, I showed I could still do it, huh?"

Cipriano didn't grin back. "Yeah," he said. "You sure did."

Loren frowned. Cipriano seemed weary. "Why don't you knock off till ten, hey?" he said. "Then I'll go home and you can take over till things die down."

Cipriano nodded. "Yeah. Okay." He pulled up in front of the City-County Building's deco griffins. Loren opened the door and put one foot on the sidewalk.

"Good bust," he said.

"Yeah, jefe. Good bust." Cipriano hesitated. "Loren," he said, "remember what happened to Roberts. He was just doing what everyone did. But the rules changed."

Loren was puzzled. "Yeah," he said.

"The rules are changing. Just try and remember that, okay?"

Hesitation fluttered in Loren's mind as he watched Cipriano drive away.

Hell, Cipriano was probably just working too hard.

He went to his office and started on his report.

Two hours later, Eloy Esposito appeared in the door and knocked on the frame. He grinned from over the neck brace. "Chief?" he said.

"I thought I'd run over to Lupe's Chili House and get something to eat. You want me to get you something?"

"Sure." That would make a change from the awful food at the Sunshine, anyway. Loren reached into his pocket and pulled out a five-dollar bill.

"Mexican plate, coffee."

"Got it. Would you mind watching the phones and the radio while I'm out?"

"No problem."

Stretching, Loren moved to the front desk. He looked down the end of the dull white hexagonal corridor tile, through the glass doors to the Federal Building on the plaza. One of the hallway's six-foot-long fluorescent lights hummed and flickered overhead. The police radio buzzed with officers returning to patrol from dinner. Loren made notes in the log at each report.

The 911 line rang. Loren picked it up.

"Atocha Emergency."

"They're at it again." The old lady's voice seemed vaguely familiar, but Loren couldn't place it.

"Who are at what, ma'am?"

"Is that you, Loren?"

"Yes."

"ATL, that's who!" The voice was indignant. "They're firing their laser beams again!"

Loren recognized the voice at last. Mrs. Mickelsson, the widow of a Riga Brothers truck driver whose brakes had given out hauling copper ore up the two-and-a-half-percent grade of the Atocha pit, and who had been run over by his own twelve-foot left front tire as he baled out of the cab.

"What are they doing with their lasers, exactly?" Loren asked.

"Trying to control my mind! I can hear their voices in my head!"

Loren winced at her volume. "I see." He held the phone a little farther from his ear. "Have you been taking your medication, Mrs. Mickelsson?"

"It makes me feel funny." Mumbling.

"You know that medication makes you immune to the mind-control lasers, don't you, Mrs. Mickelsson?"

"I don't like it."

"You're going to have to take your medication, okay? And I'll call ATL and tell them to shut the lasers off."

There was a lengthy, dismayed silence. "Do I really have to take my pills?"

"Yes, you do. But I'll have them shut off the lasers, too, okay?"

"Okay. I'll do 'er." She seemed cheerful again.

Loren made a note to have someone stop by her house later, just to make sure she was okay.

Sometimes the old people called just to have someone to talk to. And when others saw flying saucers finally showing up at the UFO field east of town, or angels towering over the City-County Building, or when the demons that lived in the drainpipes got too noisy, they called 911 to get some action.

Most of the time it was best just to humor them. They didn't hurt anybody with their visions.

After the mind-control laser alarm, there were no disturbances. No drunks, no fights. Maybe the anger had blown itself out the previous night.

Loren's heart leaped at the sound of a metallic crash from outside. Someone's car had just hit something. He stood up, began to move around the desk.

One of the two fluorescent overhead tubes winked out. Loren moved forward in the reduced light.

The glass doors banged open. Loren's heart leaped again. October wind fluttered papers on the desk.

A dead man walked through the door.

Loren stared, heart pounding, in a moment of horrified recognition. Fear poured like ice water through his veins.

The man was in his twenties. He wore blue jeans, scuffed brown cowboy boots, and a pale blue yoked western shirt with metal collar tabs and pearl buttons. The left side of his chest was soaked with blood.

The man stumbled and fell. Loren ran forward.

The man had fallen on his face. There was a pale circle on the man's right rear jeans pocket. The round can of Copenhagen therein was partially dislodged, half out of the pocket. Loren knelt and turned the man over. There was blood on the hexagonal tile where he had lain. A string of half-clotted blood drooled out of the man's mouth.

"Loren. Goddamn. Help me, Loren."

The voice was a strangled whisper. Loren reached for him, tried to check vital signs, tried to remember what the Red Cross paramed had told him to do in lifesaving class years ago. The skin was clammy and pale. The chest rose as the man tried to breathe. He made drowning sounds.

"Hang on. We'll get help," Loren said.

The man stopped breathing. Hands clutched frantically at Loren's arms, his shoulders. The eyes were yellow and terrified.

The police had been equipped with little plastic tubes that they were supposed to use while breathing for victims, so that they wouldn't have to expose themselves to blood and maybe get AIDS. Loren didn't have one with him.

He was going to have to do this the old-fashioned way.

Loren bent down and pressed his mouth over the man's mouth, pinched off his nostrils with one hand. He exhaled fiercely into the man's mouth. He had to fight against great resistance to pump air into him. Blackness beat with feathered wings against Loren's vision as he battled whatever was filling the man's lungs. The victim's chest rose.

Loren straightened, gasping for breath. Lights flashed behind his eyes. The man's chest hung there, the lungs full, refusing to empty.

Loren reached out, pressed down on the man's stomach. Dark blood fountained from the victim's mouth. It was full of little bubbles.

The man's eyes were glazed. His arms moved limply. Loren wanted to scream in frustration.

He couldn't think of anything else to do but keep trying to breathe for the other man. He bent, pressed his mouth to the man's mouth again. Blood slicked his lips. Loren tried not to think of AIDS and tried to breathe out. The man's lungs refused to expand.

Loren fought till blackness swarmed into his vision, until he could feel himself passing out from lack of air, and then he leaned back, tasting blood, gasped for air, and watched the man die.

"Jesus, what happened?" Eloy walked through the open door. There was a paper bag of takeout Mexican food in his hands. "There's a car all—oh, shit."

"Call the hospital," Loren said. Hopelessness swirled in his mind. It was too late, he knew.

Eloy's heels slipped on the blood and he made red heel marks as he ran for the radio. The red stuff was getting over everything.

A few minutes later the ambulance parameds—Bag 'n' Drag, as the police called them—made a pronouncement of DOA. They didn't take the body away yet because there was still police stuff to do with it. Begley had been called in from patrol and stood around in case someone gave him something to do. His new partner, Quantrill, was keeping people away from the car out front. Everyone went to elaborate lengths to avoid stepping in the vast seeping puddle of blood. Eloy knelt over him, brow knit as he looked at the face.

Loren watched the procedure, leaning against the wall. His heart was still intermittently thrashing against his ribs, as if it were changing gears from high to low and back again. Loren tried to will it into obedience.

Eloy rose. "You knew the guy, Chief?"

"Randal Dudenhof. I grew up with him." A rancher, Loren knew. Good ole boy, a jack Mormon. His wife was named Violet and had been two years behind Loren in high school.

He called me by name, Loren thought.

Eloy squinted at the corpse. "Doesn't look that old."

"He's not. He's . . ." Speech trailed away as Loren's mind, unable to quite absorb what had just happened, did another quick disconnect. He tried to find another track.

Procedure. What happened next?

"Get the Polaroid," he said. "It's in my office, on the shelf behind my desk."

Eloy's heels ticked on the tile as he walked away. Chain of evidence, Loren thought.

When things got confusing, you could always fall back on procedure.

He stepped closer to the body, knelt down. He unbuttoned the shirt and carefully pulled it away from the left side, then the right. There was an entrance wound on the left side, under the arm, but no exit wound was visible. Loren turned the front pockets inside out. There was nothing in them but lint. No ID.

Loren looked down into the dead man's glazed eyes. All thoughts of procedure flittered away like swallows.

He called me by name. He asked me for help.

"Dudenhof, Chief?" Ed Begley was looking at the body, a puzzled look on his face. "Did Violet Dudenhof have a kid?"

"No," Loren said.

Begley's puzzled look didn't go away. "There's a shot-up car outside. You want to look at it?"

Loren found himself reluctant to follow this suggestion. He rose from his crouch possessed of a dreadful certainty what he would find beyond the glass doors. A canary-yellow 1956 T-bird, waxed and buffed and polished, with whitewall tires and matching yellow leather upholstery with little red stripes . . .

The car was a gray BMW. Quantrill was keeping a lounging crowd of spectators at a healthy distance. The car had been run over the curb and into the cast-iron streetlamp near the police entrance. The driver's door had two bullet holes in it and the rear window had been starred by another bullet. It looked as if there were gallons of blood in the driver's seat and on the floor, a trail of red splotches leading to the door. The man had known right where to drive when he got himself shot and wanted to report a crime.

Funny he didn't drive himself to the hospital, though.

At least it wasn't the yellow T-bird. But still the cold horror that hummed in Loren's bones did not recede.

An ATL jeep was parked across the street. Two men in bulky, tailored custom jackets watched the proceedings through gold-rimmed Ray-Ban shooting glasses.

Loren felt their eyes centered like gun sights between his shoulder blades. He turned to Quantrill. "Who was the last guy to take the crime scene course at the Albuquerque academy?" Loren asked.

"Buchinsky."

"Go inside and call him. I don't want to mess up on procedure. It's been too long since we had a homicide where we didn't know who did it right away."

"Except for the guy in the car."

Loren thought about it. "That was different. Go call Buchinsky."

"He's on medical leave."

"Fuck his medical leave."

Loren stood outside the splash of blood on the pavement and peered into the BMW. There were probably a couple bullets rolling around inside, but he didn't want to search the car until he got every print off it that he could.

He straightened, feeling those Ray-Bans on his back. He looked around, seeing the crowd of spectators, the familiar and half-familiar faces. His eyes froze on a stranger, a bearded, barrel-chested man in a turban, tie, and long-sleeved sport shirt.

Probably a terrorist, Byrne had said.

Bullshit. Probably a tourist. Or an elk vampire.

He had the feeling, though, that if he called William Patience at ATL Security he would discover who the man was and where he was staying. An obvious anomaly like that would be the sort of thing the guys in the chocolate Blazers would investigate as a matter of routine.

Eloy appeared in the doorway. "I couldn't find the Polaroid, Chief. Where did you say it was?"

It was only then that Loren remembered he'd taken the camera home last Fourth of July to take pictures of Katrina and Kelly on the church picnic. It was sitting in his closet back home.

"Never mind. Use the video camera the feds bought us."

"We don't have any blank tape."

Loren turned to him. "Go down to the Rexall and buy some, then!" he said. "Get a receipt and I'll have our weasel of a mayor reimburse you, okay?"

Eloy opened his mouth, then closed it. "No problem, Chief," he said.

He went to the back of the car and looked at the license plate. It was a custom New Mexico vanity plate and read DELTA E.

Loren's mouth went dry. He looked at the ATL jeep and suddenly the security goons' presence made sense. He had no idea what DELTA E could possibly mean, but it sounded like the sort of thing that someone who worked at the Advanced Technology Laboratories might have on his car.

He took out his notebook, wrote the letters down, walked back into the hallway. He'd run the number through the LAWSAT link with the Department of Motor Vehicles computer in Santa Fe and find out who the car belonged to.

He looked down at the body again. Cold crept through his bones.

Randal Dudenhof. It was Randal right down to the can of Copenhagen snuff in the back pocket.

One of the parameds approached him, a tall young woman with horn-rim glasses and long brown hair pinned neatly at her nape with a tortoiseshell clip. She had a big leatherette notebook and was filling in information. "What did you say the patient's name was?"

Loren looked at her. "John Doe."

The medic's eyes widened. "I thought you said—"

Loren could feel dried blood flaking off near his mouth. "It couldn't be Dudenhof," he said.

The woman was persistent. "But you said—"

"Randal Dudenhof died almost twenty years ago. He was headed home to his ranch after drinking too much bourbon at the Happy Steer Steak House and he skidded on the black ice and drove his yellow Thunderbird off the Rio Seco bridge on Highway 103. The steering column speared him through the chest. I watched him die."

The paramed looked at him for a long moment, then shrugged and turned away.

Loren looked at the body again.

He knew me. He called me by name.

It was Randal, all right.

S I X

Two mumbling ten-eighteens were pulled out of a police cruiser and hauled off to jail. Despite scrapes, skinned knuckles, and freely bleeding noses, dusty gimme hats were still plastered firmly to their disordered hair.

Drunks, Loren thought, don't stop beating each other up just because somebody else got himself killed.

"Hey, Chief." Buchinsky's voice. "Found something."

Loren bent and crawled into the BMW's back seat. Buchinsky grinned up at him and held up a slug in fingers stained with flaking blood. It was a semi-wadcutter pistol round, the crimping still clear around its base, deformed from having hit the back window and then the back of the passenger seat. The metal casing, shattered in the impact, showed bright gleaming fragments around the dusky core of the bullet.

Loren could smell a faint powder residue.

"Funny size," he said.

"Bigger than nine-millimeter."

Loren took the bullet from Buchinsky's fingers and peered at it. "Not a .45, either. It's got to be a .41, or eleven-millimeter."

"Not many people have guns of that caliber. Not around here."

Loren rolled the bullet between his fingers, then gave it back to Buchinsky. "Bag it," he said.

"There's gotta be another round in here."

"We'll find it."

The evidence thus far, besides the corpse and the bullet, consisted of a crumpled bag from Dunkin' Donuts, a small packet of Heinz ketchup, an empty V-8 vegetable drink can, a container that once held a McDonald's quarter-pound hamburger, and a whole lot of bloody footprints. Otherwise, it looked as if the car had been cleaned recently.

Loren reached under a seat, and a bolt of pain went through his lower spine. Thirty years of walking with a heavy pistol on one hip had done things to his hip placement and his lower back. He clenched his teeth and backed out of the BMW and straightened, pressing the heel of one hand into the small of his back. As he rose he gazed straight into the angry, resentful glare of Buchinsky's wife, Karen, the blond, narrow-faced woman who wanted her husband to be a truck driver in Albuquerque. Loren's gaze moved over the crowd of onlookers. The man with the turban had gone. Loren hitched up his gun belt and turned back to his work.

The ATL jeep was still there. The two occupants were eating takeout Mexican food out of cardboard trays.

The shiny, waxed surface of the gray car was covered with grainy black fingerprint powder. The car had been washed fairly recently and there weren't many prints on the outside, though the inside had come up with a fair number of latents, including what Loren figured were those of children.

Timothy Jernigan's children, presumably.

Timothy Jernigan was the owner of the BMW and the DELTA E vanity plate, the name brought up a few seconds after the LAWSAT queried the New Mexico DMV. Jernigan lived in Vista Linda, and was presumably connected in some way with Advanced Technology Laboratories.

Loren would have been knocking at his door long since if he hadn't had to supervise the car search.

A Fury cruiser pulled up, and Cipriano jumped out. Loren could see anger in his face.

"There's a homicide and you don't call me?" Cipriano demanded.

"I wanted you to get some rest."

"Shit, man." He scratched his neck furiously. "I had to hear about it from my wife, and she heard about it from her mother on the phone."

"We don't know anything yet. I would have called you if there had been anything for you to do."

"When there's a homocide in this town, I want to know about it."

Loren sighed. "Yeah, I'm sorry. I should have called even if it was to let you know that nothing was happening. Tell you what." He looked at the assistant chief. "How about I put you in charge of the crime scene? That'll give me a chance to brace the guy who owns this car."

Cipriano was unappeased. "How about *I* brace the car owner, jefe?"

"Maybe we can do it together. But for now, let's take a look at the victim. I want to know if you see what I see."

A resentful Cipriano followed Loren into the police entrance. The body was still lying there in its spatter of blood, Bag 'n' Drag still standing around waiting for permission to carry it away. White plastic bags with the Rexall imprint had been fixed with rubber bands round the body's hands and feet to preserve physical evidence. Cipriano's brown eyes rested for a moment on the dead face.

"Huh," Cipriano said. "Sure looks like old Dudenhof, doesn't it?"

Loren felt relief trickle into his mind. He hadn't been seeing things. "That's what I thought," he said. "He's even got Copenhagen snuff in his back pocket."

"That ain't unusual around here."

"I guess not. But it was the only thing in his pockets at all. No ID, no coins, not even a hanky."

He called me by name, Loren was about to say, but he was interrupted.

"Chief." Eloy calling from the desk.

"Yeah?"

"I just got a call from that Timothy Jernigan guy. He wanted to report a stolen car."

Loren felt a distant hum in his bones, like a dynamo rumbling up to speed from a cold start. The cover-up, he knew, was starting. He looked at Eloy.

"What did the guy say?"

"Said he looked out the window and his car was gone from his driveway."

Loren smiled, the internal humming building in volume. The guy's story was lame. It wasn't going to hold up; he knew that already.

If he could get Jernigan alone, before he got his story straight, he could crush him. He knew that with absolute certainty. He pictured himself confronting the guy in some book-lined study, sweat pouring down the suspect's face as he tried to hold his cover story together. If he got to the guy's house, he might even be able to find evidence.

"He said he'll be right down as soon as he can get a ride," Eloy said.

Loren's train of thought jumped the rails. "He's coming *here*?" he said. "What the hell did you tell him?"

"I told him we had his car here."

Loren's voice rose to a shout. "*Did you tell him anything else?*" Anger tore at his throat.

Eloy's eyes widened. He tried to shake his head in the tall foam collar, failed, gave a nervous laugh instead. "No, Chief. Just that we had his car."

Loren tried to give some consideration to what was going to happen. "Okay," he said. "That's good."

Jernigan was coming here, Loren thought. That might be all right. He could get the man in his office and take his story apart there, on his own ground, while the suspect was still disoriented.

"You didn't tell the guy," Loren said, "that we had a dead body, right?"

"Nope. Just that we had the car."

"Good." If Jernigan had shot the guy, Loren thought, then he wouldn't know for sure whether Randal Dudenhof—no, not Randal, he thought insistently, John Doe—was dead. Even if he figured Doe was dead, he wouldn't know if Doe had accused him before he died.

All Loren had to do, he figured, was to apply pressure till Jernigan cracked.

He turned to Cipriano. "We're gonna break the guy," he said.

Cipriano was still looking moodily at the corpse. "He might come with a lawyer."

"Why would an innocent man show up with a lawyer?"

"He might not. On the other hand, he might actually be innocent."

Loren shook his head. He started walking to the exit. "My working hypothesis is that he's gotta be connected to this guy somehow. Maybe he didn't pull the trigger, but any other explanation is too complicated." He stepped out the door. "Look," he said, "we won't tell him the John Doe is dead. We'll take him into the building through the main doors, not the police entrance, and that way he won't see the body." He looked behind him and saw that Cipriano wasn't following, was instead staring at his own feet with a moody expression. Loren pushed back through the door. "You coming or what?" he said.

Cipriano looked up. "Yeah. Right."

Loren stepped out into the night again. He had enough to do tonight without catering to Cipriano's moods.

For half an hour Loren waited with increasing impatience, his back throbbing as he wished he could just jump in his Fury and confront Jernigan in the man's own house. In police work there was a principle called the 24/24 rule, which held that the most important moments during a murder investigation were the first twenty-four hours of the investigation and the last twenty-four hours of the victim's life. Go back any further than that, stories started getting confused, witnesses' memories unfocused; and the longer the investigation took, the colder the trail got. Loren could feel time eating away at him as he pictured the killer cleaning up evidence, getting his story straight, obscuring things, shoring up his alibi. Loren wanted things to start happening.

He wanted not to have to think about Randal Dudenhof.

While he waited, Buchinsky's search of the BMW came up with a bobby pin, a few dusty coins, and another bullet. It was the same caliber as the first, and more thoroughly deformed, having gone through the door and then bouncing around the interior of the car before finally ending up under the back seat.

Loren was examining this latest find when he heard the squawk of a radio in the ATL Blazer, then saw the driver answer. There was a brief conversation, of which Loren could only hear the incoherent white noise of the radio and the murmur of reply, and then the driver started his engine and pulled out.

Loren felt a degree of relief. No one was second-guessing him anymore.

And then another ATL Blazer pulled up into the same place, and two men got out. Reflexive annoyance buzzed like a wasp through Loren's brain.

The driver was William Patience, the head of ATL's security. He was wearing the same bulky jacket, spit-shined shoes, and gray slacks as his goons, though he allowed himself a pastel-blue shirt instead of the standard white. His cuff links and tie clip were plain steel blackened military-style.

Patience's face looked as if it had been shaped with an adze. His straight, graying black hair was worn long and was tied into a modest ponytail behind. Loren knew that Patience had been in some kind of under-the-table counterterrorist special forces outfit identified only by an acronym, that he lived alone in a small apartment in Vista Linda, that he climbed rocks for a hobby, that he had few material possessions and taught a yoga class at the community center.

Prescription, Loren thought, for a tight-ass control freak jerk. Who furthermore, to judge by the samurai ponytail, had seen too many Steven Seagal movies.

Loren smiled heartily as Patience approached. "Hi, Bill," Loren said.

Patience smiled back, a lizard smile: no teeth, no lips. He offered a hand and Loren shook it. "Heard you got a stiff," he said.

Loren scuffed a toe on the concrete while Patience shook hands with Cipriano. For some reason Patience made him want to be as folksy as the dumb country hick that Patience probably assumed he was. "Where'd you hear that, Bill?" he asked.

"My guys could see the body through your glass front doors."

Loren concealed a flare of annoyance. "I guess they could, at that."

"I thought I'd offer some help in this situation."

The second man hovered nervously behind Patience, looking as if he were waiting for someone to tell him what to do. He was a couple inches taller than Loren and about fifty pounds lighter, a balding blond bean pole in black plastic-rimmed glasses and a close-trimmed beard, tweed sport coat, and tie.

Loren smiled again. "How were you planning on offering to help, Bill?"

"I thought I'd bring Tim Jernigan in to meet you."

"That's damn thoughtful of you, Bill," Loren said. His mind whirled, tried to make connections, while he went on grinning, scuffling, playing the hick. He looked up at the thin man, into dark, flickering eyes obscured by thick spectacles.

Sometimes you just knew. You knew when people were lying, you knew how things were. Like he'd known about Robbie Cisneros and the Texas twosome. Something was wrong, clearly wrong, with this setup.

"Tim called me when he saw his car was gone," Patience said, "and I told him to call you. Then he asked me for a ride down here."

"That's nice of you."

"He's got a meeting at the Hiawatha later tonight. With a colleague. So I thought I'd take him to that after you've talked to him."

"This may take a while," Loren said quickly.

"That's okay. I haven't got anything better to do."

"Uh-huh." Loren looked at Jernigan, found his gaze falling once more into the shadowed, depthless obscurity of the thick spectacles. He couldn't make eye contact with this guy.

Jernigan shifted his weight from one foot to the other, then shifted it back.

"I guess I'd better start by asking if that *is* your car over there."

Jernigan looked, blinked, looked again. "Yes," he said. "It's mine."

Loren stepped around Patience, moved closer to the tall man. He heard Cipriano's footsteps behind, moving on his right shoulder. "You work for ATL?"

"Yes." Blinking again.

"In what capacity?" Loren stepped closer.

"Uh." Blinking. "I'm a particle physicist."

"That's what the plate's about, right?" Loren stepped even closer, trying to intrude on the man's personal space, see if he could make him nervous.

"The what?" Jernigan stepped back. He was rolling his shoulders awkwardly, as if there were an itch between his shoulder blades.

"The license plate." Loren followed. "DELTA E. That's something in physics?"

"Oh. Right. Delta E charts change in energy."

Change in energy, Loren thought, okay. Whatever that meant. Maybe that was something Jerry would know about. Loren came forward till his breastbone was maybe an inch from Jernigan's. "Let's go to my office," he said softly.

Jernigan's shadowy spectacles blinked back at him. The physicist didn't say anything.

"This way," Loren said, right into the man's face. He turned and began moving back toward the police entrance. Cipriano walked ahead of him. No point in going in the big front doors—Patience had to have told Jernigan that the John Doe was dead.

"Loren," said Patience. "I should point out that Tim has a top-security clearance, that some of his work is highly classified."

Loren gave his hick smile again. "I'm not going to ask him about his work, Bill. I wouldn't know what to ask him, anyway."

"Still, I think we have a legitimate security interest here."

Cipriano looked over his shoulder and gave a disbelieving smile. "Come off it, Bill. We got a dead man lying in the lobby."

"And the security of the labs needs to be protected."

"Hold on," said Loren. He paused between the big copper griffins and turned to Patience. "Let me ask you formally then. Do you have any knowledge of this crime?"

"No." Stiffly.

"Do you know the identity of the victim?"

"I haven't seen the body, but I assume not."

"Do you have any knowledge that Mr. Jernigan is connected to the crime in any way?"

Cold resentment lined Patience's face. "No," he said. Loren stepped closer to him, looking down at the shorter man, anger warming his nerves.

"Then get outta my investigation, Bill!" he shouted. "There's a murder here, and I'm gonna find the shooter. All I want from Mr. Jernigan is the answers to a few questions about where he was when he misplaced his car."

Patience looked up at Loren with flat, angry eyes. "I'd like to be able to participate."

"No. I appreciate your bringing Mr. Jernigan here, but this is my investigation and I don't need your participation."

They looked at each other for a moment, then Loren climbed the stairs and walked in through the open glass door. The body, the western shirt and denim failing to conceal the utterly boneless look of the dead, lay cooling on the white tile. Loren stopped and looked down at it, then up at the two ATL men.

"Either of you seen this man before?"

"No," said Patience. His voice was cold.

Jernigan looked and blinked and shook his head.

Loren glanced down at the body again. "Bullet hit a lung," he said. "The man drowned. There are probably a couple gallons of blood in his lungs."

Loren looked up at the two ATL men once again. Patience was looking down at the body with an expression of frigid contempt on his face. Perhaps the dead man didn't meet his expectations.

Jernigan seemed uncomfortable. He stared down at the body as if he'd never seen one before. Loren decided to see how far he could push Jernigan, if he could make him nervous and off balance enough to let something slip. "Lot of blood in a man," Loren said. "It gets all over the place. I've probably got it on me."

Patience looked up at him. The contempt wasn't about to leave his face. "Let's get moving, Loren. Tim has an appointment."

"This way."

Cipriano led the way into Loren's office. Loren noticed his neck was growing red from scratching. Cipriano stood by the door until Loren and Jernigan entered, then pointedly closed the door on Patience. "You mind if we record this?" Loren said. Without waiting for an answer he went to the cabinet and took out a portable disk recorder.

"Uh," said Jernigan. "Guess not."

Loren made sure there was a new disk in the recorder, held down the Record and Play buttons. "This is Chief Loren Hawn," he told the recorder, "and this is the recording of an interview with Dr. Timothy Jernigan, at—" he checked his watch—"eight thirty-four P.M."

He put the recorder on his desk. He sat on the desk next to the recorder, then asked Jernigan to sit on one of the straight-backed chairs in front of him—he could be close to Jernigan that way, and sitting on the desk he could loom over the taller man, be intimidating if he had to. Cipriano hovered in the background, behind Jernigan, in hopes of making him nervous. Cipriano scratched his neck again, then opened his pocket and took out his notebook.

"Full name?" he asked.

"Timothy Eldridge Jernigan."

"Age?"

"Thirty-four."

And so on: occupation, education, his marriage to someone named Sondra, his two children, length of residence in New Mexico. Jernigan did not seem any more at ease during the routine questions than he had while he was staring at the body. Loren began to wonder if he was always like this, some kind of mutant scientist geek who was totally incapable of interacting in a normal way. He remembered people like that in high school.

Hell. His *brother* was like that. The difference being that Jerry wasn't holding down a job that would earn him a BMW.

"The gray BMW sedan, license plate DELTA E, is yours?"

Jernigan nodded.

"Could you answer for the recorder?"

"Oh. Sorry. Yes. The car's mine."

"Could you describe your activities yesterday?"

"Friday?" Jernigan seemed surprised that Loren would ask about the previous day.

24/24, Loren thought. Start twenty-four hours ago.

"Yes," he said. "Friday."

Jernigan blinked. "I got up, uh, a little late, because I knew I'd be up all night. I got to the lab around ten. We were supposed to start an experiment at ten-thirty, but we had computer problems so we didn't start till a little after noon. The experiment ran till about four in the morning. After that I took Dr. Singh to the Hiawatha, then went home and to bed."

"There are witnesses to your presence at the lab?"

Jernigan looked up and gave a twitchy smile. The first time he'd smiled at all.

"Oh, yeah. We have to check in and out with security people at the gate. And I was with colleagues the whole time."

"Can you name your colleagues?"

Jernigan scratched his beard. "There were about fifty of them, and maybe a hundred technicians. But the two project leaders, besides myself, were Joe Dielh. Joseph. He's my project director at ATL. And—"

"Can you spell that?"

Jernigan obliged. "And Amardas Singh. That's S-I-N-G-H. He's from Caltech, but he's currently doing work at New Mexico Tech in Socorro."

"What was the first name again?"

"Amardas. A-M-A-R—ahhh." His face fell. "D-A-S, I think. Maybe there's an H in there somewhere, I'm not sure."

"What kind of name is that?" Cipriano asked in a quiet voice. He was over Jernigan's left shoulder, and Jernigan jumped at the sound.

"He's from Pakistan. A Sikh. But he's an American citizen now."

Loren remembered the bearded man in the turban he'd seen in the crowd around the BMW. Another anomaly explained. A visiting scientist, and not, apparently, a blood-drinking terrorist.

"He's the man you took to the Hiawatha?"

"Yes. He's staying there for the weekend."

Loren cleared his throat. "If it's not gonna endanger the national security, could you give me some idea what the experiment was about?"

"It was—" Jernigan groped for words. "Fairly routine, actually. An accelerator run."

"Uh-huh?" Loren tried to be slightly encouraging. Now that he was talking about something in his professional sphere, Jernigan was loosening up a bit, speaking and gesturing in a more natural manner. If he relaxed, maybe he'd make a mistake.

"We really didn't have to be there, the whole run could have been programmed into the computer and supervised by assistants. But Joe—Dr. Dielh—and I don't get a chance to work with Dr. Singh very often, so we spent most of the time in the control room with the holotanks, watching recordings of past runs, and, ah, talking shop."

"Did you see or talk to anyone between the time you dropped off, uh, Singh at the Hiawatha and the time you arrived at home?"

"No."

"Can anyone confirm the time you arrived at home?"

"My wife. I guess. She was asleep."

"And then?"

"I had something to eat and went to bed. I got up at noon. I drove to the lab after breakfast to pick up some of the data from the run so that I could have a conference tonight with Dr. Singh. I was at the lab about four or five hours while the computer printed out what I needed."

"Can anyone confirm that?"

"The gate guards. And Dr. Dielh. He was there. We spent the time talking about the spectra. The experimental results, I mean."

"And Dr. Singh wasn't there?"

Jernigan blinked. "No," he said.

Loren leaned forward, his mind humming. He knew this was important, though he wasn't certain why.

"Isn't that funny," he said slowly, working his way into it, "that you'd be sitting there talking experimental results with one of the other project managers, and the third project head is sitting in a motel just a few miles away and you don't make him a part of it?"

"We were going to see him, anyway."

"But you said he was the visiting guy from out of town and you don't get to talk to him often. So why didn't you pick him up at the motel and drive him, or just have him walk to the station and catch the maglev right to the labs?"

"Well." Jernigan's mouth gaped open like a fish, but no sound came out. Panic fluttered behind the thick spectacles.

"Well?" Loren said.

"Well. We were supposed to meet this afternoon, actually. But the experiment ran late and we all slept late and we hadn't got the data yet, so I called Dr. Singh and we postponed the meeting to the evening."

Cipriano gave a contemptuous snort. "So why didn't you invite Dr. Singh this afternoon?" he repeated.

Jernigan looked for an answer for a long, paralyzed moment, then gave a helpless shrug. "We just didn't."

Loren looked at him for the space of two heartbeats, trying to figure out where to go from here. When he'd taken Jernigan into the office he'd had a picture of crushing the man, destroying him, but somehow he couldn't find the piece of specific information that would allow him to do it. Even though he'd caught him in a contradiction, in blatantly inconsistent behavior, he couldn't figure out what to do with it.

And even if he just flat told Jernigan that he didn't believe him, even if he jumped up and yelled and tried to intimidate him with his size and conviction, the man had brought a *bodyguard* with him, a man who was probably hovering just outside the door waiting for a chance to intervene.

Loren shook his head. "So what did you do then?"

"Went home for dinner. Ate a quick meal out of the icebox."

"About what time?"

"Six, six-thirty."

"And then what?"

"I took the printouts and went outside and into the driveway for my car. And it was gone."

"Right from out of the driveway?"

A nod.

"For the recorder, Mr. Jernigan?"

"Yes." Jernigan cleared his throat. "It was gone."

"About what time?"

"Around seven. My appointment with Dr. Singh was at seven-thirty."

"And what did you do then?"

"Called Mr. Patience."

"And he told you to call us?"

"Yes."

"And then gave you a ride down here?"

"Yes."

"Don't you have another car?"

"Sorry?"

"Another car. Aren't you a two-car family?"

Jernigan licked his lips. "Yes. My wife has a Chrysler New Yorker. But she had already taken the children to a movie at the mall."

"When did they leave?"

"Just before I did."

"And they didn't notice the car was gone?"

There was another moment of paralysis before Jernigan found an answer. "I guess not."

"Or maybe it wasn't gone yet."

"I . . ." Jernigan cleared his throat. "Possibly. I can't say."

Loren looked at Cipriano, who looked back and gave a twisted smile. Jernigan certainly *acted* guilty. If nervousness alone could convict a man, Jernigan was headed for death row.

"I want to tell you something, Mr.—Dr.—Jernigan. We will be talking to witnesses. We will be gathering evidence. And I will talk to you again, okay? And when I talk to you again, I will know certain things."

Jernigan gaped up at him.

"I will *know* what happened, okay? There's no way I won't. So if you have anything to add to this, it would be best if you did it now. It would look a whole lot better."

Jernigan shrugged. "I don't know anything else."

Loren looked at the physicist. He couldn't see this man for a killer.

"Do you own a firearm, Mr. Jernigan?" he asked.

Jernigan shook his head. "No. I don't believe in it."

Loren felt a reflexive annoyance. This was not an attitude that found its way out West very often. "Does anyone in your family own a gun?" he said.

"No. We wouldn't know how to use one."

"Do you have any idea who would steal your car?"

A mute shake of the head. Loren didn't bother asking for a verbal answer.

"Any enemies? Any rivals?"

"No."

"Do you have any reason to suspect that your wife might have been unfaithful?"

Jernigan looked as if he'd been hit with a hammer. It was some time before he could assemble an answer.

"No."

"Do you use drugs?"

"No."

"Does your wife?"

"No."

"Your children?"

Jernigan assembled an expression of indignation. "The oldest is in eighth grade!" he said.

Loren gave him a skeptical smile. "It's been known to happen."

Jernigan shook his head.

"Would you object if we tested your hands for gunpowder residue?"

Jernigan's mouth opened, then closed. "Go right ahead," he said.

"We'll have to ask you to sign a statement that you took the test voluntarily. Does that bother you?"

Jernigan shook his head. Loren looked up. "Would you take care of that, Cipriano?"

"I guess. Where's the Shibano kit?"

Loren thought for a moment and didn't know the answer. "Better ask Eloy."

Cipriano led Jernigan away. He would use the new Shibano test, the one recommended by the FBI, swab the hand and wrist thoroughly with Solution A, allow to dry, then swab with Solution B. Any gunpowder residue would turn bright red.

Loren stood, stretched, adjusted his gun. He took the recorder from the desk and was about to press the Off button when he noticed that the red LED above the Record button wasn't lit. He pressed the Test button and the green battery light didn't go on.

The batteries were dead.

Loren looked at the dead recorder and put it down gently and wondered whether the department was ready for any of this. The Polaroid in his bedroom closet when he needed it, the gunpowder test kit stored somewhere where it couldn't be found, evidence bags borrowed from the Rexall store, dead batteries loaded into the disk recorder . . . Maybe there was something to Jerry's theory about a germ of incompetence that lived in the water here.

At least, in his experience, the germ usually infected the bad guys, too.

There was a knock on the door frame. William Patience gave an inquiring look. "Busy?" he said.

Loren looked up. "Not this second, no."

Patience slid into the room. His jacket was open and Loren could see the hardware under his left arm. "How'd Tim do?"

"He's very nervous."

"I know. Most of the researchers are pretty regular people, but

some of them never developed much in the way of social skills."
Patience sighed. "Tim's one of those. That's why I thought I'd better bring him in myself."

"For what it's worth," Loren said, "I don't figure he shot anyone."

Patience nodded. "I didn't think so, either."

"Maybe he knows who did," said Loren.

"I doubt it." Patience scowled. "You don't know who the dead man is, right? Maybe nobody does."

Loren gave the smaller man his hick grin. "What makes you think nobody knows who the guy is?"

Patience looked up. "What do you mean?"

"He talked before he died."

"What did he say?" Casually.

He called me by name.

Loren shook his head. "Words," he said.

Patience's glance flickered away. "Hell of a weekend for you," he said.

"As violent as they come."

"They don't get much worse."

Loren gave a laugh. "You should have been here during the Big Strike against Riga Brothers. It lasted five months. Nobody died, but the governor had to call in the state troopers and the National Guard. There were more broken heads than there were beds in the hospital."

Patience looked up. "Who won?"

"Nobody. The company lost, the union lost, the town lost. If anybody won, it was the copper miners in Chile. And ATL came in to use the pit's excess generating capacity."

Patience shook his head. "They shouldn't allow that kind of thing anymore. The unions just got too strong. Somebody had to knock them down a peg."

"Shit, Bill," Loren said. "That wasn't it. The unions weren't too strong, it was the companies that got too multinational. If they can play Chilotes off against American workers, then they can keep the profits and pay the miners like peons no matter which bunch of 'em are working."

Patience looked at him. "I guess we disagree."

"I guess we do."

Patience ambled over into the corner, where Loren's trophies and photographs were set up. "Somebody told me you were a boxer," he said.

"When I was in the service."

Patience peered at the photograph of Loren in his belt. "U.S. Army heavyweight champion of Korea." He looked over his shoulder at Loren. "That was after the war, right?"

A stab of pain raced through Loren's back. "After the war?" he said. "It was twenty-five *years* after the war. How old do you think I am?" He eased his gun around to the front.

Patience looked at Loren over his shoulder. "Guess you've still got the moves," he said.

"A few."

"All my men are trained in hapkido. That's a Korean style of karate."

"Is that one of those where you jump up in the air all the time? I never thought those would be very useful." Loren limped to his chair and sat in it. Relief swam through his lower back. "I mean," he said, "the time it takes one of those guys to get his foot up into the air, I could pop him in the face about twelve times."

"We try to emphasize the practical side of things. I teach my people to immobilize the enemy before trying any high kicks."

Loren shifted his weight in his chair and gave a sigh of relief. "That's sensible," he said.

Cipriano appeared in the office door. "Test's done, jefe." He shook his head. "Negative."

Loren shrugged. The test, he knew, was good; it would have picked up traces of the powder no matter how carefully the man had washed his hands. "Thank Mr. Jernigan for his time," he said. "I guess he's got a meeting to go to."

Patience shook everyone's hand and left with the physicist. Cipriano stood in Loren's office, his arms akimbo, a dubious expression on his face. "There's something going on, jefe," he said.

"I know."

"I wish we could have kept on that guy's ass a little longer."

"Me, too. But we didn't have any reason to question him further. And I couldn't think of questions to ask anymore."

"So what now?"

"I go home and go to bed. You stay on till the bars close."

"Thanks a lot."

"In the morning we do police work. We go to everyone on Jernigan's block and ask what they saw. And we talk to Singh and Dielh, and to Jernigan's family. And if we have anything that contradicts Jernigan's story, we nail him with it."

Cipriano nodded. "Shit," he said, "I hate this."

Loren heaved himself out of his chair. "Me, too, pachuco." He headed out, then paused in the office door. He turned to Cipriano. "He called me by name," he said. "He asked me for help."

"Who?"

"The John Doe."

Cipriano looked surprised. "You know this guy?"

"Not unless he was Randal Dudenhof."

Cipriano laughed. "Yeah, sure."

"He knew me," Loren said.

"Maybe he read your name tag."

Loren looked in surprise at the plastic name tag pinned above his right breast pocket. "I never thought of that."

"It's right there in blue and white."

"Funny thing for a dying man to do."

Cipriano shrugged. "Dying men do funny things."

"I guess so." Loren walked out into the corridor, then to the front desk. The body was still sprawled on the white tile in front of the doors. Someone had put a blanket over it.

Loren turned to Eloy. "Tell the Bag 'n' Drag they can take him away."

"Right, Chief."

Loren felt a sudden tenderness welling up in him. Despite the dead batteries and the forgotten Polaroid, the department had done very well tonight, had performed on a par with any department anywhere. He put a hand on Eloy's shoulder.

"You did real good," he said.

Eloy looked up in surprise. "Thanks, Chief."

"Take care of your neck. Do what the doctors say."

"Sure."

"Have a good night, now."

"You, too."

Loren limped out of the building, pain nagging at his back. He paused on the front steps, breathing the October air that touched his face and hands with its invigorating chill.

He looked down at the BMW, its gleaming surface defaced with fingerprint powder.

Time to go home, he thought.

The Days of Atonement were just beginning.

S E V E N

"It's a well-documented phenomenon," Jerry said. "Sometimes people just catch on fire. I read it in a book. Could you pass the waffles?"

Breakfast coffee scalded its way down Loren's throat, forcing open his eyes through sheer pain. He hadn't slept well. Images of John Doe's body still sprawled through his mind, Randal Dudenhof in an accordion of sharp-edged metal, impaled by the steering column, one or the other or both gasping for breath on the white tile floor.

"There was this one guy—" Jerry was enthusiastic. "He caught fire in his car in the middle of traffic. He burned up completely before they got to him. All that was left was his feet."

"Yuck," said Kelly.

"Most people who burn up are fat old alcoholics, but this guy was *young*."

Loren looked up from his coffee cup. "Sounds like he was freebasing cocaine," he said, "and the torch got away from him."

"This was *before* cocaine. I mean, before they started doing that kind of thing with it."

Loren considered the thought of a pair of smoldering feet found in an automobile. The insurance company would call it an act of God, and perhaps they were right. People, he thought, shouldn't be afraid to call something a miracle when there was no other explanation.

This specific instance, however, did not convince him. Miracles ought not to be this frivolous. "Where do you find this stuff?" he said.

"Books."

"There are books and there are books," Loren said. "People *lie* in those kinds of books. Sometimes people just tell good stories."

Jerry shrugged. "Maybe. But it could be relevant."

"To what, for God's sake?"

"There's a fire danger now, right? There are always these fires up in the national forest. And range fires around town. Suppose it isn't just humans who spontaneously combust. Suppose all those fires are caused by animals just *blowing up*."

"Exploding gophers." Kelly rolled her eyes. "Give me a break, Jer."

"Jerry," said Loren, "the cause of those fires is always investigated. And nobody's found an exploding animal yet."

"Have they *looked*?"

"Someone would have noticed by now."

"Mom." Katrina looked at her plate. "This toast has butter on it. I wanted dry toast."

Loren looked at her. "You're not fat," he said.

"Yes, I am."

"You're not."

Skinny Kelly smirked. "Yes, she is."

Loren poured himself more coffee. Katrina had inherited her mother's sturdy bone structure—no diet could change that—but Katrina hadn't accepted it. She was on some manner of fast most of the time and worked out continually, a nonstop combination of track, aerobics, and the high school drill team. At least, Loren thought, the weight obsession had made his daughter into an athlete.

Katrina went into the kitchen to make herself more toast. Loren stared at his plate and swallowed coffee.

He remembered Randal with the steering column through his chest, blood bubbling out of his mouth. Back then the department didn't have the equipment to cut him out of the car, the heavy cutters they called the jaws of life.

A few weeks after the accident Loren had started a fund for the city's first pair of cutters. He hadn't wanted to see anything like Randal's death again. Loren was just a patrolman then and he didn't have much money, but he would have paid for them out of his own pocket if he'd had to. Instead he'd gone to Luis Figueracion and pointed out how with a few thousand dollars he could preserve the lives of any number of voters. Luis had seen the point, and the cutters he'd bought were still in operation.

"Jer," said Kelly, "I wouldn't talk too much about those exploding gophers. What if terrorists find out that they can use fat alcoholic gophers as *weapons?*"

Jerry grinned. "Gopher grenades," he said.

"Gopher cocktails."

Jerry's eyes widened in imitation awe. "The *G-bomb*," he said, his voice breathless. Kelly burst out in giggles.

Loren looked down at his plate and realized he'd left his waffle untouched. He took a bite, chewed slowly, then turned toward the kitchen, where Debra was making more waffles. Kelly was still fighting her fit of giggles.

"The waffles are wonderful!" he shouted.

"Thank you!"

"Heard you got a body," said Jerry.

"Did . . . it . . . *blow up?*" Kelly asked, her words popping out from around bursts of giggles.

Loren put down his fork. "Not at table," he said. "No politics, no police business."

"Sorry," said Jerry. "Forgot."

"Who'd you hear it from?"

"Frank Sanchez took me west last night."

"And what did he say?"

Jerry shrugged. "Not much." He looked at Loren. "I thought you didn't want to talk about it."

Debra returned from the kitchen with a new plate of waffles. "No police business," she said.

"Absolutely," said Jerry.

* * *

The Roberts family was not present this morning, but there was another specter haunting the church steps.

"Loren," said Mack Bonniwell, "I need to talk to you."

Bonniwell stood on the steps of the church, gazing angrily at Loren from behind black-rimmed spectacles. His expression was grim.

"Let's make it quick," Loren said. He gestured for his family to continue on into the church. "Get a pew," he said. "We're late."

"When you called the other night, you said you'd had to arrest my kid," Bonniwell said. "You didn't say you'd beat the pulp out of him."

"I hit him twice," Loren said. "That's not beating the pulp out of anybody."

"You kicked a seventeen-year-old kid in the crotch," Bonniwell said, "and you yanked his ears half off and kneed him in the face and broke his nose. That's pretty goddamned brutal if you ask me."

Loren looked into the church. "The service is about to start."

"I don't give a shit, Hawn," Bonniwell said.

Loren turned to him. He didn't want to have anything to do with this. "A.J. had a gun," he said.

"*My* kid didn't."

"I couldn't see whether your kid did or not. I had to take him out."

"You're a bully, Loren Hawn!" Bonniwell stood very close. Loren flinched from the spittle that landed on his face. "You always *were* a bully, even back in school! I remember how you used to push other kids around! Sneak around, find out their secrets, then confront them when they were at a disadvantage!"

Heat flickered over Loren's skin. "Are you finished?" he said. He looked left and right to see if latecomers were in view. The church choir began to sing.

"That badge doesn't allow you to knock my family around!" Bonniwell screamed. "It doesn't allow—"

There didn't seem to be anyone looking. Loren slapped Bonniwell hard in the face. Bonniwell fell silent, eyes wide in stunned surprise. If the guy made a move, Loren intended to drive an elbow into his face and then sweep his feet. Dump him on the church steps and secure him.

No move was made.

"Shut your dentures, Mack," Loren said, trying to keep his voice low, "and listen very carefully. *If* your kid had a gun, and *if* I'd given him a chance to use it, your kid would be facing death row right now, because if he killed an officer he'd be tried as an adult, okay? Now, if I were you—"

"You're *not* me, thank God—" Bonniwell seemed to have found his tongue again.

"If I were you," patiently, "I'd just shut my mouth and pay the fine and tell my kid not to hang with trash, okay?"

"I'm going to complain," Bonniwell said. "You can't get away with this."

"There's a procedure for complaint, okay," Loren said. "You can follow it if you want. But let me point out that Judge Denver won't want this business reopened since he's already given a sentence, and he might just revoke your kid's probation and make him do time, and—"

"*Are you threatening my son?*" Bonniwell's voice was raised again.

"I'm telling you what'll happen. Nothing more."

"Hitting me on the church steps! Threatening my kid! I'm not going to forget this, Hawn."

"I hope you don't. Because—"

"I'm not interested in what you've got to say, you goddamned bully."

Loren looked him in the eye. "Walk away from it, Mack."

Mack stared at him for a long time, fists clenched, within a centimeter of violence, and then he turned and walked into the church.

Loren took a few deep breaths as he turned angry little circles on the porch, then headed into the big church and sat down with his family.

Last time he'd ever do an old friend a favor, he thought. Next time he'd just see the kid was tossed in jail and forgotten.

He contemplated, in some detail, breaking several of Bonniwell's bones. The details were graphic and very pleasant.

It totally escaped him now why he'd been so reasonable during the confrontation.

"I had a sermon already written out!" Pastor Rickey proclaimed. He pronounced the last word *owt*. "And then I saw last night's news on the TV and threw the whole darn thing away!" *Dahrn*.

"You're grinding your teeth," Debra said.

Loren glanced up in surprise. He'd forgotten where he was.

"That sermon was a good one, too!" Rickey said. "Maybe I'll impart it next year."

There were chuckles from his audience. Loren wondered blindly what the pastor was talking about.

"Because on the news last night was a perfect example of why gluttony is considered a Deadly Sin, as opposed to some less significant kind."

The pastor lowered his voice, becoming intimate. "I only know what I saw on the news," he said, "and since this is a legal matter I want to give you a caution here. I only know what I saw. I don't *know* that the people charged are guilty, and since some of you may serve as jurors someday, I want to remind you that you don't know, either."

Uh-huh, Loren thought. This was getting interesting.

"But *if* the news reports are correct," Rickey said, "then what this community has experienced is a cascade of sin, one leading to another.

"The first was gluttony." Raising a finger. "Not gluttony in its ordinary sense, but gluttony in the sense of a craving for drugs. Drugs are not simply bad for you—drugs are *sinful*! I want to make that clear!"

Rickey banged a fist on his pulpit. Loren watched with increasing interest. This guy might make a preacher yet.

"Drugs are sinful because they make you *turn away from God*! Just as excess pride makes you turn away from the Lord, so drugs make you care abowt nothing but yourself and your own craving! God's mercy is the *only answer*—there are no answers in chemicals!

"So that was the first sin—gluttony for drugs. And because of their gluttony—that *Deadly Sin*—the people who use drugs don't much care where the drugs come from. And because they don't care, they encourage their suppliers not to care much, either."

Rickey leaned back on his stool and took a long breath. "So the *gluttony* for drugs led to a *demand* for drugs that led to a robbery in order to get the *cash* to buy drugs! Now, about how many sins have we got so far?" Rickey held up a fist and stuck out a finger. "Theft—that's against the Commandments!" A second finger. "Pride, because they thought they could get away with it. Covetousness of money and drugs—that's another Deadly Sin." Fingers kept rising till he was working on his second hand. "Envy of those who had money—Deadly Sin again! And anger, a Deadly Sin, because they had to be angry to do their part in the robbery and point guns at people in the first place and steal all their dollars." *Dahlers*. "All because of gluttony, which doesn't seem like much of a sin until you think about it."

After the service, Loren walked down the aisle feeling as if he were on fire. He had broken this web of crime and evil, ended the cascade of sin, crushed the ringleader with the Lord's name on his lips. He shook Pastor Rickey's hand.

"That was the best sermon I've ever heard you give," he said.

Rickey smiled. "Thank you. People always seem to pay more attention when you talk about current events."

"You tied the current events to God."

"I heard you got a body." Rickey peered at Loren through rimless spectacles. "Any luck at finding out who did it?"

Loren felt the fire inside him leap higher. Was the Almighty looking at him through those spectacles? "We're in the middle of things right now," he said. "But I'll be working on it today."

"Good luck," said Rickey.

Sword and arm of the Lord, Loren thought.

Time to get to work.

E I G H T

Loren bounced up the steps of the City-County Building three at a time. Splotches of dried blood marred the white tile just inside the door. Loren moved past the mess and found Cipriano in his office. The assistant chief was listening to a pre-football sports program on the radio and doing paperwork. A book about the New Mexico water war lay open, facedown, by his hand. He looked up at Loren's knock.

"What's up, pachuco?"

"Nothing new, jefe," he said. "Begley's taking the cargo of drugs to Albuquerque. Chip Lone from the mortuary is taking the body to the Albuquerque medical investigator's office at the same time."

"Good," Loren said. "Anything from Jernigan or Patience?"

"Nope."

"Any idea why Patience is taking such an interest?"

Cipriano shrugged. "Because he's an asshole, jefe." He looked up and grinned. "And he's not even a half-competent asshole. They've found cattle wandering around their security areas down there."

"Cattle at ATL?" Loren was delighted by the thought. "Cattle got past those cameras and through alarmed chain link fences?"

"That's what Begley said. He goes shooting with one of their security guys, and the guy told him they run across cows every so often. They're so embarrassed the cows got through security that they just shoot them and bury them right there on the facility."

"Waste of good beef."

"That's what I thought. Oh." Cipriano looked surprised. "I forgot something. That-weasel-the-mayor wants you to call him."

Loren felt his good mood start to slide away. "What did he want?" he asked.

"Guess."

Loren sighed and went to his office to call the mayor. He used the DialComp code for the mayor's mobile phone and caught him just as he was setting off for the town's nine-hole golf course.

"I wanted to talk about that body you found," Trujillo said.

"That body more or less found me, Ed."

"Any idea who the guy was?"

"Not yet."

"Or who did it?"

Loren cleared his throat. "Same answer."

"Because the city can't afford a big investigation. The way I look at it, if no one knows who the body was, nobody's going to get upset if we don't go out of our way—"

"He looked like a local to me. There *are* a few of the ten thousand people in this county that I don't know by sight. And that body didn't drive very far, Ed. Someone in this county, maybe even in town, pulled the trigger."

Trujillo's voice demonstrated an exaggerated patience. "What about the last body, Loren?"

A cold wave of guilt poured like ice water down Loren's back. "That was different," he said.

"I don't see how."

Two years ago the county cops had found a dead man in the trunk of a car. He'd been killed by someone who had emptied a .45 automatic into the trunk. He'd been dead a week, and a television news helicopter hovering over the scene blew most of the evidence away in the propwash. After that Shorty lost the rest of the evidence, including the murder weapon, just in the act of getting it from the crime scene to his office. Probably one of his men ripped the gun off for a souvenir. There was no ID on the body and the car had been stolen in Boston fourteen months before, so no leads there. The crime was most likely drug-related and probably had nothing to do with anyone in the county.

"You and Shorty ruled that one suicide," the mayor said.

Loren cleared his throat again. Guilt bounced around in his skull like a rocketing rubber ball.

"The coroner ruled it suicide," he said. "And there's a difference, Ed."

"I don't see any essential difference. A stranger killed in a stolen car."

"The difference is that the guy didn't die of gunshot wounds *right in police headquarters*, Ed. It's kind of hard for us to ignore it under the circumstances."

"It's not that I don't appreciate the efforts of your department, Loren. Don't misunderstand me there."

Loren frowned at his BUY AMERICAN sign. "I understand you perfectly well, Ed," he said.

"But we've got to store the drugs in Albuquerque, and we've got a bill from the mortuary—"

"You'd get that in any case, Ed. Whether we investigate or not."

"—plus we have to bear the costs of transporting your body to Albuquerque for an autopsy, and maybe burying it when it gets there."

"If we find any next of kin, that last will be their problem."

"If they're solvent. I have no confidence in that."

"Ed, there ain't much we can do about any of these things. It's our *job* to do all this."

Trujillo paused for a moment. "Could you just keep the overtime to a reasonable amount?"

Loren smiled. "I'll do my best, Ed," he said.

He called the Hiawatha and asked for Amardas Singh. The sleepy voice that answered the phone had an accent far more Californian than Pakistani; Singh said he would be happy to talk to the officers if he could just take a shower first.

Loren used the extra time to buy new batteries for his disk recorder.

The Hiawatha was a U-shaped two-story motel that, like the Geronimo bar, featured a giant feathered Indian of green and red neon. Cipriano drove under the waving, flickering tomahawk and into the parking lot. He pulled up next to an Infiniti sedan that featured a bumper sticker reading HEISENBERG SLEPT HERE OR SOMEWHERE ELSE NEARBY. More physicist humor, apparently. Loren got out of the passenger seat and looked for a long moment at the neon Indian.

"Why Hiawatha?" he wondered suddenly. "Didn't Hiawatha live in Minnesota or something? Why not an Indian from around here?"

Cipriano knocked on Singh's door without giving the neon Indian a glance. "Tourists wouldn't understand if this place was named after Mangas Coloradas," he said.

"I guess."

"Maybe they should name it after Heisenberg. Whoever he was."

Loren ambled to the door just as it opened and stared at the room's inhabitant in surprise.

Like the man Loren had seen the night before, this man was big and dark-complected; but unlike the turbaned figure Loren remembered, this character had a wiry beard reaching almost to his navel and long pepper-and-salt hair that hung almost as far. Give him a bed of nails and a robe instead of his T-shirt, jeans, and moccasins, and he could have passed for a guru on his way to pick up some converts among the rich and fashionable who had, in recent decades, occupied Santa Fe in much the same fashion, and with more or less the same attitude, that the U.S. Cavalry had once occupied hostile Indian country.

"Hello," the man said. "I am Amardas Singh. Please come in, sirs."

Despite the somewhat formal language, this was still the Californian voice Loren had heard on the phone. The room smelled of fresh coffee. Loren and Cipriano took the two plastic seats available. "Would you like some French roast?" Singh said. "I just made some."

Both accepted. Singh poured from a portable plastic coffeemaker that he had obviously brought with him. Loren noticed, as Singh handed him his cup, that the man had a steel bracelet on his wrist. Singh sat down on a print bedspread with a fake Navajo design. He smoothed the pattern and looked at it with a smile.

"I remember this pattern from Pakistan," he said. "Odd to see it here in the western U.S."

Loren looked at it. "Looks Navajo to me," he said.

Singh shrugged. The gesture looked odd in a bushy-haired exotic. "I suppose the pattern could have been developed independently." He turned back to Loren. "Dr. Jernigan said you would call."

"I suppose he told you why."

"He said you would wish me to verify his movements."

"If you could." Loren sipped the coffee. It had been made with the hard tap water and tasted dreadful. Waste of good beans.

"Do you mind if we record this?" he asked.

"Please go ahead, sir."

"Could you give your full name for the record?" Starting the recorder.

"Amardas N.M.I. Singh."

Amusement trickled through Loren. N.M.I.: no middle initial. Singh must have got used to official interviews during his years of dealing with immigration.

Loren spoke into the recorder. "This is an interview with Amardas N.M.I. Singh, commencing at ten-forty A.M. Interviewing officers are Loren Hawn and Cipriano Dominguez." He looked up at Singh. "Birthplace?"

"New Delhi, India."

Loren frowned. "Someone told me you were Pakistani."

"I was born in India. My grandparents were killed by Hindus in a riot following the death of the dictator Indira Gandhi. My surviving family fled to Rawalpindi, in Pakistan."

The words were matter-of-fact, said with a slight smile. Loren tried to picture Atocha divided along those kinds of bitter ethnic lines, with Apostles battling the LDS over their varying interpretations of early Mormon history, and armed Knights of Columbus cruising the plaza armed with shotguns, blasting Baptist heretics with iron pellets . . .

Atocha wasn't as much as part of the Third World as Jerry liked to think.

"You're a U.S. citizen now?"

"For seven years, yes."

"How old are you?"

"Twenty-nine, sir."

Loren sipped more of the horrible coffee. It tasted almost as bad as Coover's at the Sunshine.

"And you are employed where?"

"I'm on the faculty at Caltech, but I'm sort of on loan to New Mexico Tech in Socorro."

Loren blinked. "Why is that?"

"New Mexico Tech has this lightning lab up on a mountain—Langmuir?" Singh smiled hopefully, waited for a reaction from Loren, and didn't get it. He shrugged. "Anyway, there's a lot of hot science going on right now relating to the kind of plasmas that can be formed by lightning, so I thought I'd get in on that."

Loren decided to stick to the facts. "Could you tell us what you remember of your movements?"

Singh cleared his throat. "I drove here from Socorro on Thursday night. I arrived around ten and called Dr. Dielh from the motel to let him know I was here. Dr. Jernigan picked me up the next morning and took me to the lab."

"In his BMW?"

"Yes. License plate DELTA E."

"You remember that?"

A modest smile. "It's my job to keep track of Delta E."

Whatever that meant. "Okay," Loren said. "Do you remember the time?"

"Ten o'clock, I think."

"And then?"

"We went to the labs. The experiment was supposed to start at ten-thirty, but there were computer delays, and the run started after noon."

"And the nature of the experiment?"

Singh paused for a moment. "How much about high-energy particle interactions do you know, sir?"

"Assume," smiling, "that I'm totally ignorant."

"Very well, sir." Singh pushed back his long hair with his hand, the one with the bracelet. "The new room-temperature superconductors have allowed us to see particle interactions at a higher energy level than before. But there has been a problem. During some interactions, at apparently random moments, the level of energy just seems to drop away, then resume. It's really remarkable. If you put it on a graph, the energy dives clean off the scale in just a tiny fraction of a second." One hand sketched a drooping line in the air. "Everything gets cooled down, and all the experimenters get really pi—get upset."

Loren took another sip. At least the awfulness of the coffee would keep him from falling asleep.

"There have been several theories concerning what may be occurring," Singh said. He seemed to have gone into a reflexive teaching mode: his tone was different, as if he were lecturing to students. "The most obvious thought was that the instrumentation was simply wrong—we *are* dealing, after all, with very tiny particles that exist for only a very tiny amount of time. The energy drops might conceivably lie within the span of experimental error. And Tim Jernigan suggested it might be a result of some unknown form of flux creep. But all of that was ruled out." Singh halted his lecture for a moment, then offered a self-conscious smile. He'd realized he was lecturing. "Have patience, guys. This won't take long." The voice, and vocabulary, had returned to southern California.

"That's okay," Loren said. "Take all the time you need." Even if he didn't quite understand any of this, there might be something here he could trip Jernigan with.

"I had a theory as to what was happening. The run here was to test that theory."

"That's all?"

"It occurred to me that the energy might be filling up interstices in the Penrose tiling of the ceramic superconductors."

Loren didn't have any idea what had just been said. There was a long moment while he tried to work out what to ask next.

"So does it?" he said finally.

"Guess not, man," Singh said. "The idea behind our experiment was to run the accelerator for enough hours, and at a high enough energy rate, so that the interstices would be filled and the power dropouts would not continue. Either my theory wasn't correct or the interstices can pack an awful lot of particles."

"So you were invited to watch the experiment because it was your theory that they were testing?"

"Yes. That and the fact that I played a part on the design team that built the superconductors used here on the accelerator facility."

"It's your design?" Surprised.

"Mine and a few hundred other people, yeah."

Loren noticed that the formal vocabulary had eased, and that the "sirs" had vanished completely. Singh had forgotten he was talking to the authorities, and that was good—he'd feel a lot more inclined to talk freely.

"In that case," Loren said, "why aren't you working for ATL?"

"Ah." Singh smiled again. "Too much of the work here is classified. I can't get a security clearance."

"Why not? You're a citizen now."

"I'm a Sikh!" Singh's voice was almost jolly. "My grandparents were killed solely because they were Sikhs. As a consequence of this I have never ceased to work for the establishment of a Sikh homeland in the Punjab. My political activities put me at odds with the policies of the U.S. government, and the FBI's been all over my ass for years, and I couldn't get a clearance."

Huh, Loren thought. Maybe he *is* a terrorist.

Cipriano, working through the information, reached a conclusion before Loren.

"You mean the experiment wasn't classified?" he asked.

Singh shook his head. "No. There are loads of experiments done at ATL that have no national security application."

Cipriano and Loren looked at each other, then at Singh. "Do you have any idea," Loren said, "why ATL is trying to invoke national security in this?"

Singh shrugged. "Sorry," he said. "I've no idea. Maybe it's a bureaucratic matter. Maybe the head of security wants this to become his investigation."

Right on the money, Loren thought. Singh didn't know William Patience but he sure knew the type. Maybe there were bureaucratic claim-jumpers in the sciences as well.

Loren tried to think of any further questions in this line, but couldn't come across any. "You were at ATL how long?"

"We were in the control room or at the buffet till early the next morning. Three or four o'clock, I think."

" 'We.' That's you, Jernigan, and Dielh?"

"And about fifty other guys, yeah. When a major experiment like that goes down, there are a *lot* of people who want to be a part of it—hook up their photon detectors and go crazy with the data. The list of authors on some of the papers is longer than the contents."

"What then?"

"Dr. Jernigan took me home."

"You planned to see him the next day? That would be yesterday?"

"Yes. We were going to repeat the experiment, but Dielh called it off. He said it would be more useful to reduce the data from the first experiment before beginning another." Singh fell silent for a moment. "What an asshole!" he added cheerfully.

Loren looked at Cipriano. Jernigan hadn't mentioned this. "When did this happen?" he asked.

"Yesterday morning. Perhaps ten o'clock. He said we would get together in the afternoon to go over the printouts from the first run."

Singh looked a bit deflated. Loren looked at him. "How'd you feel about that?"

"I wanted to do the experiment at least twice. It decreases the chance of experimental error and makes the conclusions more certain."

"Did you argue against the decision?"

"Yes. Dr. Dielh said we would schedule the second experiment for later, but I didn't relish another drive all the way from Socorro in order to do something I could have done this weekend."

"And then what happened?"

Singh looked annoyed. "I got another call a couple hours later that it would take some time to assemble the data, and I wouldn't be able to see any of it till evening."

"And you thought?"

"I started getting tired of these people pissing around. And then when I was walking home from dinner I saw Dr. Jernigan's car crashed in front of the courthouse, and I figured there'd be more delay."

Loren was surprised. "I don't remember seeing you in the crowd."

Smiling. "I was in my turban."

"I did see someone in a turban, but he wasn't you. Are there Indian tourists in town? Did you see the other guy?"

Singh laughed. "I'm afraid that was me, sir. Normally I braid my hair and beard and put it up in the turban."

"Oh."

"I washed my hair this morning." He fluffed out his beard with both hands. "It was getting a little gamy."

Cipriano cleared his throat loudly. Loren looked at him, then back at Singh.

"I suppose we should get this back on track," he said. "When *did* you see Dr. Jernigan?"

"Eight or nine o'clock. He brought the data."

"And Dr. Dielh?"

"I never saw him after we concluded the experiment."

"Really?" Loren looked at him in surprise. "Did he ever say why?"

"He called yesterday afternoon, just before I went to dinner, to say that he'd been called to Washington on some kind of classified job. He took the ATL plane to Albuquerque."

There was a long moment of silence. "Funny," Loren said.

Singh smiled ruefully. "A little odd, yeah. But then Dielh's a world-class jerk, anyway."

Loren was amused. He'd never thought scientists spoke of each other in this way.

"What did Dr. Jernigan tell you?"

"He said that his car had been stolen, that the man who stole it was shot—not by him—and that he hoped I'd confirm his story."

"He didn't tell you what story he wanted you to confirm?"

A tight smile. "No. I've told you exactly what happened."

"What's your impression of Dr. Jernigan?"

Singh grinned. "He's a brilliant man in his field. One of the best. But he lives in the microatomic world all the time—I envy his brilliance, but not his life outside the lab."

"Ever known him to be violent?"

Singh laughed out loud. "I doubt he would know how!"

"Do you know if he drinks? Does drugs?"

"I've never seen him take anything stronger than soda pop. He's a Dr Pepper man."

"Do you know his wife? Family?"

"Slightly."

"Do you think his wife would have an affair?"

"Wow. I wouldn't know. I never heard anything."

"Do drugs? Drink to excess? Become violent?"

Singh shook his head. "Based only on a very brief acquaintance, my impression of Sondra Jernigan is that she's someone who wanted nothing more than to be a housewife and raise children. Dr. Jernigan was the safest man she could find to marry. He'll never run around on her, and he'll bring in a big paycheck every two weeks."

"How about Dr. Dielh?"

Singh cleared his throat. "I know Joe somewhat better. I think he's probably a better politician than a scientist."

Loren thought about that one. "Political how?" he said.

"Not national politics. Office and science politics. He's very good at explaining science to bureaucrats and writing grant proposals, that sort of thing. And if you can be useful to him, he courts you. Pays you lots of compliments, lots of attention, goes out of his way to be nice to you." He shrugged. "That's why Tim's here. Dielh went out of his way to get him. And that's why I'm here, I guess. Joe thinks it's useful to have me coauthoring his papers."

"Have you ever known him to be violent?"

"Not really, no."

"What d'you mean *not really*?"

"He's never hit anyone that I know of. But he can be abrasive. Opinionated. Especially when one of his projects is threatened."

"Does he do drugs? Drink to excess?"

"He drinks the odd social martini. I've never seen him drunk."

"Does he have a family?"

"He's divorced. No children. I think the wife lives in San Diego."

"Does he have a girlfriend?"

"It wouldn't surprise me. But I don't know."

"Did you meet William Patience last night?"

"I don't . . . think so. What was the name again?"

"He's the head of ATL Security. He was driving Dr. Jernigan last night."

"Oh." Singh shook his head. "No, he didn't come in. Dr. Jernigan said when he left that he was going to take the maglev train back home."

"What time was that?"

"About three this morning. We went over the results as thoroughly as we could."

"Did he leave the data here?"

"It's on the table next to you." Loren looked in surprise at a stack of wide computer printout. Cipriano hurriedly removed his coffee cup from the pile. Loren flipped through it, saw nothing but meaningless figures and graphs.

"What does it all mean?"

Singh gave a shake of his head. "It means I'd like to do another run before I publish."

Loren looked at Cipriano and saw Cipriano looking back with the same questioning expression. Nothing left. Loren turned back to Singh.

"Last question. There's been a lot of changing of plans going on with your colleagues. Not to mention a body turning up in Dr. Jernigan's car. Do you have any idea what happened?"

Singh shrugged. "The confusion must have been caused by something coming up on one of ATL's other projects," he suggested. "The accelerator run couldn't have been the cause of any of this—it's a big experiment, but it's nothing out of the ordinary. And as for the body, I have no idea."

Loren reached out for the disk recorder. "This is Loren Hawn, ending the recording at"—looking at the watch—"eleven-seventeen A.M." He turned off the recorder and turned to Singh. "Thank you," he said. "And thanks for the coffee."

"You're welcome." Singh started to rise from his seat, then dropped back. "I have a question, if you don't mind."

"Sure."

"Somebody at the labs told me that there was a UFO landing field outside town. How do I get to it?"

Loren told him.

"And a flying saucer supposedly landed there?"

Loren and Cipriano grinned at each other. "Depends on who you talk to," Cipriano said.

Loren looked at Singh. "See, back in '99 there were all these millennial movements?" Singh nodded. "One of these guys, this guy named Westinghouse, had a vision, or whatever—"

"A saucer landed and told him," Cipriano said.

"Yeah. And the mother ship was supposed to land here, in New Mexico, on January 1, 2000, and pick up all the good people, and teach them how to deal with the chaos that would follow when this *other* group of *bad* aliens started bombarding Earth with evil rays."

"Zeta rays," said Cipriano.

"Westinghouse—except he changed his name to Millennium 2000—was ordered to build a field for the ship. So he rented some land from one of our local ranchers—"

"Luis Figueracion," said Cipriano.

"Yeah, Luis. So Millennium's followers built this concrete pentagram out there, so the saucer would know where to land. And they sold tickets for six thousand dollars apiece for rides on the mother ship."

"And suits!" Cipriano added. "Don't forget the suits!"

"Yeah. He also sold flying saucer suits—he called them ascension robes—for five hundred bucks each. So that the mother ship would know who to pick up first. It turned out they were white gowns, like kids wear for graduation."

"This is fascinating," said Singh.

"He had to fence off the field to keep gate-crashers from getting a free ride on the saucer. And Cipriano and me had to help with crowd control, because there were a lot of curious and hecklers and good ole boys with a skinful showing up . . ."

"Cops work on New Year's Eve, anyway," Cipriano said, "so we're used to it."

Singh leaned forward. "What happened? I assume the mother ship didn't arrive."

Loren grinned. "That was the great part. He got all his followers to start chanting, mantras or whatever they're called. After he got all the chanting going for long enough, he interrupted and told everyone that the mother ship *had* showed up and *had* taken everyone away."

Singh seemed confused. "But how—?"

"He said that people who are taken off for flying saucer rides usually have amnesia afterward, and that all the saucer literature proves it, and that they'd all remember their ride eventually. And he said that the mother ship would be back the *next* year for *another* ride, and they should all tell their friends."

"And then he got the hell out of Dodge with his money," Cipriano said, grinning with his long yellow teeth.

"The thing was," Loren said, "he *was* back the next year, with a bunch of the same people in robes. Only a few hundred this time. The ones who said they *could* remember the saucer ride."

"But he never did get back for the third year," Cipriano said. "I think there were a bunch of lawsuits."

"It's classic," said Singh.

Loren looked at him. "Why are you interested?"

Singh gave an elaborate shrug. "I come from India, which is famous for all the attention it pays to religion. But I've never seen so many religions as here in the States, or such a wide variety of believers. Southern California, then New Mexico—is the whole rest of the country like this?"

Loren and Cipriano looked at each other. "We wouldn't know," Loren said.

"And all the *new* religions claim to be scientific. And they wouldn't know science if it bit them. But science has *become* religion, at least for the masses—they don't know the difference between science and magic. UFOs and the space shuttle are like the same thing to them." He shrugged again. "I'm interested, anyway. I'll probably take a look at the place on my way out of town."

Loren rose from his chair. "Thanks very much."

"I hope I could be of some help."

Loren and Cipriano blinked in the bright sun as they stepped out of the motel. "At least he talked to us," Loren said.

Cipriano's voice was disgusted. "Only because he didn't know a fucking thing, jefe."

"Yeah."

"Dielh's flown off to Washington. I don't know if I wanna believe that was coincidence."

Loren shook his head. "Maybe he was just reporting the fact that Jernigan got involved in something that resulted in a dead body. I still think it was his family that started this—wife, kids, somebody."

"Yeah. But Patience knows something he's not telling us."

"That's my impression."

"So what are we gonna do?"

The neon Indian waved its tomahawk back and forth. Sword and arm of the Lord, Loren thought. He walked to the car and got in the passenger seat.

"Let's give Jernigan his car back," he said.

Jernigan stood on his driveway and stared at his BMW. He wore blue jeans, sandals, and a T-shirt with an MIT logo, and his expression suggested he strongly wished he or the car were elsewhere. The floor and driver's seat were still covered with dried blood, the shattered back window had crashed into the back seat on the drive to Vista Linda, and the bullet scars on the car's flank were even more obvious in daylight.

"I thought you'd clean it up," Jernigan said. His eyes blinked nonstop behind thick lenses.

"That's not our job," Loren said. "Maybe your insurance will cover it."

The battered auto stood in violent contrast to Vista Linda and its coddled ambience. Immaculate green lawns, difficult and very expensive to maintain in New Mexico, lay like sheets of green velvet before ranch-style tract homes. The hard local water, brought up from the ground at great cost, hissed gently, forming rainbows, as it sprayed over the smooth green. Lawn mowers, the signature tune of suburbia, buzzed quietly in the background.

It didn't look much like the Southwest. More like a piece of Pennsylvania sliced out of its bedrock and transported to the high desert by one of Millennium 2000's flying saucers.

Jernigan's lawn was half green grass, half crushed lava rock that matched the color of the blood on his car seat, with a neat curved border of white brick separating the two. Sitting in the middle of the lava rock, as in a Japanese garden, was a stunted piñon.

There were child-sized footprints in the lava rock where kids had run across it rather than use the sidewalk. Pebbles were scattered up and down the driveway. Loren hadn't seen the children as yet.

"Can we talk to you, Mr. Jernigan?" Loren said. "We've got a few things to clear up."

"I guess so." Jernigan was still staring at his car, teeth nipping at his upper lip.

"Shall we go inside?"

"Oh." Scratching his beard. "Yeah."

Loren and Cipriano followed Jernigan into his house. A boy of maybe twelve, graying white sneakers propped up on a hassock, sat in the living room. He was wearing a video helmet on his head and had sensor gloves on. Both were connected by wires to a computer deck on the table in front of him. The gloves were dancing in the air, manipulating objects in the artificial reality of whatever game he was playing. His head was bobbing in the odd, syncopated way of some blind people. "This is Werner," Jernigan said.

Loren looked at the kid, smiled, and nodded. "Hi," he said.

Werner's head kept bobbing in its odd disconnected way. "Hi," he said.

"My other son is Max," Jernigan said vaguely. Loren looked left and right. Max did not seem to be present.

"I have a daughter Werner's age," Loren said. Neither Jernigan nor Werner acknowledged this.

Loren felt impatience building under his belt. Jernigan's disconnected communications habits were going to drive him right over some certifiable edge in another minute or two.

Loren looked at Cipriano, then, more meaningfully, at Werner. Cipriano nodded and walked to stand next to Werner, pretending an interest in the equipment.

Loren followed Jernigan down the back hall into a study. It was spacious, lined with books and bound magazines. *Science*, Loren read, *Nature*, *Science News*. *Physical Review Letters*. A computer, black with gold baroque designs, sat atop a Victorian walnut desk. Above the computer hung a framed black-and-white photo of Albert Einstein on a bicycle. A large whiteboard stood on delicate polycarbon struts, its surface covered with red and blue felt-tip hieroglyphics. At least half of it seemed to be in another alphabet. Greek? Loren wondered. Russian? Inside a red circle, underlined several times, he saw a thing like a blue triangle followed by a cap E—okay, he thought, Delta E. And this was followed by another blue delta followed by a lowercase t, and then a sign that Loren remembered from high school as being less than or equal to, and then a thing like a lowercase h with a slash through it. Delta E times Delta t is less than or equal to—to whatever the slash h meant.

Jernigan sat in a black leather swivel chair and blinked up at him. Loren closed the door behind him, hitched his gun around behind, and started the disk recorder. He went through his usual preface, then looked at Jernigan.

"I spoke to Dr. Singh," he said. "He confirmed your story, but he added a few things you didn't mention."

Jernigan looked at him.

"He said you'd originally scheduled a second run for yesterday, and that it was called off. Why was that?"

Jernigan was silent for a long time. Loren was about to repeat the question at the top of his lungs when the man finally answered.

"Joe—Dr. Dielh—that was his decision."

"Why'd he make it?"

"He—got called—away."

"What's that got to do with it?"

"He—" Jernigan hesitated, then started over. "Dr. Dielh got called to Washington on some classified business, so he canceled the run."

"When was this?"

"Yesterday."

"When yesterday?" It felt good to raise his voice. He leaned forward over Jernigan, arms on his hips, glaring down into the thick spectacles.

"Morning?" Jernigan peered up inquiringly. "Ten o'clock?"

"You asking or telling?"

Jernigan leaned back, his face closing like a door. "I don't remember."

"Why didn't you tell me?"

"It seemed simpler that way."

"Why'd he get called to Washington?"

Ask the questions, Loren thought. Ask fast. Patience isn't here to protect him and you can bust him wide open.

"I don't know," Jernigan said.

"Something to do with the run?"

"Something classified."

"Why was the run called off?" Repeat. Repeat until the answers were different.

"I told you."

"What happened at the first run?"

Silence.

Loren felt his blood bubbling like Perrier. Patience wasn't here to protect the man and Loren was going to rip him apart.

"What happened?"

"Nothing." A mumble.

Loren beat on the arm of Jernigan's chair with one big fist. *"What happened to the Delta E?"*

No answer. Loren looked at the blackboard, saw the symbol circled and underlined.

"What happened to Delta t?" he demanded.

There was a flash of something in Jernigan's expression, something that Loren triumphantly read as terror, not fear but utter terror, clear as spring water and as horribly fundamental and real as a razor drawn scraping along a nerve; and then the door opened and a tall, plump woman entered, her expression as fixed and ferocious as the neon Indian at the Geronimo. Behind her was Cipriano, his face carefully expressionless.

"What are you doing to my husband?" The voice was shrill.

Loren swung on her. "Trying to find out why somebody died," he said.

"Get out of here!"

"You must be Mrs. Jernigan. I'm Loren Hawn. I'm chief of police at—"

"Get out, you bastard!" She swung toward her husband. "What were you thinking about?" she demanded. "The other goon was interrogating Werner!"

An uncertain alarm worked its way onto Jernigan's features. He looked as if he were about to say something.

"Can we calm down here a minute?" Loren said.

"Out. Or I'll call the police."

Loren gave her a moment to think about what she'd just said. "A man was murdered last night," he said.

"We don't know anything about it!"

"I thought maybe you could identify the body."

"I don't know him! Get out."

Try to get a foot in the door, Loren thought. "How do you *know* you don't know him?" he said.

That stopped her for a moment. Loren tried to pry the door open a little farther.

"I mean, you haven't seen the body, right? So how do you know that you don't know who he is?"

She turned to her husband. "Will you tell them to leave?" she demanded.

Jernigan rose. "Time to go," he said.

"Fine. Fine, I'll leave." Loren bought another few seconds while Sondra Jernigan and Cipriano danced around each other in the doorway.

"I should point out something," Loren said, watching the dance. "I'm going to go on working this case till I get a killer, okay? Now, I don't think your husband shot anybody . . ."

The two in the doorway finished their promenade and Loren followed them down the hall. The parade moved past the computer game and the oblivious adolescent in the living room.

"But there's such a thing as accessory after the fact," Loren went on, "and I think Mr. Jernigan knows more than he's letting on. If I find the killer without his help, I'll try and see that your husband is prosecuted, and that will mean time inside. And Mr. Jernigan—" He stepped into the front hall, then swung toward the physicist. "You are *not* the type to survive long in the slams, okay? A bunch of real crude guys are gonna enlarge your sphincter by about fifteen inches just to watch the expression on your face when they do it."

Jernigan stared at him with what appeared to be a mixture of disgust and horror. "Get out," he said.

"Mrs. Jernigan," turning to her, "I strongly advise that you find yourself and your husband a lawyer. Then tell him exactly what happened the night the man died and follow his advice very precisely, okay?"

She spoke from bloodless lips. "Get out of my house, you crude fucker."

"I'm just giving you the best advice I can."

"Out."

"The man talked, you know."

He said my name.

"Out."

Loren stepped out into the bright suburban sun, blood singing in his ears.

Maybe Mrs. Jernigan had been listening. If she had any sense, she'd follow his advice.

Two children, one dark, one blond, had the driver's door of the BMW open and were examining the interior. Both were about ten.

"Max!" Mrs. Jernigan shrilled. "Get in here!"

"I'm just looking at the—"

"*Max!*"

Max's dark eyes got big. He ran into the house. His straw-haired friend seemed undecided about whether to follow.

Loren closed the door of the BMW. "Let his mother talk to him for a while," he said.

"Okay."

"Ever seen a car with bullet holes in it before?"

The boy reached out to touch one of the bullet scars. He was wearing a Cybercops T-shirt. "It's real frigid," he said admiringly.

Loren smiled down at him. "Want to see our police car?"

The blond kid grinned. "Sure."

Loren and Cipriano followed the Cybercops shirt down the driveway. "What's your name?" Loren asked.

"Richard."

"You live around here?"

"Down the street." A vague wave of an arm.

Loren opened the driver's door. "Go ahead," he said. "Get in."

Richard slid into the black imitation-leather seat and peered out above the wheel. "Frigid," he said again.

"You good friends with Max?" Loren said.

A shrug. "I guess." He looked at the shotgun propped between the two front seats. "Can I look at the rifle?" he said.

"It's a shotgun. Hang on a sec." Loren reached over the boy and took the shotgun out of its rack. He propped the gun on one hip and worked the pump until he emptied the magazine into his hand. Richard's eyes shone at the businesslike *clack-clack* sound. Loren handed the shotgun butt-first to the kid and stuffed twelve-gauge rounds into his jacket pocket.

"Cool," said Richard. Frigidity forgotten.

"You get along okay with Max's dad and mom?" Loren asked.

"We get along okay. My mom and his mom go to church together 'cause our dads aren't interested. They're both in the choir." Richard raised the shotgun to his shoulder level and took aim at a mailbox across the street. The gun was heavy and the barrel wavered.

"Bam," said Richard. He tried to work the pump but his arm was too short, so he dropped the gun to his lap and slammed the action back and forth. He liked the sound so he did it again. Then he looked up at Loren. "You ever shoot anybody with this?" he said.

"I never shot anybody at all," said Loren.

"Oh."

"It's never a good thing to shoot someone," Loren said. "Someone got shot in Mr. Jernigan's car and it wasn't a thing you wanted to have to see."

Richard frowned down at the gun. The Cybercops weren't reluctant at all to shoot people. Loren tried to regain his interest.

"Let me show you the radio," Loren said. "Cipriano, you wanna do a radio check?"

Cipriano got in the passenger seat and demonstrated the radio. Richard's interest returned.

"The Cybercops have these implanted in their mastoids," he said.

Loren didn't know what a mastoid was, and he suspected Richard didn't, either. Loren took John Doe's picture out of his pocket.

"This is the guy who got killed. You ever seen him?"

Richard looked at the dead face. "Don't think so," he said. "This guy's dead, right?"

"The picture was taken after he died, yes."

Richard studied the picture with intense interest. "This is the guy who stole the car, right?" he said.

"Maybe. We don't know. You've never seen him hanging around?"

"I don't think so."

"We got some helmets and armor in the trunk. You want to see it?"

Richard's face lit up. "Yeah!"

Loren led the boy around the car and opened the trunk. "Were you around here last night when the car was stolen?"

"Naw. Max and Werner and their mom went to the movies."

Loren took out one of the vests and draped it on the boy. His blond head grinned up from the mass of black armor.

"Did you see anything unusual happen? Anything at all?"

Richard shrugged. "Nothing. I saw Tim come back from work, that's all."

"Tim? Timothy Jernigan?"

Richard busied himself buckling on the armor. "Yeah. Him and Sondra like everybody to call them by their first names."

Some of *those*, Loren thought, not quite knowing what he meant by it.

"You saw him drive home from work?" Loren said.

"He got dropped off."

Loren looked at the boy for a long moment. Something weighty and implacable was moving in his brain, rolling like a flywheel. Sprinklers and mowers hummed in the background.

"Who dropped him off?" Loren asked.

"One of those jeeps. The ones that the security guys drive around in."

Loren looked up triumphantly into Cipriano's bleak eyes. Lie number one, he thought. The cover story is starting to come apart.

Cipriano didn't look happy at this turn of events.

"You sure about that?" Loren said.

"Yeah. You can't miss old Tim, you know. Not as tall as he is and the way he moves." There was condescension in his tone. "Can I put the helmet on?"

"Sure." The blue helmet came down over the boy's eyes. He pushed the helmet back and peered out. "Wish I had my shades," he said. "I got mirrorshades just like the Cybercops."

"Did you see who was in the jeep?" Loren asked.

Richard's head shook back and forth in a no. The heavy helmet atop the head barely moved at all.

Loren asked a few more questions, but they didn't help. He put the gear away and Richard ran off to tell his friends about the police stuff he got to play with.

"I don't like it, jefe," Cipriano said.

"It's going to be hard relying on a ten-year-old as a witness," Loren said. Triumph bubbled through him like champagne.

"That's not what I meant."

"We gotta get confirmation." Loren looked up and down the street. "We're gonna interview every person in this neighborhood. Every single one."

"And if we're lucky we can nail William Patience and his whole security force as accessories after the fact? Jesus, jefe."

"We nail whoever we nail."

"And guess who's watching." Cipriano gave a deadpan look down the street. A chocolate-brown jeep had just come around the corner and pulled over to the curb.

"Who gives a shit?" Loren said. He slammed the trunk down. "Let's find our witnesses."

"I don't like it."

"24/24," Loren said. "Let's get humping."

He hitched his gun forward, then picked the house across the street and headed for it.

It was great, he thought, the way things were breaking.

N I N E

"Pay me."

"The dice hate me."

"Pay up."

Skywalker's soft voice chimed in. "Welcome to the bankruptcy club."

"Chite," Kelly said in Spanglish, after which she handed over three hundred dollars' worth of Monopoly money. Buddy Mandrell, one of her older sister's suitors, smirked and dropped the money onto his stack.

"Watch your language," Jerry said, rolling dice. "Your dad's here."

Kelly glanced over her shoulder. "He's not listening," she said.

Loren sat on an easy chair across the room, watching television and doodling on a pad. "I can hear perfectly well," he said. "And that word had better have been chiste."

Kelly blinked for a moment. "Sí, patrón," she said. "I was just making uno chiste, that's all."

"Roll the dice, Ivor," said her sister.

"Just a second." Ivor Thomas left the folding table in the living room and stepped through the front door. The screen closed behind him on hushed hydraulics.

Ivor and Buddy were among the candidates to replace Katrina's last boyfriend, whom she'd dumped about a week ago—Katrina changed boyfriends more frequently than she changed the color of her lipstick. Her tomboy tastes, fortunately for Loren's peace of mind, led her to local kids, good ole boys in training . . . Loren figured he knew how to handle ole boys, all right.

The only problem was that sooner or later all apprentice ole boys start to dip snuff. Judging by the worn white circles on the back of Ivor's and Buddy's jeans, that stage had been reached by both of them.

Ivor reentered, dabbing at the corner of his mouth with a blue print handkerchief. Loren looked up at him.

"You want me to get you something to spit in?" he asked.

Ivor shambled to a surprised stop. "Uh," he said. "No, sir."

Loren always brightened at the way young ole boys always called him "sir." He looked over his shoulder at the Monopoly game. "How about you, Buddy?"

"No, sir."

"Sorry to interrupt. Go right ahead with your game."

You had to let ole boys know right from the start that they couldn't hide anything from you. Then keep demonstrating it, in case they weren't bright, because often they weren't. And the ones that were smart—and there were more smart ones than a stranger might think—had got into the habit of acting dumb, because that was what the role required.

The phone rang, and Kelly ran to answer it. She was wearing a lot of makeup tonight, Loren noticed, scarlet lipstick and lurid purple eye shadow, nails done in a different but equally violent shade of purple. A T-shirt that read NOTHING SUCCEEDS LIKE EXCESS.

Dressing up for her sister's boyfriends. The difficulty with Katrina's habit of trying out several boyfriends at once was that they all got used to hanging around the house, and when Katrina made her choice from the pack, the rest of them often as not decided to hang around Kelly, something Kelly was all too willing to encourage. Her parents had declined to let her out on solo dates—group dates were okay—but the problem was a constant one.

"Hi," Kelly said, answering the phone. "Tuesday? I'll ask." She came back to the living room, her body twisted in a coltish, ungraceful stance, ankles crossed, a stance that mirrored the social awkwardness of her position. "Daddy," she said. "It's Mrs. Trujillo. She wants me to sit Tuesday."

Loren looked at her. "No."

Her stance grew more awkward, more unbalanced. "What am I gonna tell her?"

"Tell her that you forgot that you already have a sitting job." Loren reached into his pocket and pulled out his money clip. He took ten dollars off it and handed it to Kelly. "Tell her you've been paid in advance."

"Okay!" brightly. Kelly spun about, the awkwardness gone, smiling around her braces. She danced back to the phone on winged heels.

"I don't believe it," said Katrina. "Ten bucks! Are you gonna actually—"

Loren scowled over his shoulder. "This," he said, "is not a matter for discussion."

The Monopoly game continued, a bit subdued. Bursts of mechanical hilarity came from the TV set, which was pulling in an Australian sitcom off the satellite. Loren returned his attention to the white recycled legal pad in front of him.

JOHN DOE, it said in big letters, right in the middle. Just below, in much smaller letters, were the initials *r.d.*

Loren had put the letters in lowercase so that they would be less intrusive. He didn't even want to think about what they might represent.

If he did his police work, he thought, he wouldn't ever *have* to think about it. If he could find the killer, get the proper evidence against him, it wouldn't *matter* who the victim was.

ATL was at the top of the page, in medium-sized letters. Names—Diehl, Patience, Jernigan—were connected to ATL by radiating lines, then by another set of lines to John Doe.

Delta E was written and circled. So was Delta *t*.

Loren wished he could talk to Debra about it. Sometimes just talking helped to clarify things. But Debra was off helping to costume a production of *The Gondoliers* at the Presbyterian church, a favor to a friend.

Loren looked at the pattern and couldn't find anything new in it. He put the pad down and stared at the TV. Someone had just made a joke and the canned audience was finding it hilarious. Loren did not understand why.

His skin felt as if it were radiating mild heat. He touched his forehead lightly with his fingers; they came away warm. He'd got a slight sunburn that afternoon, going from door to door in Vista Linda.

He hadn't found a thing. No one had seen Jernigan return home, no one had seen John Doe, and no jury was going to believe a ten-year-old's evidence about something he hadn't really been paying attention to.

Maybe the autopsy would tell him something he didn't know, though he doubted it.

He'd just have to keep putting pressure on people. Sooner or later, someone—most likely Timothy Jernigan—would inform. That was how most cases got broken—people ratted out their comrades.

And a good thing, too.

Loren put his pad down and went into the kitchen for a grape soda. He closed the refrigerator door with its commanding GUARD THE EARTH! poster and then saw that Skywalker had followed him into the kitchen.

"You want something?" he asked.

Skywalker shook her head, a gentle wave rolling through her long, straight hair. Her T-shirt had a cartoon of a humpback whale in combat fatigues and helmet, clutching an assault rifle. PROTECT THE EARTH! it said.

"No," Skywalker said. "I've just gone bankrupt."

"Sorry."

"I'm not." A bit defiantly, her lips pressed together. "I don't want to be a success as a land developer, anyway."

Loren grinned. "Good for you."

"I'd rather play a more ideologically sound game. Like Monkeywrench or Balance of Nature or something." She shrugged. "I got outvoted."

Ideologically sound, Loren thought. Jesus. He sipped grape soda. "Do your parents agree with you? Is that why they live in town instead of Vista Linda?"

She nodded. "Yeah. They're both active members of the Eco-Alliance."

"Good for them." They were on the right side of a few things, Loren thought, even if they were fuzz-brained enough to name their kid Skywalker.

"I mean, we drink *bottled water* in this town because of what the mines have done to the water table. And we've had three years of drought in a row, and the water table's even farther down, and industry still won't believe about the greenhouse effect. You'd think people would *notice* this stuff."

"You'd think they would."

"And all the timber industry can do is blame eco-saboteurs for starting forest fires that were clearly started by lightning strikes. Monkeywrenchers wouldn't put *more* carbon dioxide in the air, for Christ's sake. Industry can't even keep its lies *consistent*."

Loren nodded. "I hadn't considered that."

She scowled. "It really gets me annoyed."

Loren looked at her. Every time he had a conversation with Skywalker, he had the impression he was talking to an adult, not a fifteen-year-old. His own children seemed so much younger.

And a lot more carefree.

Her parents, he remembered, worked at ATL. And Skywalker was bright, obviously kept her eyes open.

"I suppose you've heard about our murder," Loren said.

Skywalker gave a little smile. "I thought you had a rule about discussing police business at home."

Loren shrugged. "I thought you or your parents might know some of the people involved."

"Oh." She seemed surprised. "You mean this is an *interrogation?*"

"Sort of. Do you mind?"

She shrugged. There was an amused light in her eyes. "I guess not."

"Do you know Timothy Jernigan? Or his wife, Sondra?"

She shook her head. "Sorry."

"Amardas Singh? Joseph Dielh?"

Two more shakes of the head. "I guess I'm not much help, huh?"

"Where do your folks work, anyway?"

"My dad's a specialist in crystal growth. I don't think he deals with any of the people you're talking about. My mom's a particle physicist working in the black buildings, and she doesn't talk much about any of the people she works with. She's not allowed to, basically. And I don't see her very often in any case."

"She's working all the time?"

She shrugged. "She and my dad separated. I live with my dad."

"I didn't know." Uncomfortably. "Sorry."

"That's okay. I'm glad it happened, to tell the truth. Things were getting tense." She gave a deep sigh. "Except now there's a big custody fight. My mom wants custody just to keep Dad from getting me. It's not as if she ever pays attention to me or anything."

"Did they ever talk about William Patience?"

"The security guy?" Skywalker gave a laugh. "He's an anal-retentive jerk, if you ask me."

A gust of laughter broke from Loren. "You've heard about him?" he said.

"I've *met* him. He lectured to our church group—we're in the Earth Church—about mountaineering and showed some slides. He's one of the climbers who try to leave a clean mountain behind, picks up all his spikes and stuff. You know."

"Not really."

"With some people it's respect for nature, but for him it's just another way of being tight-assed. My mother used to complain about him all the time, about how the security people were always listening in on her phone conversations or getting on her case about putting her work in the safe every time she went for a cup of coffee. Everybody *hates* the guy.

"Of course," nodding her head, trying to be reasonable, "it's his *job* to be a tight-ass."

"There are ways of being nice about it."

"True. And he's not nice at all." She seemed happy now that she'd found a legitimate reason for disliking Patience.

"How come," said Kelly, appearing in the doorway, "you let *her* use words like tight-ass and I can't—"

"Because," Loren said, "this is an *interrogation*. I have to take note of her exact wording and phraseology."

"A *what*?" Disbelieving.

"I needed what your friend knows," Loren said. "And now I do."

The two girls caught each other's eyes and burst into laughter.

Loren returned to his television and his pad, gazing for a long time into the unanswered scrawls that were his questions.

"Try and watch the tooth grinding, okay?" Debra put her spectacles on the night table and reached for the light.

"I'll try," Loren said. He was lying in bed but he didn't feel like sleeping at all. Thoughts, images, disconnected ideas kept rolling through his mind. William Patience staring at Loren's boxing trophies, the look of fear in Jernigan's eyes, Mack Bonniwell standing with clenched fists on the church steps, Randal Dudenhof with his chest transfixed by his car's steering column, the blood-spattered steering wheel bent and broken in front of his chest like a crumpled target symbol.

Debra turned off the light. "I can't get over it," Loren said.

"Over what?"

"How that dead man looked like Randal Dudenhof."

There was a moment of silence in the darkness. "I haven't thought about Randal for a long time," Debra said.

"Do you know what happened to his wife?"

"Violet? She hung onto the ranch for a few years, then sold out to Luis and moved to Utah."

"I knew that."

"Provo, I think. Remarried and raised a lot of little Mormons."

The T-bird smelled like Canadian whiskey, Loren remembered. Randal had won sixty dollars in the poker game at the Copper Country and had bought a fifth to celebrate. He'd probably been swigging from the bottle when he skidded on black ice and went off the Rio Seco bridge.

It wasn't even illegal back then. You had to be some kind of communist to suggest a guy shouldn't have a few drinks on his drive home. The jack Mormons and the other good ole boys could handle their liquor and they could spit a quid of tobacco right between the eyes of a sidewinder at ten feet and they could drive forty miles above the speed limit on icy roads and handle every slide.

They died in droves, pierced and crushed by velocity and metal that crumpled like paper, weeping and filling their drawers as their spirits bled away. Loren had cut enough of them out of crushed vehicles to know. So much for good ole boy machismo.

"First man I ever saw die," he said.

"I know."

"Damn. What a waste." Meaning all of them, all the bodies torn by metal.

Suddenly Loren wished he had a cigarette. He'd never smoked— at the age when most kids in Atocha took up smoking or snuff, he'd been on the football team under a strict Mormon coach who would cut a player for drinking, smoking, or (he said) masturbation, though how he intended to enforce the latter proscription was never clear. (He could have, come to think of it, at least with the Mormons on the team—he was a bishop, and had the spiritual authority to ask them questions about their sex lives and demand straight answers.) Loren had never taken up smoking—drinking and strangling the goose were something else—and in Korea he used to give his free G.I. cigarettes away to the locals.

But for some reason he had a powerful urge to smoke now, to lie in bed and hold his wife's hand and think aloud about what was happening in his town. The image of himself doing that struck him as impossibly poignant.

He took Debra's hand. Her fingers were cool.

"Do you suppose he could be Randal's son?" he asked.

"I was wondering that."

"He used to run around on his wife a lot, Randal."

Debra was silent for a moment. "That's what everyone said."

"But who the hell would he have a kid with?"

"I never heard anything."

"Me, either."

The words faded into the darkness. Loren remembered Randal at Connie Duvauchelle's one night trying to make a deal with one of the girls to perform some sexual act, just about *any* sexual act, for the four dollars and change Randal had left in his pocket after pissing away the rest playing poker at the Copper Country.

"It couldn't be the real Randal," Loren said. "The guy was too young."

The words seemed to hang in the dark, refusing to fade, and a sudden wave of panic struck Loren. Had he actually said that aloud?

Implied that the dead man might be the real Randal, even in the darkness of his own bedroom, to his own wife?

He could never say that, not even here. It would be taken as evidence he was losing his grip.

But Debra didn't reply, and Loren felt a current of relief.

Tomorrow, he figured, he'd have to start applying pressure.

Roberts was back on his box across West Plaza for the early Monday service, swaying slightly with drink as he condemned the church by his presence. As Loren passed by he called out, "Miracles happen every day!" in a cheerful voice. Loren didn't answer.

The church was only two-thirds full. It was perhaps appropriate that the sermon was on sloth. Sloth, the pastor maintained, was a sin that prevented people from doing their duty to God and their fellow human beings. Loren thought that even so, sloth was a pretty boring sin, all things considered.

Loren didn't need the sermon to fire him up for duty. He drove his family home, changed from his church clothes into his uniform, and then took the cruiser back to his parking place. Sword and arm of the Lord, he thought.

Eloy was in place behind the front desk. Loren gave him a cheery wave as he walked buoyantly up the hall. "Hey, Chief," Eloy said, "the custodial staff are back from their weekend and want to know if they can clean up the hall."

"Of course," Loren said. He hadn't given the old bloodstains a single look.

"You got some headlines, boss." Eloy pulled out a folder and opened it to reveal a headline from that morning's Albuquerque paper. POLICE CHIEF LEADS CHARGE ON DRUGS, it said, with a photo from the press conference, Loren in his helmet and armor, holding up the confiscated Mac-11.

Loren admired himself for a moment. "Mind if I take this?" he asked.

"I made a bunch of copies. Take all you need." Eloy grinned up at him. "You noticed something funny about the headline?"

Loren looked at it. "No," he said. "It's a nice headline."

Eloy gave a laugh. "It makes it sound as if you were on drugs when you led the raid."

Loren looked at the headline again and the double meaning jumped out at him. He scowled. "Some asshole wasn't doing his job at the damn paper."

"Huh."

"I should call and give them a piece of my mind. Letting the story go under a headline like that."

"That kind of thing happens all the time."

"Pisses me off." Loren felt like waving a fist. "Finally we get a chance for some good publicity, and instead people are going to be laughing at us. I guarantee that."

"Hey, Loren. Good bust."

Loren looked up at the sound of the new voice and saw Salomon Tafoya, the chief of the police at the Apache reservation. Salomon was a barrel-chested, muscular man with a close-cropped Marine D.I. haircut. His bearing was straight-spined and military, and his uniform was black with silver flashes, reminiscent (if anything) of Hitler's SS. He was not one of the gentle, pollen-scattering, Earth-loving Indians beloved by recent Anglo immigrants, but rather an Apache in an older style, practical, unsentimental, and as ruthless as he thought necessary.

Loren shook Salomon's strong, capable hand. "What're you doing in town, Sal?" he asked.

"An errand or two. And I'm picking up that troublemaking son of a bitch George Gileno."

Loren nodded. "What's Gileno's problem, anyway?"

"The problem," Salomon said, "is that he's a troublemaking son of a bitch." No humor intended.

"Buy you a cup of coffee?"

"Thanks, Loren, but I've got to pick up Gileno and get back to the rez."

"Say," remembering what he'd seen the other day, "I saw a group of young Apaches out on the plaza the other day. Some older man was pointing stuff out to them."

"Part of the young men's initiation," Salomon said. "They have to memorize all the water sources in the territory."

Loren looked at him. "What water source?"

"There used to be a spring on the plaza about a hundred years ago. We figure it'll be there again."

Loren contemplated his surprise. "Guess that explains why the Federal Building basement is always having these leaks."

Salomon allowed himself a cold smile. "Water's funny in this country. It comes and goes. Folks come and build, they should ask the people who've lived here for hundreds of years."

"They had to take all the records out of the basement and move them into the old dance hall on Railroad."

"Why am I not surprised?"

Loren shook Salomon's hand again and said goodbye, then went to his office and sat at his desk. The paperwork from the double deliveries to Albuquerque, drugs and a body, were waiting in his In box. He ignored them and called the Office of the Medical Investigator in Albuquerque. John Doe's autopsy, he discovered, was under way. The M.I. would call as soon as he was done.

Loren thought for a moment, then called an old fishing buddy named Larry, who worked at the Riga Brothers power plant, and told him he wanted to fish for some facts. Larry checked the weekend logs and confirmed that ATL had ordered full generating capacity for Friday, beginning at ten-thirty, but that the actual order for the power hadn't come till six minutes after noon. ATL had taken all the power the old facility could provide till just before three the next morning and had announced its intention of buying more power beginning at ten-thirty that same morning. The power order had been postponed till two in the afternoon, then canceled altogether.

Loren thanked his informant and promised to catch some trout with him before the weather turned chill.

Loren looked at the figures he'd jotted down. Jernigan and Singh's report of the first accelerator run, and the cancellation of the second run, were now confirmed. He hadn't really ever thought their stories false, but if the stories had been lies, he would have had something to hang the liars with.

He looked up Joseph Dielh in the phone book and telephoned, encountering an answering machine tape. He left a message asking Dielh to call, then called ATL and left another message with his secretary. He was about to call Patience with a few questions, but there was a knock on his door.

"Photo opportunity, Chief," Cipriano said. "Pedro and his buddies are being arraigned in ten minutes."

"Be down in a minute. Which courtroom?"

"Santos."

Loren heaved himself out of his chair and went to the men's room to comb his hair and make sure his navy-blue uniform didn't have too much lint. Then he made his way to Judge Santos's court and sat in the back.

Television cameras squatted on tripods like one-eyed Martian invaders. Shorty was wearing his white suit, star, and Stetson. District Attorney Castrejon had shown up in person instead of delegating things to Sheila Lowrey, who was nevertheless present in her broad-shouldered suit. Mayor Trujillo pumped hands and passed out buttons among the spectators. Santos, the judge, ignored the circus and went on handing out sentences to the weekend's drunks.

Robbie Cisneros, the Texas cousins, and the drug dealers were brought in shackled. Their attorney was a guy from Albuquerque named Axelrod, a man Loren knew by reputation as a syndicate mouthpiece. There was a story that he'd had a judge's legs broken once for the man's having found him guilty on a traffic citation.

Apparently the dealers' connections had bought some high-class legal muscle. Axelrod wore, Loren considered, too many rings on his thick fingers, and had a few too many glossy waves in his dark hair. His manner, as glossy as his hair, made Loren want to take him into an alley and twist his head off.

Axelrod had made some effort to put his clients in coats and ties for the event, but even so they looked no more respectable than would Geronimo and his Apaches had they been likewise dressed. Robbie looked ghastly, eyes swollen shut, yellow and purple oil slicks seeping down his face. A walking bruise. The two Mexicans, Medina and Archuleta, were not being indicted for the drug-running charges—that would happen later, in federal district court—but on charges of firearm possession. Axelrod moved for separate trials for everybody, with translators provided for the two Mexicans. The two were alleged not to speak English, though when busted they seemed to have understood things well enough. Santos, a dignified, sleepy-eyed member of the Democratic apparat, took everything under advisement and set bail at $150,000 apiece.

The gavel banged—a recess—and all the extras filed out, leaving behind the usual shabby assortment of weekend drunks waiting to take their legal medicine. The two Mexican nationals were turned over to federal marshals, who marched them, chains and all, across Plaza Street to the Federal Building, to be arraigned on the drug charges. Shorty and Castrejon and Loren and the mayor, lined up in the hallway outside, each spoke their piece for the cameras before the reporters drifted off.

Loren, microphones jammed in his face, doing his rhetorical bit for law 'n' order, saw Sheila Lowrey waving at him from behind the press of reporters. He finished and waded through the mob to her side.

"Can I buy you some coffee, Loren?" she asked.

"If it's quick. I'm kind of busy."

"Let's go to my office, then."

Sheila pushed through a heavy fire door and Loren followed her up a flight of stippled steel stairs toward her office. She poured him a foam cup of coffee from a mineral scarred coffee machine waiting in the hallway, then led her past her secretary into her office.

It was a comfortable book-lined place, with shabby old furniture drawn from county storage and an untidy collection of paperbacks occupying the top of the bookshelf above the law books. One of the two old varnished wood chairs was draped with her jogging outfit: T-shirt, shorts, white socks, and shabby running shoes, white with blue stripes. Loren had seen her bounding around the plaza at lunchtime. Loren's gaze modestly shrank away from the halterlike arrangement she strapped about her breasts when running.

He hitched his gun around and sat on the other chair. He knew better than to actually drink his cup of coffee. He put it on her desk and left it there.

Sheila took off her horn-rims and waved them casually in his direction. "I think we're in trouble on the Cisneros indictment."

Loren looked at her in surprise. "Just because he got that syndicate hotshot from Albuquerque? We can—"

"Medina turns out to be the cousin of one of Mexico's biggest drug dealers. The ones the papers call kingpins? The guy can spend millions if he has to in order to get the guy out of jail."

"Let 'em see if it works here."

"Axelrod has requested medical reports on all his clients."

"'Cause Robbie resisted and got clocked? He—"

"And he'll go to town on that warrant. An anonymous call, for God's sake! And it didn't come in on a 911 call, so it wasn't recorded."

Heat flared under Loren's collar. He remembered the call, Eloy's recognizing his voice. And he remembered that every call into the station was logged, though only the emergency calls were recorded.

Have to talk to Eloy, he thought.

"That warrant was legal," he said. "Denver signed it."

"Axelrod will try to have it overturned. And you can damn well bet he'll charge police brutality. All he has to do is win *one* of those and the case gets thrown out. Robbie and the Texas boys walk. And he'll *try* to get the drug shipment thrown out on the same grounds, fruit of the poison tree and all that—"

"Now, wait a minute!" Loren began.

Sheila held up a hand. "Give me a second, Loren. He'll *try* to get that evidence tossed, but he probably won't succeed. You didn't search the truck on the grounds of that warrant, you searched it because you got a warning off the LAWSAT, and that's legal."

"You bet it is," Loren glowered.

"Here's the deal," Sheila said. "One of the things we can do to really nail the Mexicans is to get one or more of the Texans or Robbie to turn state's evidence. But if the indictments get tossed out, we won't have any pressure to put—"

"They're *not* going to get thrown out," Loren insisted. "The case is going before Santos, for Christ's sake!"

Sheila pursed her lips. "That's what Castrejon thinks."

"Well, he's the D.A."

"He figures all he has to do is deal with his cousin the judge and all the fellow cousins and Democrats in the system—and maybe he was right so long as Robbie's lawyer was one of our sterling local public defenders, also cousins of the judge or cousins of Castrejon or cousins of *somebody*. But I disagree. I think it's gonna be a bitch."

"Just because of that Axelrod? He's—"

Sheila put on her spectacles and leaned forward. "He plays by different rules than the local boys, Loren. Justice in this county is like a private club—things get done in this building in a certain manner because they've always got done that way. I don't belong to the club, and working here has really opened my eyes."

"Sheila . . ."

"But *Axelrod doesn't belong to the club, either!*" The spectacles were off again, jabbing at Loren like a penknife. "And Axelrod is being paid a lot of money by *somebody*, not just to flout the club, but to *burn the clubhouse down!*"

Loren felt tongue-tied by this vehemence. "Hey," he said. "I'm on your side."

The spectacle-knife sliced twice, disemboweling invisible foes. "The only way he can get his two boys off is to completely discredit the police force that busted them, okay? He can try to suppress the warrant, and he'll either file a civil suit against you on behalf of Robbie, or he'll file a civil rights complaint."

"Civil rights complaint?" Outraged filled Loren's heart. "On what fucking grounds—!"

"Robbie's Hispanic, right?"

"I didn't beat him up because he's Spanish!" Loren said. "I beat him up because he's a fucking thief!"

"Loren. Watch what you say around me, okay?" Sheila flung herself back in her chair. Her look was grim. "For a minute there it almost sounded as if you beat up Robbie Cisneros because you felt like it, not because you had difficulty apprehending him in the course of an arrest."

Loren glared at her, knuckles turning white as he gripped the arms of the old wooden chair.

"Because if you *did* beat up Robbie just for the fun of it—" She peered at him nearsightedly. "—and I'm not saying you did, okay? But if you did, with someone like Axelrod on the defense, it's going to come out in court."

"Bullshit."

"Let me tell you what Axelrod is going to do, Loren. He'll get expert medical testimony that will indicate—well," with a shrug, "that *might* indicate—that Robbie was beaten while he was in handcuffs. No defensive wounds, handcuff marks around the wrists, that sort of thing. He'll fly his own doctor into town if he has to. Then he'll depose every witness—you, Shorty, every officer present—and he'll ask you to go through your story piece by piece. He'll be hoping to trip someone up on the sequence of events. 'And then what happened, Officer?'" imitating Axelrod's glossy tenor. "'The chief handcuffed the suspect,' " another voice. " 'What?' " —back to Axelrod's voice again— " 'He handcuffed the suspect *before* Mr. Cisneros was struck?' "

"Loren," seriously, "you *know* what he can do with that. He'll tear us apart."

Loren just looked at her.

The spectacles came jabbing forward again as Sheila leaned toward Loren. "If there's a problem with this bust," Sheila said, "I want you to tell me now. I can plea-bargain Robbie and his buddies and nothing will ever come out in court."

"There's nothing wrong with it." Flatly.

"Loren," warningly, "*think* about it."

"Nothing wrong," said Loren.

Sheila gave a long sigh. She put her spectacles on and leaned back in the chair. "Funny that I'm the only person in this building who doesn't belong to the goddamn Atocha Men's Dinosaur Association, and I'm the only one who knows how to defend it." She picked up a pen and began writing on a white recycled legal pad, making notes to herself. "What I want to do is rehearse every witness. I want to do it *before* Axelrod can get to them." Her level eyes rose from the pad and gazed steadily into Loren's. "I want it clear to everybody that Robbie Cisneros tried to run away, that he resisted arrest and received all his injuries before he was handcuffed."

"That will be made clear," said Loren. "Absolutely clear."

"And in your written report?"

"Almost done. I'll get busy on it."

She made a tick mark on her pad. "I want all the officers concerned to make appointments with me in the next day or so. I'll also want to talk to everyone involved with the George Gileno arrest, because if Axelrod goes the route of the civil rights complaint, he'll want to show that you beat up Indians, too."

"That's all?" Loren shifted in his seat. He just wanted to get out of there.

"No." She was looking weary. "I happen to know that Mack Bonniwell is going to make a complaint against you for hitting his kid."

"At least Len Bonniwell and A.J. Dunlop are Anglos."

"Want to bet Axelrod offers his services to the father free of charge?"

Loren felt a tingling in his spine. They were lining up against him, his enemies, coming together, like the Deadly Sins all marshaled in Samuel Catton's visions by the Master in Gray . . . Bonniwell and Dunlop and Cisneros and Timothy Jernigan and William Patience and Axelrod the legbreaker . . . He hadn't quite seen the pattern before.

Atocha was under siege. Its enemies wanted to alter its ways, take away the rightness that, with all its faults, nevertheless underlay its existence. Of that Loren felt an absolute moral certainty.

"Axelrod is going to try to make this last weekend seem like a bloodbath," Sheila said.

"If that's the way he wants it," said Loren.

She looked up sharply. "We're going to have some absolutely clean cops here," she said. "We're going to have absolutely clean cops until this trial is over."

"Cops here have always been clean."

Her eyes were searching. "That's not what the rumors say, Loren."

Loren shrugged. "People always talk."

"Fortunately," Sheila said, "what people say, and what can be said in court, are two different things."

"Fortunately," Loren echoed. He stood up. "Thanks for the coffee."

Sheila looked at the cooling, untouched cup that sat on her desk. "You're welcome." Her eyes turned up to his. "If you think I was hard on you, picture what Axelrod's going to do. I hope you're ready for that."

"When the time comes."

"The time is *now*, Loren. He'll be waiting for you to slip up, waiting every second. Till this whole thing is over."

"I'm always ready, Sheila."

She looked at him, a small frown on her face. "I hope to hell you are, Loren."

Loren made his way to the front desk, where Eloy was chatting on the phone. "Just a sec, Gloria," he said, cupping the mouthpiece, and looked up at Loren.

"Business, Eloy," Loren said.

"Right away, Chief." Eloy excused himself from Gloria, whoever she was—certainly not his wife—and hung up the phone.

"Been ringing all morning," he said. "People with missing children. They heard we had a John Doe, everyone's scared it's *their* John Doe. Pretty damn sad."

"Sheila Lowrey wants to see you, about the anonymous tip that led to Robbie Cisneros's arrest."

"Oh. Sure." Grinning.

"Now. I'll answer the phones while you talk." Loren cleared his throat. "The thing is, you have to be absolutely positive that the call was anonymous. That you have no idea who it was that called."

Eloy winked. "Sure, Chief. No problem."

Loren looked stern. "No winking, Eloy. Not at Lowrey, not at me, not at anyone. We could lose the bust."

The grin faded from Eloy's face. "Right, Chief. What you say." He rose from the chair. "By the way. The M.I. up in Albuquerque called for you. That London guy."

"Autopsy's over?"

"Yep. He said to call back."

Loren sat at the chair and waited for Eloy to leave. He turned the pages of the phone log and looked at the entries for two days before. The 911 emergency calls were recorded on disk, but those coming into the desk were simply logged by the man on the desk. *09:03*, the entry said, *Chief Hawn, personal.* This was crossed out with a neat blue ballpoint line, with *Refused ID, tip re: armed robbery* written in a smaller hand in the remaining space above.

Loren looked at the tiny handwriting. He had been taught all his career to preserve evidence.

He looked left and right, then tore the sheet out. He folded it in quarters and put it in his pocket, then flipped the page back to Monday's calls.

He called Shorty's office, and the sheriff himself answered.

"I want to talk to you about the drug bust," he said.

"Go ahead, cousin." Shorty's voice was genial.

"Sheila Lowrey thinks we might have some problems," Loren said, "now that Archuleta and Medina and Robbie Cisneros have this guy

Axelrod." He gave a brief explanation of what Lowrey thought Axelrod might try to do.

"The thing is," he said, "we have to make certain that everyone in both our departments is clear on the series of events and how Robbie got his injuries."

"No problem, cousin," Shorty said.

"I mean," making himself as clear as possible, "you'll have to talk to your people."

"I already have, cousin," Shorty said. "I talked to my men the minute we delivered those guys to the jail."

Surprise performed a slow, ominous dance on Loren's heart.

"Thanks, Shorty," he said.

"No problem, ése."

Loren put the phone in its cradle. There was a sour taste in his mouth.

He wondered if he had been wrong. And if he had been wrong, how wrong had he been?

He looked up the medical investigator's number in the massive desk Rolodex and dialed the number. He eventually got one of the examiner's assistants, a man named Esquibel.

"London's working on another popsicle," Esquibel reported. "But I was present at the John Doe autopsy and I've got the tape here. Lemme play it through headphones, and I'll summarize it." Loren heard the sound of shuffling papers, the snap of a recorder button. "Okay, here we go. The body is that of a well-developed, well-nourished young adult Caucasian male, weight a hundred fifty pounds, seventy-three and one-half inches in height, age approximately twenty-two to twenty-eight. The body is received within a white body bag, with the closed end of the zipper covered by a 'State of New Mexico, Office of the Chief Medical Investigator' evidence label—"

"Skip that," said Loren.

Esquibel went on to describe John Doe's clothing, including the worn spots on the knees of his jeans, the little white circle on the back pocket consistent with a can of snuff—the Copenhagen can was described separately—and the metal collar tabs on the yoked shirt. There were no powder burns on the clothing, and Loren made a note of that. Esquibel continued with the state of rigor, postmortem lividity on the dorsal surfaces, length of scalp hair (5 cm. max), the width of pupils (0.35 cm.), the tobacco stains on the teeth, and the fact that Doe had been circumcised.

"Beneath the left arm," Esquibel said, "is a 1.2-centimeter circular defect, with five stellate tears radiating from the center point." *Circular defect* was M.I. talk for *bullet wound*. "These extension tears vary from 0.7 to a maximum of 2.1 centimeters in length. The tissues are extremely swollen, blue-purple and discolored . . ."

This went on for some time, as the M.I. opened the body with his standard Y-shaped incision, removed the organs, and weighed them. The liver weighed in at 1,700 grams, the spleen 130. "What happened," Esquibel said finally, "is that the guy got shot under the left arm, the missile tracking slightly downward"—*missile* was M.I.-speak for *bullet*—"and then the missile ricocheted off the fifth rib and was directed slightly upward. The missile bounced around inside, making some pretty crazy zigzags through the torso. Not uncommon, by the way. From the way the missile was flattened and its casing shattered, and from its erratic course, it's a decent guess the missile came through the door of the car first and was tumbling when it hit Mr. Doe. The missile punctured both lungs and nicked the descending aorta. What we think happened is that he was able to function for a while after he was shot, but that eventually the aorta eroded and burst. It filled his lungs in a minute or two and he drowned."

"The bullet?"

"We found it in his thorax. Caliber .41, but I'm just a damn ignorant pathologist, so you'll have to talk to criminalistics to make it official." Loren heard the sound of flipping pages. "No alcohol or drugs in system. No powder marks on hands or arms. Palms show calluses related to manual labor. Blood type: A positive. Body normal: no tattoos, no sign of previous wounds. Defensive bruises on both forearms, like he was trying to protect himself against somebody swinging a baseball bat."

"Or he got in a car crash and braced against the wheel with his arms."

"I was about to say that. No other bruises, no signs of restraint, bite marks, ligature marks. Skin abrasion on the first two knuckles of the left hand, possibly indicative of fistfight. Small scar on left forearm, scar on right shin, scar on ball of right thumb. All the scars were old. Smallpox vaccination scar on upper right arm, which would probably indicate he was left-handed. Silver fillings on the following teeth."

Loren jotted down the complicated dental jargon while trying to remember if Randal Dudenhof was left-handed.

"Nothing under the nails that you want to hear about. Mild gastritis at two locations in the stomach. That's from your coffee or alcohol use. Stomach contents: coffee, potato chips, ham and American cheese on white bread, eaten approximately one hour prior to death. Heart normal. Brain normal. Lungs demonstrated tobacco or marijuana use. Liver showed mild cirrhosis consistent with heavy alcohol or drug use. Vermiform appendix present. Precancerous condition on the interior lower lip consistent with dipping snuff. No recent sexual contact. No semen in rectum, which I'm sure you'll be happy to know."

"Thanks. I'm delighted."

"Got any idea who shot him?"

"Not really."

"Because what you've got is a hard-drinking, fist-fighting, snuff-dipping, ham-and-cheese-eating manual laborer who got shot in somebody else's car."

"I know," Loren said. All of this, he knew, added up to someone probably not a Republican, which would make the mayor even less interested in finding out who'd shot him.

"We've sent the finger, palm, and retina prints out on the LAWSAT. Nothing yet. Some tissue samples went upstairs to the histology lab. You can call criminalistics and see if they've done the work on the physical evidence."

"They won't have. But I'll call them."

"I'll send the paperwork by the next mail. Just so you can get it all in detail."

"Thanks."

Loren called the criminalistics division and found, as he'd suspected, that they hadn't got around to examining the victim's clothing yet. Maybe they'd get to it by the end of the week, he was told; they were stacked up.

"We did look at the bullets, though," Loren was told. The voice was female and a little fussy. "Forty-one caliber, and there was more than one gun."

"Say again?"

"One of the bullets you took out of the car was from a different gun. Two people were shooting at this guy, but only one hit him."

Loren, staring at the hallway in which the man died, let this information roll over him. His informant, knowing somehow that the information was important, gave him all the time he needed.

"What caliber?" Loren said finally.

"Both .41. Five lands and grooves, right-hand twist."

"Any idea what kind of gun that would be?"

"Lots. Any Smith & Wesson .41, for a start."

"Great." Another phone call began to flash and chime on the comm board. Loren frowned at the system and tried to remember what button to push.

"That's all I can tell you. If you find a gun or some brass, we can do a lot more."

"I know. Thanks."

"You're welcome." Primly. "We'll let you know when we do the other tests."

Loren pushed a button, the right one, and answered. The call was a missing-person query from Allentown, Pennsylvania. Loren informed the querent that his male Caucasian early-twenties John Doe was not a black female Jane Roe in her mid-teens. The querent—Roe's mother—sounded weary. Loren wished her luck and wondered how she had found out about the death so quickly.

Missing Children Hotline, he thought. On computer, accessible via modem.

As he logged the call he felt depression wash over him. He didn't know whether to be relieved the woman hadn't found her daughter dead or grieved that the anguish would continue, maybe for years. He thought of what he'd feel if one of his daughters vanished and was amazed at the woman's calm. He knew that if Kelly or Katrina went missing, he'd be mad with rage and grief, mad beyond all hope of sanity, until his daughter returned to him.

Another light blinked on the comm board. Loren answered.

"Chief Hawn, please."

Loren knew the voice.

"You're talking to him," he said.

"This is Bill Patience. Are you answering your own phones now? I knew there were budget cutbacks, but—"

Loren reluctantly offered the chuckle that the comment seemed to require. "The regular guy had an errand to run. I'm filling in."

"Good." Patience's voice had a heartiness that seemed false as the devil. Loren despised it. "I'm just calling to ask if you have any information on your dead man's identity."

"None that I can talk about."

"Oh."

"Sorry, Bill."

"It's just that—well, we're supposed to look into anything weird."

"In case the guy was a spy."

"More or less." Reluctantly. Why, Loren wondered impatiently, did the guy balk at revealing what was public knowledge? It was the spies themselves who were supposed to be discreet, not the cops that hunted them.

"I guess he's a dead spy now," Loren said. "Looks more like my department."

"I also have a complaint."

All lining up, Loren thought. Axelrod and Patience and Trujillo and Bonniwell and Jernigan . . .

"A complaint?" He could hear his own false ingenuousness, as phony as Patience's camaraderie, and for an instant loathed himself for it.

"Who from?" he said.

"Mr. and Mrs. Jernigan. Something about terrorizing them in their own home."

"She asked me to leave and I did."

"She says that your partner interrogated their son."

"Asked him a few friendly questions, maybe." Loren cleared his throat. "This is a murder investigation, Bill," he said. "What's wrong with asking people questions?"

"I'm just relaying a complaint that was made to me. I informed Mrs. Jernigan that my job was not to protect her from a legitimate police inquiry, and that if she wanted to take it any further, she could complain to your superiors."

Loren wondered if she would. It would sound great, wouldn't it, her complaint coming in at the same time as Bonniwell's and Axelrod's?

"Thank you for telling her that," Loren said.

"I don't really care for people using my office as a clearinghouse for domestic complaints." There was an edge in Patience's voice. Perhaps that was the first genuine thing he'd said all along.

"I had some questions for you," Loren said. He heard footsteps in the corridor and saw Eloy walking toward him.

"Whatever."

"Can I see your logs of who was checking in and out of your establishment on Friday and Saturday? It would serve to clear a lot of people."

"Sure. I can't let the original logs off the premises, but you can come and copy them if you like. Or I can have them photocopied and sent to you."

Loren was suddenly conscious of the folded bit of phone log, the evidence he'd stolen, awaiting disposal in his breast pocket. Eloy, the log's guardian, was hovering just behind him. "I'd like to look at them in person, if I can," he said. At least he'd be able to tell if something had been ripped out.

"Just call for an appointment."

"How about this afternoon?"

There was a slight pause. "Name a time."

"Three o'clock?"

"Fine. I'll leave word at the gate."

"Another question."

"Okay." Patience sounded a bit weary.

"What kind of weapons do your people use?"

Patience's answer was prompt. "Anyone here under suspicion, Loren?"

"What I'm trying to do is clear them more than anything else."

"That should be easy, then. Our standard sidearm is the Tanfoglio TZ-M. That's an Italian copy of a Czech military sidearm, the CZ75. Thought by some," pridefully, "to be the best in the world."

Loren jotted it down. "And the caliber?"

"Nine-millimeter."

"Okay. And *all* your people carry this gun?"

"I can't say what private weapons my people might have in their homes, but when on duty our people are required to carry the Tanfoglio. We want to have a common ammunition used by all weapons. It's the same with the UZIs in the jeeps."

Loren's pen froze on the paper. "You've got UZIs in the jeeps?" he said.

"Standard UZIs. Nine-millimeter, firing the same ammo as the pistols."

"This isn't exactly known, Bill." Loren could feel his voice rising. "There's been no reason for anyone to know it."

"Where are they carried? What if some kid broke into a jeep and—"

"It won't happen."

"How can you say that?" A picture rose in his mind, A.J. Dunlop, in his torn black T-shirt, lank blond hair hanging down from his backward-turned gimme cap, standing in the darkness of the high school parking lot with a submachine gun in his hand. Yanking the bolt back and smiling and taking aim at the windows of the school.

"I can't precisely reveal the details," Patience said, "but there's a security system in place to keep those guns from getting into the wrong hands."

"I'm not encouraged," Loren said.

"I'll show it to you," Patience said. "When you're over here this afternoon."

Loren said goodbye and hung up the phone. He looked up at Eloy. "How'd it go?" he said.

Eloy tugged at his foam collar. "*Man*, Chief. She asked me the same questions about fifty different ways. I feel like I've been through an interrogation. She should work for *us*, you know. Not for the D.A.'s office."

"She's sharp," Loren said.

"Am I gonna have to testify under oath and everything?"

There was a funny tone in Eloy's voice. Loren looked at him. "Could be. You got a problem with it?"

Eloy looked uneasy. "Guess not, Chief," he said.

Another chime came from the comm board. Eloy and Loren both looked at it. "Another missing offspring, Chief," Eloy said, and reached for the phone.

Loren rose, thinking of all the missing offspring in the world, wandering from one place to another, rootless, ID-less, in worn boots and faded Levi's, to be turned into victims by person or persons unknown.

Just like John Doe.

Loren walked into his office. He was going to solve this one, he thought. For all the parents of all the Johns and Janes who would never be found, who would cluster around computer terminals linked to the Missing Children Hotline and make hopeless phone calls to every little town where some pathetic corpse had got itself shot in someone else's car . . .

TEN

The maglev was three coaches long and a burnished silver. Growing clouds overhead did not dim its luster. The streamlined coach on either end was shaped like the semi-wadcutter rounds that had killed John Doe; the one in the middle, blunt-ended, was connected to the others by a ribbed plastic shield. The gray-on-red ATL symbol gleamed confidently on each coach, like the eyes old mariners used to paint on their ships.

Even at rest the train made a loud, grating, humming sound. As if impatient to take off.

Loren took off his shades and stepped off the worn wood platform into the front coach. The inside walls were cream-colored, the wide seats—shaped plastic—were orange. The high-backed seats, tall enough to include padded headrests, faced both ways. He looked left and right. There were no other passengers. And no engineer—the maglev was entirely computer-controlled.

He sat in the front seat and looked out the window at the old AT&SF station. It was a classic southwestern design, a two-story brown adobe with a graceful little false front on top that displayed the Santa Fe logo. Though the building was still used for administrative purposes, the Santa Fe trains didn't come into Atocha anymore, only served to connect the Atocha copper pit with El Paso. And now that the pit was closed, the trains would vanish altogether, taking up the iron rails behind them. The station might be boarded up and left to the weather and the vandals, like most of the old Santa Fe stops in the Southwest, while local people removed the ties for use in construction.

Loren wondered if ATL would buy or rent the old station then, just to keep their terminus from looking ratty. Replace the blue and white Santa Fe logo with their own gray-on-red sigil, a nineteenth-century monolithic symbol with its twenty-first-century equivalent.

The scenery darkened. The bright sun had been hidden by a cloud.

"The doors are closing," a female voice said. "Stand clear of the doors."

Loren looked behind him as the doors rumbled shut. The voice repeated the instructions in Spanish. "Thank you!" said the voice cheerily. "Muchas gracias!" It sounded as if the woman were right over his shoulder, and had perhaps received her training in human relations at Walt Disney World—it had a kind of forced cheerfulness that Loren had only heard in totally artificial environments where people had to work hard at being ingenuous. Beyond that slightly emphatic quality, her voice was natural and didn't seem computer-generated. Loren might have been more comfortable had it been otherwise.

"Please take your seat," the voice said. "Please remain in your seat for the entire trip. Do not attempt to move or stand during acceleration or deceleration. The ATL Maglev Express is designed to travel in excess of two hundred forty miles per hour, though this journey is so brief that speeds will not exceed two hundred. Thank you."

The message was repeated in Spanish. The humming noise increased. And quite suddenly the train was moving, slowly because it was still in town. And the humming noise dropped away entirely, creating an illusion that the train was already going faster than sound.

The future, Loren thought. This is what all the old science-fiction movies thought the World of Tomorrow was going to be like. Everything automated, everything perfect. Silent. Efficient. Clean.

He looked behind him again. It was eerie. There was absolutely no one else on the train.

Everything was so perfect, Loren thought, that human beings

could be left out completely. There wasn't even a brakeman—scanners on the tracks were supposed to signal the train whenever there was an obstruction ahead. Even instructions to the passengers were given by a computer voice, however human it sounded.

The future. Right.

He wondered if it was a sin to plan a future without people in it, and if so which one. Covetousness?

No, he thought. Pride.

The cinder-block and galvanized-steel buildings of Picketwire passed by on the right, separated from the tracks by a sturdy chain link fence topped with razor wire. Having left untidy humanity behind, the train picked up speed. Loren felt himself pressed back into his seat. Naked desert shot by, marked by flashes of cholla, yucca, creosote. The absence of sound was striking—only when the train was passing through a cut or beside an embankment was there the sound of wind, and then only a distant, forlorn cry.

Then the train was decelerating into the Vista Linda station. Gravity tugged at Loren's belly. The humming started again, and the doors rattled open.

"One-minute stop," said the computer voice.

No one got on during the interim.

The voice spoke its piece, the doors rattled shut, and the train began to accelerate, much faster this time. Gees pushed Loren back into his seat. Brown desert blurred by. The bridge over the Rio Seco was a flash of silver. Then Loren was on ATL land, part of the old Figueracion Ranch, and the train was decelerating.

"The train will return in half an hour," the voice said. "Thank you for following instructions and being a good passenger!"

Loren, rising from his seat, found himself wanting to determine the source of the cheerful voice and crush it under his heel.

The station was marked by a dark polycarbon arch thrice the height of a man. There were little precise diamond-shaped cuts in it, matching brass scrollwork on the concrete and pebble floor beneath. The arch was an elaborate sundial, helping to keep the nonexistent commuters adhering to their schedule.

A blustery wind had come up. Half the sky was shaded by cloud. There would be a thunderstorm before long, one of those spontaneous, violent rainfalls generated in the New Mexico sky, that filled arroyos and caught strangers by surprise. Parts of the state had road signs that read WATCH FOR WATER, amusing with only a desert as backdrop, amusing till you saw your first flash flood.

Still. Any water was welcome after the three-year drought.

Beyond the arch was a booth with a pair of guards, a man and a woman. The pair were seated and listening to a portable radio. Unlike the pairs who traveled in the jeeps, these wore neat khaki uniforms and baseball caps with the ATL logo. The holstered pistols, Loren saw, were Tanfoglios.

The woman rose from her chair and suppressed a yawn. "Yes, sir?" she said.

"Loren Hawn. I'm here to see your boss."

"Could you sign in?"

Loren did so. The layout of the book, he saw, was similar to the phone log that he still carried guiltily in his breast pocket. The woman handed him a red pass with VISITOR on it and a large number 11.

"Could you tell me where Mr. Patience has his office?"

"If you'll wait a moment, we'll call and get you an escort."

Loren sighed. First the Disney World cheerfulness of the computer voice on the train, now this institutional uniformed paranoia. What did they think he was going to do, plant a bomb somewhere?

"Not necessary," he said. "Just tell me the way."

"If you'll just wait . . . ."

Loren pointed a finger randomly at one of the buildings. "*That* building, I think he said." And took off.

"Ah. Sir. *Sir!*"

Loren increased his pace and put on his shades. Right in front of him was a wide, blacktopped avenue with a green landscaped lane divider. At its terminus, right in front of the arch, was a tall modernistic piece of sculpture, long jigsaw forms of dark polycarbon and bright aluminum twisting up into the sky. Loren had seen pictures of it and knew it had some vaguely scientific name—was it *Hidden Symmetries?* Something like that, anyway.

Brown buildings flanked the avenue. Some were obviously administrative, three-storied, windowed, flat-roofed structures of cinder block, stuccoed in imitation of New Mexico adobe. Others were blank-walled, with large, heavy steel doors at either end and barrel-vaulted roofs vaguely reminiscent of Quonset huts. One of them, for some reason, had the word FIDO printed on it in huge blue letters. Presumably these contained heavy apparatus. Other buildings were low, built into the ground like bunkers, with heavy flat roofs covered with solar cells. Loren wasn't even going to guess at what might be inside these last.

Each building was painted the same desert-brown and had a large blue number twice as tall as a man. They weren't taking any chances on people getting lost.

"Sir! Sir!"

The woman caught up with him. A long blond braid, hanging down her back, swung madly left and right as she bounced up next to him. "I'll just go with you, shall I?" Her voice had a condescending, false heartiness as distasteful as that on the maglev.

"Suit yourself," said Loren. He walked past the sculpture. The wind made a hollow whistling sound as it gusted through the metal structure.

"Interesting sound, huh?" the guard said. She had to adopt a kind of skipping step to keep pace with his long strides. "Do you like our *Discovered Symmetries?*"

Loren glanced up at the structure. He'd got the name almost right. "It's okay. I don't know much about art."

"I like the noises it makes, different depending on where the wind is coming from. We want to turn left here."

They turned between a pair of Quonset-like buildings and headed down a bare concrete walk lined by naked brown soil on either side. A gust of wind funneled between the buildings and spat desert grit into Loren's eyes in spite of his shades. He blinked and put a hand in front of his face. A spatter of rain impacted the back of his hand. Other large drops exploded on the concrete nearby.

The gust fell away. Loren lowered his hand and saw William Patience appear from out of a wind-whipped cloud of dust and gravel, walking hastily with his head down and his hands in his pockets. Patience looked up as rain began falling like a barrage.

"Loren!" he shouted. "I'm not surprised you didn't want to wait! This way!"

He turned and began sprinting down the walk. Loren grabbed his pistol holster to keep it from bouncing and followed at a slow run, water spattering the lenses of his dark glasses. His escort, braid swinging, turned to run back to her station.

Loren sprinted past a large asphalt parking lot, part of which was fenced off with chain link and filled with brown Blazers, then into a large steel-walled building sitting beside it. Loren noticed a security camera set over the door. Patience was waiting for him, breathing hard and brushing water off his gray jacket. He pulled the elastic band off his ponytail and shook out his long, wet hair. With the hair hanging to his collarbones and his carefully cut uniformlike clothes, he seemed a unique combination of respectability and menace, like some retired, well-heeled drug dealer sunning away his days in Cancún.

"I've got the logs for you," he said. "For Friday and Saturday both."

"Thanks."

"They're on computer."

"I'd like to see the originals."

"It's the originals that are on computer. I'll show you."

Loren was in an anteroom that featured white ceiling tile, desert-tan steel walls, and a gunmetal desk with a dozen television monitors presumably keeping track of various sensitive parts of the complex. There was no one watching the monitors. Heavy steel doors, painted government green, pierced three walls. On the walls hung a number of posters concerning security: COMPUTER SECURITY IS YOUR RESPONSIBILITY; and YOU NEVER KNOW WHO'S LISTENING, with a picture of a couple of people, one in military uniform, gabbing on the phone with a sinister character grinning evilly as he listened on a line tap.

Rain drummed on the metal roof. Patience had a credit card-sized holocard in his hand: he sliced it through a wall-mounted holo reader next to one of the doors. There was the sound of a buzz lock; Patience yanked open the door and held it for Loren to pass through. Walking past the man, Loren had the intuition that Patience was running him through some obscure test and intently observing the results. Loren's performance so far, he suspected, had been disappointing.

The corridor beyond was empty, fluorescent-lit; there was a corkboard on one wall with notices pinned heedlessly to it, fluttering in the air-conditioning, and a camera at the far end. Patience resumed the lead.

"Did you say the original logbooks are on computer?" Loren asked. "At the station I just signed a real book."

"It *is* the originals that are on computer," Patience said. "There's a scanner at each security station—we read the information and signature into our data banks as soon as it's on paper. Then the computer compares the signatures to the ones in each employee's files." Patience turned into a brightly lit room. "You want some coffee? I could use some."

The room was a small cafeteria with half a dozen tables and bench seats. Vending machines and a couple of video games, one with a pistol attached to the machine with a cord, sat next to the wall. The video games made combat noises that were largely overwhelmed by the drum song of rain on the roof. On the walls were posters advertising elite military units, each featuring a soldier with his weapon in a combat-ready stance. Special Forces, Loren recognized, Marine Force Recon, SAS in black balaclavas that concealed everything but their eyes, somebody in an obvious Russian uniform, carrying one of the new Soviet bullpup assault rifles and identified by Cyrillic lettering, red stars, and multiple exclamation points.

Patience stood by a coffeemaker, pouring into a thick insulated cup with his name on it alongside a scowling picture of a Green Beret. The Green Beret was wearing camouflage face paint.

"It's good coffee, by the way," Patience said. "We filter our water."

"In that case," Loren said, "I'll have some."

"Cream? Sugar?"

"Black." Loren looked at the vending machines. One was for soda, one for snacks—peanuts, chips, crackers—and a third for plastic-wrapped sandwiches. Loren looked closer at the last one.

Coffee, potato chips, ham and American cheese on white bread. John Doe's stomach contents.

An electric current crackled in Loren's nerves. He crouched to look at the labels on the doors of the sandwich machine. Egg salad, tuna salad, ham and cheese. There it was.

"Want something to eat?" Patience asked.

"No. Thanks." Loren realized he was still staring at the

cellophane-wrapped sandwich, and he straightened. There was a crackle from the stolen log sheet in his breast pocket and he gave a start at a sudden, guilty memory of his theft.

Patience, he observed, was watching him intently.

"I'd like to see the original logs," Loren said.

Patience cocked his head slightly, then cast a look up at the roof. "Let's wait till the rain dies down a bit," he said, "and I'll run out and get them. In the meantime I'll show you how the computer works."

He handed Loren his coffee and gestured for Loren to follow him. They went down the corridor again, past closed steel doors with cardboard tags inserted in metal slots in the center of the door. Loren read people's names on individual office doors, then ARMORY, all in caps, and DETENTION. He paused by the last one.

"You keep prisoners in here?" he asked.

Patience gave a dry little laugh. "It's never been used. It's intended mostly as a drunk tank. If one of our employees gets loaded and has to be held until he sobers up."

Loren looked at the heavy buzz lock. "You don't have powers of arrest," he said.

"When someone works here, they sign a waiver giving up certain rights," said Patience. "We can hold them for up to twelve hours."

Loren scratched his jaw and looked at the door. "I don't think that's legal. Waivers get broken in court all the time. A person can't give up his right to due process just by signing his name."

An unreadable expression flickered across Patience's face. "Let's just call it a gray area in the law, okay?" His voice was flat, brooking no further argument. Loren decided the point wasn't worth contesting. If Patience wanted to court a lawsuit from the ACLU, that was fine with Loren.

Patience led him past the office of his secretary—a trim middle-aged woman whose bearing seemed as military as that of her boss. She had decorated her room with large travel posters. Patience opened another buzz lock with his card, then led Loren into his office. "You can use my terminal," Patience said. "I've got it set up for you."

"Thanks."

"Sit down here." Indicating the dark fine-grained leather of his padded chair.

There was a Turkish carpet on the floor. The lighting was from floor lamps, not overhead fluorescents, and the lamps had intricately designed brass-framed lampshades in the same style as the carpet. There was an elaborate brass coatrack and two bookshelves crammed full of books. The desk was a wide, modern hardwood rolltop, designed to hold a computer terminal. In one corner stood an American flag, the pole capped with a gold-plated eagle; in another corner was a flag Loren didn't recognize. There were a pair of filing cabinets in military matte black, and on the wall were framed certificates and a plaque with the Special Forces shield and the motto DE OPPRESSO LIBER. There was another plaque featuring a black stylized helicopter on a blue background, with a bloodred lightning bolt, all in murky colors that made the design hard to make out. UNIT 77-112, it said. ABRACADABRA.

There was a picture on the wall of a young, round-cheeked Patience with short hair, a mustache, and a green beret, and a second photo of a ten-man Special Forces team. In both photos the young man's expression was intense, unsmiling, and uncompromised— essentially unchanged from the older Patience who used the office. There was another photo on another wall, a picture of a hawk-nosed, eagle-eyed man in a gray uniform.

"Who's he?" Loren asked.

"Mushegh Abovian. Armenian freedom fighter."

Loren looked at the flag he hadn't recognized. "And the flag? It's Armenian, too?"

Patience tapped keys on his computer. "We had a big interest in the Armenian revolt when I was in Special Forces."

"Huh. Which side were we on?"

Patience glanced up, gave another quick, humorless smile. "I can't say. Everything's still classified. You know how to use a mouse?"

"Yeah." Loren sat down at the computer and put his coffee cup on the desk. There was a picture of Timothy Jernigan on the screen, staring at Loren through his thick lenses. Patience hovered over Loren's right shoulder, pointing at icons on the screen. Loren detected the faint scent of gun oil from the pistol under Patience's arm.

"I've called up the file on people going in and out the last few days," he said. "Here's Dr. Jernigan's name, ID number, job assignment, signature, and comparison signature from computer memory. We use a hypertext system that can call up additional information—here." He leaned forward and punched the button on the mouse. The flickering image on the screen changed, began to scroll down an image of a standardized form. "Here's Jernigan's employment file and personal history. You won't be able to get at anything that's classified, but with this system you have access to everything else."

"How about Sondra Jernigan?" Loren asked. "I've been wondering if our John Doe knew her rather than her husband."

"Just use the hypertext. Here." He pressed the button again; the screen altered again. Sondra Jernigan's picture appeared. She was smiling prettily, with faintly flushed cheeks—not Loren's view of the woman at all. "Here's our file on the wife. We don't have much. If you want hard copy of anything, just tell the system to make one for you. Or if you want to copy something onto disk to read later, you can do that." He gave Loren a disk.

"Thanks." A cold suspicion filled Loren. Patience was making this all too easy, giving him vast amounts of data. It would take weeks to check everyone's story, and in the end it would probably amount to nothing.

Patience straightened. "I don't envy you," he said. "We had thirty-odd extra Ph.D.'s on base during that accelerator run. Some flew in from California, Massachusetts, and Illinois."

On base, Loren thought. An interesting slip. Patience went on:

"After seeing this, you still want the original logs?"

Loren looked at him. "Sorry, Bill. But yes."

Patience looked at him for a long, intense moment. Jesus, Loren thought, doesn't the guy ever lighten up? "Okay," Patience said finally, and opened a drawer on a cabinet to pull out a plastic bundle wrapped with a large rubber band. He pulled off the band, then shook out the bundle. A hooded plastic poncho in desert camouflage.

"I'll be back in a little while," he said. "Annette can look after you in the meantime."

"Thanks," Loren said.

Patience didn't answer, just breezed out through the heavy door. Loren pondered for a moment how awful it would be to have William Patience as a boss, then rose from his seat. He stepped over to the bookshelf beneath the window, then scanned the titles. *Shooter's*

Bible. Improvised Munitions Black Book—three volumes. *Escape and Evasion Manual. Guerrilla Warfare and Special Forces Operations (FM 31-21).* Loren's eyes dropped a few shelves. *History of Modern Turkey. The Armenian Struggle for Statehood. Disintegration of the Soviet Empire. History of the Transcaucasian Republics 1918-1921. The Glory and Resurrection of the Armenian Apostolic Church.* Armenian, Russian, and Turkish dictionaries and phrase books.

Nothing here. He looked out the window and caught a glimpse of Patience dashing across the parking lot in his hooded poncho, his polished wing tips leaving brief footmarks on the wet asphalt before being obliterated by the downpour. He thought about looking through the man's desk, but knew there'd be no point to it. If there were anything to find, Patience wouldn't have let him in here, let alone let him stay here by himself.

He was just here to be impressed by Patience's computer system and Patience's personality.

Assholes, he thought, always advertise.

Loren circled the room, the soft Turkish rug cushioning his steps. UNIT 77-112, he read as he looked at the plaque. For someone who had participated in an undeclared, top-secret Special Forces action as part of a unit that didn't even have a name, William Patience sure did everything he could to let everyone know about it. It enhanced the mystique, no doubt.

ABRACADABRA.

The certificates on the wall were from an M.A. in psychology from Boston University and a number of graduation certificates from survival courses. One of them graduated him from the "Advanced Course" on "Interrogation Resistance and Escape Techniques."

Great. The guy had himself tortured on his vacations just to see what he was made of.

Loren looked at the other bookshelf. *Managing Stress. Breath Control for Yoga Mastery. Fifteen Deadliest Strikes. Sharpening Your Mind for Effective Action. Relax! Survival in a Desert Environment. Manual of Sudden Death* (three volumes). *Secrets of Concentration. How to Beat Ulcers.*

Ulcers, Loren thought, no shit. The guy was so tightly wrapped it was a miracle he hadn't detonated by now.

He returned to the computer and began putting data on disk, his eyes scanning the screen and his fingers working the mouse while his thoughts drifted elsewhere.

Detention. Ham and cheese sandwiches. Coffee.

Right. Suppose that at some point Friday or Saturday Patience or his men put someone in the detention room. Suppose they fed him dinner, and when a guard arrived to take away the tray, the prisoner clocked him, scraping a couple knuckles in the process. Suppose the prisoner ran out into the parking lot, yanked Jernigan out of his car, and drove off. Suppose he got shot making his escape.

No, Loren thought, because it doesn't make any *sense*. ATL had a perfect *right* to shoot at someone in those circumstances. If that's what happened, why hide it?

The drumming on the roof diminished, then ceased. There were footsteps in the outer office, then the sound of the buzz lock. Patience came in carrying a pair of ledger-sized books. He'd left the wet poncho outside.

"Here you go. I've marked Friday for you."

Loren looked up. "Thanks."

Patience looked over Loren's shoulder. "Getting anywhere?"

"Vastly increasing my paperwork."

"My sympathies. But you did volunteer." Patience walked to the center of the office, then bent and took off his shoes. He took off his coat and shoulder holster, then put them both on the coatrack. "Unless you have some questions," Patience said, "I'm going to do some stretching."

"Fine."

Patience lowered himself to the carpet. The desk blocked Loren's view of most of what he was doing, but whatever it was seemed to require a lot of grunting, as if someone was hitting Patience repeatedly in the breadbasket. Breath control, Loren thought, for torture subjects. Maybe Patience could write a book about it.

He finished loading his disk and removed it from the drive, then turned to the two logbooks Patience had brought, one from the vehicle entry, the other from the maglev station. He opened the first to the spot Patience had indicated with a white slip of paper, saw scribbles of signatures in blue or black ballpoint, the confusion of names, addresses, and ID numbers. He paged through, looking carefully, guiltily, at the binding to make certain nothing had been torn away. Apparently nothing had. He looked at the other logbook and found much the same. He hefted them both and peered over the desk at Patience.

"Is there a place where I can Xerox these?" he asked.

Patience was lying on his back with his knees bent and feet under his butt, a position Loren recognized from his high school football days as one that could tear out every knee tendon if you weren't limber enough. His long hair was spread out on the carpet like that of a swooning Victorian maiden. There was a light dotting of sweat on his forehead.

"Just ask Annette," he said.

Loren rose and went into the secretary's office. Patience's poncho dripped rainwater in one corner. The secretary—Annette, he presumed—pointed out the Xerox, a beige box sitting beneath a swirling color photograph of masked Chinese dancers. Loren declined her offer of assistance and made copies, then returned to Patience's office.

Patience was on his feet, tying his hair back. He was breathing hard, dabbing sweat with a handkerchief.

"I guess I've got what I came for," Loren said.

Patience looked out the window. Sunlight gleamed off puddles on the asphalt. "Would you like a look at the proton accelerator?"

"Very much."

"We'll take my jeep. You wanted me to show you how the SMGs are stored, anyway, right?"

Loren had forgotten. "Sure," he said. "Thanks."

They left by a back door that opened by a push bar, like a door in a theater. It led directly into the parking lot. Loren considered how easy it would be for a fugitive to slip through the door without anyone necessarily seeing him.

The sun blazed on the parking lot, reflected on spilled oil and puddles. A dark shroud of water obscured the mesa east of them, but here the thunderstorm was over. It wasn't enough, Loren thought, to alleviate the drought conditions. The lightning would just start more forest fires.

Patience led him to a gate on the fenced-off chain link parking lot, then opened the gate with his holocard. The fleet of Blazers, together with the weaponry in them, was fenced off from anyone not possessing a card. Like, Loren thought, escaping prisoners.

Patience led Loren to one of the jeeps, opened the door with a key, and got in. Loren got in the passenger seat.

"We keep the UZIs in here," Patience said. His knuckles rapped a featureless black aluminum box set between the front seats, just abaft the emergency brake. He pulled on the front box lid and the box folded back on hinges. Beneath lay two submachine guns with their pistol grips up, a position that allowed them to be seized easily in an emergency. Each had a magazine inserted in the pistol butt, and additional magazines were clipped underneath. Both weapons were locked down with a heavy metal bar that crossed just forward of the trigger guard. A ten-key pad, white plastic keys beneath a red LED, sat atop the bar.

"That bar is heavy alloy," Patience said. "Hacksaw-proof. You'd need to work at it with a torch for ten minutes. In order to open the lock you have to know the right three-digit combination." He reached for the pad, his index finger pointing.

"Let me," said Loren.

The hand hesitated. "Okay," Patience said.

Loren reached down and punched 571. The red LED went off and a green one winked on. Loren yanked up on the pad, pulling the bar away, then took one of the UZIs by its grip and pointed it at Patience.

"Bang," he said, "you're dead."

Patience stared at him, eyes wide. Loren smiled.

Patience's hatchetlike face froze in an expression of vast, cold anger. "Who told you?" he said. His voice had a tremor in it, a stammer on the *t*—he'd been *scared*, Loren thought, when the muzzle came in line. And Loren didn't blame him.

Loren returned the weapon to its cradle. "No one," he said.

"I'll fire the son of a bitch."

"Look at the keypad," Loren said.

Patience's eyes dropped reluctantly to the locking device. Loren slammed the bar down on the SMGs. The red LED winked on, the green off.

"Three of the keys are dirty," Loren said. "It had to be that combination or one of a couple others."

Loren heard the breath going out of Patience, a soft hiss. Then a humorless laugh.

"You've taught us a lesson, Loren. From now on everyone gets a bottle of Windex to keep the keys clean. Thank you."

"You can thank me more by keeping these guns out of my town."

Patience gave him a quick glance, then an almost imperceptible shake of the head.

"You're gonna have some of these stolen sooner or later. I don't care how good your security system is. The thief'll probably be some snot-nose kid who'll use them to shoot up the high school or some other kid's car, but I don't even want a minor-league bad-ass in my town with that kind of firepower."

"I can't remove the guns," Patience said. "It's not consonant with my mission."

Loren squared himself in the seat and looked out a windshield spattered with connect-the-dots raindrops. Futile anger buzzed in his brain like a wasp battering its brains out against a car window. "We'll see," he said.

Patience looked at him for a moment, then replaced the metal box over the machine pistols. He started the Blazer, backed out of his parking place, hit the button that would open the fence. The route took him back to the main drive, past *Discovered Symmetries* again, then down the boulevard past an administrative building and a pair of the barrel-roofed structures, including the one labeled FIDO.

"Black labs," Patience said. "Where they do the classified work."

One of the bunkerlike structures was labeled PRINCE. Another was SHEP.

"Black labs," Loren said. "I get it."

Patience gave him a puzzled look. "Get what?"

"Black labs."

"Yes. They're black laboratories. What about it?"

"Black labs? As in Labrador dogs? SHEP? FIDO? Physicist humor. Get it?"

Comprehension dawned in Patience's eyes. He gave a polite and completely humorless laugh. "I see it now. A pun. I see."

Loren watched beaded raindrops bleeding across the windshield. What kind of person was this? he wondered. He must pass by those buildings every damn day.

He probably just assumed it wasn't his job to figure it out.

"I don't know exactly what they do in there." Patience sounded aggrieved.

"You don't need to know, do you?"

"I guess not. But if I hear someone with black-lab access talking shop to someone in a bar, I don't have any idea whether he's blabbing classified information or not."

"Depends on who he's blabbing it to, I suppose," Loren said. "If it's someone in a baggy suit with a Russian accent, I suppose you've got a problem."

That humorless laugh came again. "Bloc spies haven't worn those baggy suits in forty years. You know it was Kim Philby who taught them how to dress? And most of the scientist types are so happy to talk science, they'll talk it with anyone. And though they don't necessarily disregard security classifications, they'll just talk around the classified stuff and leave it to their audience to infer what they're leaving out."

Not Jernigan, Loren thought. The guy just sweated and stuck to his story. And it looked like Dielh wasn't going to talk at all.

The Blazer reached the end of the boulevard, then turned left. At the end of a quarter mile of blacktop was a low flat-roofed building, poured concrete painted brown, that looked like an Indian pueblo built by monomaniac German perfectionists. Beyond the building the high desert with its surreal towers of interweaving ocotillo spines and waving tufts of yucca.

"Why's this one by itself?" Loren asked.

"The black labs and administrative buildings are clumped together for security reasons. This one's closer to the boonies because that's where the accelerators are. And the TOKAMAK and the high-explosive site are *way* the hell out by themselves."

"High-explosive site?"

Patience parked in front of a wooden blue-on-turquoise sign that said LINAC. "Yes." Yanking back the emergency brake. "Down at the MCG—magneto-cumulative generator. You create a magnetic field in a specially shaped chamber, then compress it with an explosion. Channel the force onto a target. It's something the Russians got a head start on." His fingers did a little dance in the air, tracing an explosion. "Boom. Target vaporized."

"Great." Without enthusiasm.

Loren followed Patience toward a pair of twelve-foot-tall steel doors set into an alcove in the front of the building. Patience didn't need his holocard to open the lock; he just pulled back on the unlocked beige steel door and stepped inside. Loren was surprised.

"No security out here?" he asked.

"Nothing classified goes on in this building. So all they do is lock it at night if there's no one around."

"Huh."

"But someone's almost always here. These guys keep all kinds of hours—you'll see that when you get a chance to study the logs. People check in at two in the morning and pull eighteen-hour shifts."

The interior walls were nonprettified concrete with the impressions of the wooden forms still on them, all painted a sickly government green. Corkboards hung on them, and the boards were full of notices, put on four or five deep. Some announced conferences on one obscure subject or another. Many were headed A CALL FOR PAPERS. Some appeared to be the papers themselves. Loren squinted at one of them. *Insights into the Nature of Classical and Quantum Gravity via Null-Strut Calculus*. Loren gave up on that one and looked at the next. *Multi-Megampere Plasma Flow Switch-Driven Liner Implosions*.

No help.

The first few rooms they passed were empty offices with whiteboards, corkboards, and steel desks with computer terminals. In the intervals between these and pastel-green steel bookshelves were more travel posters. Loren wondered if ATL bought the posters wholesale. He was beginning to feel oppressed by the constant overhead fluorescent light in all these installations.

"In here," Patience said. He opened another of the doors, one with CONTROL ROOM stenciled on it. Below the stencil was a bright fluorescent green-on-orange bumper sticker with the by-now-familiar message about Heisenberg and where he may or may not have slept.

"Good Lord," Loren said. He had stepped into what looked like a Pentagon situation room, at least half the length of a football field, all subdued lighting, dark consoles, unwinking high-resolution monitors. All that was needed was a giant map of Russia overhead.

Loren was standing on the second level, on a kind of balcony running around the entire room. Ventilators made a continual, hushed white-noise sound. Thirty-inch television monitors, lining the walls, gazed at him with bright, unblinking eyes. Brushed-aluminum railings set into polycarbon supports kept any hypnotized bystanders from toppling into the lower level. The area below was lined on all sides by matte-black control banks and more monitors, most of which showed only a test pattern, a computer-generated version of the ATL logo that went through constant, slow changes in color to prevent phosphor burn. Half the monitors were holotanks on which the logo rotated slowly, in three dimensions. There was another bank of monitors in the center of the room, each side sloping toward the center, permitting two sets of technicians to face one another during operation.

It's the goddamn starship *Enterprise*, Loren thought.

Intent on one central-bank monitor were two young men, both muttering intently as they leaned forward from contoured leatherette chairs to stare deeply into a holographic image. Plush carpet absorbed Loren's footsteps as he followed Patience down a cantilevered stairway and out onto the floor.

"You're losing it!" one of the men said. He was Asian, dressed in a T-shirt and jeans. "You're gonna crash and burn."

"Motherfucker!" A flash lit the other man's face from below. He was a burly man, with corded muscles and a thick neck, obviously a weight lifter.

"Commit!" the first man urged. "Commit!"

"I don't have my ears on!" Frantically tapping keys.

"You don't have a choice!"

"Shit! Shitshitshit!" Another flash highlighted his profile. Both men slowly relaxed, reluctantly leaning back in their padded chairs. Both appeared to have suffered an inconsolable loss.

"Sixteen thousand," the first said. "That's not bad."

"I've done better."

"If I can interrupt," said Patience. Both men glanced up.

"Hi." The first man, the weight lifter, rose from his seat. He wore Levi's, brown work boots, and a flannel shirt with the sleeves rolled up to show off the curve of his biceps. He had a turned-down brown mustache and wore dark-rimmed spectacles—he looked like a well-off rancher on his way to town.

"I was looking for someone to give Chief Hawn a tour," Patience said.

The man looked at his friend and grinned with a silver front tooth. "I guess we can spare the time." He stepped forward and offered a hand to Loren. "I'm Kelly Steffens."

"Loren Hawn."

"Yoshi Kurita."

Loren shook hands with them both. Kurita had a thin, enthusiastic face and spectacles held together with tape over the bridge of the nose. His T-shirt had a holo picture of the *Galileo* explorer firing an instrument package into one of Jupiter's moons. It looked as if there were a square, black hole in his chest, with planets and the probe floating eerily inside.

"Nice shirt," Loren said.

"New process." Grinning. "You'll see it on every street corner in six weeks."

"I bet."

"I've got some phone calls to make," Patience said. "I'll be back in a few minutes. Don't worry, I'm just going upstairs."

I won't worry, Loren thought, but didn't say it.

Patience went back up the stairs two at a time. Loren felt as if he were swimming deeper into quicksand. He knew now he wouldn't find out anything important. The tour was like the computer files—if there was anything important to discover, Patience wouldn't have left him alone with it.

Loren put his Xeroxes down on the smooth cool surface of the control bank. At a loss for what to do next, Loren looked into the holotank and saw, in gleaming chrome-steel letters on a background of depthless blue sky and scudding cloud, the words HOLO CYBERCOPS III. A computer game.

"So," he said, "this is what the taxpayers' money is going for."

Steffens grinned. Holo images glowed in his silver front tooth. "I'm being paid by one of the contractors, not the government."

"That's *okay*, then."

"Actually, I'm just a techie, not a Ph.D. They pay me to fix things, but they didn't manage to break much today."

"We completed our checklist," said Kurita. His tone was defensive.

"Was there anything in particular that you wanted to see?" Steffens asked.

"I don't suppose you were here on Friday."

Another grin. "*Everyone* was here on Friday."

Rolling through Loren came the realization that Steffens had a cleft palate. That's why he had a missing tooth. And the mustache covered the scar on the upper lip.

"Dr. Jernigan?" Loren asked. "Dr. Dielh?"

"*Especially* them. They were running the show."

"Amardas Singh?"

"Sure. He's someone you can't miss."

"And," looking back over his shoulder at the softly closing door, "Mr. Patience?"

Steffens gave a puzzled little scowl, then looked at his partner, who shrugged. "I didn't see him."

"Hey," said Kurita. "Show him the Big Bang."

"Good idea. You want to see the creation of the universe? We've got a recording, and it's pretty good."

Loren looked from one to the other and tried to make up his mind whether they were playing some kind of joke.

If they were, he thought darkly, woe unto them.

But they were both bending over the console, tapping with rapid-fire enthusiasm on the keyboard.

"There," Kurita said. "We're out of the games file."

"Use Version D. That's the most complete." Steffens looked up at Loren. "It's got great special effects."

"Look up there," said Kurita, pointing.

Something had come into existence atop the long console, a cube-shaped shift in the light, a quality of emptiness, marked by brief specks of light, somehow different from the emptiness that had been there before. Like Kurita's T-shirt, it seemed a window into something else, an emptiness that was somehow projected from another place, perhaps another world . . .

"Another new process," Kurita said.

"Holography without tanks," Loren said. "I saw it on the news."

"Right."

"Fire one," said Steffens. Kurita hit the Enter button.

There was a dazzling flash of white light in the empty cube. Bits of brightness seemed to scatter, tumbling, some of them doing weird loops like uncoiling springs. Loren blinked. Steffens gave a playful open-handed slap to the back of his friend's head.

"Idiot. Use slow motion."

"That *was* slow motion." Rubbing his head resentfully.

"Another order of magnitude."

"Just a sec." Tapping keys.

"Make that *two* orders of magnitude. Slow it right down."

Steffens glanced from Loren to the holographic cubes and back again. "With the room-temperature superconductors, our linear accelerators can get higher energies than the Supercollider, and without any damn silly ninety-mile circle, either. And the whole thing happens at far less expense in electricity—the Supercollider takes enough power for a major city, and it's used mainly to run the compressors and pumps for the old-fashioned superconductors, and we don't use those."

"So what are you doing now?" Loren said. He felt he'd been lost the second he walked into the room. "You're using the accelerators?"

"No." Loren saw that silver-winking grin again. "It takes a lot of coordinated effort to run the accelerators—this room would be full of people. We're just rerunning the highlights of Friday's party."

"Oh. It's recorded. I see." A trickle of interest lifted Loren's spirits. Maybe he'd see something, after all. He frowned at the empty holo cube. "What was that you said about the beginning of the universe?"

"Oh, yeah. See, if you cook matter hot enough, you can duplicate the conditions just after the Big Bang, when the universe consisted of very energetic particles combining, coming apart, and recombining under conditions of extreme heat and pressure."

"The Bang plus maybe a zillionth of a second," said Kurita.

Loren looked at him. "Say again?"

"We can't duplicate the exact conditions of the Big Bang. We don't have enough energy. But we can get within a fraction of a second."

"A zillionth?" Loren said. He gave a laugh. "That's a scientific term?"

"Well." Steffen's eyes turned vacant for a moment. He seemed to be mentally rewinding his conversation, recalculating, starting over.

"Ten to the minus thirty-fifth second, which is a ten with a decimal point and thirty-five zeroes in front of it."

"A one with a decimal point and thirty-*four* zeroes," said Kurita. "Let's not make it more difficult than—"

Steffens slapped him on the back of the head again. Loren could hear Kurita's teeth clack together. "A damn short time, anyway," Steffens said. "The theory is that the further back you go toward the beginnings of time, the more simple and symmetric nature becomes. The electromagnetic force and the strong force haven't split off, though gravity has, so you get all kinds of particles and conditions that don't normally exist in our relatively cool universe. You've seen *Discovered Symmetries* out on the Fairgrounds?"

Loren nodded. "Fairgrounds?"

"What we call the main area. There's this famous statue called *Broken Symmetries* at Fermilabs in Illinois, which is supposed to represent the way nature became less symmetric and more, ah, fractured after the first few seconds of existence. Instead of having one unified force controlling things, you have electromagnetic force and gravity and the strong and weak nuclear forces. And assuming that you give any credence to Kaluza-Klein theories, you get eleven dimensions falling into four, because there isn't enough energy to sustain the others."

"I don't understand any of this," Loren said.

"At ATL we're supposed to be able to crank up the LINAC to the point where the symmetries start becoming visible again. So we've got a more optimistic sculpture." He bent toward Kurita, who was still working at the keyboard. "Thank you," he said, "for not interrupting."

Loren watched this well-honed routine with a familiar amusement. Put a couple gimme hats on them and drinks in their hands, they could hold their own in the rustic comedy contest with Bob Sandoval and Mark Byrne down at the Sunshine.

"You're making it too complicated," Kurita said. "Kaluza-Klein theories are unnecessary to your point. And otherwise you're too vague."

"Hard to be both complicated and vague at once, huh? I must be a genius."

"If you were a genius," smiling maliciously, "you'd have finished your thesis three or four years ago."

"You can't finish a thesis when everything that happens at work changes my fundamental understanding of the things I'm writing the thesis *about*."

Kurita looked up at Loren. "He has lots of excuses."

Enough of this comedy, Loren thought.

"How do you—" Loren searched for a way of phrasing his question. "How do you *do* all of this, exactly? Cook your particles, or whatever it's called."

"Okay. We've got two linear accelerators, and they're aimed at one another. We fire protons out of one and antiprotons out of another, and the two meet and annihilate one another. It's like—" He peered at Loren. "Do you ever go duck hunting?"

"I'm going later this week."

"Me, too. Now suppose we went duck hunting together. Suppose we put the muzzles of our shotguns together and pulled the triggers at the same instant."

"Suppose we don't," said Loren.

Steffens went on as if he hadn't heard. "There'd be an explosion as all the bird shot and the chemical and heat energy collided. That's what we do with the LINACs. We slam bird shot—protons and antiprotons—into each other and take pictures of the explosion. And annihilations produce a lot of energy and heat and elementary particles and further annihilations and energy and so on, until you get to ten to the twenty-ninth degrees Kelvin, which is nearing the heat of the Big Bang that created the universe . . ."

"Okay. I see your point."

"And the profusion of particles that constitute matter are simplified to a few, and perhaps we get glimpses of the higher seven dimensions as predicted by Kaluza ninety years ago or whenever . . ."

Kurita looked up again. "Leave Kaluza-Klein out of it, okay? You don't *need* it in this explanation."

Steffens raised a hand as if to slap the back of Kurita's head again, then thought better of it and dropped his hand. "It's my thesis topic, okay?" He turned to Loren and gave an apologetic look. "It's something I've been waiting to find confirmation for. But there's no evidence so far. Everything keeps falling into what Tim calls this energy sump."

"Tim Jernigan?"

"Yes. The energies keep falling away. No one knows what's happening."

Kurita looked up again. "The energy doesn't fall away all the time. It's intermittent. That's why everyone's so perplexed. Why my *colleague* is annoyed"—that malicious smile appeared again—"is that on those occasions when the experiments have worked perfectly, he still hasn't found his six extra spacial and one extra time dimension."

"It's hard to find them," Steffens said, more to Kurita than Loren, "because we're using four-dimensional detector arrays and we can only detect the *shadow* of extra dimensions in our space, not the real thing."

"I appreciate the explanation," Loren said. "But this extra dimension stuff goes way over my head."

Kurita smiled sunnily. "My colleague's head, too."

Steffens looked at him. "I haven't noticed a published thesis from you, either, bucko."

"Mine's further along than yours."

"Huh. We'll see."

"I've got the simulation cued up."

"Then *run* it, moron!"

Loren decided he was going to have to introduce these guys to Sandoval and Byrne. They were clearly competitors in the same Bozo Sweepstakes.

Loren turned back to the holo cube as Kurita pressed Enter. A dim line, a silver trail, appeared along the center of the cube.

"That's the angle of the beam pipe," Steffens said.

In the bottom of the cube chrome-bright numbers rolled, a minus sign followed by a big number 10 with smaller numbers above the right-hand corner of the image, the scientific notation that Kurita and Steffens had been using and that Loren only dimly remembered from high school. The number reached zero, and the minus sign turned into a plus.

There was a sudden speeding brightness, a horizon filled with primal fire, and then blasting out of the center of the explosion, like shrapnel from a grenade, were tiny objects—perfectly focused spheres, unblurred by motion and hyper-real, almost offensively real. Suddenly the image froze, hovering over the dark surface of the console like the harbinger of an apocalypse. The time counter was frozen at 10^{-36}.

"The interaction's almost ideal," Steffens said. He stepped closer to the image. "Symmetry's already broken, because gravity's broken off from the superforce, but there's plenty of other things to look at. The physicists haven't had time to identify but a few of these particles—lookee here." He crooked a finger at Loren, who obediently stepped closer. Steffens put his hand into the image. A dark tiger-striped cloak shimmered over his palm and fingers—strangely, the hand looked less real than the frozen image.

Steffens pointed at a blue marble. If Loren looked close, he could see a lowercase d written on the surface. "That one's been identified as a d quark. Quarks possess this quality called color, okay, but the actual color of quarks in this simulation doesn't signify anything—all quarks are coded blue in this simulation, and most of what's been identified so far are quarks, because that's mostly all that can exist at these temperatures." Loren wondered idly what a quark might be. Steffens's finger moved to a little orange sphere with Z written on it. "There's an intermediate vector boson. If you look closely when we start the simulation again—I saw this earlier—you'll see it decay into an electron-positron pair and a Higgs particle. Hey." He peered into the image and gave a little hop, trying to see better. "Is that a Centauro event?" Speaking to Kurita. "Would you rotate the image one-eighty?"

"Which axis?"

"Y."

Steffens turned back to Loren. "Bet no one's noticed this yet."

Kurita tapped keys and the image rolled over like an obedient dog. Steffens pointed at a bright fan of shining spearlike tracks. "See here? This spray of particles? That's—" He hesitated, remembering his audience. "Well, it's something you hardly ever see in nature." He looked at Kurita. "Mark this and log it, okay?"

"I sure as hell will." Kurita wore a smirk. "That's *my* thesis."

A cube appeared in the center of the holo image, then tracked (Kurita tapping keys) until it stood over the event. Kurita kept tapping keys.

"He's got to log it in four dimensions, counting time," Steffens said. "Then we can get on with it."

Kurita finished and the cube disappeared. The image rotated again until it regained its former alignment.

Steffens pulled his hand back. "Okay. Next."

Kurita tapped a key and the simulation advanced, the bright fragments coiling outward like a time-lapse video of a thundercloud forming over an isolated New Mexico peak. The action was still happening too fast for Loren to follow, even assuming he knew what to look at.

"Stop!" said Steffens.

The image froze. Time was 10^{-29}.

"Here's where it all goes to hell," Steffens said. His voice was heavy with disgust. "See these guys?" He waved his hand through an expanding cloud of tiny bright particles. "Photons! Electrons! Neutrinos!" He pointed an accusing finger deep into the mass. "And there's a neutron! We shouldn't *have* these things yet!" Another ferocious stab with his finger. "And over here's a *proton!*" There was disgust in his voice. "They should exist only for an instant and then be blown apart!" He withdrew his hand and shrugged. "In a little while we'll start forming deuterium, and then it's all over. At this stage there should be a *lot* more energy in here. But it's gone—most of the energy from this interaction got dumped somewhere."

"The energy sump," Loren said.

"That's what Tim calls it, yeah."

Kurita tapped a key again. The explosion grew, the brightness lessening as it diffused. Particles shot out of the frame of the holo. In the end there was nothing, just the shadowy image of the beam pipe. The cube disappeared. End of demonstration.

Loren tried to decide how he felt about all this. A vast complex, with the latest technologies, and all for the purpose of cataloguing the behavior of things no one could see. Was it salvation or a sin? And if sin, which one? Vanity?

They were trying to cook up the Creation. And what the hell did *that* mean?

It annoyed him that he didn't know the answer.

"What happens if you get all the way back to the Bang itself?" Loren said.

"We won't," said Steffens.

"Do you see God?"

Steffens started to answer, then didn't. He seemed uncertain what attitude to take to this question.

Kurita rose from his chair. "What do you mean, *we won't*?" he said. "Remember what Pascual Jordan said back in World War II? He said he could create a star out of nothing, because at the point zero its negative gravitational energy is numerically equal to its positive rest mass energy."

Steffens waved a hand near his ear, as if to brush off a mosquito.

"If you create a star, from there it's just a tiny step to creating a new universe," Kurita insisted. "With inflation theory it should be *easy*."

"I'm serious, here," said Loren.

"I'm not a cosmologist," Steffens said. Loren couldn't tell which person he was talking to.

"Create yourself a star," Kurita urged, "you could become your own god."

"Go back far enough," Steffens began, definitely talking to Loren this time, "back before symmetry breaking, back before Kaluza's eleven dimensions start to fade, and there the universe is simple and elementary, and if you don't see God, you can at least see his handwriting. Because you'd see the fundamental laws of the universe, and you can't get any closer than that."

A spectral chill washed up Loren's spine. These people, the two comedians and their superiors, were approaching the divine. Or had the divine, instead, approached them?

Loren was beginning to suspect that it had.

"Of course," Steffens added, shrugging, "I'm an atheist, so I'm not exactly an authority on matters theological." He fell silent for a moment, then added irrelevantly, "I was raised Quaker, though."

"I was raised Baptist," Kurita blurted, "but so what? Listen! We can make a *universe*! It'll be terrific! Some thesis, huh?"

Steffens looked at him patiently. "Shut up, Yoshi."

"What's it like working with Tim Jernigan?" Loren said. Time, he thought, to get this interview back on track.

"I don't work with him much," Steffens said.

"Our job," said Kurita, "is to fix things when they break. Not talk about experimental physics with Ph.D.'s. But I *have* talked to him. For a big shot, he's pretty approachable."

"You have to talk to him on his level, though," Steffens added, "and his level is pretty high. He's friendly, but the quality of his thought is kind of intimidating."

"He's brilliant," Kurita said. "He and Singh are right at the top. Even Dielh talks to him."

"Doesn't look like Dielh's going to talk to *me*," Loren said.

"I'm not surprised," Steffens said. "Joe Dielh is working hard on getting his Nobel, and he's not dealing with anyone who can't help him."

"He'll never get it on his own," explained Kurita, "so he's harnessed Tim and Singh to get it for him. That's why he doesn't do any research on the classified side—he couldn't publish and get himself invited to Stockholm."

"He doesn't?" Loren was startled.

"No. The military offered him a lot, but he's always turned them down."

"I've been told he's in Washington on a classified mission."

Steffens and Kurita looked at each other, their puzzlement plain. Kurita was the first to speak.

"First we've heard of it."

"Think for a minute." A pain shot through Loren's back and he hitched his gun around, straightened one leg, stretched the muscles. "Did anything unusual happen on Friday or Saturday? Anything out of the ordinary."

"There were a lot of people in and out," Steffens said. "I didn't know very many of them. I had to replace a malfunctioning calorimeter on the detector array, but that was last Thursday night, before anything started. And then Friday night I had to fix a ventilator in the conference room, where the buffet was set up." He shrugged. "That's all I can remember."

"I can't remember anything unusual other than the large numbers of people," said Kurita.

"Can I see the accelerators?" Loren asked.

Steffens looked uncertain. "You can, I guess."

"They're miles from here, is what he means," Kurita said. "This is just the control room. The accelerators themselves are way out on the mesa."

"There's not much to see," said Steffens. "Other than the proton synchrotrons and the small storage rings, there's mostly just a long tunnel with a pipe in it."

Loren stretched his leg again, pain nagging at him. "Why isn't the control room near where the collision takes place?"

"We've got a lot of electronics in here," said Kurita. "It could interfere with the experiments. So the LINAC is way out on the ranch, and we control it by fiberoptic cables to minimize interference."

Loren glanced around as he tried to think of another question, taking in the bright monitors, the workstations, the balcony from which supervisors could observe their underlings. It looked more like a motion picture set than anything real, and the objects the room was built to study seemed more unreal even than a movie.

"Wanna see the Cray that runs the show?" said Steffens. "It's impressive."

Loren took his Xeroxes and followed the two back to the upper level and then out of the room. A few bearded men in jeans and T-shirts passed by in the corridors and offered greetings to his guides. Another barnlike room, this one brightly lit and filled with desks, niches, and terminals, offered as its centerpiece the Cray, which was a two-foot-high clear-plastic tetrahedron largely filled with a black-as-midnight carbon solid on which bas-relief circuitry could dimly be seen. Other techs stood by like proud new fathers showing off their offspring. Someone had stuck a piece of cardboard on the Cray's base, with an arrow pointing upward to the computer, that featured in red crayon the words *Heisenberg Sleeps HERE*.

Loren was surprised by the tall transparent tubes that arched above the computer, filled with clear coolant. "Makes your computer look like a McDonald's," he said.

"Fast data, not fast food," said one of the techs.

"It got knocked out by a fast-moving electron Friday morning," Steffens offered.

Loren looked at him. "I heard there were computer problems."

"See, the whole universe is full of electrons that we can't see. *Besides* the ones in matter, I mean. That's Dirac's idea."

Maybe Dirac, Loren thought, was on the log sheets somewhere.

"And sometimes an electron jumps out of this invisible sea and interacts with matter. It happens about once each week in the Cray. And crash goes the computer." Steffens grinned. "Interesting, hey? That we can build a computer so sensitive that it can be knocked out by something invisible?"

"I guess. Do I really need to know this?"

Steffens looked sympathetic. "Probably not."

Loren's tour continued, to Steffens's workshop, full of half-assembled equipment and crumpled potato chip bags, and another big room, filled with tables and benches and vending machines, where the buffet had been set up during the run. As they walked, Kurita kept on trying to convince Steffens of the value of creating their own universe.

"What happens," Loren asked, "to *our* universe when you create your own?"

"We get blown away," said Steffens.

"No offense," said Loren, "but I hope your experiment fails."

"Wait!" Kurita said. "Not necessarily!" He looked confidingly at Loren. "That's why I need my colleague here. He's the expert on Kaluza-Klein theory."

Steffens scowled. "What's that got to do with it?"

"You just arrange for different dimensions to collapse, see," Kurita said. "You've got nine spacial and two temporal dimensions to work with, right? And ours are collapsed to four. So when you create the new universe, you arrange so that it collapsed into *another* four spacial dimensions and the *second* time dimension. And then the new universe won't interfere with ours."

"I don't believe I'm hearing this," said Steffens. "How do you make these arrangements?"

"That's what I need you for," said Kurita. "You're the expert."

"Uh-huh."

They found William Patience in an office near the entrance. He was talking on the phone, looked up as he saw them in the hallway, nodded and waved, then went back to his business. Loren tried to eavesdrop, but the conversation didn't seem relevant—something to do with Patience straightening out someone's overtime. The man's intensity gave the impression he was saving his employee from the electric chair. Outside in the corridor, Steffens and Kurita kept up their act.

Patience hung up. "Seen everything?" he said.

"I guess," Loren said.

"Take you to the train?"

"Sure."

Loren shook hands with Steffens and Kurita and thanked them, then followed Patience out into the parking lot. The sunlight was blinding. The parking lot was dry and there was no sign of the downpour only a few hours ago. Loren put on his shades.

Patience got in the Blazer and started it. "What did you think?"

"Those two guys should be wearing greasepaint and putty noses."

"They're just techs. You should see the damn scientists." Patience backed out of his place, swung out of the lot. "I remember one of them asked me to repair his stapler once. His Swingline was broken, and I happened to be passing, and he wandered out of his office and asked if I could fix it for him." He shook his head. "Sometimes I wonder who's in charge of the asylum."

There should be humor in that, Loren thought, but somehow there wasn't. Loren had the feeling that what Patience really meant was that *he* should be in charge, and that if he were, changes would definitely be made. Not least of all to the staplers.

Loren wondered if he should try to see Jernigan again, then decided against it. He'd try to corner Jernigan without either of his watchdogs, Patience or his wife.

"Did you see Vlasic on the maglev?"

"There was nobody."

"It hardly ever gets used," shifting into third. "A pity, since the technology's so nice."

"Yeah. People love their cars too much."

"I guess some of the maintenance staff use it."

"Yeah. The peons from town."

Patience gave him an odd look.

"This Vlasic," he went on, "he's a theoretician of some sort. Came over a long time ago from Eastern Europe. And he likes to ride the train. Back and forth, all day sometimes, if he's working on a tough problem. He sits right up front in a coat and tie and watches the world go by. It says it helps him visualize how things move at relativistic speeds."

"I didn't see him."

The Blazer moved past *Discovered Symmetries* and toward the station. Loren handed in his visitor badge and shook hands with Patience.

The maglev was waiting. Loren got in the front compartment and saw that he was sharing it with someone. Sitting right up front was a small, bald, pink-faced man in a neat blue three-piece suit, complete with red tie. He was sitting hunched slightly forward, folded hands in his lap, like a contrite schoolboy. When Loren entered he glanced over his shoulder with watery blue eyes.

Loren nodded at him as he sat across the aisle. The man, Vlasic presumably, nodded back, then returned his abstracted gaze to the front.

Loren thought about the Xeroxes, the data he'd gathered from Patience's files. All probably useless, unless Patience had let something slip, and that was unlikely.

He'd have to think of something else to do.

The train rose, humming, and began its fast ride into a former century.

E L E V E N

"So I called Violet Dudenhof," Loren said, later.

"Did you!" Debra dried lettuce with several paper towels. A laxative commercial boomed from the television in the next room.

"I was tactful." Defensively. "And Jesus, Randal died decades ago. She should have got over any shyness about his behavior by now. So I asked her if Randal had any relatives left in New Mexico, any in that particular age group—"

"That is tactful. I guess."

"And she said no. No relatives at all that she knows of, not since his brother died of AIDS in San Francisco. And he was gay."

"That doesn't mean he couldn't have had a kid twenty-odd years ago." Debra opened the door of the microwave oven and brought out a bubbling enchilada casserole.

Loren thought about it. The thought of someone who changed sexual orientation was not a comfortable one for him. A man should discover what worked for him, he figured, then stick to it.

"I suppose not," he said.

"But still. No one's heard anything."

"No. But I'll keep asking."

"I wonder," an idea striking him, "if *Patience* is gay."

"Did he give you that impression?"

"He's got more machismo than all the Magnificent Seven put together. But that could be overcompensation. And the Turkish carpets, the long hair, the . . ." He groped for concepts. "The gun fetish. The clothes fetish. He's never been married. Maybe John Doe is a lover he's bumped off."

"Sally Manson told me that he asked her out."

"Did he?" He looked at her. "Did she say yes?"

"She went out with him a couple times. But all the machismo and narcissism put her off."

"Narcissism! That's the word I was looking for." He sighed. "I'll keep asking around."

Keep asking around. That was his strategy now. Sooner or later he'd be able to find someone—someone besides a ten-year-old, anyway—who could provide some useful evidence.

"Right now I'm going to start looking into the wife," he said.

"Jernigan's." Following his jump in subject.

"I got her file from Patience, but I haven't looked at it yet."

"So you think he's connected with the murder."

"I think he knows more than he's telling." Loren frowned at the thick bubbles rising in the casserole. The scent of onions and green chiles sharpened in the room. "I hate to think he's connected with the killing in any way," he said.

As if on cue, the sound of weapons fire came from the television. Small, hollow-sounding bursts, not dramatic enough to be fictional. The nightly news had started.

"There were two people shooting at your John Doe," Debra said.

"Two people with identical weapons. Like the two guys who travel in each ATL jeep. Or who guard the gate."

"Except the caliber's wrong."

"And the caliber's *weird.* Hardly anyone around here uses .41. It's some kind of pointless intermediate caliber, anyway, for people who think nine-millimeter is for wimps but who don't want to carry something as heavy as a .45."

Debra removed the pot of Spanish rice from the stove and stirred it. She left the spoon in the pot. Loren got a pair of plates from the cupboard.

Katrina and Kelly were with Skywalker tonight, leaving their parents to dine alone on leftover casserole. Loren and Debra took their meals into the living room, the sound of gunfire growing louder, and sat in front of the television. Debra reached for the remote control and turned down the volume. The announcer was describing the civil war in Natal. Chile sauce scored Loren's palate as the camera panned over flyblown corpses scattered in a minefield. LIVE BY SATELLITE, said the small letters in a corner of the screen.

"Are you going to be costuming tonight?" he asked.

"Yes. We're getting close to the deadline and I still have half the chorus to fit."

"Is Sondra Jernigan in the play?"

Debra looked away from the TV, her eyes interested. "Yes," she said. "In the chorus."

"And the chorus is rehearsing tonight?"

Debra nodded.

Mortars walked up and down the televised veldt. The camera jerked as its operator sought cover. "Good chile," Loren said.

"Fresh from Hatch."

The Lord, he thought, was providing.

He drove Debra's Taurus, a less conspicuous flag to corporate goons. No one answered the door at Jernigan's, and neither of the cars was present in the driveway. Loren occupied his time by going up and down the block, knocking on doors, finding people who had been away yesterday and asking the same questions he'd asked then. He heard nothing new.

He walked away from the last query, hearing a carved oak door close solidly behind him. He halted at the sidewalk, where an elaborate wrought-iron grid, reminiscent in its way of *Discovered Symmetries*, held aloft a mailbox; and he let Vista Linda rise to his senses. Water still sprayed here and there over the mossy, expensive lawns; lawn mowers still roared in the background. A preadolescent boy sped by on a moped, a red strip of fluorescent tape on the back of his helmet. Somewhere a car with a broken muffler rumbled. There was a brisk October coolness adrift in the darkening sky and Loren turned the collar of his jacket up.

He stood silently and let the time and place wash over him. God talking, maybe.

A tall silhouette was moving up the street and it was some moments before Loren realized it was Jernigan. He'd never seen an adult walking anywhere in this suburb: there was no place to walk *to*. Except, of course, the maglev station, which Jernigan would naturally use while his car was being fixed. Loren steered an interception course, crossing the street. Jernigan recognized him and quickened his pace.

"Hi, Dr. Jernigan."

Jernigan kept his long legs moving, his gaze fixed resolutely on the haven of his own front door. He was swinging a narrow leatherette case on the end of one arm. "I don't have to talk to you," he said.

Loren had to adopt a shuffling, skipping pace to keep up to the tall man, just like the woman guard had adopted with Loren that afternoon. Concrete scuffed under his shoes as he hopped along. "I just want to tell you some stuff." A bit breathlessly. "For your own good."

"I'm not interested."

"I wanted to give you the name of a good lawyer. Since you're going to need one."

Jernigan just gave him a look over his shoulder, a look of contempt.

"See, I've been talking to witnesses. I told you that I would. I found someone who said you didn't drive home Saturday night. And that, combined with what the dead man said before he died . . ."

Jernigan kept moving, but the movement turned jerky, spastic almost, as if his brain weren't sending out quite the right signals. He gave a Quasimodo lurch into the blood-colored lava gravel of his rock garden, taking a more direct line for his front door.

"Listen to me," Loren said, feet crunching on gravel as he skipped alongside. "I think you've been getting the wrong kind of advice. I think you need to talk to a real lawyer."

"*Leave me alone!*" Jernigan shouted. He spun around, gravel spraying from his feet. Loren stepped back to avoid the case at the end of Jernigan's thin arm.

"Will you see a lawyer?" he said. "I don't think you're a killer, but you keep acting like a suspect. And I keep finding things wrong with your story."

"Just keep away!" Jernigan said.

"Oliver Cantwell," Loren said. "He's a good attorney, and he's just a phone call away."

Jernigan stared at him. Loren could see the pulse hammering in his throat.

"I have to go in now," Jernigan said. His voice was conversational. "I have to talk to Dr. Dielh by modem." He held up his case as evidence. Presumably there was a modem in it.

"Oliver Cantwell," Loren repeated. "Remember the name."

Jernigan nodded, then turned around and walked from the rock garden across the driveway toward his house. Bloodred gravel dribbled down the driveway, trailing from his loafers. Loren regarded him for a long moment, then turned and headed back into the growing night.

Time to knock on more doors.

Before he was through there was a presence on the street, the dark, waiting, expected silhouette of an ATL jeep. Loren ignored it as he went on knocking on doors, asking questions. Kept on knocking till it was full dark.

In silence, it followed him home to Atocha.

As he drove, Loren could look in his rearview mirror and see the glow of a fire in the national forest to the north, deep orange outlining the black column of smoke rising above it. Helicopters, searchlights stabbing down through the murk, circled the smoke cloud like moths hypnotized by a lamp.

The ATL Blazer was right behind him, not bothering to try to hide. Uncertainty crawled through Loren's heart. For some reason he didn't want to lead Patience's goons to his home, to have their intruding presence within the peacefulness of his querencia, and so he passed his turn and drove down Central heading toward the Line. The town was quiet on Monday night, with only a little vehicle traffic and a few pedestrians, mainly young people, walking in small, cheerful groups down the streets.

Before he got to the Line he turned around in the high school parking lot and headed back, forcing the Blazer to make a U-turn behind him. He grinned into the rearview mirror as his followers swayed back into his trail. You couldn't do a proper tail job with a single car.

A figure appeared out of the darkness, a tall man wrapped in a blanket: Roberts the Prophet, trundling home from the Line with a bottle in a brown paper bag. His daily dose of inspiration.

Miracles happen every day. Roberts's slogan.

The big thermos-bottle-shaped towers of the Apostle church reared up on the right, silhouetted by the glow of the town plaza. Behind the church, the porch light of the parsonage was on.

An impulse swung Loren and his car into the right lane, then brought him to a stop. Loren waited behind the wheel for the Blazer to pass him—it kept on going down Central—and then Loren stepped out.

Loren hadn't done his spiritual duty for months now.

A car drove past on jacked-up rear wheels, an Arab rhythm booming from interior speakers. Loren tried to ignore it.

The Ordinances of the Apostles commanded each member of the community to regularly visit the pastor and "make his report" on the state of his spiritual health. Exactly how often was "regularly" was up to the pastor, the church elders and deacons, the parishioner, and the latter's conscience. In his wild days Loren had let years go by between visits. Now he reported every two or three months, at least for the amount of time it took to announce that his spiritual state seemed, on the whole, pretty good.

Now he didn't know precisely what his soul was telling him. Questions bubbled up in his heart, questions he did not dare ask lest they betray him as a lunatic. He swung open the white picket gate, walked up the short flagstone path, and knocked. Only then did he wonder exactly what it was he had come here to say.

Pastor Rickey's expression, on answering, seemed only mildly curious. In the few times Loren had seen him in this capacity, his questions had been as pro forma as Loren's answers. Maybe he only tried to match his parishioner's mood.

"Hi," Loren said. "Is it too late? Can we talk?"

Rickey's expression didn't change. "Come on in." Rickey swung open the door and Loren followed him into his study.

"Are you here for your regular visit?" Rickey said as he walked. *Yower.* "Or is this some special particular occasion?" *Pahrticular.*

"I'm not sure," Loren said.

"Sit down. Would you like some tea?"

The study had a strange little tented tin ceiling with winglike deco motifs, and a plastered dado that featured deco symbols of a more or less religious character: zias, crosses, swastikas, Egyptian sun symbols with streamlined Raymond Leowy wings. The pastor's desk, bookshelves, and chairs were of light wood, the uprights carved with branching zigzag lightning bolts clutched in the hand of God or Zeus. More 1920s modernism.

"No tea, thanks." Loren hitched his gun around under his jacket and sat down in one of the lightning chairs.

Rickey tugged at the knees of his pair of brown cords and sat. He was wearing a light blue shirt open at the collar. Part of the next day's sermon lay flickering on the amber screen of a VDT just above his keyboard.

"We're alike in a way," Loren said. "You and me."

Rickey looked at him with polite regard.

"We both keep other people's secrets," Loren said. "We both know more about our neighbors than anyone else."

Surprise glittered behind Rickey's spectacles. His balding head inclined to one side.

"I hadn't considered that."

"Sometimes more than we *want* to know."

"I suppose so." He leaned forward encouragingly. "Is that what you wanted to talk to me about? How to deal with other people's secrets?"

"Not exactly." Loren cleared his throat, shifted his weight to the other hip. "What I'm worried about isn't a secret, exactly. Well"— changing his ground a bit—"it *might* be a secret. It's something I can't talk about directly."

Rickey absorbed this. His brow furrowed as he considered. "Can you perhaps give me an indication of its general nature?" he asked.

"What—" He paused for a moment, licked his lips, went on. "What is the church's position on miracles?"

Genuine surprise danced in Rickey's eyes. He smiled and nodded. "Miracles are an established part of doctrine. Twelve people witnessed the ascension of the Master in Gray. The first president of the church recorded his miracles in his diary."

"Miracles happen every day."

Rickey grinned. "Have you been speaking to poor Mr. Roberts? That's his slogan, I believe."

"Al Roberts is going over the edge."

"He's *gone*. Long gone." Shaking his head again. "Perhaps a miracle would have saved him."

"Maybe." Loren looked at the pastor suspiciously. He couldn't quite tell whether Rickey was being flippant or not.

Miracles. How could he get there from here?

"I was down at the labs today," he said. "Looking at some of their equipment."

"Ah." Rickey settled into his seat, fingers steepled in front of him. Loren peered at him again. How significant was the "ah"?

"They say," starting again, "that they can come close to remaking the Creation. One of the techs even told me it was possible to create a whole universe." He gave a little dismissive shrug. "Though maybe that was all bull. I think it was. I couldn't really tell."

"Whatever they can do," Rickey said, "it's not the Creation. It's just a material reconstruction. The Creation—and any genuine miracle, by the way—requires the divine spirit."

"Yeah." Loren cleared his throat again. "That's not the miracle I was talking about, anyway."

"Oh." Rickey frowned. "I thought perhaps that science had shaken your faith."

"No. I don't think so." He shook his head. "Definitely not."

"Science, read properly, should build faith." Rickey was laughing. The amber words of the next day's sermon glowed over his shoulder. "The evidence is good. I've looked into it, and science reaffirms the most essential tenets of our religion."

Loren looked at him, despair tugging at his heart as he tried to figure out how he was going to get through this without seeming a lunatic.

"The evolution business gets in the way, always. People get upset over whether we're descended from apes, or whether the Creation actually took place on October 22 of 4004 B.C., like Bishop Ussher said. What twaddle!" Rickey waved a hand dismissively. "That's picayune literalism! It's just modern-day Pharisees picking over the minutiae of a religion that they and people like them tried their best to kill in spirit ages ago—and thank God they didn't succeed. Why be *literal* about the thing?" *Literahl.* "What matters is that the Creation actually took place, however it did! What matters is that we're *here*!"

Loren tried to smile at him. A smile at least seemed required, the pastor seemed so cheerful. Even if he was totally missing Loren's point.

"The scientists look at nature and find randomness, and that's the same kind of literal-mindedness that the latter-day Pharisees engage in—they won't believe in anything unless it's spelled out for them. Heisenberg's Uncertainty Principle—it demonstrates free will! I've looked into it!"

Aggravation griped along Loren's bones. "Hey," he said, "does everybody know about this Heisenberg guy but me?"

Rickey laughed again. "I studied physics for a while, till I decided to go into philosophy instead. And with ATL being built down the road, I reacquainted myself with modern physics on the principle of know-your-neighbor. I suppose I thought I might have the chance to convert a scientist." Loren nodded. Rickey went on. "Heisenberg was a physicist, and he demonstrated that you cannot determine both the position and velocity of a particle." *Pahrticle.* "One or the other has always to remain uncertain. Heisenberg's Uncertainty Principle."

Loren thought about it. "Okay," he said. "I understand the bumper sticker now."

Rickey looked puzzled for a moment, then shrugged, his enthusiasm returning. "A man named Schrödinger illustrated the principle with this lovely parable about a cat and a bottle of poison—but my point is this: in classical physics, all is ultimately knowable. If you can understand the present, know it really well, unto the tiniest particle and its velocity, then the future is predictable. As foreordained as the most depressed Calvinist would have it. If the present is unknowable —if you can't demonstrate certainty *even about the present*—then it follows that the future is unknowable. And that means, my dear sir, that free will exists! We are *not* predestined robots! We exist, and our actions have consequences. *Church doctrine is proved.* Samuel Catton was right. QED."

Loren looked at him. The man was looking at him expectantly. Maybe he was anticipating applause.

"That's good, Pastor," he nodded.

It had been a mistake to come here, he knew. He searched his mind for a graceful way to make an exit.

"And as for miracles—they *do* happen!" Rickey's openmouthed smile revealed his tongue probing at the back of his teeth, as if searching for answers. "They happen not every day, but every second! Look at what happens when an electron absorbs a photon and moves to a higher energy state—the electron doesn't just migrate to the higher state, it sort of fades out in its old location and fades into a new one." Rickey dropped a fist on his knee, banging the point home. "That's a *miracle*, son! And that's a miracle that happens every teensiest fraction of a second to billions upon billions of electrons in the whole goldarn universe. Be joyful!"

"I'll do my best," Loren said. His head was swimming. A thoroughgoing nostalgia rose in him for the former parson, who would have quoted some stern Old Testament injunction or other, told him it was not his place to question the ways of God, and then sent him on his way. And who would certainly not have given him a physics lesson, of which he'd had a clear overabundance in recent hours.

"Miracles," Rickey said, "are a demonstration of God's grace. In our fallen world, a world filled with evil and uncertainty, with impure motives and questionable deeds, miracles are like a voice in the wilderness that crieth out *God is here!*" His voice was earnest now, not bubbling over with enthusiasm as before. He leaned forward, gazing intently into Loren's eyes. "Large miracles—macroatomic miracles, if you like—appear when all else is hopeless. When things are so tangled and confused that *God himself must intervene!* When there is no other way to God's grace, miracles point the way!"

Loren thought about it, wondered what it meant for him. "Have you ever seen a miracle?" he asked.

Rickey grinned. "No. It was the *absence* of miracles that convinced me of their existence." He leaned back, cleared his throat. "I was brought up an Apostle, of course, back in Susquehanna, but I didn't take much stock in matters of faith." *Apahstle, Seskehanna.* "The idea that God sent an angel to some half-literate farmer in upstate Pennsylvania in order to deliver a worldwide revelation—pretty silly, don't you think?" He grinned self-consciously. "And the *good* things that were associated with the church, the welfare and community work and so on, were being undertaken by the federal government."

He shook his head. "So I joined the Peace Corps. I got sent to Africa—Uganda. And that was a disaster—well, you've seen the television."

Loren nodded.

"After that," Rickey continued, "I moved to Los Angeles and went to work in a shelter for the homeless. I thought that the relief effort had just been mismanaged, that if I couldn't be a part of the effort abroad I could at least help people here at home. And you know what?" There was a hot desperation in his glance. Loren saw a gleam of moisture on his upper lip. "*I couldn't help.* You can't *imagine* how hopeless it was. The AIDS plague has absorbed so much social funding that there's not much left for anything else. A city the size of L.A. has tens of thousands of indigent—we'd fill our facility every night and close the doors in the faces of hundreds. And we didn't just serve old rummies—we'd give priority to families with children, and even so there'd be little kids sleeping in the streets of our neighborhood, because we didn't have places for them.

"And the *diseases*." There was remembered horror in Rickey's eyes, and Loren knew the pastor wasn't seeing his comfortable little study, but the sick bay in his Los Angeles shelter, children lying on ancient iron beds, old donated mattresses, mended white sheets. "Stuff we should have got rid of years ago. Diphtheria. Scarlet fever. Polio, for heaven's sake! If we'd had leprosy and schistosomiasis, it would have been as bad as Africa. But the social services were all overwhelmed by AIDS, and even basic vaccinations for children weren't being done."

He cleared his throat, then coughed into his fist. "We were in a gentrifying neighborhood, and the people living there weren't pleased by our presence. They wrote to their representatives, complained to the media; some of them even picketed. They didn't want to live next to poor people! Thought it brought down their property values!" *Prahperty.* Rickey gave a little mad grin; his eyes gleamed. One hand was scrubbing his thigh, a robotlike gesture without awareness. "And one night somebody burned our place down! Arson!"

Ahrson. "Jesus," Loren said—and then was acutely mindful he'd broken a Commandment. Rickey continued, seemingly unaware of Loren's transgression.

"There was a proper fire alarm and a sprinkler system—our place was up to code!" Rickey mopped his brow. "No one should have been hurt. *No one should have been hurt!*" He seemed to want to insist on that. "But some of the alarm components had been stolen by our clients, to sell for liquor or food or bootleg antibiotics, and the alarms and the sprinklers didn't go off. Twelve people burned to death. Most of them children from the sick ward." He gave his crazy little smile again. "No one caught the arsonist. They said he was a transient, and maybe he was. Nobody looked very hard. Developers built a strip mall on our location. And I went back to Pennsylvania, to Catton College."

"I never knew any of this," said Loren.

Rickey slapped a hand on his knee. He was smiling. "Do I believe in miracles? You bet I do!"

Loren looked at him. "Because the rest weren't burned, you mean? Other than the twelve who were killed?"

Rickey gave a twitchy shake of his head. "Because there's no other answer," he said. "Nothing else works. All that planning, all that relief effort, it failed. Federal intervention is a joke. Mankind is fallen and so are all our schemes. All, as Ecclesiastes says, is vanity and vexation of spirit." His ropy arms lifted, brandishing fists. "God's grace *has* to be the answer. Because otherwise it's all a desert. Extinction. If God isn't the answer, nothing is. God is the only hope."

Loren felt heat flashing through his body. Rickey was right. Loren was a public servant, he knew how rotten it all was, how much the world needed belief. But he had other things to believe in—faith wasn't his last resort. Images of his children shimmered before him. He wasn't like Rickey, with all his work gone for nothing.

"If you had children," he said, "you might feel different."

Rickey looked at him from shrunken eye sockets, a skeletal smile on his face. "I had *lots* of children, Chief. Some starved, some were crippled by polio, some burned to death. They are much better off with God." The skull's smile widened. "Auden, I believe, said that not to be born was the best. Failing that, I recommend faith. As, I believe, did Auden."

Loren started to answer, realized he had nothing more to offer. Nothing except that he believed in his family as much as he believed in God, and Rickey wouldn't accept that.

"I almost forgot to ask you." *Ahlmost forgaht.* Rickey gave a self-conscious chuckle. "You've performed a miracle? Is that what this is about?"

"I haven't done one," Loren said. Knowledge of his own sins plucked at his heart. "I'm not a prophet or a saint," he said. "But I think I may have witnessed a miracle."

He called my name.

"I'm somewhat relieved," Rickey said. He produced a handkerchief and mopped his brow. He was breathing hard. Loren thought of children burning in a sick ward, Randal Dudenhof pierced through with the steering column, all the unexpected horror that could shatter life's peace.

"I'm not sure how I would deal with someone who said he *worked* miracles," Rickey said. "A witness, though, that's another thing. You're a trained observer, and that helps, too. A man of the world, not a mystic. I've met mystics, and you can fool them with parlor tricks. Prestidigitation. They want to believe so much." He gave a shaky smile. "So who performed this miracle?"

"No one that I saw."

"Hm." Rickey looked at him quizzically. "But you can't tell me what it was?"

"I would prefer not to. And I don't know for certain that it *was* a miracle. There are other possibilities I have to eliminate. But—" He spread his hands.

Still, he called my name.

"But it still troubles you." Rickey took off his spectacles, wiped them on his handkerchief.

"Yes."

Myopic eyes flicked to Loren. "Why does it bother you?"

Loren opened his mouth, closed it. *Because I'm afraid.* He didn't want to confront this matter of miracles. He wanted a straightforward police investigation, with John Doe killed by Timothy Jernigan because he'd caught him in bed with his wife or some other answer equally simple and satisfactory.

"If it *is* a miracle," he said helplessly, "what does it mean?"

Rickey flashed a smile as he slipped his metal bows over his ears. "I thought we settled that. God's grace."

"God's grace for *who*? For me?"

"An impetus to belief. For you, for anyone."

Loren's head spun. "The miracle was there. And h—and it was taken away. Before it could be seen by anyone but me." He looked up at Rickey. "So what was the point? What's the point of a miracle that no one sees?"

Rickey stared at him levelly. The amber eye of his monitor glowed with spiderwebs of scripture. "You saw it, yes?"

"I saw it. No one else."

"Maybe it was for you."

Loren blinked. An ache began to throb in his heart. "I don't want to hear that," he said.

Rickey cleared his throat. "You have to understand that our church has always been torn between its gnostic origins—Samuel Catton's revelations and miracles—and its own establishment impulse. With the death of Catton and the foundation of the college, the church establishment became dominant. Miracles, you see, *change* things. They tear things up, turn everything upside down. An established church doesn't *like* tales of miracles, at least not outside of scripture, in the here and now. They're so . . . *uncontrolled*. That's where the Mormons are going wrong, in my view—they're trying hard to become an establishment church, and they're just *not*. They were revolutionary in their day—the Book of Mormon addresses every single political and spiritual question that beset New York in the 1820s. Maybe that's why it's so hard to read now." He flashed a smile. "And the Apostles were rebels against even the Mormons, which should make us even more antiestablishment. Our social programs were a century ahead of their time."

Impatience welled up in Loren. "I don't know what any of this has to do—"

"What can this miracle, this vision or whatever it was, mean to *you*? To *your* spirituality? That's what our gnostic tradition addresses, just you and God and no one in between. If you were the only person to see this miracle, then God was talking to *you*."

"*I don't know what it means!*" Loren realized he was shouting,

216

waving an arm. He dropped his hand into his lap. "It wasn't like one of the miracles in the Bible, where it's obvious. Wheels in the air, angels appearing, prophecy, the walls of Jericho falling, a rain of blood and toads . . ." *The dead rising.* "The meaning was unclear," Loren said.

"Think about it. Offer prayer. An answer will be granted."

Loren thought of Randal spitting blood that reeked of bourbon. More blood fountaining from John Doe's gasping mouth. "I don't know."

Rickey gave a barking laugh. "Trust me on this one. I'm an authority."

"Okay." Loren passed a hand over his brow.

"Is there anything else you need to talk to me about?" *Abowt.*

"I guess not."

"You haven't made your report in a while."

It would be a relief, after all this. "I guess we can do that," he said. "Sure."

A slight smile ghosted across Rickey's face. "Have you then, in the words of Mr. Catton, 'any matter which disturbeth the minds of the elders or the heart of the congregation'?"

Loren gave Rickey a look. Had he just heard a touch of irony? He couldn't quite tell.

"I can't think of anything," he said.

"It's been a violent weekend."

"I haven't done anything I'm ashamed of."

Rickey was looking at him intently. Loren felt himself shift under Rickey's gaze.

"Any violence done by me," he said, "was justified."

"Even when you hit Mack Bonniwell on the steps of the church?"

"Who told you that?" Loren demanded. Outrage plucked at his nerves. He dismissed the action with a slice of his arm. "Mack's crazy over what happened to his kid. Len broke the law and Mack wants to blame me."

"So you didn't hit him?" Rickey's gaze was intent.

Loren opened his mouth to deny it, then saw Rickey's look and figured out he was about to be bushwhacked.

"I slapped him," he said. "An open-handed slap."

Rickey nodded. "I'm glad you said that," he said. "Because I saw it from where I was standing. I was looking back to see if it was time to close the doors."

Blood hissed in Loren's ears. The hairs on his arms prickled. Alertness swept through him, an intentness like that he'd had in the ring, those midnight smokers at the old Ringside, when he locked eyes with a tattooed, battle-scarred opponent from the state pen and realized for the first time the kind of danger he was in.

"He was working his way up to hitting me," Loren said. "If I hadn't slapped him down, he would have swung at me, and I would have had to haul him off to jail."

Rickey's expression remained intent. "In other words, you hit him because if you hadn't, you would have had to jail him for assault."

"Yes." Loren leaned back in his chair and crossed his arms. "That's exactly what I did."

Rickey tilted his head and considered this line of reasoning. "A preemptive punch-out. I'm not quite sure how to put it in terms of ethics."

"I don't know much about ethics. But it's a small town, Pastor. I do things informally when I can. You probably do the same sort of thing yourself."

Rickey gave a thin-lipped smile. "Hit people? I don't think so."

"I mean," hastily, "deal with problems outside of channels. The thing was, Mack's words and body language were threatening. I had to deal with it."

"And you don't have a problem with it."

"No."

"And Len?"

"I thought he had a gun. I was wrong, but things were moving fast and there was no way of knowing. In a big city, they probably would have shot him."

Rickey nodded. "From what I've seen, that's not unlikely."

"And if I'd let him shoot me, he would have been executed."

"And you'd be dead."

Loren barked a laugh. "That, too."

"So it was another preemptive strike, if you like. To keep Len from going to death row."

"Yep."

They stared at each other for a moment, Rickey's look probing, Loren's defiant. Finally Rickey shook his head.

"I have examined your conscience, and it would seem to be at peace. I have no way of knowing whether it *ought* to be at peace, and therefore can say nothing further."

Loren restrained an impulse to shrug.

"Is there any other matter that falls within my sphere? A family matter, say?"

"My family life," Loren said, "is perfect anymore."

Rickey looked at him. "Why do people out here use that expression?"

"What expression?"

"'Anymore.' When what you really mean is 'now.'"

Loren shrugged. "I didn't know people *didn't* use it that way."

Rickey nodded. "Very good." He rose from his chair and offered his hand. "Thank you for making your report."

Loren rose and shook the hand. "Thank you."

"Tell me how your miracle turns out. I would like to know."

"If I ever figure it out." Grimly.

Loren left the parsonage and stood on the walk. The door closed softly behind him and the porch light winked out.

Cool, still October surrounded him. A slight breeze tugged gently at his senses. He looked upward, at the high stars, and asked them what to do next.

A sawmill snore answered him. Loren stepped forward, opened the gate, saw Roberts the Prophet lying propped up against the rail, his paper bag in his hand.

"Aw, shit."

A snore answered him. Loren opened the passenger door to the Taurus and then turned to lean over the former mayor. He shook Roberts by the shoulder.

This man was once my boss. The recollection had a taste of surprise.

"Hey, Al. Wake up."

The prophet mumbled, shifted, knocked over his bottle. The scent of bonded bourbon tainted the air. Roberts' flock was apparently bringing in enough money to enable him to enjoy the good stuff.

Loren grabbed Roberts' clothing and shoved him rudely back and forth.

"Wake up, Al!"

The prophet's rheumy eyes leaped open. He gave out a cry of fear, shrank back, then blinked up twice.

"Hi, Loren." His expression softened.

"Can you get up? I'll take you home."

"God loves ya, Loren."

The man's knees wouldn't support him. The bottle went skating into the gutter as Loren dragged him across the sidewalk. Loren wrestled the prophet into the passenger seat, then stood. He was panting for breath.

"Puke in my wife's car," he told the prophet, "and you're history."

Roberts waved a hand. "Bless you, my son."

Loren closed the passenger door, then walked around the car and got in. Roberts' smell was appalling, all bonded bourbon and body odor. Loren rolled down his window and started the car.

Roberts and his clan lived in a three-story house built in the Queen Anne style, complete with a conical-roofed Charles Addams turret, a house saved from the wreck of 19th-century Atocha in 1924 and carried on a big Riga Brothers truck to a block and a half from where Loren lived.

The lawn was shadowed by a dead elm and overgrown with mature weeds, Russian thistle, and brown range grass. Miscellaneous junk, an old cabinet, a car transmission, a screen door and a broken toilet bowl, gleamed in starlight among the weeds. Loren pulled up and got out of the car.

He had barely opened the passenger door before a couple of the faithful, Roberts' wife and his pregnant concubine, were out the front door. They were dressed in simple ankle-length homemade dresses. Loren looked into the blank face of the pregnant girl and remembered those sad calls to the switchboard that morning, all the parents seeking their lost children, and wondered if this girl was being looked for, or whether she was here because there was simply no place else.

The two women began to move Roberts out of the car, throwing his flailing arms over their shoulders. "Can I help?" Loren asked.

Amy Roberts looked up, her thin face defiant. "He's not always like this."

"I remember him, Amy. I worked for him."

"He's the messenger of God." Insistently. "You remember *that*, Loren Hawn."

"Okay, Amy." Shrugging.

Her sharp voice lifted in anger. "You always were an evil son of a bitch, Loren. I *never* liked you. *Never.*"

Surprise rolled through Loren at the unexpected anger. He watched in silence as Amy Roberts dragged her drunken prophet down the walk.

Never liked me, he thought. He remembered the way her lips had opened under his, her hot tongue stabbing into his mouth; he remembered her moving under him, naked and wet atop a beach towel stretched out next to a hot spring on the Apache reservation. He remembered the sulphur smell of the spring, the funny way she made noises, the sounds that seemed to force their way out of her, odd little baby noises, a small child whimpering.

Hell, he thought. Coulda sworn she liked me then. At least a little. Before she threw me over for a guy with a college degree who looked like he was going places, who kept regular hours and didn't spend his days training to turn cons into hamburger at midnight county smokers.

Maybe there was some kind of justice here, after all.

He got in his car. Rising into his mind came thoughts of Amy, young and wet, moonlight playing on her skin. And then guilt stabbed him to the heart.

God was talking to *you*. Rickey's voice.

Loren decided he needed to find out.

He drove to Len Armistead's service station on the east of town. As he drove, he watched carefully to see if he was being followed. No one appeared to take any interest in him.

The station was in the process of closing. When Loren turned off the highway he drove around back, parking out of sight behind Armistead's wrecker. It had a bumper sticker reading OUT OF WORK? NO MONEY? GETTING HUNGRY? EAT YOUR IMPORT! A bulldozer, a snow-removal blade for Armistead's jeep, and a backhoe, the type with a scoop on one end and a blade on the other, stood quietly rusting behind the building. Loren got out of the car.

The bear hunter came around the cinder-block corner of the building. One bulging cheek was loaded with tobacco. "What's up, Loren? You need something?"

"I need to rent your backhoe."

"Sure. Tomorrow?"

"Tonight. Right now."

Armistead looked surprised. "Okay," he said. "You know how to operate it?"

"Sure. You got a shovel I can use?"

"I guess." He spat a quid of tobacco onto the decaying blacktop. "What you need this for, exactly?"

Loren looked at him. "Something confidential. An investigation."

Armistead tilted his gimme cap forward and scratched the back of his head. "Okay."

"How much?"

Armistead told him.

"Can I write you a check tomorrow?"

"Sure, Loren." The big man grinned. "I reckon if you don't pay, I can always get the law on you."

Loren put on his jacket inside out, so the big gold letters that spelled POLICE wouldn't show. He got the bolt cutters and a long four-battery flashlight out of the Fury and put them in a metal toolbox on the backhoe. He strapped the shovel on the backhoe with a bungee provided by Armistead. He started the backhoe, turned on its lights, and drove farther east on 82. No one in the few cars paid him any attention, an anonymous figure in dark clothing. He turned down the side road to the cemetery, then stopped by the big metal gate.

Southwestern cemeteries were always more forlorn than most. No green growing, just dust and weeds and fading artificial flowers. He was glad that this one was dark. The stars were beginning to come out, their images wavering in the rising warmth of the land.

The cemetery gate, Loren found, hadn't been locked. No one came out here except for a funeral. He wouldn't need the bolt cutters.

The Dudenhofs' grave marker was easy to find, marked by a gray weathered Mormon angel with a trumpet, a copy of the gold Moroni

222

atop the Salt Lake City temple. Loren brought the backhoe up to the grave, reading the carved words in the light of its headlights. HERMAN, the stone read, FATHER. PATRICIA, MOTHER. ADAM, SON. RANDAL, SON. And dates. And little white headstones marking the grave of each.

Loren blinked at the third name and calculated figures. Randal had a brother besides the one who had died in San Francisco and been cremated there, an older brother who had died at the age of six, when Randal himself was maybe two. Loren hadn't known.

Only three children. Small for a Mormon family. And all died young. The graves were untended by anything except dead brown grass. The mounds had compacted into smooth concave depressions. Loren found Randal's headstone in the dust and positioned the backhoe.

By the time he struck the coffin he was sweaty, covered in dust, and deafened by the sound of the backhoe. Cars had flashed by on the highway, but none had shown any interest. Loren pulled the backhoe away, killed the engine, left the lights on, and took the shovel and flashlight.

He got the coffin open finally, after a furious, sweating ten minutes. Violet had bought the most expensive box she could find for her worthless husband, hoping perhaps to increase his value thereby. It was a round-topped bronze thing with a lead lining, its exterior now different shades of green, rippled and textured like an impressionist sea. Loren beat Armistead's shovel into a lump of metal by the time he finally pried the inner lid up and gazed down at what lay on the rotten satin pillow.

Loren's sweat pattered into the metal box as he turned on the flashlight. His breath grated in his throat. The body wore a blue suit with gold threads. The nails and hair were long, and there was a short beard on the face. The flesh was shrunken, browned, nothing more than a thick layer of varnish over the bones. Though it wasn't completely recognizable, the body seemed more reminiscent of Randal than not.

Loren knelt and played the flashlight beam over the body. There was a musty smell in the coffin. Loren's heart gave a little lurch as he saw, through translucent skin, the little delicate stitches that held the eyes shut. A gold wedding band was on the desiccated hand. He

223

closed his eyes and tried to imagine Randal, call his image to his mind, but all he kept seeing was the man dying on the old white tile of the police foyer.

He opened his eyes again. He couldn't honestly tell.

He reached out and took the corpse's nearest hand and moved it to the side. It was surprisingly light and there was no resistance. He did the same with the other hand. Then he flipped up the corpse's tie, opened his jacket, opened his shirt.

And there it was, black and tattered, broken ribs lying under the sutured varnish of skin—the deep wound where the steering column had entered Randal's chest. Loren gave a little sigh.

He'd dug up the grave for nothing.

If John Doe was Randal resurrected in body, resurrected by the divine hand as in the Book of Revelation, there should be no body here at all. The papery flesh would have been reanimated and the broken chest restored; Randal would have walked the Earth in his old skin.

If John Doe was another type of resurrected Randal, a Randal taken from a time before his death and brought forward by some bizarre side effect of the big accelerator run at ATL, then Loren figured this body should not be here, either, because he would not have died on the Rio Seco crossing and not been buried. And in that case the headstone and coffin wouldn't be, either, because history would have changed, and Loren would remember Randal as a missing person, not an accident victim.

John Doe was a stranger. There had been no miracle. Loren had not been on the receiving end of any messages from God.

Loren didn't know whether to feel disappointed or not.

He closed the coffin and climbed out of the grave and used the blade on the front end of the backhoe to push the earth back onto the mortal remains of Randal Dudenhof. He ran the backhoe back and forth over the grave for a while, making sure it was level, and then returned the backhoe to the service station. The station was closed, and Loren just parked the backhoe in its place, dropped the keys through the mail slot, and drove home.

The Fury cruiser wasn't home, and that meant Debra was still doing her costume work. The streetlight shining through the front-yard ocotillo threw crazy corkscrew stripes across Loren as he beat dust from his clothing. He opened the screen door and stood just inside the house. Middle Eastern bass rhythms thudded from Katrina's back room. Loren could feel the vibration rising up through hardwood floors.

Home, he thought. Querencia. He could feel the tension easing from his neck and shoulders.

A long night, he thought. He looked at his watch.

A little after eleven. Long past the girls' bedtime.

He closed the door behind him and the phone rang. It was Cyrano Dominguez, another of Cipriano's cousins, one Loren didn't know well.

"Hi, Cyrano," Loren said.

"Hi, Loren. I figured I'd give you a call, because I need to pass a message to your brother. You gonna see him anytime soon?"

"I'll see him tomorrow morning."

"Okay, good. You know that old GMC camper pickup I got?"

"Not offhand," Loren said. A rising dismay sighed through him. He had a feeling he knew where this was heading.

"It's an old truck. I don't drive it very often. Anyway, a couple months ago it blew a head gasket."

"And Jerry said he'd fix it." The dismay was solidifying.

"Yeah. He's had the truck ever since it blew, and I haven't heard from him. And I gave him twenty bucks to cover expenses."

Jerry probably hadn't started the job yet. And a head gasket should take a couple hours, tops.

"I'll remind him, Cyrano. Okay?"

"I'd like it by Friday. I wanna go duck hunting this weekend."

"I understand. I'll give Jerry the message."

"Sorry to bother you."

"That's okay."

Loren hung up the phone and thought about the burden of being his brother's keeper. "My family life is perfect anymore," he'd told Rickey.

Well, maybe not.

Music was still thumping from the back room. He went down the back hall to the little addition they'd built for Katrina five years ago.

The only way into the room was through Kelly's room and the bathroom they shared, that and the window, which—a bit ominously —he'd sometimes seen tomboyish Katrina use.

An ad for Wrangler jeans, showing hard-muscled young men in cowboy hats, occupied most of the door. Loren could hear the discordant dervish wails of some weird Arab bagpipe. He knocked.

"Lights out!" he yelled.

Bagpipes and drumbox diminished. Loren heard laughter, and then the door opened and a grinning Skywalker came out, carrying a macramé schoolbag in one hand and a worn Levi's jacket in the other. Loren's daughters followed behind her.

"Hi, Chief Hawn," Skywalker said. She frowned as she looked at him. "You're all covered with dirt."

"Very observant of you."

"What have you been doing?"

"Something connected with work."

She shrugged. "Sign my petition?"

"Depends." Loren followed her through Kelly's room and the hall to the living room.

"It's to our senators," Skywalker said. "Urging them not to pass the new trade agreement with England until Great Britain agrees to abide by the London Dumping Convention of 1972."

"Till they what?"

Skywalker turned and dug into her macramé bag. "The Brits are dumping heavy metals, fluorides, mercury, and atomic waste in the Atlantic. Again. They stopped for a while, but it looks as if they were just waiting for the world's attention to flag." She pulled a tattered petition from the bag and presented it to Loren. "They're dumping it off the Irish coast, which doesn't have Ireland happy, either."

"I imagine not." Loren took the petition, glanced at the text, found it simple and straightforward enough.

"Mrs. Hawn has already signed," Skywalker said.

"So I see." Loren unclipped his pen from his pocket, put the petition atop an algebra textbook presented by Skywalker, and signed.

"Thanks!" Skywalker flashed a rare, sunny smile, spun, headed for the door. Katrina and Kelly followed to say their goodbyes.

It used to be, Loren thought, that the only petitions he'd see were for installing a traffic light near the grammar school, preserving a historical building that was scheduled for demolition, or closing down Connie Duvauchelle's. Now most of what he saw had to do with national, often international, politics. Support for the Plastics Convention, bans on Chilote copper, protests against radioactive dumping, attempts to close down Sam Torrey's elk ranch, support for aboriginal populations in Central America and/or Africa . . . a long, saddening, seemingly endless list of the world's problems flashing at the speed of light into the satellite-linked neighborhoods of Atocha.

Loren admired Skywalker for her intelligence, her commitment, her knowledge—certainly she was the brightest kid he knew—but he was wearily thankful he didn't have her for a daughter. Skywalker, somewhere, had lost her childhood; his own daughters, happily, had not.

He had given Katrina and Kelly a secure childhood, as perfect and safe as he could make it, standing like a ferocious dog between them and the things that could hurt them. Surely, he figured, that was worth the commission of any number of sins.

He came awake the instant Debra made her stealthy entrance into the room, leaping from black sleep to total alertness in half a second. Policeman's reflexes.

"What time is it?"

"Almost midnight." Her tread was louder; she'd given up trying not to wake him.

Loren propped himself up on an elbow. "Rehearsals go on this long?"

"No." He heard the hiss of clothes sliding on skin as she began to undress. "Some of us went over to Lois Johnson's. We had some coffee and talked."

"How's the play coming?"

"Aside from the temper tantrums of the soprano, we're doing just fine."

Loren smiled and lowered his head to the pillow. Unfortunately there was only one woman in Atocha with a voice suitable to the part, Sandy Odell, and she and everyone else knew it.

"It's her moment of fame, I guess," Debra said. She opened the closet door and began hanging her clothes on the pegs set into the reverse side. "She's not gonna get any others. If she doesn't play prima donna now, she'll never get another chance."

"Phil still hasn't found a job."

"And benefits have run out. Her job at the Dairy Queen is only part-time. If it weren't for Calamity Fund, they'd really be in trouble." She dropped her nightgown over her head, worked it down over her hips. She dropped into bed and giggled. "I thought the music director was going to run her through with his baton, though."

"The last few days have been violent enough."

He leaned toward her and kissed her, lingering a bit more than usual for the good-night peck. Her lips tasted of coffee. He withdrew a bit, seeing his reflection looming in her spectacles, a blackness outlined by starlight. He put his arm around her, feeling her against his chest, soft human warmth beneath a layer of sensible flannel. The erotic mood stirred in him by memories of Amy Roberts, never faded entirely, began to grow in intensity.

"You don't seem too sleepy," he said.

"Too much coffee, I guess."

He kissed her again. She put her arm around his neck. He deepened the kiss, felt her tongue flutter against his. She gave a laugh and drew back.

"Your breath is steaming up my glasses." She took them off, put them atop the flat bookcase bedstead, then returned for another long kiss. Her hand slid over his back.

"I'll be right back." She pulled away, then left the bed and went into the bathroom to put in her diaphragm.

Loren rolled onto his back, pillowing his head on his hands. Anticipation beat like a pulse in his cock. He remembered Amy Roberts and other guilty pleasures, the mayor's secretary Irene, some little blonde girl at Connie Duvauchelle's with a zealous joggle to the way she'd moved her ass, like her hips were double-jointed or something, and who'd popped her gum right through it . . .

And Debra, who was perhaps not as adventurous as some of his other partners, but who was at least as enthusiastic. He felt comfortable with her. Wild oats once successfully sown, he figured, you didn't want an acrobat, you wanted a partner.

Certainty rose up around him like warm, enveloping mist. Querencia. Whatever he'd done to shore all this up, he thought, it was worth it.

The phone tore Loren from his postcoital sleep. He reached to the nightstand and picked up the receiver.

"Loren Hawn," he said. Debra gave a long sigh, rolled over, and began to breathe regularly.

"This is Alan London."

"Yeah?" Loren glanced at the watch on the nightstand. Dr. Alan London was the medical investigator in Albuquerque.

"It's kind of late for you to be calling, isn't it?"

"Things are a mite unusual." London gave a little smoker's cough: people in the OMI tended to smoke constantly to deaden their sensitivity to the smell of formaldehyde and cadavers.

"Your John Doe has disappeared," London said.

"What," half laughing, "the body's gone?"

"That's right."

It still seemed funny. "Did you bury it by mistake?"

"No, we did not." London's voice wasn't the least amused. "It was here just a few hours ago. Somebody got past my assistants into the cold room and took off with it."

"Are you serious?" Loren sat bolt upright in bed. Debra's body gave a little jerk, and then Loren felt her turn over to look at him. "Why would—I don't understand."

"I don't either. I thought I'd call and see if you had any notion why someone would—"

"You've got the fingerprints on record, right?"

"That was the first thing I thought of. But I still have the prints, both on computer and on card. And I still have photographs of the body."

"I have them, too. It's still possible to find out who Doe was."

"Assuming his prints are on file somewhere, yes." Coughing. "Or that someone can ID the picture."

"This is weird."

"That's not the half of it." London's voice took on a bemused quality. "The internal organs are gone, too."

"They—" Retracking. "Say again?"

"We take out the internal organs and the brain during the autopsy, okay? And some samples are sent upstairs to the histology lab and the rest are either returned to the cadaver or preserved in jars."

"And the jars are gone, too?"

"Not the *jars*." London was nearly shouting. "The *jars* are still there. It's the *organs* that are gone. And the *blood*."

"The organs and the blood," dully repeating. He looked at Debra and saw the opalescent glimmer of her eyes. She was paying careful attention.

"The formaldehyde in the jars gets discolored from the blood, okay? But it isn't cloudy anymore. Not even a taint. Whoever did this poured out the jars completely, cleaned them, and partially filled them with formaldehyde again."

"Or replaced them with new jars."

"Could be. I hadn't thought of that." London's voice cracked, was superceded by a fit of coughing. "One other thing," he added. "They left the toe tag."

Ghostly feet ran cold up Loren's spine. Up till this last detail the whole episode had existed somehow in the realm of burlesque, soft-footed intruders slipping into the M.I.'s office, tossing a corpse over one shoulder, playing games with jars of formaldehyde—all like characters in a good-natured horror film. Now everything had turned eerie, spectral, significant. Visions of quiet, efficient CIA spooks moved like black cats through Loren's mind. Or the Men in Black that the UFO freaks believed in. Or the Cybercops. *Left the toe tag behind* . . . Unseen supermen had done this, and they liked to play games.

The line gave a little click. Paranoia surged through Loren's veins. Was somebody listening? he wondered.

Time to be a cop.

"When did it go?" he asked.

"The cadaver? It was in its drawer at shift change, at four-thirty. The assistant coming on duty—tonight it was Esquibel—normally he checks every drawer as he comes on, and he remembers seeing it.

Later we got a hit-and-run, and instead of checking the card file to see which drawer was free, Esquibel just started pulling them open till he found one empty—and then he saw that there was paperwork on that drawer, that it was supposed to be occupied."

"When was that?"

"Around eight-thirty."

Loren felt like he was flying high and fast, blinded by dense cloud glowing with an eerie light. Lost, lost in time or meaning. At eight-thirty he'd been pushing dirt back into Randal Dudenhof's grave.

He was, he remembered, a cop. First, eliminate the obvious. "You've looked in the other drawers, I assume."

"Yeah." London's answer was cut by a fit of coughing. "It's not a mistake. The body's definitely gone."

"No one was in the cold room the whole time, right?"

"No. But Esquibel was just next door, in the office, and in order to get to the cold room you have to go past the office. Although they *could* have got through a locked, alarmed fire door."

"Yeah!" Loren recognized Esquibel's protesting voice in the background. "I woulda seen 'em. And if they'd used the fire door I would've heard. Them things are *noisy*. And I was in and out of the cold room, anyway."

"There were two DOAs," London said.

"Yeah!" Esquibel's echo. "DOAs! I was in and out!"

"And the samples have disappeared from the histology lab as well. And that's not even on this floor."

"Shit!" Esquibel's comment.

"The problem is," London said, "is that the circumstances cast a certain light on my assistants." Esquibel's voice shouted something indistinct in the background, then was followed by a round of coughing. Loren pictured the two of them at an autopsy, smoking Cuban cigars and hacking up lungers into someone's abdominal cavity.

"I trust Esquibel, of course," London went on. His tone suggested he was saying this only to be polite. "And I want him and the other assistants removed from suspicion. So if you have any reason to suspect anyone else in the removal of this body, the APD really needs to know."

"*I* wanna know!" Esquibel shouted. "I'll kill the motherfuckers!"

I don't know what to make of it, Loren thought.

"If you get anything at all," London said.

"Sure. You'll be the first to know."

"And hang on to those fingerprints. Make lots of copies."

"Honestly," the M.I. said, "it's as if the guy never existed."

Loren hung up and stared for a long moment at the ceiling.

As if the guy never existed.

Maybe he never had.

Maybe someone—or Someone—had done this for a purpose, just to preserve Loren's faith in miracles.

TWELVE

Dust swirled across the mesa in the wake of a merciless, unseasonal warm wind from Mexico that piled tumbleweed at every fence and leached the remaining moisture from the dry country. Soon there would be more forest fires. Junkyard dogs barked and pranced and flung themselves bodily against Loren in hopes of attracting attention. He rubbed their heads absently and crunched across the oil-spotted ground toward the GMC pickup parked behind Jerry's trailer.

He thought of dust trailing across Randal Dudenhof's grave. He realized he wanted to open the grave again and make absolutely certain the body was still there.

The GMC was battered, rust-streaked. Drifts of dust lurked in its defilades. Loren opened the hood and saw the V-6 engine with the valve covers and valve assemblies removed, pistons frozen in their cylinders, awaiting new gaskets. Loren walked around the truck to look in the window in the back of the camper shell. Tools and the valve assemblies were laid neatly on a piece of canvas, and had probably been sitting there for two months or more.

Jerry's trailer door boomed open. Loren walked around the truck again, slammed the hood down. When he turned, Jerry was standing there, head tilted back as he fumbled with the knot in his tie. Wind tore at his dark, curly hair, flew it like a flag over one ear.

"That's Cyrano's truck," he said. "I'm doing some work for him."

"I know. He called me."

"What about?"

"He wants his truck back by Friday. Better make that Thursday night. So he can go duck hunting."

"Okay." Shrugging.

The wind was eroding Loren's patience. "You'll do it by then?"

Jerry turned and started walking for Loren's car. "Sure. All I have to do is install a couple of gaskets."

Loren walked after. Hopeful dogs bounded around him, ears and slobber flying. Irritation danced through Loren, and he knew he should just drop the subject and take Jerry home for breakfast. But somehow he couldn't stop, couldn't stop trying to puzzle out Jerry's mode of thinking.

"Why didn't you do it before?" Loren asked.

"Didn't do what?"

"The gaskets."

"Oh. He said I could take as long as I want."

"I don't think he meant two months."

"Three." Jerry's voice was vague. He opened the Fury's passenger door. "Closer to three, I think."

Jerry and Loren got in the Fury. Loren smoothed his hair back with his fingers, blinked grit out of his eyes.

"I don't know why Cyrano called you, anyway," Jerry said.

"You don't have a phone."

"He could've come out."

Loren gave him an irritated glance. "Maybe he figured talking to you wouldn't do him any good."

"I woulda done it sooner or later." Another shrug.

Loren started the car, stared forward through the windshield. Anger grated in his bones. Trying to talk to Jerry was like trying to reason with a buffalo: you chattered on forever and then the animal did whatever it wanted.

Try and be a human being! he wanted to shout. Pointless.

"Hope we don't get a range fire," Jerry said. Tumbleweeds had built in large drifts against the junkyard fence, obscuring the Hamm's beer ad. Loren drove onto the highway, headed back into town.

" 'Better hope no gophers explode.' " Jerry looked at him. "That was *your* line."

"Guess I have something else on my mind."

Jerry's voice rose. "Get off my case, will you, Loren?"

Loren looked at him. "I didn't say anything."

"My business with Cyrano is my business with Cyrano. That's all I'm saying."

"It's your business till Cyrano calls *me* about it. Now it's my business."

"He shouldn't have called you. He could have dropped by."

"Maybe he did. Maybe you weren't there."

"He only called you because you have this thing about looking after me."

Loren looked at him again. "Somebody's got to."

"I can take care of myself."

"Oh, really."

"I can." Jerry sulked back into his seat. The Earth Church, empty, alone on its windy ridge, sailed past on the left.

"I saw that friend of Katrina's the other day," Jerry said. "Skywalker."

Loren glanced over his shoulder at the adobe building. "At the church? I know she belongs."

"No. Out in the arroyo behind the yard. She and some older people were in a four-wheel drive."

Loren looked at him and wondered if Jerry was implying something illicit. "What were they doing?"

"Just driving down the arroyo, heading south. Real slow, about three miles an hour. I waved, but I don't think they saw me."

"I think her dad has a jeep."

"It was probably him, then."

Loren stared at the road and tried to reconstruct Jerry's line of thinking. What did Skywalker and her jeep expedition have to do with anything?

Probably nothing. The Skywalker story was probably about as useful as Jerry's other stories.

And he had a lot of other things to think about.

* * *

"Lust!" Rickey let the shouted word echo through the church for a moment, then leaned forward to peer at his congregation through glittering spectacles. "Have I got your attention now?" he asked.

There was nervous laughter from the congregation. Rickey grinned.

"At college," he said, "people used to joke that it's customary to preach on lust right in the middle of the Days of Atonement, in order to maintain a higher rate of attendance." He blinked at his audience. "Happy Tuesday!"

More nervous laughter, testifying, perhaps, to the fact that the congregation *was* larger than usual for midweek. Loren looked up at the pastor and thought of children dying, starving in Africa, burning in Los Angeles. The man he had seen the night before—hollow-eyed, driven, insistent on the hopelessness of worldly life—had transformed himself into a rustic comic.

Rickey brushed a nervous hand over his thinning hair. He glanced at his notes, and Loren remembered the text of the sermon glowing amber over Rickey's shoulder.

"Human beings," the pastor said, "are moved by appetites. These appetites are appropriate to the preservation of the individual and the species. For instance," glancing up, "pride. We've already spoken of pride as being something that we all desire, in that we all want to be thought well of. But an excess of pride, once it becomes vainglory, is not simply a sin but the greatest of sins.

"Likewise with the appetites of the body. It is natural for the body to desire food and drink, but when we desire food and drink to excess, we risk gluttony. The body desires rest after labor, but sloth is rest carried to extremes.

"So it is with sex." Loren glanced at Debra and saw her own sidelong look at him, the memory of the previous night passing between them. She swiftly looked away, her color rising. Loren suppressed an urge to grin.

"Sexual intercourse is desirable on two counts," the pastor said. "It is desirable for the preservation of the species, and it is desirable insofar as it heightens the feeling of love between husband and wife. Love is a special thing—love is a gift of the divine."

Loren looked up at Rickey and wondered again about the man. He'd never been married, apparently, and that was very unusual in this religion that stressed family life above all else. Not that this necessarily implied abstinence: as custodian of most of the town's secrets, Loren had all too clear a notion as to the fallibility of the clergy. There were plenty of woman parishioners, church workers, and secretaries and the like—married, most of them, and hence safer—who were willing to give their all for Jesus or, in his absence, his local representative. There had been rumors, not necessarily true, about the last pastor, Baumgarten, and a couple of the married laywomen. Loren had been inclined, for all sorts of good reasons, to disregard the stories, and in any case there hadn't been any complaints. Unlike, for example, the case of the Evangelical Baptist minister he'd hauled off to jail for statutory rape. Loren had been careful to use only soft-tissue strikes then, gut and groin and kidneys, driving in with the end of his baton—no chance of broken bones to embarrass the department, and scarcely any bruises. Whether the girls had consented or not—and in this particular case it appeared they had—Loren knew damn well they were still someone's daughters.

But concerning Rickey, Loren had heard nothing. Maybe he was too new, maybe the rumors hadn't had time to start yet. Maybe the town gossipmongers, like Loren himself, hadn't quite figured out how to take the new pastor, and were waiting to make up their minds before they gave their suspicions any particular spin.

Maybe the man was a complete ascetic. Unusual in a religion like the Apostles, which preached moderation in material things rather than denial, but not entirely without precedent.

"Sex," Rickey said, "is a spiritual good." He paused a moment, as if anticipating an argument from someone, then looked down at his notes. "'Thy navel is like a round goblet, which wanteth not liquor; thy belly is like an heap of wheat set about with lilies. Thy two breasts are like two young roes that are twins.'"

"Jeez," muttered Kelly. Loren felt a quiet shock. He'd never in his life heard anyone quote those verses.

Rickey looked up. "That's the Song of Solomon. That is the loving and inspired and godly voice of human sexuality."

No shit, Loren thought. He looked uncomfortably around. There were *children* in here.

"Where does this divinely ordained love become lust?" Rickey asked. "At what point does it become sin?"

Rickey paused, straightened, frowned at the congregation. "I have tried, in these sermons, to relate the subject matter to our lives. It's good ole New Mexican, down-home lust I propose to discuss this morning." *You're all guilty*. That's what Loren read in his look. *I've got your number*.

"Sex becomes sin," Rickey said, "when it becomes an act of commerce. When it is an act of revenge. When it is forced. When it is an act performed in defiance of marriage; when it is performed as an *escape* from marriage; when it is done lightly, on impulse, without concern for precautions or safety; when it becomes an act of self-punishment; when it becomes a way of punishing someone else. When it becomes a way of raising yourself above someone else, particularly someone helpless, someone who is dependent on you . . ."

Rickey's voice was cutting. *I've got your number*. Fellow custodian of the town secrets, he wasn't about to let his parishioners off easy.

"Let me be more specific," Rickey said. Cold dread stirred in Loren's stomach.

His early adulteries had been impulsive, spur-of-the-moment things, old habits resurfacing. His later ones, during Debra's pregnancies, when they'd had to avoid sex if they wanted to keep the child, and after her miscarriages, when she had been too depressed to think about sex at all, had been deliberate, planned with care by someone who knew exactly how to keep a town from discovering a secret. Running away, as Rickey would have said, from marriage.

In a cold monotone Rickey anatomized Loren's sins with careful, ruthless precision. The parson seemed as driven as he had been the previous night. Loren stared at the pulpit, careful not to glance up at Rickey, afraid of meeting his eyes and giving the preacher confirmation of his guilt. His heart throbbed uneasily in his chest. He couldn't look at his family.

Rickey had his number, sure enough.

The service, subdued, staggered to its conclusion. "I didn't think sex was that complicated," Kelly said as they walked out. Loren, sweatily following, thanked the Lord for that.

"Good," he said at the doorway, shaking the parson's hand. "Real good."

"Thank you." Rickey's glance was sharp. Loren compelled himself to smile. The hot Mexican wind blew in his face.

My family life, he wanted to say, is perfect anymore.

And it was going to get *better*.

The park across from the church was empty: Roberts and his cult had not shown up.

"Chief." A well-known voice, a feminine singsong. "Chief, could I *talk* to you?"

Heart sinking, Loren turned to face Mrs. Caldwell.

Antonia Caldwell, the widow of a former councilman, was nothing if not a caricature, a small-town shrew whose energy and high-mindedness were matched only by her viciousness and capacity for turning ordinary gossip into something ugly and wounding. Loren loathed her, hated the soft-voiced singsong in which she delivered her bile; and he hadn't thought much of her husband, either.

Loren compelled himself to smile at her. "I'm sort of busy now, ma'am."

"It's official *business*, Chief." Mouth simpering, eyes glittering steel behind blue-tinted spectacles. Her voice was low, and Loren had to bend over her to hear her words over the hissing wind. "Surely you have time for official *business*."

Loren turned to his family. "I'll be right there."

"I think this is an *appropriate time*," Mrs. Caldwell sang, "to bring up the matter of *Connie Duvauchelle* and that *horrible house* of *ill repute*."

Lord, Loren thought. Not again. "There's a jurisdictional problem there," he said. "The ranch is out in the county. You could talk to the sheriff."

"I *have*. He says the ranch is part of the *city*." Her mouth twisted into a pursed smile. "I'm *sure* you can deal with *illegality* wherever you *find* it."

"There have been no complaints."

"But *I* am complaining *now*."

"But you've never *been* to the Wildfire Ranch, right?"

"I *would* not soil . . ."

"Then you have no official knowledge of what goes on there, do you?"

Mrs. Caldwell's eyes flashed. "*Every*one knows what goes on there."

"What everyone knows and what you can persuade a judge are different things, ma'am."

Mrs. Caldwell had ceased to smile. Her voice had ended its coy singsong. "All of this is just enough to make me wonder," she said, "if the rumors are true."

Loren had just had his sins anatomized by someone who, to his way of thinking, had the moral right to do it. He was not prepared to put up with it from someone who did not.

"I wouldn't know what rumors those would be, ma'am," he said.

They glared at each other for a few moments. Mrs. Caldwell broke the silence. "How they *let* that woman in the Rotary, I can't imagine."

Loren could imagine it perfectly well. He suppressed his smile. "I'll tell you what I'll do," he said, and grinned. "I'll go out there this morning. In person."

Mrs. Caldwell looked at him suspiciously. Loren smiled at her. *Got you now*, he thought.

"If I see anything illegal going on, I'll make arrests," he said.

The shrew considered this for a moment, could find nothing to object to. He was doing just what she asked, right?

"Well," she said. Her eyes narrowed as she looked at his chest. "I *see* you are still *wearing* the *Star* of *Baby*lon," she said.

"I'm afraid so."

"The *sight* will *com*fort Satanists, I'm sure."

"I haven't met any. I wouldn't know."

"*I* know who *they* are," she warned darkly.

I just bet you do, Loren thought. "I'll be right out to the ranch as soon as I change," he said, and smiled again. "Good talking to you, ma'am."

Just because her husband used to spend time there, he thought. He couldn't blame Caldwell: he had to get away from his misery somehow.

Maybe sometimes escape from marriage was justified.

His family were already in the Fury. Loren hitched his gun around to the front and got in the driver's seat. He looked at Jerry.

"Drop you off at the auto parts store?"

Jerry gave him a sour look. "Guess you might as well."

"What did the Horror from the Tomb want?" Katrina asked. Kelly laughed.

"Wanted to report a lawbreaker," Loren said. He started the car, pulled out onto Church Street.

"I remember when she was trying to get *Huckleberry Finn* and *Catcher in the Rye* banned from the school library."

"Catcher in the what?" asked Kelly.

"You were in sixth grade." Katrina pulled off her scarf. "Mrs. Caldwell thinks everybody but her are idiots."

"*Is* idiots," said Kelly. Her voice was smug. "'Everybody' is singular." She giggled. "Idiot." Katrina jabbed her with an elbow.

"An interesting sermon," Debra said. She was sitting behind Loren and her voice, like that of conscience, was unexpected.

Guilt scalded Loren's veins. He'd happily forgotten all of that. "Yeah," he said.

"I've rarely seen Rickey that passionate about anything."

The thought surprised Loren. "I hadn't thought about that."

There was something personal going on in that sermon, something driving Rickey. Was it, he wondered, some kind of confession? Had he been so ruthless because he was touched with what he condemned?

No doubt, Loren thought, he'd someday find out.

But he knew he didn't really want to.

The Wildfire Ranch was out behind Las Animas, right on the city-county border, down half a mile of gravel private road. The place was a dusty clump of mobile homes surrounded by chain link. Old auto tires, strewn atop the flat roofs of the house trailers, kept the roofs from tearing away in the wind.

Loren parked his car by the trailer labeled OFFICE. Memories echoed in his head. He hadn't been here in years.

He got out of the car and walked to the office door and banged on it. Wind whipped his hair into his face, little needlepricks on his forehead. When Buck, the latest in a long series of young bodybuilders who lived with Connie and acted as bouncer, opened the inner door, the aluminum screen door was almost torn from his hands. Buck fastened his massive grip on the door, looked at Loren, nodded, stepped back. Loren entered, looked at Buck, and wondered where she got them all.

Connie Duvauchelle stood in the foyer. She was an old woman, in her eighties or beyond, but her green eyes were bright and cold and missed nothing. She wore a bright red bouffant wig, crimson lipstick, and a Stewart tartan suit over flat-heeled house slippers. "You're early," she said. "Just come from church?"

"You were expecting me?"

"Tuesday is Lust Day down at the Apostles, right?" She had an eccentric southern voice, one that sometimes sounded Arkansas, sometimes almost English. "Sometimes thinking about it all morning gets the congregation all worked up. Hope your damn police car don't scare away my customers."

Loren sighed. "I'm here on a different kind of business, Connie. And I just heard Rickey's sermon, and I don't think it'll do your business any good."

"Come into my office." Loren followed Connie past Buck and through the parlor, where two sullen young women in lingerie were smoking cigarettes and watching a soap opera, a Mexican novela off the satellite, and then past the wet bar and into Connie's office. It had cheap paneling and was adorned with dozens of old photographs. The badge of the Rotary flaunted over the desk.

"Shut the door," Connie said. "You want some Southern Comfort?"

"No."

"Joined the gang of virtue, huh?"

"It's just early for me."

Connie poured herself a glass from the bottle in the lower right drawer of her desk and reached into a box for a hand-rolled cigarette. She lit it and sat down in a padded chair. The odor of the amaretto-flavored pipe tobacco she used in her cigarettes began to invade the room.

"It's early for *them*, too." Waving the cigarette toward her employees. "They're not used to early hours." She sipped her drink. "Stupid junkie bitches. Not like the old days."

Loren had heard all this before and had found it only moderately interesting the first time. "It's some of the old days I want to talk about, Connie," he said.

"The twenties and thirties were good times, Loren. During the Depression we gave a home to a lot of good women down on their luck. They gave the place a higher tone. And when the NRA came in, we did our bit for the economy." She cackled, then hacked a cough. "Raised the price of short-time from two dollars to three. Those were good days here in this town. The pit gave everybody a lot of money, even in the Depression."

If you wanted one of Connie's girls, you had to pay. If you wanted Connie's company, you had to pay in a different way—you sat in a growing cloud of sweet pipe tobacco while learning about the Golden Age of Prostitution, an era in which Loren was disinclined to believe. According to Connie, she'd been born to a high-class French-Creole hooker in a Storyville whorehouse and grown up there, then migrated West to seek her fortune when Storyville was shut down. Loren, curious, had once looked it up and found out that Storyville had been closed by the Navy during World War I.

The story wasn't true. Connie wasn't *that* damn old, and Loren suspected she'd never been within five hundred miles of New Orleans. That stuff about raising the price when the NRA came in had to be something she'd heard from older people in her line of work. She was creating herself a legend to live in, cloaking herself in a rose-hued past in which her life was glamorous, part of a glorious mythology.

Loren had asked around, and heard that Connie Duvauchelle had first shown up in Atocha during World War II, when she stepped into the management of Maybelline's, a classic gabled western palace of pleasure that sat by itself on a bluff north of town, with a player piano in the parlor downstairs, a billiard table in the lounge, red-flocked wallpaper, and brass spittoons. Connie's patron was supposed to have been Benjamin Siegel, better known as Bugsy. Among the innovations offered by Connie was her assistance to the morale of the local high school—after every winning game, the most valuable player on the team got his ashes hauled for free.

There had also been freebies to the winners of the Ringside smokers. Loren remembered the parties careening on forever, his relief and the endorphin high and victory champagne keeping the celebration rolling on past dawn. All the gamblers flinging their money around, the officials assuring him of his future with the police department. He wondered if there were still parties like that here.

The law got after Connie Duvauchelle in the 1960s, and she closed the old building, turning it into a restaurant called the Ore House, with photographs of naughty Edwardian nudes capering on the walls next to sepia images of nineteenth-century Atocha. It was a good restaurant. Families dined there after church. Prostitution was a quaint curiosity provided it happened a century ago, behind bead curtains and to the sound of a ragtime piano, a vice only if it was practiced today. Connie's status as a restaurant owner, massive donations to local charities, and a certain amount of discreet blackmail had made Connie a member of the Rotary.

Connie opened the Wildfire Ranch after closing Maybelline's. The enterprise was carefully situated on the city-county boundary, and Connie went on paying her graft to Luis Figueracion as per normal. The less flamboyant location—at least it didn't overlook the whole town—and the legal ambiguity concerning its location made her safe from the law. The Wildfire Ranch was officially a massage parlor. Her employees never stayed in town for very long, two months at the most before they were replaced by new girls. There was a kind of vice shuttle going on, run by what FBI bulletins on the subject referred to as "organized crime," that moved the women in and out. Connie paid her taxes, or at any rate some of them. And she kept other kinds of vice out—no gambling, no theft, no disease transmission. That was part of the deal cut with Luis Figueracion when Bugsy Seigel had moved her into town. And, other than what was necessary, she kept on good terms with the law.

"You wouldn't believe some of the girls I get now," Connie said. Tobacco smoke hung blue above her. "Third-generation junkies. They not only try to steal from the customers, but from *me*. They're too stupid to get away with much, but what can you do?"

"Those two." Loren jerked his head back toward the parlor. "Are they users?"

"One of 'em uses Dilaudid. The other does love beads." She tilted her head, looked at Loren through narrowed eyes. "Is that what this visit is about? Has their supplier been dealing in town?"

"Not that I know of. And if he sells in town, I'll bust him."

Connie gave a sneer. "If he sells in town, I'll let you know where you can find the son of a bitch. And I've told him that. He didn't like that much."

"I bet."

"I consider myself a good citizen." She paused, then peered at him. "So what's this about? You never come here for fun anymore."

"Antonia Caldwell lodged a complaint. So I came up here to see if anything illegal's going on."

Connie barked a smoky laugh. "Look around all you like!"

"I think I've seen all I need to."

"That Caldwell cunt. Just because her husband used to come up here for a little relaxation. And she *still* drove him to an early grave." She stubbed out her cigarette and took a sip of Comfort. "Now you're off duty, can you drink?"

"It's still too early. And I have a couple other things to ask you."

She reached for another cigarette. "Go on."

"You heard about my John Doe."

"Yep."

"Any strangers been through here?"

Connie shook her head. "Nobody but the regulars."

"Nobody waving guns around? Doing a little bragging?"

"Heh." A cold smile. "They wouldn't dare."

Loren, looking at the smile, believed it. "Mind if I ask your girls?"

"Suit yourself."

Loren took a breath. "Okay," he said. "Now here's the funny thing about the body—"

"He looked like Randal Dudenhof."

Surprise flickered through him. "You heard."

"I hear everything sooner or later."

"Who from?"

She flicked ash in the general direction of her Cinzano tray. "A customer."

"I guess it doesn't matter. The thing is—Randal used to hang around here a lot."

Connie's lip curled. "Tried to freeload a lot, you mean, after he lost his pocket money at poker. And he was a lousy tipper."

"How about the brother?"

"Did Randal have a brother? I don't remember."

"He was supposed to be gay. He moved West."

Connie shook her head. "I don't remember him at all. I don't think he came around."

"Did Randal get anyone pregnant?"

Connie seemed surprised. She picked a piece of tobacco from her lip and reflected. "You mean the John Doe might be his kid? Hadn't thought about that."

"I figured you'd know if anyone would."

She shook her head slowly. "I don't think so."

"It didn't have to be one of your girls. Maybe he came to you asking for help 'cause he got some girl pregnant . . . ?"

"Shit, Loren. Abortion was legal back then, remember? He didn't need me for that."

Loren shrugged. "I thought I'd ask."

"If I hear anything, I'll let you know." Connie sipped her Comfort again, leaving red lipstick on the glass. She got a bunch of keys from her jacket pocket, opened her desk drawer, took out a metal cash box.

"Collection day's tomorrow," she said, "but if you like, I can give you the department's share now."

Loren looked at the box and remembered the syndicate attorney at the arraignment Monday morning, the way he smoothed his gleaming hair with ringed fingers. Remembered who it was who shuttled Connie's girls in and out.

"I do not know what you are talking about," he said.

Connie looked at him cynically. "I remember your bagman days, Loren."

"Put the fucking box away, Connie."

Connie shrugged and returned the box to its drawer. "You sure changed, Loren. Since I took that picture up there."

Loren looked up and saw his face on the wall, grinning after one of his victories at the Ringside. His face was bruised, one eye puffy. Naked women stood, one on each side of him, and there was a champagne glass in his hand.

No guilt, he thought. I buried that guy.

There were other people on the walls as well. Benjamin Siegel, Virginia Hill, Mickey Cohen—people who had helped set her up in business. Sheriff Shorty Lazoya, the district attorney Castrejon, Loren's predecessor in the chief's job, members of the Figueracion family. A young, mustached Cipriano Dominguez, Judge Denver, a couple of governors, most of the town's mayors, state senators, a congressman, the longtime head of the state police. John Begley, his new patrolman, grinning from under his shock of blond hair, one arm around a redhead with a wicked smile, the other around a male friend Loren didn't recognize. Candid shots taken during parties, the men waving liquor glasses while women in various stages of undress cavorted alongside. None of them were hiding or covering their faces—Connie had a way of getting her subjects relaxed before bringing out her old Konica.

Connie knew how to stay in business, all right. Nobody on her wall was going to try to shut her down.

"You got a picture of William Patience?" he asked.

Connie snorted. "*That'll* be the day. That tight-ass jerk came in a year ago and offered me a reward of a hundred bucks to tell him if any of his men came for a visit."

"And what did you tell him?"

"I got Buck to throw his ass out of here."

"Discretion is your middle name, Connie."

"Damn straight." Spitting tobacco off her lip.

"Timothy Jernigan?"

"Never heard of him."

"Joseph Dielh."

She narrowed her eyes, cocked her head. "Why you asking?"

"I figure he knows something about John Doe, but isn't telling."

"He's a regular."

Loren waited. Connie took another drag on her cigarette, let it out. "Brags a lot," she said. "About his money, about how much he gets in grants. About how he's a big shot at the labs, going to win a Nobel, and about how great he is in bed—and he's not, I'm told. Pays with a Status Card. Complains about his ex-wife gouging him." She curled a crimson lip. "A typical john."

"Assholes always advertise."

Connie laughed, then coughed into a fist.

"Has Dielh been in lately?"

"Not since the middle of last week. He's overdue—he usually comes in at least twice a week."

"He may be out of town."

Connie shrugged and blew amaretto smoke. "Couldn't say."

"When he comes in, tell him I want to talk to him." That should jolt him, Loren figured.

Her eyes narrowed again. "I'll think about it."

Loren looked at her. "Cooperate, Connie. Somebody got killed. I'm not doing this for fun."

"I said I'll think about it."

An idea occurred to Loren. "How about Rickey, the pastor? You ever see him?"

Connie blinked in surprise. "No. What has he got to do with anything?"

"Nothing. I just heard his sermon on lust, and it wasn't exactly abstract. So it made me wonder."

"This is the age of AIDS, Loren. Explicitness is a virtue." She paused, Comfort halfway to her mouth. "Did my name come up?"

"Only from the Caldwell broad. Rickey wasn't as concrete as all that."

"Good." She sipped, then picked up a red business card out of a stack she had lying on her desk. Loren knew it had a silhouette of a black, winking cat on it and the words CATHOUSE: ADMIT ONE FREE. Connie held it out to Loren. "Want a freebie?"

He remembered the first time he'd come here, the sweaty red card in his hand, a birthday present from an older friend. He'd turned fifteen a month before, but it had taken him weeks to work up the nerve to take the drive to the ranch. In the end he decided he needed the experience; he thought his girlfriend was showing signs of wanting to go all the way and he wanted to know what to do if she did. The girl he picked wore straight blond hair and was dressed in a long print skirt and buckskin vest, Summer of Love fashion a few years late. The two of them shared a joint out in the trailer before she lit a stick of incense and got to business. The lesson had to be enjoyed for its own sake: his girlfriend dumped him a few days later.

"No," Loren said.

"You sure? It's been years, and you used to have a real taste for it."

Sixteen years precisely. Since Katrina was born. He'd seen his daughter in her cradle, the red-faced little miracle, and among the bright rush of sensations had been the thought that, when his girl grew up, he didn't want her knowing certain things about him. And the best way to ensure her ignorance was simply to quit.

"You were a real believer," the old lady said. "Like there was some kind of secret here, and you were gonna find it out."

"Maybe I figured out what it was," Loren said.

Smoke drifted out of her mouth as she spoke. "I doubt it."

He was somewhat surprised, in spite of his resolution, he wasn't in the least bit tempted. Whatever Connie's girls were, he thought, they were still someone's daughters.

"You could give it to your brother. I still see him from time to time."

"He can get his own damn card."

At least, Loren consoled himself, Jerry still maintained some contact with something approaching a normal human desire.

He stood up. The thick amaretto smoke was making him ill. "Thanks," he said. "I'll just ask your girls about Dielh."

Connie put the red card back in her pile. "Suit yourself."

The Mexican soap opera still yammered from the television, but one of the girls had gone, presumably with a customer. The other watched the novela without even a flicker in her eyes. No one home, Loren thought.

He asked his questions. She remembered Dielh, but didn't have anything to add to Connie's comments. Buck, polishing glasses behind the bar, didn't have much to say, either. Loren was trying to decide whether or not to wait for the second girl when the outside door banged open in the wind.

"Ése bato!"

It was Bob Sandoval, his unshaven face grinning from under his gimme cap. He had a bottle in a brown paper sack. Connie's other employee followed him, shrugging out of a down jacket.

"Hey, Chief," Sandoval said. "Can you give me a ride back to the Sunshine?"

"I guess," Loren said. "Would you mind waiting outside? I have to talk to people here."

"Sure, Chief." The old man waved the hand with the bottle in it. "See ya, Connie." He turned to his indifferent purchase. "Bye bye, dearie. It was nice."

He wandered out. Loren looked at Connie.

"Half my customers are over sixty," she said.

Loren thought about it. "Good for them," he decided.

"Their wives aren't interested anymore."

"If they ever were," said Sandoval's girl. Coldly, as she lit her cigarette.

She had nothing new to say about Dielh, so Loren said goodbye to Connie and Buck and left the trailer. Sandoval was sitting in the passenger seat of the Fury, swigging from his bottle. Loren got in and started the car.

"Where's your buddy?"

"He don't come very often. He's afraid his wife'll find out." He gave a dismissive growl. "Enculado," he said. Meaning a kept man, that being the local slur for someone faithful to his wife.

"You're not worried about your old lady?"

"I don't give a shit, ése. She ain't had nothing good to say to me for years, anyway."

I bet, Loren thought.

Loren pulled out of the parking lot and headed down the gravel drive. Windblown dust danced against his windshield.

"There was this guy in the Sunshine yesterday," Sandoval said. "He was asking about you."

Loren's nerves hummed alarm. "Yeah?" he said. "Who?"

"Said he was an investigator. Wore a suit. He said that he'd found out that a call had been made from the Sunshine on Saturday morning and he wanted to find out who'd made it."

Loren's mouth felt dry. A stone clunked against the Fury's floorboards.

"What did you tell him?"

"Didn't tell him shit, bro. Neither did Mark or Coover."

Loren turned to him. "Listen," he said. "That guy's poison. He works for a syndicate mouthpiece." *And he works fast*, Loren thought. Monday would have been the earliest he could have got access to the phone company records and backtracked that call.

"Man!" Sandoval said, impressed. "I thought he was a fed."

"He didn't show you a buzzer or anything?"

"A badge, you mean? Naw. Just said he was an investigator."

"He's working for Axelrod, the guy who's trying to get those drug dealers off."

"Chite! I should've asked him for money!"

Loren looked at him. Sandoval grinned. "Just kidding, ése."

"You better be."

Loren drove the old guy to town, mind buzzing. He was going to have a talk to Coover, get him to warn the old drunks himself. Then talk to Luis Figueracion, get the word out that Axelrod's man was in town, looking for witnesses.

Damn, he thought. This was getting too complicated.

THIRTEEN

Luis Figueracion sat before a patterned tin wall covered with yellowing election posters of FDR, Harry Truman, and John Kennedy. Loren had come to think of it as the Wall of Dead Democrats. Luis lit another cigarette, swept lank gray hair back off his forehead, looked at Loren over the rims of his glasses. "Patronage," he said. "That's what we lost. Things went to hell when we couldn't get a voter a job anymore."

"Yeah, Luis," Loren said.

The old man's eyes flashed through his thick spectacles. His hair flopped down on his forehead again. "They don't wanna let us take care of our own! God damn the civil service laws, anyway!" He brandished his cigarette. "That's why we got a Republican in City Hall. No patronage to keep the voters in line!"

Loren resigned himself to the fact that this was going to be his day for sitting with old people while they journeyed down Memory Lane. Luis leaned back in the creaking leather-padded chair that was probably as old as his Roosevelt poster. "This country went down the tubes," he said. "When the political machines stopped delivering. Not here." He stabbed his desk with a thick finger. "Not in Atocha County!" He smiled proudly. "Here we deliver. For over a hundred years, we've taken care of business."

Luis Figueracion took his job as patrón seriously. He spent his days dressed in baggy slacks and flannel shirt in a dusty old storefront office with creaking floorboards and flyspecked windows, and there he peered through his thick spectacles as he listened to complaints, settled disputes, and dealt out unofficial justice with the confident and undisputed authority of a Mafia chieftain. It was a job that ran in his family, and he did it well and with pride.

During the late eighteenth century the Figueracions had stolen title to a land grant in northern New Mexico, a theft achieved partly through adroit manipulation of colonial politics in Mexico City, partly through a bunch of Figueracions physically occupying the grant along with their families, their crossbows, and their guns. The land had remained theirs for three generations, only to be stolen again in the 1870s by the Catron Ring, which had a conclusive superiority in firepower and owned the local military commanders and the Republican judges, those being the only kind the state possessed. The title ended up by the end of the twentieth century in the hands of Mormon land developers from Utah, who cleared off indigenous sheepherders by running over their flocks with bulldozers and were now building vacation condominiums and blighting the environment as fast as their ever-expanding credit would permit.

The dispossessed Figueracions—those the Catron Ring left alive, anyway—poisoned the water sources on their old land in a final act of spite and went into the freighting business in Atocha County, their ox-drawn wagons bringing overpriced salt, flour, and mining equipment to prospectors, returning with two-hundred-pound crudely cast ingots of gold and silver. They also ran cattle over most of the county and bought protection from the Apaches by selling them antique, rusting, dangerous firearms and third-rate gunpowder, which had the multiple beneficent effect of making the Indians happy, militarily less effective than if they'd stuck to bows and arrows, and dependent on Figueracion commerce.

When the silver boom ended and Riga Brothers came looking for copper, they found the burned timbers of the abandoned Mexican diggings on the Figueracion Ranch. The Figueracions were happy to give them the surface rights to the Atocha pit in return for a political understanding: Riga Brothers ran the mine, the Figueracions ran everything else.

Now Riga Brothers was gone, and a Republican sat in City Hall. Luis considered the latter a greater threat.

"I'm gonna *smash* that son of a bitch!" he said. He drove his cigarette into the ashtray as if it were a stake into Edward Trujillo's heart. "Next mayoral election, this damn town's gonna be wallpapered with our posters! And no laid-off miner is gonna have any reason to love Edward Trujillo!"

"Trujillo's tight with ATL," Loren said.

Luis put a liver-spotted finger by his nose. "Most of them guys don't vote in Atocha. Trujillo'll be outflanked. He thinks he's the only man who can talk to company presidents? Shit, I can call up the president of Riga Brothers any day I want! And I dealt with a lot of ATL guys when they bought my land to put their plant on."

"It's not a plant," Loren said. "It doesn't manufacture anything."

Luis waved a dismissive hand. "No difference."

"There *is*. There's no one there to *talk* to. The guys who bought your land, they're off doing other things now, making acquisitions elsewhere probably. There's no one person that sets company policy—it's all this free-form information-age networking stuff. All they produce is knowledge, and they're a consortium, owned by other companies that have nothing to do with us."

"Crap. There's *always* someone to deal with."

"The only people who interact with our town are P.R. people, Luis. They don't want to help us out; they just want people to *think* they're helping us out. They'd just as soon we all went away."

"They'll deal. Everybody always deals." Luis stuck his nose in the air like FDR and smiled. "I got my irons in the fire. I'm not worried."

Loren looked at him. "I wish you were, Luis."

"Everyone deals. And Figueracion delivers. That's the rule here, and everybody knows it."

Loren felt his heart give a little tug. Trujillo had outmaneuvered Luis twice now, and all Luis did was sit in his office and wait for people to come to him. His power came from the people in the county who acknowledged his leadership, and those people were fewer every year. When the pit shut down, so did a lot of Luis's power base—all he had left was the prestige he had from being the largest rancher in the territory. And half the people who worked at ATL probably didn't eat red meat, anyway.

"You heard about this guy Axelrod?" Loren said.

"He and I done business once or twice."

Loren paused for a moment, then decided he didn't want to know. "He's defending Archuleta and Medina, the two drugrunners I popped the other day. And he's defending Robbie Cisneros, too."

"He'll lose." Luis seemed unconcerned.

"But he's gonna make us look bad. That's his only hope of winning."

A shrug. "What can he do?"

"First, he's going to challenge the warrant I got. It was an anonymous call, and he's going to try to prove it was me who made it." He cleared his throat. "Me or one of my men. And *then* . . ."

"Denver's the judge who gave you the warrant, right?" Luis squinted at him. "Fair and square, right?"

"Then he's gonna try to prove police brutality, because Robbie tried to escape and I had to hit him a few times."

"You hit him a few times." Luis repeated. He frowned. "Was it one of *them* escapes, Loren? I don't know how many times I've warned you about your temper."

Guilt raised hairs on the back of Loren's neck. He smoothed them back down and gave a deliberately weary sigh. "It doesn't fucking matter, Luis. The point is that he'd got some investigator wandering around town letting people think he's a fed, and if he ever gets around to passing out money, he'll get all the witnesses he needs."

Luis tapped thoughtful fingers on his little potbelly. "I dunno, Loren. People in this town are loyal to their own."

Loren figured he knew exactly how far to trust this statement. "All it takes is one rotten apple. And you know the Cisneros family."

Luis scratched his chin and said nothing. Loren kept talking.

"He's gonna try to smear the police, Luis. That's the only way he can win this case. And Medina and Archuleta are connected down in Mexico; he's gonna do everything he can to get those boys off."

"You think so. Man, I got all the judges their jobs. You think they're gonna listen for a minute to any of this shit?"

"Cases can be appealed. But think for a minute. You want some kind of reform movement started about the police and sheriff's department? That's half the patronage you have left."

Luis's calm face, over a period of several seconds, turned slowly to stone. "You got a point, Loren. I'll put the word out."

"Put the word out *now*. Before somebody does something stupid."

"I'll send it out with the mail tomorrow."

Loren's nerves tingled. He smoothed his nape hair down again. "About that mail, Luis."

"Yeah?"

"I don't think the mail should go out to the police tomorrow."

Luis cocked his glasses back on his long nose as if to study Loren more carefully. "Why d'you say that?"

"This investigator. He doesn't know anything about our life here. All he's looking for is dirt. And if he finds out the mail goes from your office to police headquarters every Wednesday . . ."

"I'll work out some other way."

"There's no other way that's safe. Other than to hold up the mail."

Luis's face twitched. "That's not how this county works. I do favors for people, other people do me favors. You do favors, I do favors, everybody does favors for everybody. And the mail goes through."

"You want to lose that last piece of patronage, Luis? That Axelrod is *smart*."

"Neither snow or sleet," said Luis in a singsong, "or gloom of night, shall keep the whatever-the-hell, the mail anyway, from going through." There was a goofy smile on his face.

"Just hold up the mail till after the trial, okay?"

"What are your boys gonna say about it?"

"I figure they'll work out the reasons for themselves. It's in their interest to understand. And it's not like it's anything but pocket change these days."

Luis scowled. "You think you're not getting enough, ése?"

"I didn't say that, Luis."

"This is how it *works*! Everybody gets his piece of the action and everybody gets to keep his job!" His voice turned to a roar, and he thumped a fist on his desk.

"I'm not complaining, Luis." Loren waved his hands.

"*My job is making people happy, God damn it!*"

"Will you listen to me?" Loren could feel his blood turning to steam. "I'm just saying that I don't want anything going on when that son of a bitch Axelrod is poking around!"

"Who got you your job, Loren?" Luis's face was purple. "Answer me that!"

"You did!" Loren shouted.

"I been sending you the mail for twenty years, and you say you're not grateful!"

Loren raised both fists, slammed them down on Luis's desk. "I'm grateful as shit!"

"You fucking well better be!" Luis put a hand over his heart. He fell silent and gasped for breath. His hair stuck out like a scarecrow's. Jesus Christ, Loren thought, he's gonna have a heart attack and die right here.

"I'm just asking you to hold up the mail," Loren said. He tried to keep his voice down but he knew he was still louder than he wanted to be. "That's all. Who the hell gets hurt?"

Luis shook his head, still gasping. "Not how it works, ése."

"Too many people know about the mail. Maybe Axelrod knows already, maybe he deals with the people who supply Connie Duvauchelle her girls."

"Connie's been around. Connie knows what's what."

"She offered me cash this morning. Right in her office. For all I know there was a wire in there."

Luis's face did that slow transformation again, angry red-faced geezer to stone statue. "That's interesting," he said.

"There could be some guy in a car outside this office, listening to us with a rifle mic. Or maybe he's bouncing a laser off your storefront window so he can listen to the backscatter and find out where the mail's going."

Luis's eyes flickered. He didn't look out the window. "Is that possible?"

"Hell, yes. That's why I want to hold up the mail."

Luis gave a nod. Dead Democrats approved his sentiments from the wall behind him. "Okay. But you explain it to your people, okay?"

"Fine."

"And otherwise nothing's changed."

"Yeah."

"Join me for lunch?"

Loren rose from his chair. "I got a murderer to catch."

A smile twitched across Luis's face. "Go get 'em, killer."

257

"Yeah."

Loren stepped from the office and blinked in the sunshine. The hot wind tore at his hair. He put his shades on and somehow was reluctant to get in the car and drive off. Thinking about it now, he couldn't tell how serious he'd been about the laser mic, whether it was a fantasy he used to snow Luis or whether he was really as paranoid as he wanted Luis to believe.

He thought about how John Doe's body had disappeared. If that wasn't reason enough for paranoia . . .

He looked across the street, saw no mysterious operatives in dark sedans. He glanced up at the power poles, saw no apparatus that shouldn't have been there.

He thought about Connie Duvauchelle offering him money in her office and his nerves sang a little warning. Best to be cautious.

Had he really gone to Pastor Rickey the night before babbling about miracles? If anyone found out about it, he was in a world of shit. That had been a perfectly crazy thing to do.

So, he concluded, was standing here in the blowing dust. He got in the Fury and drove to the Sunshine for lunch.

He checked his rearview mirror every few seconds. When the ATL jeep pulled out of a side street and began to follow, there was a part of his mind that wasn't surprised.

There was a shiny rented pickup truck parked in front of the Sunshine with a dead elk in it. The man who had shot it was inside drinking Coover's greasy coffee. He wasn't dressed like a hunter—he even wore a knit tie beneath his L.L. Bean goose-down vest. He had paid twelve thousand bucks for the privilege of walking into a stock pen, raising a state-of-the-art Perugini-Visini nylon-stocked hunting rifle with a hunter-killer laser sight featuring IR and night-enhancement options, and there shooting an elderly, tame elk at point-blank range, all for the purpose of using the head and rack of horns to impress the hell out of his golfing buddies.

At least, unlike the Chinese and Koreans, he probably didn't intend to eat the horns and drink the blood.

The sight of this distinguished sportsman did not put Loren in a good mood. More annoying were Bob Sandoval and Mark Byrne, who rolled their eyes at each other and winked broadly while they jabbered witlessly about anonymous calls and pretended to pass drug money back and forth under the counter. Loren told them and Coover that the investigator that had approached them yesterday worked for a syndicate lawyer who was out to hang every cop in Atocha County and that anyone who talked to him had better find a new place to live. Then he ate his burger and left.

A five-ton truck filled with velvet elk antlers was maneuvering into a parking space across the street. Two Asian men were inside. As they got out, Loren saw that the white shirt of one was stained with blood.

The ATL jeep was parked on West Plaza. Ray-Bans followed him past the deco griffins into the City-County Building.

Eloy was on the phone as Loren boomed through the glass doors; he waved frantically as Loren approached him and put his call on hold. He held out a thick wad of message slips.

"Lots of calls for you, Chief. Cantwell, Castrejon, Lowrey, Axelrod."

"Axelrod?" Loren flipped through message slips written on coarse recycled paper. "What's the shyster want?"

Eloy gave him a dubious look. "He probably wants to complain about the missing page in the logbook."

Loren almost grinned but caught himself in time. "What missing page is that?" Feigning casualness, flipping through his messages.

"He sent one of his investigators here to subpoena our records about that anonymous tip."

"You don't say."

"I gave him the logbook, left the desk, and went to the toilet," Eloy said. "When I got back, the guy said the page had been torn out."

Loren looked at him over the message slips. "You think he tore it out himself?"

Eloy tilted his torso back to smile at Loren over his neck brace. "I was on the shitter, of course. But I think a case can be made."

"Good."

"I missed the page yesterday. That's why I went to the can when I did, so I couldn't say whether he took it or not."

Loren looked at Eloy, impressed. Maybe the man's brains weren't scrambled, after all. "Very good," he said. "Any call from the OMI?"

"Nada. You got any idea why someone would take our stiff?"

None he wanted to speak out loud, anyway. "Beats me, ése," he said.

The phone rang. Eloy gestured for Loren to remain, answered the line, put the caller on hold.

"They've been calling all morning. John Doe ended up on the Child Support Net."

"Why?" Loren was surprised.

"Lots of guys have run off and left their wives and kids in the lurch. If Doe's their boy, maybe they can get insurance or more public assistance or something."

"Jesus. I hadn't thought about that." A vision flashed before his eyes, tens of thousands of hard-bitten women in faded maternity clothes, snot-nosed kids in striped T-shirts that didn't quite cover their navels, all sitting in fleabag apartments or tin-walled house trailers, praying for Daddy's death.

"Any luck?" Loren asked.

"Not really. Anyway, I wanted to tell you—Lowrey *really* wants to talk to you."

"I'll call her right back."

"She's out running. Wait till after one."

"There was something I needed to tell you." Loren cleared his throat, suddenly uncomfortable. "The Wednesday mail—it isn't coming tomorrow."

Eloy blinked. "It got delayed or something?"

"No. It's gonna be held up until Axelrod and his investigator stop poking around."

"Oh." Eloy seemed to want to know what to think about this.

"We don't want them knowing about it. They'd hang us up by our balls."

Eloy's eyes flickered. "Okay."

"The mail's just being held at the post office. You'll get all your letters."

"Okay."

"What I need is for you to tell everybody going on swing shift, then all the guys coming off shift."

"Okay."

Loren had about had it with this passive response, this long chorus of "okays."

"It's not my fault, God damn it!" he said. "Blame the shyster, not me!"

Eloy tilted his braced body back in his chair and looked at him. "I got some ladies on hold, Chief."

"Right."

Loren moved down to his office. A lousy fifteen bucks, he thought. That's what Eloy's take amounts to. What, he couldn't live without it for a while? At least he had a job. In this town, that was something.

The anger faded as soon as Loren entered his office. Guilt began to throb in his temples. If he hadn't beat up Robbie Cisneros, Eloy wouldn't have had to cover for him, and Axelrod wouldn't have any ammunition to use on him.

Still. It wasn't as if Robbie didn't deserve it.

Neither, however, did Eloy.

Loren decided not to think about it any more. He booted his computer and used the LAWSAT antenna to connect himself with FBI LAWNET, a bulletin-board service run by the feds in Washington. It featured chitchat on various law enforcement topics, as well as services where you could ask questions of various experts, chief of whom was a free-lance criminalistics expert who called himself "Dr. Zarkov" and who advertised that he was "the East Coast's foremost expert on blood spatters, patterns, and the velocity of blood in flight." All no doubt of fascination to some.

Loren bypassed all that and went to the data library on firearms. He looked up the Tanfoglio TZ-M and discovered that it was, as Patience had said, an Italian version—the file called it a "near copy"—of a 9mm Czech military sidearm. He then moved to another section on .41-caliber weapons. The list was not very extensive.

He scrolled down the list, looking for a barrel with five lands and grooves and a right-hand twist—it was most of them. And then his eyes lit on something in the "Descriptions" section and a cold hand touched the back of his neck.

A company called U.S. Military Sidearms, it said here, made a .41-caliber replacement barrel for the Tanfoglio.

Loren looked at the screen for a long moment and felt his mouth go dry. He wrote down the information in his notebook and logged off.

Where do we go from here? he wondered.

He picked up the phone and called Oliver Cantwell at the number given on his message slip.

Cantwell was an attorney and had been a year behind Loren in high school. The two of them had hung together when young, driving fast cars, roaring from one place to another along the Line, heading to Connie Duvauchelle's on occasion or taking their girlfriends out to the hot springs on the rez . . .

Years ago. Nowadays Loren didn't see Cantwell much except in court, but Loren figured they were still friends.

"Who's this Sondra Jernigan cooze?" Cantwell demanded.

A little hum of triumph sounded in Loren's nerves. "Why do you ask?" he said.

"Because she's been calling every *other* attorney in town asking about me. It seems you mentioned my name, and she wants to make sure she isn't being sandbagged."

Loren restrained the impulse to shout hallelujah. "Have you heard from her yourself?"

"Yeah. She and her husband are coming in at four-thirty."

"Good."

"This ain't some kind of divorce matter, is it?"

"Nope. I think they're just in over their heads on something."

"Can you give me a hint?"

"I was just about to. I think they know something about the John Doe that got killed here a few days ago. He was shot in Mr. Jernigan's car."

"Ah."

"My working hypothesis is that they didn't have anything to do with the shooting, but that they know more than they're telling."

"Yes."

"Tell 'em that whatever it is they were doing, I'm not interested in prosecuting for that. I just want the shooter."

"You can't give guarantees like that. I'll have to talk to Castrejon."

"Talk to him. I think he'll agree in return for a chance to put away an honest-to-God murderer."

"I'll talk to this Jernigan guy first."

"I doubt he's done anything serious. But I don't think he's got much connection to the real world, so he might think that whatever he's done is a lot worse than it is."

After Loren hung up he felt like dancing. Things were finally starting to look up.

He was dealing with paperwork when Sheila Lowrey knocked on his door. She had just finished her run and was wearing shorts, Nikes, and a T-shirt that said CASTRATING BITCH. There was a Diet Coke in her hand.

"Can we talk?"

"I was just going to call you. Sit down."

Breathing hard, Sheila took a chair, pressed the chilled soda can to her sweating forehead, then her upper sternum.

"Axelrod's going crazy on the missing log sheet," she said.

Loren shrugged. "His own guy probably stole it."

She looked at him, held his eyes. "Do you believe that?"

"Doesn't matter what I believe," Loren said. "It matters what can be proved to the satisfaction of the judge."

She opened the Diet Coke and took a long drink. Loren watched her little Adam's apple bob up and down as she swallowed. She sighed, lowered the Coke, looked at Loren.

"Axelrod's doctor saw Robbie Cisneros. My best indication is that they took some very good photographs of the damage done to him, including the raw stripes around his wrists that would seem to support the theory that he was wearing handcuffs when he was damaged."

"He went berserk when I put the cuffs on him. That was in my report."

"Berserk enough to be hit a minimum of fourteen times with the butt of a rifle? That's what's on the report from the emergency-room doctor, I might add. God only knows what Axelrod's doctor would have found."

"It was a shotgun. And it happens."

She looked at him levelly. "I'm going to advise Castrejon to plea-bargain."

"Don't do that, Sheila."

"They'll still be found guilty of most of the charges."

"Don't do it, dammit!" Rage burned through him. "Robbie's a fucking traitor to the town!"

She stood up, took another drink of her Coke. "It's up to the D.A. But I'll tell him what I'll tell him. Which you might well consider the next time you're tempted to hit a suspect fourteen times with a shotgun."

Loren watched her leave and wanted badly to break something in half with his bare hands, very possibly Sheila's spine. Instead he went back to his paperwork, jabbing his mechanical pencil so hard into the blotter that the lead snapped off. He threw the silver thing across the room.

Right on cue, the mayor came in.

"Loren?" Pretending he hadn't seen the pencil go flying. "I left you a message."

"I was just going to call you. I figured you were out for lunch."

"I had a pita sandwich in my office."

Trujillo sat down without being invited, tugging at the knees of his tan corduroy slacks. "We need to talk," he said. "I've been getting complaints."

"Who from?"

The mayor's mouth gave a little twitch. "It doesn't matter. But there have been complaints as regards your behavior on this John Doe murder."

Loren vented a contemptuous laugh. "What do you mean?"

"I've been told that you're wandering around Vista Linda harassing people."

"I've been knocking on their front doors and asking if they've seen anyone who might have committed a murder. That's harassment?"

Trujillo licked his lips. "I want you to lay off the ATL employees. I'm involved in negotiations that have reached a delicate stage."

Loren leaned back in his chair. "I don't give much of a damn, Ed. I'll conduct the investigation as I see fit."

"Be reasonable, Loren."

"I'm being perfectly reasonable. *My* question is, who've you been talking to and why is he so concerned about the murder of some nobody?"

Trujillo's lips thinned. "I am ordering you to lay off any investigation outside of this jurisdiction. It's absurd to be wasting department resources for an investigation of someone who hasn't even been identified."

"Who've you been talking to, Ed? Over at ATL."

"It doesn't matter!"

"How do you know he's not a killer?"

"Don't be absurd." Trujillo stood. There was a steady little twitch in his thigh. "Will you follow my directive or not?"

Loren looked at him. "Elisa Hawking," he said.

Trujillo looked abruptly away. The twitch was making his knee tremble. "It wasn't what it looked like," he said.

Loren smiled up at him, savoring the moment. "It looked like you porking the baby-sitter in the front seat of your LTD. That's what it looked like."

"God damn it!" Trujillo stuck his hands in his pockets and began to pace. He looked over his shoulder at Loren. "It was just a little slip. I'd been drinking that night."

"She was fifteen, Ed."

"She didn't say no."

"I doubt you gave her much chance. And anyway the law doesn't much care."

Trujillo approached Loren's desk. "Look," he said, "I appreciate what you did. Not telling anybody."

"And I appreciate your not interfering in department business, Ed. And submitting budgets that don't make me lay off any more of my people."

"I've got a press conference tomorrow." Trujillo's words came rapidly. "ATL is going to announce the sponsorship of a museum of high technology. Three-D holo theater, the works. Here in town."

"Good for them."

"It may help to save our economy. This is a three-million-dollar project! But I can't let it be jeopardized by bad relations between ATL and the town."

"I don't have any bad relations with ATL."

Trujillo paused, took a breath, let it out. "I'm glad to hear you say that, Loren."

"But I'm going to conduct a murder investigation the way I see fit."

"You'll never get her to talk!" Trujillo exploded. "If she hasn't complained by now, she won't ever!"

Loren looked at him again. "If I have a little chat with her, Elisa will talk. She doesn't have the brains not to. She'll sing like goddamn Joan Sutherland."

Trujillo stared at him a moment. His face was drained of color. Then the mayor turned and left the office.

Win some, Loren thought, lose some. Thinking of his last two visits.

He decided to win two out of three.

He got out of his chair and walked from his office and past Eloy's desk and down the foyer to the glass doors. He went through the doors and past the griffins and across West Plaza to where the chocolate-brown Blazer waited.

There was only one person inside, a thin-lipped thirtyish man with short black hair slicked back from his forehead. Hiding behind his Ray-Bans. He didn't show any surprise when Loren knocked on his window. He rolled down the glass.

"Yes?"

"I'm the chief of police," Loren said.

"I know."

"You're under arrest."

There was, to Loren's ultimate satisfaction, surprise on the goon's face. "What for?" he asked.

"Carrying automatic weapons. There's a city ordinance against it."

"Bullshit!"

Loren opened the door, gestured with his hand. "Out of the car," he said. "And don't do anything to make me nervous."

When somebody pushed, Loren thought as he handcuffed the man and marched him across the street, you pushed back.

It only stood to reason.

The goon's name was Vincent Nazzarett. He wouldn't give the combination to unlock the UZIs, so Loren had to bring in someone in with a torch. It took a full twenty minutes to cut through the retaining rod and liberate the guns.

While that was going on, Loren ordered his patrolmen to bust every other ATL vehicle in town. It turned out there was only one. Two more bewildered company goons were added to the lockup, and two more UZIs were cut free. It was only after the guns were cut free that Loren realized that he might have just pressed the same number's he'd used while visiting the labs, that Patience might not have got around to changing the combination.

Nazzarett tested positive on the Shibano test for gunpowder residue on his hands. "I went to the company range and fired off fifty rounds on Sunday," he said. "What about it?"

"Did anyone see you?" Loren asked.

It seemed for a moment that Nazzarett didn't have an answer for that one. "It's of no relevance," he said.

The other two tested negative.

It was almost three-thirty, over two hours, before William Patience showed up to bail his men out. His eyes were ice and his face was so taut that his cheekbones were sharp as flint.

"You've really fucked up this time," he said to Loren. Loren had followed him downstairs into the jail, watched him hand his company credit card through the bars to Ed Ross, the jailer.

"Seems like you forgot to tell me something. You forgot to tell me that U.S. Military Sidearms makes a .41-caliber barrel for the Tanfoglio."

Patience's narrow eyes flickered. "This is the first I've heard of it."

"Seems to me I told you not to bring automatic weapons into my town."

Patience turned to him. "This ends my cooperation in any investigation. If you want any documents from me in the future, you can subpoena them."

"Answer me a question. Did you tell Nazzarett to follow me around? Or did someone give *you* an order?"

Patience's lips twitched back from his teeth, like he wanted to snarl but didn't quite allow himself the satisfaction. "I'm not cooperating anymore, remember? So take your tin-pot small-town badge and shove it."

"Shove it yourself. If you think you can."

There was a brief magnesium flare in Patience's eyes. His hands, holding Ed Ross's paperwork, tightened. Loren felt readiness filling him, licking his nerves with little flaming tongues. In another few seconds, William Patience was going to need plastic surgery.

Patience let the air in his lungs hiss out, turned away, and hunched down over his paperwork. Loren felt a little rush of disappointment.

Pity. It would have been interesting.

Edward Trujillo was waiting upstairs for Patience to emerge. The two of them walked out together, down the long white-tiled corridor. Loren watched them from next to the front desk and had the feeling that Trujillo was apologizing. He became aware of Cipriano standing next to him.

"I dunno, jefe," Cipriano said.

"Dunno what, pachuco?"

"I dunno if that was wise."

Loren looked at him. "Fuck wisdom."

Cipriano frowned and gazed toward the mayor. Loren looked at Patience, then turned to Cipriano. "The guy who told you about the cows," Loren said. "Who is he?"

"What?" Distracted.

"The cows that got through the fence at ATL. Who told you about that?"

"That was Begley. He goes hunting with one of the ATL people."

"Is Begley on duty?"

"Swing shift, I think."

"What else did he tell you?"

Cipriano looked at Loren, his face screwed up in thought. "I don't remember what all, jefe. I wasn't paying a whole lot of attention. All I remember is this thing about Patience."

"What about him?"

"He pretends to be this big Special Forces covert operations guy. But Begley's friend got a look at his actual army record. Patience broke a leg in training and never did anything."

Loren stared at him. "He told me he went into Armenia!"

"The team he trained with did. But Patience was laid up in the base hospital with a compound fracture."

Cold mirth waltzed through Loren. He looked at Patience again and grinned. "You should see his office. It's a goddamn shrine to Armenia. Flag, carpets, pictures of his special-ops unit."

"Guess he wishes he'd gone."

"It's more than that. It's pathological. The guy's a nut case."

"Could be, jefe."

Feeling buoyed, Loren went back to his office and opened the big nineteenth-century walk-in safe where he kept evidence. A musty marijuana scent wafted out, a reminder of all the years he'd kept contraband there. Four submachine pistols were sitting on the top shelf, each in a plastic bag and tagged with the name of the violator. Below was the sawed-off and the pot he'd seized from Robbie Cisneros. The Ingram Mac-11 was bagged on another shelf, along with the other weapons taken from the Mexican couriers.

Evidence of an interesting week.

Out of the corner of his eye he saw the video viewer that he kept in the safe to keep people from fooling with it. He took it out, put it on his desk, and got the disk from the file with Saturday's date and the name of John Doe, the video that Eloy had shot of the crime scene.

The quality of the video wasn't very good. The blood was redder than it had been in real life and the skin of the corpse was jaundiced.

It was still Randal Dudenhof. Even in the video, that was clear.

A warm fist closed around Loren's heart. He found himself whispering to himself, words just coming to the surface. He realized he had no idea what it was he was saying, but that he knew he was praying.

There was a knock on the door. Loren looked up and saw Eloy.

"Big accident, Chief. The maglev hit a truck on the Rio Seco bridge."

Even as he absorbed the words, as his nerves sparked and his pulse began to race, he knew what had happened.

And he knew who'd been on the train.

F O U R T E E N

Velvet elk antlers, hundreds of them, littered the bottom of the Rio Seco, scattered like shrapnel on the brown sand. The maglev train dangled off the bridge, the lead car crushed like a beer can under a fat man's foot. One of Sam Torrey's five-ton trucks had been parked on the ATL side of the railroad bridge and the train had plowed right into it. The truck had split in half and tumbled into the arroyo, somehow without catching fire.

Loren had to park his car on the auto bridge, next to an expectant volunteer fire truck, and walk the quarter mile to the wreck along the edge of the arroyo. Once there, there wasn't much he could do. Sheriff's deputies were already at work with the jaws of life, trying to extricate something or someone from the first car.

Pointless, Loren thought. Even if the guy hadn't been crushed, he'd been bounced around the interior of the train at close to two hundred miles per hour.

Some of Patience's men were standing around, jabbering into walkie-talkies, looking self-important in their suits and shades and otherwise contributing nothing. Hot wind traced swirls of dust in the air. Loren looked at them and felt a ghostly hand brush his spine.

Which of them had done it? Which of them knew?

Loren hitched up his gun, approached the bridge, and carefully slid down the steep slope of the concrete abutment and into the arroyo. He hit bottom and a little jolt of pain went up his back.

The train, partly hanging over him, seemed enormous, far larger than when he had actually ridden in it. The gray-on-red ATL symbol hovered in the air. There was a strange burning-plastic smell: parts of the train had been heated on impact and partly melted. Shattered polycarbon struts had fired black splinters into the walls of the arroyo. Loren slogged to where the sheriff's deputies were trying to cut into the front car. A carpet of glass shards below Loren's feet reflected the diamond-hard light of the high desert. Directing operations was Shorty Lazoya's brother Ramón, another tall man, potbellied, not as frail or myopic as his older brother.

"How many?" Loren asked.

"At least one. We can't really tell. ATL says not many, because the shift hadn't ended yet."

"Got any ID?"

"Not yet. All we can see in that mess is an arm and some bits of clothing."

"No pulse in the arm, right? Shit." Loren looked over his shoulder at one of Patience's men, standing silhouetted on the edge of the arroyo.

"We didn't find anyone in the truck," Ramón said.

"I didn't think you would. Who was first on the scene?"

"Some of the ATL guys."

"Which ones?"

Ramón shrugged. "I don't know."

Loren looked over his shoulder again. Patience had been late bailing his men out of jail: that meant he had been setting this up. They would have had to steal Torrey's truck, bring it here, drive it across the desert to park it across the tracks. Presumably they would have also had to disable some sensors on the bridge so as not to trigger the automatic safeties that would have ordered the train to brake.

That would have taken hours. Which meant this wasn't a reaction to Loren's arrest of Patience's men: this had been planned in advance.

He wondered how Patience had made John Doe's body disappear.

Patience had to have known that Jernigan was going to see Oliver Cantwell. And he would have known that Jernigan was taking the maglev to work, since his BMW couldn't have been cleaned yet.

"We're in." The deputy crawling out of the wrecked car looked a little green.

"Let me see," Loren said. "I think I know this guy."

"Be my guest."

Loren bent to peer into the hole the cutters had made. He knew he'd have to be careful of the sharp bright edges of metal left by the cutters.

The metallic smell of death came from inside. Loren remembered the stench hitting him in the face as blood fountained from Randal Dudenhof's mouth. The T-bird had crashed just a quarter mile from here, plunging off the auto bridge.

Many years ago. But the smell was the same.

Wary of sharp edges and broken glass, Loren carefully inserted his upper body into the hole. The interior seats had been jammed together but hadn't broken. Two of the seats were tilted so as to be braced against one another and form a tunnel. Loren could see an arm in a blue wool jacket propped on the end of the seat. A large gold cuff link closed a white cuff with a subdued red stripe. Loren put his weight on his elbows and shimmied forward.

The arm was not attached to a body. The smell was very bad. The person to whom the arm had once been attached was about four feet away, sandwiched between his seat and a razor-edged tangle of metal. The face was covered with blood and Loren had to look at it a long time before he recognized it.

Loren backed out of the tunnel dragging the arm behind him. He dropped it onto a white plastic body bag that the Bag 'n' Drag had already laid out on a stretcher.

"His name is Vlasic," Loren said. He took in air, let it go. "He's a physicist. He liked to ride the train back and forth because it helped him think."

Ramón got out his notebook and frowned into it. "How d'you spell it?"

"Don't know." The hydraulic cutters went back to work.

The dangling train made crackling noises as it swayed slightly in the wind. Loren kept looking up to see the ATL people standing silhouetted on the edge of the arroyo. Hopelessness oppressed him. He knew he needed to do something, but he couldn't think what.

272

He looked up as Cipriano slid into the arroyo, his heels leaving black marks on the slanted white concrete of the abutment. "I talked to Sam Torrey," Cipriano said. "He didn't know his truck was missing till I told him. They finished cropping the antlers this morning and just left the truck sitting out by one of their pens. It was out of sight of the main building, and anyone could have taken it."

"We'll dust for fingerprints," Ramón said.

Vlasic's body was carried out, laid in the body bag, zipped out of sight. There was a hydraulic hiss, then a crash as the cutters chopped out a big piece of metal.

"Oh, man," said a deputy. "Number two." He turned and, with an air of mild concern, vomited cleanly onto the sand.

Loren walked around the hanging car and saw Timothy Jernigan's bearded head resting on the ragged silver piece of metal that had decapitated him. It hadn't sliced cleanly but at an angle, and one ear and part of a jaw were gone. Jernigan's lip was curled in an uncharacteristic sneer of defiance. The rest of the body was not visible, and not likely to be for some time. The metal here was crumpled like an old piece of newspaper.

"Recognize him?" Ramón asked.

"Never seen him before," Loren said. His heart was pounding in his chest. Urging him to run.

Loren turned and walked over the antler-strewn sand to the concrete abutment. His shoes made frantic scraping noises as he scrambled up it, sounds like the pawing of a trapped animal. He made it to the top and stood for a moment, trying to catch his breath.

"Jefe?" Cipriano's voice. "You going someplace?"

Loren turned and looked down at him. "Not much to be done here," he said.

Cipriano looked dubious. "You want me to hang around and, you know, look after stuff?"

Meaning, Loren knew, keep the sheriff's posse from hopelessly fucking up any evidence.

Loren didn't think there was going to be any evidence.

Well. Maybe there'd be something in Jernigan's briefcase.

"Fine," Loren said. "Do that. I'll be in touch."

Loren began the walk back to his car. William Patience stood on the brink of the arroyo, his face impassive behind his Ray-Bans. Nazzarett stood with him, arms folded, his jaw working on a piece of gum.

Loren passed them by without saying anything. He could feel Patience's contemptuous gaze on the back of his head. Probably Patience thought he was running from the sight of blood.

Maybe he was.

He got in his car and drove to Vista Linda. Besides a couple of chained bicycles, the Jernigans' other car, the New Yorker, was the only vehicle in the maglev parking lot. Sondra Jernigan sat behind the driver's seat, waiting. Loren parked next to her and saw her sour look of distaste as she looked at him. He knocked on her window. She rolled it down, blinking as the hot wind blew grit in her face. She was wearing a gray suit, ready to visit the lawyer.

"Mrs. Jernigan?"

"What do you want?" The voice was hostile.

"I've got some news for you. About your husband. Can I get in the passenger seat?"

She looked at him coldly while weighing her decision, then decided she was tired of having dust blown in her face, closed the window, leaned across to open the passenger door. Loren walked around the car, opened the door, hitched his gun around, and sat.

Sondra Jernigan was looking at him. One finger tapped impatiently on the steering wheel.

Get it over with, Loren thought.

"There's been a crash on the maglev," he said. "I'm sorry to tell you this, but your husband has been killed."

She stared at him as if he'd just made a joke in ghastly taste. Loren could smell her expensive perfume.

"Do you understand what I just told you?" he asked.

Her eyes flickered away, then back. "Are you sure?"

"Yes. I've just come from the site."

She looked away again. She shifted her body to face squarely forward in the car, put both hands on the wheel. Ready to drive away.

"They said there were so many safety devices," she said. Her voice trailed away.

"It was sabotage," Loren said. "Mr. Jernigan was murdered."

Her expression didn't change. Her blunt fingers slid lightly up and down the steering wheel. Mentally driving away from it all.

"I think someone wanted to stop him from talking about the murder the other day. They must have known he was going to talk to a lawyer."

She didn't think to ask him how he knew. She turned toward him. "Somebody . . . killed him?"

"Another man died, a man named Vlasic who happened to be on the train. The saboteurs didn't care who got killed, so long as Mr. Jernigan was stopped."

Sondra Jernigan considered this. "Vlasic? Kazimierz Vlasic?"

"I guess."

She sighed, looked away again. "Poor man." Said in a small voice.

"Can you help me, Mrs. Jernigan?"

She didn't answer. Loren's mouth was dry. He tried to summon saliva, then words.

"Can you help me, Mrs. Jernigan? Can you tell me about the man who was killed the other day?"

She didn't say anything, just looked forward at the little train stop. As if she were expecting the maglev any second. A fat tear rolled out of her eye, traveled unnoticed down her face, fell with a pattering sound onto her suit jacket. She gave a long, extended sigh.

"It happened at the lab," she said. "Tim wouldn't tell me any of the details."

"What did he tell you?"

Another long, long sigh, breath hissing out of her till there was none left. For a moment she forgot to breathe at all, then she took in air. Slowly, the same way she'd let it out. "He was scared. That's all I knew. He said that the cover story, the story about the car being stolen from out of the driveway, that the security people at the labs invented that. It didn't happen." She looked at him. Tears tracked down her face, streaked her gray suit. "He's really dead?"

"I'm afraid so."

"He was going to talk to the lawyer."

"I know. That's why they killed him."

If he kept repeating it, maybe it would make sense to her.

"What else did he tell you?"

"Just that he was scared. That you'd scared him. I don't know much else. He spent Saturday morning and afternoon, and Sunday too, on the phone in his study. And last night, too, after he came home from work."

"Do you know who he was talking to?" He'd have to check the phone company.

"No. Except that I—I heard an argument on the phone with Dielh."

"Joseph Dielh."

"Yes." She licked her lips, tasted her own tears, seemed vaguely surprised.

"Is Dielh in town?"

She shook her head. "He's in D.C. Tim was on the phone with him. Tim was in his study, though, and I didn't hear the words. The door was shut. I just heard him raising his voice." She took a long breath, let it out again in another long, long sigh.

"Can you remember anything?"

"No. Yes." She blinked tears. Her voice had a little whimper in it. "He said that something—the t-thing—was sym—symmetric?—in the calculations. No, in the equations."

"Do you know what that means?"

"No. It wasn't t-thing, it was something else. T-axis. I only remember it because he kept repeating it."

"Can you remember the exact words?"

She screwed up her eyes as she tried to remember. Tears fell. " 'The t-axis is symmetric in the calculations.' No, in the equations. Then he repeated the word 'symmetric' several times. And he said, 'We didn't appreciate that.' " And—and—" She reached in her jacket pocket for a tissue, found one, wiped tears away. A keening sound broke from her.

"What else?"

"He just kept saying, 'We didn't appreciate it.' " She keened again, holding the tissue to her face. "I'm sorry," she said. "I'm really sorry."

Everything she had told him, Loren realized, was hearsay. Inadmissible. Unless it could be read as a dying declaration, and a friendly judge conceivably could rule favorably in that instance.

Still. It confirmed things.

"Did he have any paperwork at home that might have anything to do with this?"

"Maybe on the computer." Wailing.

"May I see it? Can I drive you home?"

She didn't answer, but she opened her car door. Loren got out of the New Yorker, locked the door, walked around to the Fury. Sondra Jernigan sat in the passenger seat, weeping silently. Loren drove her home.

By the time he pulled into the driveway, negotiating around a candy-apple-red kid's bicycle, the crying jag was over. She wiped away a few last tears, sniffed, pushed her hair back out of her face. Ready to face the kids.

The younger one, Max, was sitting cross-legged in front of the television. He was eating a sandwich. A stern-voiced male on the holoset was telling him how he'd sworn to use his powers only in the cause of justice.

Sondra Jernigan stood in the entryway for a moment, blinking down at her boy. Loren pictured Debra in the same situation, trying to figure out a way to tell Kelly and Katrina.

Loren told himself to stop thinking such things.

"Your husband's office?" Loren prompted.

"Oh. Yes." Patting her hair nervously.

A series of explosions punctuated the television show. Sondra Jernigan led him to the office. Middle Eastern music boomed from one of the back rooms, presumably where the other boy, Werner, was amusing himself. The whiteboard occupied an entire wall, still filled with arcane formulae drawn in different-colored ink. Loren recognized the Delta t's and Delta E's and nothing else. He looked at it doubtfully.

"I suppose I could copy that down."

"You don't have to. It's a Panaboard."

She went up to it, pressed a button. A full-color photocopy of the whiteboard's contents hissed quietly out a slit in the board's base. She pressed another button and the whiteboard screen scrolled horizontally, bringing more calculations into view. She made another copy.

Made by Panasonic, Loren saw. Hot damn.

There were seven screens in all, of which five had writing. Sondra made copies of each, then handed them to Loren. He folded them and put them in his breast pocket.

"You know," Loren said, "you might want to call your minister. You're Presbyterian, aren't you? He's experienced at breaking news like this to children and family members. Or I could call the police chaplain."

Who was Rickey, Loren thought. He tried to picture Rickey here, babbling intently about miracles in his Susquehanna accent.

She blinked for a moment. Performing the automatic task on the Panaboard, she had been able to momentarily forget what had happened on the maglev. Now she had to switch tracks again, back to the one that led to tragedy. "That's a good idea," she said.

"Would you like to call? There's a phone here, I see."

"Sure."

Jernigan's office was very neat. Einstein still grinned from atop his bicycle. Loren looked in the wastebasket first, saw only a few crumpled memos of the "dentist 12:30" type. Searching the desk, Loren found nothing but unused memo pads and a pile of canceled checks held with a rubber band. Apparently Jernigan did most of his work in his head, on the whiteboard, or on the little Hewlett-Packard calculator that sat carelessly atop the fake-Victorian rolltop. Then Loren opened the desk, looked at the compact little computer that sat inside. He pressed the power button. Behind him, the widow looked up a telephone number and pressed keys on the phone.

The computer came up. Loren seated himself in front of it and called for the directory. Einstein smiled at him sunnily.

Alphabetic chaos swarmed before his eyes. What the hell was GAGESYM.NABEL? And that was one of the more understandable ones—most were on the order of VoTACH.EMISH3. There were even file names that featured letters in the Greek alphabet.

He'd have to copy everything the computer had on the hard drive. He started looking for blank disks, which turned out to be in one of the desk's little cubbyholes.

Maybe, he thought wearily, he could just borrow the computer for a while. He turned to ask Mrs. Jernigan and saw she was still on the phone to her minister. Tears were rolling down her face again.

He was about to turn back when there was a loud hammering at the door. Loren's heart turned over. He jumped to the window, saw one of the chocolate ATL jeeps parked by the curb, and quickly pulled back.

He seriously considered for a moment whether or not to draw his gun. Maybe they'd come to finish the job.

Not likely, he decided. They'd have to kill the whole family.

But still.

He reached for the telephone, took it from Mrs. Jernigan's hand. She looked at him with surprise.

"Pastor?" he said. "This is Police Chief Hawn. Could you do me the favor of hanging up right now, dialing 911, and asking for police backup to Mrs. Jernigan's house in Vista Linda. Tell them that I need assistance right away. The address—?"

He looked up. Sondra Jernigan's face was drained of color. Tears still hung on her face. "328 Hawking," she said.

Loren repeated the address just as William Patience appeared in the door. Nazzarett hovered behind him, as did the younger child, Max. Both ATL people were carrying cardboard boxes.

"What are you doing here?"

There was no inflection at all in Patience's voice.

"Making sure no more people connected with my murder case get killed," Loren said.

Patience absorbed that without comment, without even a flicker of expression. He put the box down on one side of the door, straightened. "We're here to secure Mr. Jernigan's papers and effects," Patience said. "To determine whether there is anything that effects the national security."

"Mr. Jernigan didn't do classified work."

"I can't know that one way or another."

"Let's see the warrant," Loren said.

"Mr. Jernigan's contract with the labs covers this contingency," Patience said.

"Then let's see the contract."

"You don't need to see it."

"Yes, I do." Brutal anger sang through him. "I am here to view the same information from the point of view of the murder of John Doe on Saturday. I am here to collect that information with Mrs.

Jernigan's permission, and I am in possession of it now. If you want to look at any of this stuff, you better show me some kind of contract that supersedes my jurisdiction."

Patience's eyes were level with Loren's. Loren wondered how long the man could go without blinking.

Jurisdictional disputes, Loren thought. A lot of county sheriffs and city marshals used to shoot each other over this kind of thing back in the 1800s. Sometimes they were so busy blowing each other's brains out that the prisoner they were fighting over got clean away.

Maybe things hadn't changed much since then.

Electric tension buzzed in Loren's nerves. He knew it would take him too long to get to his gun: the holster safety strap was buckled and Patience probably had one of those spring-loaded quick-draw shoulder holsters, anyway. If Patience made a move for the gun under his arm, Loren figured to lunge forward, clamp his left hand over Patience's arm to keep him from drawing, and drive a couple stiffened fingers into Patience's eyeballs. That would still leave Nazzarett to deal with, but with luck Patience would be so shocked by the loss of his vision that Loren could get the gun away from him and use it.

Anyway, he couldn't anticipate everything.

Patience licked his lips. "Vista Linda isn't in your jurisdiction," he said.

"Firstly, it doesn't matter, because I'm here with Mrs. Jernigan's permission. Secondly, the murder *was* in my jurisdiction. And thirdly, I don't think the sheriff is going to mind. Shall we call him and ask?"

"Where's Dad?" asked Max. He sounded frightened.

Patience turned to Nazzarett. "Get on the phone to Personnel. Get a copy of Mr. Jernigan's contract, and get our attorney out here."

A little tension went out of Loren's nerves. Whenever people started calling for lawyers, issues would take a while to settle.

"Where's Dad?" Max asked again. Loren's heart gave a wrench.

"Mrs. Jernigan," Loren said. He never quite dared take his eyes off Patience. "Why don't you take Max into Werner's room and have a talk with them both."

"Yes."

Pale, her hands trembling, she moved past Patience in the doorway, put a hand on Max's shoulder, and guided him down the corridor.

There was a stab of music from Werner's room as the door opened, then the noise lessened.

Loren heard the whooping sound of a police siren. Relief eased into his body.

"I believe that's my backup," Loren said.

"I didn't think you were stupid enough to do this."

"I don't see you walking out of here with anything in your box. How stupid can I be?"

"Pretty stupid," Patience said, and for the first time he smiled, "since the sheriff's department probably just solved your murder for you."

Loren's mind spun like a brakeless flywheel as he tried to work out what Patience was saying.

"One of the sheriff's boys found a case in the train wreck," Patience said. "It had a pair of pistols in it, both .41 Tanfoglios. We figure that Jernigan killed Doe and hid his pistols somewhere in his office. He was taking them home with him when the train crashed. Of course that will have to wait for lab tests to see if these are the pair that shot Doe, but I'm fairly confident."

Loren's mind whirled. Green spots flashed through his vision.

Patience's smile broadened. He walked into the room and picked up the phone. "Now, why don't you call your city attorney," he said, "and have him come here and talk with our company attorney? And I'll call the mayor, and he can call your city attorney, and your city attorney can give our attorney everything we want and make it official, okay?"

It's not true, Loren hoped desperately. But his heart had already fallen into his boots.

Patience held out the phone. "Or shall I dial for you?" he said.

Loren took the phone.

He had lost.

FIFTEEN

Patience's scenario played itself out just as he had described it. Loren left the Jernigans' house with only the five photocopies from the Panaboard folded in his breast pocket. Mrs. Jernigan and the children were left with the Presbyterian pastor. Loren drove to Atocha and found Cipriano taking a brown briefcase out of the big walk-in safe. Cipriano heard Loren coming in, turned, held out the case.

"I've been calling you all afternoon. Looks like Jernigan plugged the guy, after all. His pistols got found in the wreck."

Loren looked at him. "Do you believe that?"

Cipriano looked dubiously at the case in his hands. "You got some reason not to believe it?"

"Where was it found? Just lying in the wreckage, right? Like maybe we were meant to find it? And who sabotaged the train?"

"Eco-terrorists, somebody was saying. People who didn't like Torrey's game ranch."

"I think Patience and his goons did it. Because Jernigan was on his way to visit Cantwell and spill what he knew about the John Doe murder. And it's my working hypothesis that Patience did that killing, too."

Cipriano thought for a moment. "That's pretty wild, jefe," he said. "You got evidence for any of that?"

"Jernigan passed the Shibano test on the night Doe was killed—and that'll show positive if you've used a firearm in the last few weeks, and do it no matter how many times you wash your hand. Primary traces penetrate most clothing, so wearing gloves wouldn't help. And Jernigan's wife says that his alibi was cooked up with Patience's help."

"That doesn't necessarily mean Patience did it."

"Why would he help Jernigan establish an alibi if he weren't covering his own ass, too? He and one of his other men killed Doe and then pulled the train sabotage to cover it up. Think about it. The ATL people are the only people around here who would *know* how to sabotage that train. It wasn't done by just parking a truck across the tracks. They had to disable a whole sensor array."

"Can I sit down for a minute, jefe? I gotta think about this."

"Sure."

Cipriano put the briefcase on Loren's desk, took one of the old wooden seats under the BUY AMERICAN sign, and stuck his legs out. Loren sat behind his desk and reached for the briefcase. "This been dusted for fingerprints?" Loren said.

"Yep. Not a one."

"Isn't that a little suspicious?"

"It shows that if the guy was a killer, he was careful to clean his gun." Cipriano frowned and stared at his boot tips. "Jefe, I got a problem with your scenario."

"Shoot."

"If Patience did the killing, why did Jernigan agree to help him cover it up? If he was so goddamn innocent."

"Maybe Patience threatened him." Loren opened the briefcase and took out a green plastic box. Inside the box were a brace of pistols and spare magazines. He hefted a pistol and sniffed at the barrel, smelling only gun oil. He dropped the magazine and pulled the action back and looked down the barrel. Clean as a whistle.

"He coulda gone to the D.A. and got protection," Cipriano said.

"That's the part I've got to work on. Something happened at ATL between Friday night and Saturday night. Once I find out what it was, it'll explain everything." He picked up the dropped magazine and popped one of the bullets out. Black fingerprint powder marred the gleaming brass: .41 caliber, Blazer brand.

"There's a messenger waiting for that gun in my office, jefe," Cipriano said. "I'm sending it to the lab in Albuquerque. We should have news by tomorrow noon."

Loren let the action snap shut, put the gun in its box, then in the briefcase. It was a cheap case made of brown leather, with a little brass clasp. He looked at it for a moment, then reached into his bottom drawer for the phone book. He looked up the Jernigans' number and called it. Sondra Jernigan answered.

"Mrs. Jernigan? This is Loren Hawn again. I'm sorry to bother you, but did your husband own a brown briefcase?"

"No."

"Thin leather, like a document case. Brass clasp."

"Nothing like that."

"Thank you." He put the phone down and looked at Cipriano. "She says not. Patience's guys planted the case for us to find."

"She also says her husband didn't have a gun. If she never saw the gun, it would only be logical that she wouldn't see the case he kept it in."

"How d'you beat the Shibano test?"

Cipriano thought for a moment. "The guy was a scientist. Maybe he knew enough chemistry to neutralize the test."

Irritation griped at Loren. "Whose side are you on, anyway?"

"I'm just saying what Patience would say. Or Little-Eddie-the-mayor. Your theory ain't got no proof, jefe."

"Could he beat the Shibano test on such short notice? We gave him the test just a couple hours after the shooting. With all the bullets fired into the car, his hand and arm should have been covered with gunpowder traces. Even if he was wearing gloves."

"Like I say, he was a scientist. Ask another scientist if the test can be beaten."

"Okay. I'll get on the LAWSAT and query the FBI lab in Washington."

"That messenger's waiting, jefe." Rising from his chair.

Loren handed the guns to Cipriano. Cipriano put the case under his arm and left the room. Loren dialed the front desk.

"Begley checked in?"

"Yeah, Chief. He's sitting here waiting for Quantrill to bring his car in. We've been shooting the shit."

"Send him this way, will you?"

"Can do, boss."

Begley appeared in the door, a blond shock of hair hanging in his pale blue eyes. He brushed it back with a freckled hand. Loren remembered seeing him grinning on Connie Duvauchelle's wall. At least he hadn't been in uniform when the picture was taken.

"You wanted to see me, Chief?"

"Sit down for a sec. I wanted to ask you about the guy you know who works for ATL."

Begley rearranged his gun, flashlight, and baton, then sat. "Paul Rivers? What about him?"

"What's his job, first of all?"

Begley shrugged. "He works for their security service. Plainclothes, not a gate guard. Cruises the town, the perimeter. Escorts VIPs, that kind of thing."

"When did you last see him?"

"Saturday afternoon. We went dove hunting."

"How'd you do?"

"We each got about a dozen."

"A good afternoon. Do you know whether he was on duty later?"

"No. I was, but he said he was going out on the Line for some fun." Begley frowned. "That's kind of funny, though. He was supposed to have the day shift on Saturday, so on Friday night I borrowed his springer spaniel so that I could go hunting by myself, but he called me early Saturday morning to tell me he'd been taken off the day shift and he could join me."

Loren absorbed this news with quiet triumph. Something had happened on Friday night to change everybody's plans.

"Did he say anything about what happened on Friday night?"

"There was some kind of alert or something. I remember he was cruising the town and caught a squeal about closing off the facility, and he was ordered to come out and patrol the perimeter in his jeep to look for intruders. But they lowered the alert level at midnight and he went off shift and went to bed."

"Did he see anything on the perimeter?"

"Not even a cow." Grinning. "You heard that story?"

"Yeah."

"It drives Patience crazy. He thinks Luis Figueracion or somebody is playing practical jokes on him. Hoisting cows over the fence with cranes or something. And people rag him about it, and that *really* pisses him off."

"I bet." Loren thought for a moment. "How unusual was that Friday night alert?"

"Patience is always coming up with some chickenshit drill or other. Paul really hates it. He thinks Patience is a walking anus."

"Do the other security people agree with him?"

"Paul has to be careful who he talks to. Some of the guys think Patience is God. The rest just think he's a pain in the ass."

"Do you know if Paul's on duty right now?"

"Day shift all this week."

"So he'd be home later."

"Uh-huh."

"Thank you. I'll call him and ask him a few things."

"He's real friendly, Chief. I'm sure he'd be happy to answer your questions."

We'll see, Loren thought. After I arrested three of his cuates.

Begley left and Loren used the LAWSAT antenna to log on to FBI LAWNET and posted a message on a bulletin board on "Ask Dr. Zarkov," the forum run by the New Jersey blood-spatter expert. In addition to handing out arcane criminalistics information, Zarkov filled his bulletin board with bizarre pathology trivia and an endless round of gruesome morgue jokes. Loren posted a message asking whether or not there was a known way of beating the Shibano test. It was after 1700 hours in Jersey, so he wouldn't get the answer till the next day.

He logged off and stared for a moment at the old gray walls. *They killed my witness,* he thought. *My witness and some guy who wasn't even connected with the case.*

Anger simmered quietly in his blood.

I had Vlasic's arm in my hand!

Patience had to be out of control. A rogue. His superiors couldn't have endorsed any of this.

Then he thought about John Doe's body disappearing and wondered who had authorized *that.*

He wondered who was in charge at ATL. And whether *that* person knew what this was about.

How well had Patience covered himself?

He thought about Jernigan's head sneering out from its nest of crumpled metal, and remembered pink-faced Vlasic nodding at him politely as he got on the maglev.

He remembered the convict's head butting up against his nose in the fight at the Ringside. The way heat lightning seemed to roll across his stunned brain while his cornerman screamed at him to get his head down and cover up.

Randal Dudenhof, lying on the yellowed old tile with foamy blood pouring from his mouth.

No. Not Randal. John Doe.

Keep this, he thought, at a level somewhere near sanity.

He needed a drink. He locked his office and checked out and headed home. The house was full of the warm scent of cooking chiles, garlic, and onions. The girls were in their rooms doing homework and Debra was on the phone. Loren got a bottle of Cutty Sark out of the liquor cabinet—a Christmas present from Bill Forsythe, he remembered—and poured himself three fingers. He dropped two ice cubes in the glass and took it into the living room. He sat in front of the dead television set and let the drink scald its way down his throat.

Bits of bodies floated through his thoughts.

Loren took the five sheets of Jernigan's writing out of his breast pocket and looked at them. The incomprehensible mathematics danced hopelessly in front of his eyes.

Debra got off the phone and started work in the kitchen.

John Doe's death played itself out in Loren's mind. He remembered the taste of the slippery blood in his mouth.

Randal's blood.

The Cutty was fire in his veins.

He lurched out of his chair and went to the phone. He got Sheila Lowrey's name up on the liquid-crystal directory and pressed the Dial button.

"Lowrey." As if she knew it was business.

"Sheila. This is Loren."

"You got what you wanted, Loren. Your little thugs are going to trial."

Loren tried to concentrate. "Who?"

"Wasn't that what you called about? I talked Castrejon into trying to plea-bargain Cisneros and his friends, but Axelrod turned us down flat. He didn't even consult his clients. Just refused the offer."

"Castrejon tried to plea-bargain?" He hadn't thought the D.A. would actually follow Sheila's advice.

"Axelrod is going to try to nail your balls to the courthouse door, my friend. That's the only way he can save Medina and Archuleta. To make it an issue of your character and fitness."

Loren licked his lips, tried to get his mind on track. "Castrejon really thinks we should plea-bargain, huh?"

"Yeah. Because just before the clerk's office closed this afternoon, Axelrod showed up with a civil suit and official complaint from Cisneros and from Mack Bonniwell and A.J. Dunlop's dad about the way you beat up their kids. You'll probably get the subpoenas tomorrow."

Probably delivered by one of my own men, Loren thought.

"I hope this makes you happy, Loren," Sheila said.

Castrejon tried to plea-bargain. Loren's mind spun as he tried to think about it.

Maybe Castrejon had been right. And Loren had other things to worry about now that he had three murders to concern himself with.

"I can arrange for them to plea-bargain," Loren said. "If you really think that would be best."

"What? How?"

Sheila's voice turned suspicious. "Loren, what the hell are you up to? You could get us in a lot of trouble here."

"No trouble will result," Loren said. "But what I called you about is something different."

"Okay." Still dubious. "What other bad news have you got?"

"I wanted a legal opinion," Loren said, "on whether it's possible to prosecute a person for the murder of someone who's already been declared dead."

There was a moment of silence. Then, cautiously, "Could you make this a little more clear?"

"Let's talk hypothetical case, okay?"

"Let's."

"Let's say John Smith has been killed, okay? And is declared dead and buried. And then at some subsequent point John Smith turns up having been murdered. Is it legally possible to prosecute someone for killing John Smith?"

She thought for a moment. "John Smith was killed, and he turns out to have been murdered? You'd have to prove that the death wasn't accidental, probably exhume the body for tests, then prove that the killer did it."

"No. You mis—you don't understand me. John Smith's death, his *first* death, really was accidental. His *second* death was murder."

"You're right. I don't understand you."

Cutty swirled in Loren's mind. He tried to make himself speak clearly. "He was killed twice, see . . ."

"Okay, *I* see. It wasn't really John Smith who died the first time. Somebody else died in his place."

"That's not what I . . ."

"You'd have to exhume the first body and prove that it wasn't John Smith. Then prove the second body *was* John Smith, then connect the killer to the murder."

Loren contemplated this action. "Jesus," he said. "That's complicated."

"Unless of course you just found the killer standing over the second body with a smoking gun in his hand. Then it doesn't much matter who the dead man was."

"I think my chances of that just went out the window."

"You're talking about John Doe, aren't you?"

"I can't really say." For a moment he could taste Randal Dudenhof's blood again. He took a long swallow of scotch.

"You've found out who he was."

"I can't talk about that."

"I'm the A.D.A., remember? We're on the same side."

"It would sound too crazy."

Another pause. "You're not sounding exactly rational right this minute, you know."

Jernigan's head floated in front of his eyes. "Probably not."

"Have you been drinking or something?"

"I'll have to try to get him on the other two murders."

"*What?*" Sheila's voice echoed painfully in his skull. "What other two murders?"

"The train crash. You haven't heard?"

"You mean the maglev?" Disbelieving.

"Somebody sabotaged it. Two people were killed, maybe more."

"And the same person did it as killed John Doe? That's what you're telling me?"

"I'm not telling you anything, Sheila."

"Loren, we've got to talk about this. If you've got evidence, the D.A. and I can help you build the case. This shouldn't be haphazard, Loren. We can't allow any holes in this one for some smart shyster like Axelrod to drive through." Enthusiasm brightened her voice. "This isn't just some stupid robbery, *this is the big time!* A major technological innovation, a multi-million-dollar demonstration project, destroyed by some psychotic! If we can nail who did it . . ."

"Bye, Sheila." Loren hung up, drank the last of his scotch, decided to get some more.

He padded into the kitchen. Debra looked at him.

"You think the dead man was Dudenhof, don't you?"

"I can't get it out of my head." Loren opened the cabinet and reached for the Cutty Sark.

"You know it's impossible. The man who got shot was young. Dudenhof would be as old as we are."

Loren savored the bite of the Cutty, then poured himself some more. "I know," he said.

She reached out, put a hand on his arm. "It can't be Dudenhof, Loren."

Loren shrugged off her hand. "Randal was my friend, dammit!"

Debra frowned. "No, he wasn't."

Loren returned the bottle to the cabinet.

"Loren," Debra said, "you were always down on him. You always talked about how he was a drunk and gambler and ran around on Violet."

Loren headed toward the phone. "I've got to make some phone calls. Maybe Ross is still at the jail."

"You didn't like him, Loren!" Insistently. "Will you remember that?"

The jail was number six on the dialer. Ed Ross answered, and Loren told him about Axelrod refusing the Cisneros plea bargain. Then he called the front desk down at the station and got Quantrill, who had replaced Eloy as the swing shift came on line, and told him the same thing.

He hung up. Debra, avoiding his glance, had opened the oven and was bringing out a casserole dish filled with costillas, southwestern spareribs cooked in red chile sauce. The casserole dish crashed as she let it fall to the top of the stove.

"Soup's on. We've also got refritos and rice."

"You know," Loren said, "maybe we could go down the Line later and go dancing."

She leaned back against the sink and crossed her arms. She still wasn't looking at him.

"Better sober up first," she said.

"I'm not drunk," Loren said. "I'm just sick of all the dead people crossing my path lately."

She finally turned to him. "The train crash? I overheard your conversation with Sheila."

"One of my witnesses died. My *only* witness, I should say. Piece of metal cut his head off."

Her eyes softened as she absorbed this, as she realized what he'd seen that afternoon. "And you think the accident was deliberate."

"Somebody parked a truck across the tracks. That's deliberate enough."

"You think you know who?"

"Knowing and proving are different things."

Debra accepted that. "Help yourself to dinner," she said. "I'll tell the girls."

"Another phone call first."

Debra went into the back. Loren could hear her knocking on doors. He looked up Paul Rivers in the DialComp's hard memory directory and pressed the Dial button. A voice answered on the second ring.

"Is this Paul Rivers?"

"Yes."

"This is Loren Hawn. I'm chief of police down in Atocha."

"I know who you are." There was a little pause. Loren could hear a television sportscast in the background: announcer shouting, crowd roaring. *He scores!* someone yelled.

"What do you want?" Rivers asked.

"I need some information."

"I've been instructed not to cooperate with you unless you subpoena me."

"Who's gonna know? I just want to get some information about that chickenshit boss of yours."

Rivers thought for a moment. "No," he said. "It would get back to him."

Loren's family was returning to the kitchen. He took his mobile phone the other way, toward the bedroom.

"Something else might get back to him," Loren said.

"What do you mean?"

"I hear," closing the bedroom door, "that Patience has offered a hundred bucks to anyone informing him about any ATL employees who visit Connie Duvauchelle's whorehouse."

Loren heard a heavy sigh. Then the background ball game shut off.

"What do you want to know?" Resignedly.

Loren grinned to himself. It *had* been Rivers in the photo with Begley on Connie's wall. "How many people are on duty at one time?"

"Two uniformed guards at the gate. Another two at the maglev station. One person monitoring the radio, back gates, and cameras from the control desk headquarters. His supervisor. The supervisor's usually Patience on the day shift. Two people in jeeps are cruising the perimeter fence from the inside. Another two patrol the neighborhood, the town, and so on."

"What do the people patrolling the town look for?"

"Anomalies. New people. Things that shouldn't be there. The boss got this idea from the Special Forces about counterinsurgency patrols in a district—his idea is that if we hang around long enough, we'll know the town's normal behavior patterns, so that if they change suddenly, we'll know something's up."

"Like everybody in town is gonna start reading our copies of Marx some night, put on our black pajamas, take our AKs out of hiding, and go slipping through the wire?"

"I guess. It didn't make much sense to me, either. But then that's the boss. What he learned in Special Forces is gospel."

Loren got out his notebook. "Who was on duty Friday night?"

"Me. I was cruising the town with John Jacobs."

"I think I saw you. I was out front of Holliday's after a fistfight."

"Yeah. I remember checking out all the cop vehicles."

"Who was supervisor that night?"

"The boss himself. There were a lot of guests on the facility and he wanted to be on hand."

"Who else?"

"Lemme think." Rivers gave a cough. Loren heard the clink of ice on glass, the sound of sipping. "Jim McLerie on the control desk. Vinnie Nazzarett and Carl Denardis on perimeter patrol. Karen Denton and Chris Bietrich on the front gate. Bernie Patton and Paul Shrum on the maglev gate. Cosmo Vann was at the LINAC looking after the guests."

"Cosmo?"

"It's his given name."

"And Nazzarett on the perimeter." Writing it all down.

"You know him?"

"I arrested him this afternoon."

"Oh, yeah. You did." Rivers seemed to find this amusing. "That must have really pissed him off."

"He didn't seem very happy. What happened Friday night?"

"We got an alert notice around 2100 hours. Patience came on the radio and wanted us to check out the exterior perimeter. There was an intruder, he said, and he wanted us to check the fences and find out if there were any holes in them."

"Were there any?"

"No." Ice clinked over the phone again. Loren took it as a hint and sipped some of his scotch.

"Was there an intruder?" Loren's nerves gave an expectant hum.

"Apparently it was just a drill," Rivers said. "After we cruised a bunch of back roads for five hours and checked all the fences at least three times, Patience had us stand down, and the new shift came on."

New shift. Including the two men who'd watched Loren cut dead cats from A.J. Dunlop's car.

"Did the alert specify where the intruder was?"

"No."

"Or who found him?"

"No. But if there was an intruder, he would probably have been found by Denardis and Nazzarett. They were the ones patrolling inside the fence."

The hum was stronger now. The Cutty Sark was tasting more and more like victory. "What would they have done with him then?"

"Taken him to Security HQ and held him there."

"So the people at HQ, Patience and what's-his-name, McLerie, would have known about it." Looking at his notes.

"I guess."

"And anyone else?"

"Not necessarily." Ice rattled again and Rivers sipped noisily. "The gate guards and Cosmo Vann would have been on alert, but they might not have seen anything out of the ordinary."

"Have any rumors got out?"

"I haven't been on duty all weekend. But if it was just Denardis, Nazzarett, and McLerie, then forget it."

"Why?"

"They're the boss's asshole buddies, that's why." Alcohol had clearly done away with Rivers's worry about what would get back to his boss. "They think he's Jesus fucking Christ and walks on water."

"Oh, great."

"Nazzarett was Marine Force Recon. Denardis was Army Airborne but flunked out of drop school. McLerie's some kind of charismatic Christian who thinks the world is gonna end any day now, and he wants to have lots of automatic weapons around him in case he's not picked up during the Rapture."

"You should show him the UFO field."

"I have. He didn't think it was funny."

"Any of these guys actually see action anywhere?"

Rivers gave a laugh. "You kidding? We had one genuine combat veteran in the group, Crace, an older guy who'd been in Vietnam. The boss just *loved* the guy at first, worshipped the ground he walked on—Patience figures Vietnam was this noble lost cause, you know, like southerners think about the Civil War. The veterans are all forgotten heroes, all that crap. Man was barely *born* then, you know? But it turned out that Patience was disappointed by Crace. Man kept talking about what the war was really like, how totally fucked it was from start to finish. It didn't fit Patience's expectations at all. He wanted some kind of heroic John Wayne bullshit. So Patience got Crace shuffled off on the grounds that he admitted smoking marijuana back when he was in college."

"Smoking dope?" Loren figured he might as well encourage the man's attitude. "Who didn't, back then?"

"Yeah! I sure as hell did, but I was smart enough to lie about it on the forms. And I read up on how to beat the polygraph and was able to ace that part." Rivers giggled. "That poor son of a bitch Crace was honest. That's all. Patience gave him something called a lateral transfer to another ATL facility in Texas, but the poor jerk probably ended up with a janitor's job."

"What you're telling me," Loren said, "is that ATL Security is run by this crazed hard-core control-freak puritan with an inflated sense of his own importance, a whole lot of frustrated military ambition, and no goddamn common sense at all."

Rivers whooped with laughter. "That's our boy!" he shouted.

"And he's assisted by a bunch of disciples who are just as much misfits as he is, and who accept his orders like they came from Mount Sinai."

Rivers's laughter rollicked on.

"Here's what I want you to do," Loren said.

The laughter stopped abruptly. "What d'you mean *do?* I'm not doing anything!"

"Sure you are. You're getting me a list of who was on duty on Friday through today."

"You want me to *spy* for you?" Rivers was outraged.

"Of course I do." Reasonably.

"Hey, man! This ain't nice!"

Loren put slashing blades into his voice. "I don't give a shit for nice!" he barked. "I just want the fucking names, okay? And I want them by tomorrow."

"Jesus Christ!"

"That's what I want, Rivers. You can check in early tomorrow and get a look at the rosters. That's all I ask."

"I don't know if I can do it."

"You know what I want done. It's your damn job to figure out how to do it, and do it by tomorrow. Otherwise it'll be a lateral transfer to a job shoveling shit in Texas with your old buddy Crace."

Loren hung up before Rivers could bleat a reply. He carried the portable phone back into the kitchen, put it on its cradle, and sat at the table with his family.

He had ATL's personnel logs for the weekend, but they conceivably could be doctored in some way. Whatever Rivers found out would just be a bonus.

He helped himself to some ribs, saw they were too hot to eat as yet, and reached into his pocket for the scribblings he'd taken from Jernigan's Panaboard. He turned to his elder daughter. "Here," he said. "You're taking math classes. Can you make any sense out of this?"

Katrina scanned the pages, eyes widening. "We don't have any of this in Algebra II, Daddy," she said. "Honest." She handed the pages back across the table.

Loren looked at her. "Do you know what *t* stands for?"

Katrina shrugged. "Sure. It stands for time."

Cold certainty settled in Loren's bones. In spite of all the scotch, he'd never felt more sober.

"Yeah," he said. "That's what I thought."

S I X T E E N

The phone blew Loren's dream away like a prisoner from the cannon's mouth. Loren's hand snatched out to seize the phone, then he rolled out of bed and reached for his clothes with the other hand. At some point subsequent to this he actually managed to wedge his eyes open.

"We got Fucking Big Idiots all over town, Chief." It was one of Loren's patrolmen, Al Sanchez. "They're in their blue jackets and everything."

The Fucking Big Idiots, alias FuBar 1, a/k/a Fan Belt Inspectors, were known to the public as the upright, uncorruptible, ace investigators of the Federal Bureau of Investigation.

"Fuck." Loren tugged on trousers. "Where?"

"East Robin between Copper and Estes. And somewhere out on North Plaza, I'm not sure about the cross street—that's what I heard, anyway."

"That first one is right in my neighborhood."

"They're setting up to bust somebody. They won't say who."

"*Assholes.*" Reflexively. "*Assholes.*"

There were all sorts of reasons to dislike the FBI—their smug, insufferable superiority, their reliance on informants and technology instead of footwork, their high-handed appropriation of any case that might give them good publicity. All reasons enough. What Loren hated about them was the way their ops sliced through all the established networks in his town, pushed the locals around without knowing who any of them were or how they stood in relation to one another, ignored the holistic terrain in which Loren and his neighbors lived. They were outsiders: they slammed into Loren's town in the dead of night, carried his neighbors away, left people like Loren to deal with the consequences.

Debra was blinking at him through dream-fogged eyes. Loren gestured for her to go back to sleep and glanced at the clock. Five-thirty. Outside there was full darkness. The hot Mexican wind was still burning the night.

By the time he got into his clothes and drove the three blocks to East Robin it was clear that the feds' operation, whatever it was, was over. Loren's headlights revealed the street blocked off with sawhorses. A dozen men were standing around, dressed alike in blue baseball caps and flak jackets worn beneath light blue nylon jackets with FBI in large gold letters on the back. They were relaxed, smoking or sipping coffee out of paper cups, their job over. Some of them propped semiautomatic snipers' rifles on their hips, each equipped with tubelike gray light-enhancement scopes for use at night.

Loren stopped his car in the middle of the street and snapped on his bright lights. Federal men winced and held up their hands to shade their eyes. Loren got out of his car, adjusted his gun, walked up to the nearest group. The wind tore at his jacket.

"Who's in charge?"

"Special Agent Killeen."

"Huh." Loren knew Killeen, a lazy round-faced man who deserved the Fucking Big Idiot tag more than most. He had been exiled to the Albuquerque FBI office after allegedly screwing up big-time in Los Angeles, where he was supposed to have committed a moronic series of procedural errors that resulted in racketeering charges being dismissed against a Teamster vice-president. "Where is he?" Loren asked.

"In the house. Hey. Don't go in there!"

This last was shouted as Loren walked between two of the sawhorses and headed for the house in question.

Loren would have steamed right through the front door, but Killeen came out first. William Patience, in his gray polyester jacket and red knit tie, was right behind him. For a brief, wild moment Loren wondered if Killeen had arrested Patience for sabotaging the maglev and then he recognized the two prisoners that followed them out of the house.

Skywalker Fortune and her father.

Skywalker stepped out first, pale face surrounded by a disordered shroud of wind-whipped black hair, hands cuffed behind her. She was in a rumpled T-shirt, with emperor penguins on it, that she'd probably been wearing when they dragged her out of bed, and blue jeans pulled hastily up her legs. Not all the buttons were done. Her feet were bare. Two feds, both women, escorted her out of the house, one on each arm.

Behind Skywalker, her father blinked owlishly through thick glasses. He was a tall bean pole of a man, with a graying shaggy beard, his hair still tousled from sleep. Loren watched the two of them while astonishment beat a fast, angry tattoo in his head. He turned to Killeen.

"Hey!" he said. "Dickhead!"

Killeen stopped on the sidewalk, cut off in midsentence in his conversation with Patience.

"Chief," he said.

"What is this crap you're pulling in my town, Killeen?" Loren demanded. He strode up to Killeen, hooked fingers in his gun belt, stared down at the man. Set face and body to intimidate. "Running some kind of major operation without telling me?"

"We don't need you around when we serve federal warrants," Killeen said.

"The fuck you don't!" Loren felt a roar building in his chest, sent it out. Heads turned. Skywalker, behind Patience on the sidewalk, stared at him with deep eyes. "You send snipers in black outfits crawling around through people's yards in *my town*, and you didn't tell me? You're lucky some good citizen didn't figure you for burglars and blow you away with a shotgun! You're lucky one of my *own* men didn't do it!"

Killeen blinked at windblown dust. "There was no danger."

Coolly. "People in nearby residences were awakened and apprised of the situation."

"*Apprised?*" Loren wrapped his mouth around the word and bit down hard. "*Apprised?* If there was any *apprising* going on, it should have been directed at my office!"

"It reached my ears," Killeen began, with a glance over his shoulder at Patience, "that you haven't exactly been cooperating with local agencies."

Loren looked at Patience and bared his teeth. "Mr. *Patience*," he said, "does not represent a local agency. He's a private thug hired by a private concern to represent their private interests. And what the hell is he doing here, anyway?"

"We know each other." Another shrug. "I thought he might be interested in seeing a real op."

"A real op," Loren repeated. He stared at Patience, who looked back at him with an expression of refined distaste. The Mexican wind howled in Loren's heart. "That's one more real op than Mr. Patience has ever been on in his life," he said. "Guess it won't do him any harm."

Even in the darkness Loren could see Patience redden. *Got you where it hurts, asshole*, he thought.

Loren turned to look at Skywalker. She was dancing barefoot on the cold sidewalk. Her lower lip trembled. "A real op to arrest a sixteen-year-old kid," Loren said. "What'd she do? Litter on a federal highway?"

"It's the climax to a six-month-long undercover investigation. We're arresting these two and eight other members of the local Eco-Alliance chapter for terrorist activities."

Surprise barked out of Loren, an involuntary gush of air that probably sounded like an incredulous laugh. For a moment he had a hard time finding words.

"They have been arrested," Killeen went on, "in connection with a conspiracy to destroy power lines and the Vista Linda pumping station. Maybe they even wrecked the maglev yesterday."

Loren found his voice. "What the hell kind of evidence do you have for this, Killeen?"

"We have an informant."

"Uh-huh." Loren saw Skywalker and her father exchange a quick glance, and his heart sank. There was significance in that look, and fear. And secret knowledge.

They were guilty. Damn it.

"A shipment of explosives and incendiaries arrived last week from Los Angeles," Killeen said. "It's the main explosives cache for the entire western U.S., and it got moved hastily because our Los Angeles office was getting close to it. We expect to find it during one of the arrests."

"We wouldn't ever destroy that train!" Skywalker blurted. She shook her long hair out of her face and looked at Loren pleadingly. She sounded on the verge of tears. "That train was benign technology! We wouldn't ever do anything to hurt anybody!"

Loren turned to Skywalker. "I understand, honey," he said. "I know you didn't have anything to do with the train wreck. And I know that other people here know it, too."

Patience's sharp face seemed carved out of hickory. The wind wailed around the Fortunes' eaves. Killeen looked uncertain. "We'll see what the evidence says," he said.

A sudden intuition leaped through Loren. "Who was your informant?" he asked. "Mrs. Fortune?"

Another startled look passed between Skywalker and her dad. Killeen just seemed petulant. "You can attend the trial and find out," he said.

"Your informant's involved in a messy divorce with one of your alleged eco-terrorists, right?" Loren said. "There's a custody fight, right?"

"That doesn't matter," Killeen said. His tone was defensive.

Cold certainty settled in Loren. "What kind of credibility is your witness going to have," Loren asked, "when it becomes clear she was framing her ex so that she could get custody of the kid?"

Anger settled into Killeen's face. "When we find the incendiaries, it'll only confirm what the informant told us!"

"You don't even know where they are, do you?"

"We'll find them."

"Your terrorists are gonna walk, Killeen," Loren said. "Just like that Teamster." Killeen's head gave a backward jerk as if he'd been punched in the nose. "They're gonna walk," Loren repeated, "because you're too fucking federal vain to cooperate with local law enforcement."

"Your daughters hang out with a terrorist," Killeen said, "and I was supposed to cooperate with you?"

"You think I'm not professional enough to do my job under those conditions?"

"I don't know, man. Some of the things I hear about your department, I don't know how professional—"

"*What do you hear, dickhead?*" Loren bent to scream the words right into Killeen's face. "*What do you fucking hear, you incompetent fat-faced federal jerk?*"

Killeen straightened, scowled, adjusted his baseball cap and his dignity. "I'm done with you, Hawn."

Loren stood upright and glared down at the angry fed. "I'm sending a letter to your superior, Killeen," he said. "I'm lodging an official complaint about your lack of liaison and your failure to share intelligence, all of which was detrimental to law enforcement, your mission, and the safety of your men. Not to mention mine."

"Fuck you," Killeen said.

"It's my town, Killeen."

"*Fuck you!*" Killeen waved clenched fists.

"It's my fucking town." Jamming a finger in Killeen's face. "Don't trespass again."

Loren stepped back off the sidewalk and let the caravan pass. Skywalker gave him a glance as she passed. His heart went out to her.

What the hell did her father think he was doing, getting her involved in this kind of shit?

"Don't talk to these creeps without a lawyer, honey," he said. "And you'll be back in class by Monday."

She gave him a brave smile, then one of her escort put a hand on her head and pushed her down into the unmarked car that waited for her.

Loren got in his car and drove home. He was already working on the contents of his letter.

* * *

The sin of the day was avarice. Rickey's words spun like high desert dust in Loren's whirlwind mind. Things had got way the hell out of his control, a thought that wouldn't have bothered him as much if he wasn't also confident of the fact that no one else, no one at all, had a handle on the situation, either.

Eco-terrorism, by members of his community. A crime that hadn't even been invented when he'd joined the force.

He couldn't think of any way that this would not hurt him. His daughters were friends with an accused terrorist—not exactly the sort of thing calculated to raise family esteem in the eyes of the town. Worse was the paranoid thought that maybe Skywalker had been *ordered* to become friends with Katrina and Kelly, that it was one way her terrorist—was *cell* the right word?—used to keep track of the law . . .

A shipment of explosives. Jesus. If the FBI didn't find them—and he had no confidence that Killeen would—that meant a stash somewhere that would turn unstable in time, ready to blow up in the face of the first inquisitive child who stumbled across it.

Wonderful.

He wished they *had* blown up the damn Vista Linda water supply. Vista Linda was incredibly wasteful with their water, pumping down the water table for the whole district, and it would serve them right. It wouldn't have made things any worse, and probably would have kept Patience and his psychotic goons busy with something else for a while.

Rickey's Pennsylvania accent intruded on Loren's thoughts. "The desire of money is the root of all evil," he said.

Loren recalled that this would be the first Wednesday in all his years of police work that someone hadn't handed him an envelope full of graft. Good thing, he thought, with the FBI swarming all over the town.

Guilt put a cold hand around his throat. He tried to shake it off. Why the hell did he feel bad for putting a stop to the mail? He'd never liked it, never felt comfortable about it even when the money came in handy.

Was he betraying something? His town, his colleagues? The way of life he'd sworn to protect?

He ought to be feeling relief. Especially with the feds in town.

Loren slowly realized that the service was over. He rose, walked down the aisle, shook Rickey's hand, murmured something. He stood on the top step of the church and looked pointlessly across the town plaza as if there were an answer there somewhere. Wind howled around the white granite spear of the war memorial.

"Daddy?"

"Yes?" Loren was surprised by Katrina's voice. He looked down at her, saw that she was looking at him worriedly.

"Can you call somebody? Find out what's happening to Skywalker?"

"I know some people I can call," Loren said, "but it's probably too early."

"Call them, anyway," biting her lip, "would you?"

"Okay."

His family had been in a quiet state of shock ever since he'd come back for breakfast. Katrina had excused herself from the breakfast table in order to go into her room and cry. They were all convinced of Skywalker's innocence.

Loren remembered Jerry telling him about Skywalker being a passenger in a slow-moving jeep driving down the arroyo behind the junkyard.

He drove his family home, changed into his uniform, switched the small revolver for the big revolver, and headed for work. Once there he logged onto FBI LAWNET—the feds had a few uses—and found his answer from Dr. Zarkov.

"There is no known way to beat the Shibano test," Zarkov wrote. "The test is so sensitive that it has found powder residues on hands that fired weapons while wearing heavy welder's gloves. If you HAVE found a way to beat the test, for God's sake don't put it here where people can read it [but send me E-Mail NOW!!!].

"P.S.: Sorry I just blew your case out of the water."

"It wasn't my case," Loren typed in answer. "It was the theory of a psychotic who's trying to frame a man he just murdered for something he did himself. Many thanks."

He looked at the words glowing on his screen, realizing that this was the first time he'd ever put his thoughts down where he, let alone anyone else, could see them.

He had to be out of his mind.

He tapped keys and wiped his reply out of existence. He wrote a simple thank-you in its place, then filed it.

"Okay, Hawn." It was Sheila Lowrey, leaning against his door frame with one hand jabbing her spectacles at him. "How'd you do it?"

"Do what?" Logging off.

"Got our three felons to fire their lawyer, accept a friendly local public defender, and then get him into a room with Castrejon for a plea-bargaining session."

Loren smiled up at her. "Is that what happened? And all this morning? I've been in church."

"Axelrod's blown a gasket. He's claiming intimidation, that you made offers to his client without his being present . . ."

Loren shook his head. "It isn't true. I haven't seen those scumbags since I busted them."

Sheila narrowed her eyes. "Who has?"

"Other prisoners, mainly. And the jailers."

"So who told them about the plea bargain?"

Loren shrugged. "If I told you, I would only be speculating."

Because he wasn't absolutely *sure* that it had been Ed Ross who delivered the prisoners their evening meal and stopped to chat about how their attorney had refused a plea bargain without even consulting them. Nor was he entirely certain that his patrolmen, when delivering drunks or speeders or domestic violence cases into Ed Ross's willing hands, hadn't stopped to jaw with him about how Robbie Cisneros's attorney Alexrod was going to sell him and his two buddies down the river, refusing a reasonable plea bargain in hopes of using them to shake his big drug-dealer clients free in an unrelated trial. The patrolmen going on at great length, with much laughter and anticipation, about what idiots Axelrod's clients had to be in order to let their attorney sacrifice them for his wealthier and more important employers.

Said conversations taking place in the hearing of the prisoners being booked, who would soon repeat it into the ears of Robbie and his pals in the jail. By sunrise, the trio were probably boiling over what their Axelrod had done.

It would never have worked, Loren thought, if Robbie's gang were smart. But no one had ever accused the criminal classes of intelligence.

"I *know* you had something to do with this," Sheila said. "You as much as said so last night."

Loren shrugged. "So what do you want me to do about it? Go down to the jail and convince Robbie to get his old mouthpiece back?"

"This move is of dubious ethics, Loren."

Loren threw up his hands. "I didn't *do* it, Sheila. I haven't been near the goddamn jail."

She stood over him for a long moment, then put her spectacles on and pulled a chair next to his desk. She sat down and looked at him intently.

"You're a hell of an operator, Loren. I can't figure you at all."

Loren grinned. "I'm just a country boy, Sheila. A plain ole peace officer."

"And you don't know shit from Shinola. You've always made that perfectly clear. How about John Doe and the train murders?"

"What about them?"

"They're related, right?"

"I think so, yes."

"And you know who did it."

Anger twisted in Loren's belly like a knotted rope. Had he really been so indiscreet? And only one night after he'd ranted to Rickey about miracles, then dug up Randal Dudenhof's grave just to make sure. He had to stop babbling like this to people he barely knew.

"I can't prove anything, Sheila," he said.

"It wasn't the eco-terrorists who did the job?"

"No."

"You seem pretty sure of that."

"I am." He leaned back in his chair, looked at her. "It's not their style. They don't like Torrey's game ranch—nobody around here does—but they approve of the kind of technology the maglev represents. And most of the environmental extremists are very careful about not taking human life."

There was a bright gleam in Sheila's eyes. "Who did it, Loren?"

"I don't have enough to give you yet."

"If we put our heads together—"

Loren shook his head. "No, Sheila."

"This is a *major prosecution*, Loren."

"It's big-time, yeah. You said so last night. You think it's your ticket out of here. Prosecute this one, and you'll get a good job in the metropolis of your choice."

Sheila whipped off her glasses, stared at him. "Is that so bad?"

"No. But it's affecting your judgment. And the fact is, I don't have a case."

"But if we—"

"Look. Here's what happened with Cisneros, okay? I knew within hours that he and his pendejo buddies pulled the job, but I had no *evidence*. Not until that tip came in."

"So what are you doing? Waiting for a tip?"

"My only witness got killed on the train. So I'm poking around and hoping something will turn up. That's all I can do."

"And what's with all this stuff you were telling me last night, about Doe being somebody who's already been declared dead in an accident?"

"I've got no grounds to order an exhumation."

"*Dammit, Hawn!*" Her arms flew up in frustration. "*I want to work with you on this one!*"

Loren grinned. "If I get enough evidence to take it to a lawyer, you're the one I'll talk to, okay?"

Sheila stood up abruptly. "I suppose I'll have to settle for that." She set her spectacles on her nose and turned to leave, then hesitated at the door. She turned, leaned a shoulder against the door frame.

"One last thing."

"Yeah?"

"Did you really call that FBI agent a dickhead?"

"Where'd you hear that?"

"My secretary lives next door to the Fortune house."

Loren shrugged. "Hell, Sheila. Killeen *is* a dickhead."

Sheila burst out laughing. She waved an arm and left.

Which reminded Loren of Killeen. He got out a white recycled legal pad, wrote his letter of complaint to the director of the FBI, tore it off the pad, and put it in his secretary's In box to be typed when she got back from her vacation.

Then he went upstairs to the sheriff's office and got out the U.S.

Forest Service map of Atocha County. The scale was one-half inch to the mile, and the reverse side showed gridded satellite photographs of the same terrain. Every terrain configuration, watercourse, road, cattle trail, arroyo, and butte was revealed in exacting detail. The sheriff's department used the map when coordinating searches in the awful terrain of the national forest north of town.

Loren took the maps back to his office and looked at the area west and south of the city. It wasn't national forest land, but so much of the county was either forest, wilderness area, or Indian reservation that all the private land on the map was rendered in the same detail as the government property. Even individual buildings in Atocha were carefully drawn to scale.

The arroyo behind Jerry's auto graveyard was called Wahoo Wash, something Loren hadn't known, but which he didn't find surprising in view of the fact that a mile and a half down the wash was the Wahoo Mine, which Loren had heard about as long as he could remember.

The mine had produced tons of silver in the 1880s, then closed in the next decade after the government stopped its price supports. It had reopened briefly during World War II, when the price of silver went up, then closed after the war ended.

Every time silver prices rose, the *Copper Country Weekly* wrote another of its patented optimistic articles about whether the company that owned the Wahoo would reopen it. They never had, but the *Weekly* remained indefatigable in its lonely pursuit of the idea.

Loren frowned down at the map for a moment, and then reversed it and looked at the black-and-white satellite photo on the other side. ATL's installations showed up clearly, the arrow-straight lines that must be the LINAC, the cluster of flat roofs that were SHEP and FIDO and the others, the two rows of perimeter fences, clear tracks that were gravel and paved roads.

And then Loren saw something else, a thin spider trail leaving the highway and tracking, not quite straight, across the desert, and his heart gave a lurch.

It was the road—or better, the artifact of the road—that had led to the Dudenhof Ranch. Randal's driveway.

After Randal's death, Loren remembered, Violet Dudenhof had sold out to Luis Figueracion, and then when ATL came calling, Luis sold that part of the Figueracion Ranch to the company. ATL had bulldozed the ranch buildings and just piled dirt over parts of the driveway until it faded away altogether—it was a road they didn't want.

Randal had just been heading for home, Loren thought, and then what? Spotlights, commanding voices, shots in the night?

He looked at the map for a while as if it could give him the answer, and then quietly folded it up and parked it on his desk. He picked up his phone and called a man he knew in Albuquerque.

"Howard? This is Loren Hawn."

"Hi, hoss. You're calling about Killeen, ain't you?"

"Damn straight."

"What an asshole."

Howard Morton was a snuff-dipping good ole boy, one of the smart ones, who had gone to high school with Loren and played with him on the football and basketball teams. Afterward he'd gone on to law school and ended up in the U.S. attorney's office in Albuquerque. Every summer he came back to Atocha to go fishing, and Loren sometimes went with him. For reasons unclear to anyone, he alone of all people in the world called Loren "hoss." Loren knew he was leaning back in his padded chair with his snakeskin boots up on his desk, jacket open to reveal a bolo tie and a paunch encircled by a silver and turquoise belt.

"Killeen didn't liaise at all," Loren said. "First I heard about this bust was when one of my patrolmen noticed FBI—" He pronounced the name of the agency *F'bee*, since he figured it might not be tactful to call them Fucking Big Idiots in a conversation with a U.S. attorney. "—F'bee with guns crawling around in the bushes," he finished.

"From what I can tell," Howard said, "Killeen just panicked. The undercover investigation had been going on for months, but when that train got wrecked Killeen was afraid the eco-terrs had gone on a rampage, and he decided to bust everybody right away and let God and the courts sort 'em out. The raid was put together at the last second."

"Does he have a case?"

"I'm not assigned to this one, thank God," Howard said, "so I haven't seen the details of the indictments. Right now I'm just settin' in my office till the prisoners get here. But I'll help process the indictments when the prisoners arrive, so I'll see the paperwork then. My guess is they sure as shit have a case of conspiracy."

"Those are hard to prove."

"They surely are, hoss."

"How many people got arrested?"

"Eight. And Killeen found 'em all at home."

"Has he blown it again? Like he did in L.A.?"

"Hard to say, hoss. When the Full-Blown Idiots start making arrests in this kind of hurry, a lot of details are bound to slip through their fingers."

Loren grinned. So much for his tact.

"You figure they're guilty?"

Laughter. "You know better than to ask a question like that, hoss."

"I guess I do."

"You figure on gettin' yourself an elk this year? With that fancy Russian gun of yours?"

They discussed hunting for a while, then Loren hung up. He phoned Debra to tell her what he'd found out—the prisoners hadn't reached Albuquerque yet, let alone been indicted—and then took his map of Atocha County and got a pry bar and some wire cutters out of storage.

He got in his car and drove down Route 82 to the bridge over Wahoo Wash. Once there he carefully eased the Fury down the water-rutted, eroding access that had received only scarce attention from county work crews since the closure of the mine in 1945. The bottom of the arroyo was flat, sandy, and waterless, easy to drive as a highway. Early settlers had used arroyos for transport, but the smart ones kept a weather eye out for violet thunderheads in the far-off mountains that could send four-foot walls of water howling down the gullies to sweep away every lonely man-made object in their path.

But there was no water danger today, not in the third year of the drought.

There were marks of thick tires on the sandy bottom, one set leaving, another coming back. Loren followed them till the tall sides of the arroyo fell away into a flat barren plain, its sandy soil covered with salt deposits in the shape of ancient, long-evaporated ripples. On a rugged gray bluff over the dead land, next to a mound of black silver ailings, was the old mine. The tire marks came to an end below the bluff. Loren parked next to them and stepped out of his car, craning his head back to look at the site. The wind blew dust that had the tang of salt. Somewhere nearby a crow was cawing.

Surrounding the mine, built atop the remnant of older, rusting barriers, was a bright new chain link fence topped with razor wire and covered with rusting KEEP OUT and PRIVATE PROPERTY signs. The company that owned the mine was concerned about their liability in the event of accidents to explorers, and had maintained their fence better than the mine itself, which was in ruins.

The mine site consisted of creosote-black timbers partly tumbled down the hillside and half concealed by young poplar. A small house, evidently an office, had fared better—the roof was still on it, and the boards over its windows held firm.

Loren parked beneath the bluff and took his cutters and pry bar out of the trunk. The short switchback road up the face of the bluff was impassable to vehicles, the victim of decades of rockslides. Bits of it kept crumbling away beneath Loren's boots as he trudged up it. The day was hot and Loren dripped sweat by the time he got to the gate.

He paused for a moment to catch his breath. A faint wind breathed through the poplars. An old black iron padlock lay in the weeds next to the gate, and a bright shiny new lock was in its place. Loren cut the lock away with his bolt cutters and pushed on the gate. Gray tufts of grass resisted, and he had to shove the gate firmly open. A red-shafted flicker darted by, the startling scarlet undersides of its wings flashing intermittently against the bright blue sky.

Once inside he went to the one surviving building. Blind boarded windows stared at him sightlessly. Nailheads trailed rust. Small drifts of tar-paper roofing surrounded the structure like fallen snow in springtime. The black planks of the porch sagged under his weight.

There was another new padlock on the door. Loren cut it away. The lock thudded on the planks and Loren put a hand on the door.

The thought of a booby trap occurred to him. He pushed the door open slightly, looked carefully through the crack for wires, and saw none. He stepped to the side of the door frame, behind some solid timber, and pushed the door open all the way.

He heard it thud against the wall. Nothing happened. Loren took a breath and stepped into the doorway. Something huddled under tawny piece of canvas in the center of the room.

Loren stepped forward and twitched the canvas off.

Ranked neatly on another piece of canvas, each item in its own individual plastic bag, were long, careful rows of incendiaries, bombs and detonators.

Enough to blow up half the town.

S E V E N T E E N

On the table, in their own plastic bags, Loren found the same series of Special Forces manuals, *Improvised Munitions*, that he'd seen in Patience's office. Apparently it was the standard text for making bombs in attics and garages. Loren held one of the bags up to the light in a half-assed search for latent prints, found none on the label. He opened it, took the book out, paged through the text. The Green Beret motto, DE OPPRESSO LIBER, was still on some of the pages, along with the warning OFFICIAL USE ONLY. The chapter titled "Urea Nitrate Explosive" began with the instruction "Boil a large quantity of urine."

Talk about recycling.

Nothing like a government publication to inform a person the approved way of doing things, be it sowing soybeans or blowing up water plants. Loren returned the book to its bag.

Heavy glass cider bottles had been filled with a gelatinous mixture and turned into incendiaries. Wrapped in old copies of the *Los Angeles Times* were blocks of what seemed to be plastic explosive. Coils of det cord, still in factory plastic, lay on the table. Timers and delay devices—a vast array, some homebuilt out of clocks and some factory-made—occupied about a square yard. A metal box, cushioned with foam, held detonators—none homebuilt, fortunately. Apparently the local ecologists had a healthy desire to avoid suicide.

Loren put the canvas back over the evidence, then left the building and closed the door behind him. He closed the hasp over the eye, then put the broken shackle of the padlock through it. It wasn't secure, but it would hold the door closed. He shut the outer gate the same way.

He was going to make Killeen's case for him. Damn it.

It took him two tries to get out of the arroyo; the first left the Fury spinning wheels hopelessly on the soft embankment. The big car lurched out of the arroyo on the second try and Loren pulled onto Highway 82 behind a rusted-out Jeep station wagon with local plates and a bumper sticker that said DON'T TREAD ON ME: FIGHT TAXES.

Confidence hummed through him. He'd call himself a press conference, he figured. Announce that he'd found the explosive cache that the Fucking Big Idiots hadn't been able to locate.

Steal a little of Killeen's thunder, anyway. And show that asshole the virtues of cooperation.

The Jeep ahead of him slowed down to five miles below the speed limit as soon as it reached the city limits. Clearly the driver saw the patrol car behind and was being careful not to get clocked for speeding.

Loren's eyes glanced up as something—a swift shadow, an indistinct suggestion of a thrashing figure—made a sudden movement in the back of the Jeep. The Jeep gave a little lurch to one side, then recovered. Then Loren saw the flash of a knife, and a rush of adrenaline struck at his heart like a hammer.

He reached for the siren button.

Blood sprayed the Jeep's rear window. The tailgate crashed open. Loren saw a thrashing figure, spouting blood, a man crouched with a drop-point hunting blade in his hand. Loren hit the Yelp button and the lights, and then the knifeman was thrown back against the side of the Jeep and a brown and white animal, a mule doe, scrabbled out of the tailgate and flopped onto the road.

Loren slammed on the brakes, a blaze of terror in his veins. There was an impact as the deer went into the Fury's bumper. The Jeep swung toward the curb, came to a stop with a river of blood pouring off the tailgate.

Loren set the parking brake, grabbed the Remington pump, shoved his door open. The siren yammered in his ears. He jacked a round into the shotgun as he left the car. The dying doe's hooves scrabbled hopelessly on the pavement. Loren crouched behind the door and propped the shotgun on the door's window frame. The man with the knife, his arm and unshaven face covered with blood, was staring stupidly out the tail of the Jeep, the bill of his gimme cap knocked over one ear. A man walking up the sidewalk, carrying a shopping bag from Fernando's Hi-Lo, stopped, saw the shotgun, stared, then clumsily turned and lumbered for cover.

"Police!" Redundantly. "Drop the knife!"

The man, still gaping stupidly, obeyed.

"Out of the car!" Shouting over the siren. "You and the driver both!"

At the sight of the driver all Loren's fear began to drain out of him. It was Henry Sigourney, whose last visit to the jail had been occasioned by his poaching tame elk off Sam Torrey's game ranch.

Shit. A couple of poachers killing a deer out of season.

Smoky whiskey fumes gusted from the Jeep. Sigourney and his friend allowed themselves to be handcuffed amiably enough. Loren peered into the back of the Jeep and saw enough blood to fill a slaughterhouse. A mental picture of Jernigan's dismembered head queased through his mind. Two hunting rifles, in cheap plastic cases, lay in the mess. A pair of one-liter bottles of Jack Daniel's, one empty, the other not, lay as further evidence. A bag of pork rinds was broken open and scattered in the blood. Loren went to his radio, turned off the siren, called for backup and someone from the Game and Fish Department to take the dead doe into evidence.

Traffic moved carefully around the cars. Loren could see pale faces gaping at the carnage. Loren looked down at the dead doe under the wheels of his car, then at Sigourney.

"You couldn't even find a buck to shoot?"

Sigourney unloaded a gumful of Red Man onto the pavement.

"Jimmy *was* shooting at the buck. He hit the fucking doe on a ricochet. Hit her right in the head." He looked at Loren and shrugged. "So what could we do? We figured she was dead, and we didn't want her to go to waste. So we put her in the Jeep."

"And she woke up."

"Yeah. Turned out she was just stunned. And you were right behind us. So Jimmy jumped on her and tried to kill her with a knife."

"Cut her throat," Jimmy said. He kept trying to spit blood out of his mouth. "Jesus! What a mess!"

An adrenaline shudder rode up Loren's back, struck as a galloping instant of unspecific anger. "You had to go and poach a deer two weeks before the season opened?" He could feel his voice rising.

"I'm not a poacher," Sigourney said with dignity. "I'm a traditional hunter."

"Traditional hunter." Loren wanted to gag on the words. Jernigan's head stared at him, bloody lip curling, from somewhere behind his eyes. "That's just a poacher with pretensions."

Sigourney was offended. "We kill to put meat on the table," he said. Reciting the party line. "We feed our families."

As opposed to the law-abiding hunters who just riddled their deer and let them rot. Right.

Loren forbore from reminding Sigourney that his wife had walked out on him years ago, taking the kids with her, and had since remarried a miner who preferred working for a living to sneaking around the wilderness trying to bushwhack out-of-season fauna.

"And other hunters don't?" he said.

"Not those trophy hunters at Torrey's, anyway."

"You want meat on the table," Loren said, "you coulda shot grouse today, and done it legally."

"Jimmy wanted venison."

Another wave of adrenaline rose up Loren's spine. This one unaccountably turned to laughter. He looked at the dead deer under his wheels and the bloody knife on the pavement, looked at the shotgun in his hand, and laughter rose from deep inside his belly and exploded past his lips. Tears fell from his eyes. He leaned against the fender of his car.

"I thought you were Jack the fucking Ripper! Holy Jesus Christ!"

Whooping laughter tore from his chest. Sigourney laughed along with him—this would all make a good story for his new comrades in the jail. Jimmy looked resentful and spat more blood.

A pair of patrolmen arrived. One put on a Day-Glo orange vest and started directing traffic; the other assisted Loren with his prisoners and helped drag the doe to the side of the road, where her blood could drain into the gutter and she would stop blocking traffic.

Pictures of the train wreck kept floating in front of Loren's eyes. After he finished booking the prisoners, he decided he needed to spend time away from accidents, blood, and the law enforcement business, and walked across Central to the Sunshine. The tow truck from Armistead's service station was parked out front. The beefy bear hunter sat at the counter in his mechanic's overalls. Byrne and Sandoval, natch, occupied a red Formica table in the back.

Coover poured him a cup of greasy coffee without being asked. He wished that at least once in his life the man would wait for Loren to tell him he preferred a soft drink.

Byrne and Sandoval waved and cackled from their table. Loren nodded at them and sat next to Armistead. The mechanic was eating a hot turkey sandwich with mashed potatoes, gravy, and a pyramid of grayish vegetables from out of a can. The turkey looked as if it had come from a can, too.

"That the special?" Loren asked. "How is it?"

"'Bout what I expected," said Armistead.

"I'll have what he's having," Loren said.

Coover took his order into the kitchen. "Did your nephew get his bear?" Loren asked.

"Got her three times over," Armistead said. He was speaking around his lunch. "First shot went through the heart and knocked her down." He paused, holding up his fork to indicate he wasn't finished talking, and swallowed. "Danged if the bear didn't get up and try to get away. So Pooley shot her again, through the heart again, and she went down one more time. And got up again! Pooley had to shoot her a third time before she up and died."

"Hit her in the heart each time?"

"Yep."

"Lot of life in that bear."

"Yep. Gotta respect that. That bear had credence."

Loren raised his coffee to his lips, looked at it, put it down. "I just hit a deer. Right out in the street."

"I saw." Chewing again. "Good old Henry. Can't even poach a deer without fucking up."

"He's not a poacher," Loren mocked. "He's a traditional hunter."

Armistead grunted. "He's a traditional fuckup."

Coover returned with Loren's plate. Loren picked up his fork and took a bite of food.

About what he expected.

Coover put his lean arms on the counter and inclined his body toward Loren. "I heard the mayor's called a press conference for tomorrow," he said. "He's gonna announce the museum of technology that the labs want to build."

"Good for him," said Loren. The mayor's reward, he figured, for letting Patience loot Jernigan's office. And the conference was scheduled so as to allow the *Weekly* to make the museum the page-one story instead of the mine closing.

He sampled the turkey sandwich. The turkey had that cream-of-wheat texture that came only from cans. Coover had continued his policy of never serving anything that required teeth to eat. Maybe it was a courtesy to his elderly customers.

"What I hear," Coover went on, "it's gonna be in the old depot."

Loren nodded. "Good place for it. If that's true."

"The Santa Fe is happy to donate the place. Get rid of a white elephant that way."

"At least the museum will be in Atocha," Loren said, "and not Vista Linda."

"If that's true," Armistead said through mashed potatoes, "then it's the first damn thing they've done for this town."

"Yeah."

"They even call someone from out of state to do their towing."

A bright current sparked along Loren's nerves, a certain knowledge that this was significant. He looked at Armistead. "What do you mean?"

"Was driving past their gate Monday morning on my way to work from Pooley's," Armistead said, "and there was a tow truck taking a car out of there. It said right on the damn door that they was out of El Paso."

"What kind of car were they towing?" Loren asked. "One of their jeeps?"

Armistead swallowed, filled his mouth again, and shook his head. "It was under a tarp," he said, "but it wasn't one of their Blazers. Silhouette's too low. Was a small car. Sports car or something."

"Like an old yellow '56 T-bird," Loren said.

Armistead stopped chewing and turned to look at him. "Coulda been, yeah," he said. "You know something about this?"

Loren groped for a suitable answer and just shook his head. "Just saw one the other day." He looked at his coffee cup so he wouldn't have to look at Armistead, then looked at him, anyway. "You remember the name of the towing company?"

"No. The name didn't matter to me. The fact that it was from El Paso was the thing that stuck in my craw."

Got you, Loren thought. *Got you got you got you.*

He bolted his meal and ran.

Loren called up the El Paso directory on his computer, got a printout of the towing services, and started dialing. He struck pay dirt on the first, AAAAA Towing & Wrecking. Patience had run true to his methodical nature and simply gone down the list alphabetically.

"Yeah, they called us." The station owner was a man named Antony Pacheco. He had a heavy Spanish accent.

"What was the job?"

"We were supposed to tow a car from their facility down here to El Paso. I was supposed to meet a man at the gate at five in the morning, hitch up the car, drive it on out."

"What kind of car was it?"

"A vintage Thunderbird. Yellow. Maybe '56, one of the old two-seaters."

Loren felt a quiet warm triumph sing through his body, dance along his nerves, warm his blood. Confirmation, he thought. At last.

Glory.

Got you got you got you.

"Where was it?" he asked.

"It was just out on the mesa. Not near the buildings or anything. I guess the driver had been joyriding and ran himself into a rock. Had a broken right front axle, a little damage to the bodywork. It was a damn shame what happened to it."

Loren was about to ask another question, but that last comment seemed to require clarification. "What do you mean, what happened to it?"

"What I was hired to do. I had to tow the car to El Paso, crush it for scrap metal, then sell it over the border into Mexico. A damn shame, man. A little work would have fixed it right up."

Loren felt his triumphant hum diminish. The evidence was gone, crushed into a metal cube.

"Okay. This was a yellow two-seater Thunderbird, right?" Making things absolutely clear.

"Right."

"Red pinstripes, red leather upholstery?"

"Right."

"Convertible?"

"Removable hard top, yeah. With those little portholes."

"Did you get the license number? Registration number?"

"The plates were taken off. I figured everything was official . . . I mean, I was dealing with people who *acted* official."

"And who were they?"

"I don't remember his name. He paid me with a credit card."

"William Patience?"

"That's the dude's name."

A possibility occurred to Loren. "Have you crushed it yet?"

Which was as tactfully as he could phrase it. Pacheco might have decided to repair the car, sell it across the border, and pocket the money.

"Yeah, it's gone."

"You sure? It might be worth your while if you could produce it."

Pacheco's voice held unmistakable regret. "They sent a guy with me. Followed me the whole way in his Blazer and made sure I dropped the car in the crusher."

"Which guy? What was his name?"

"Cold guy. Really cold. Wouldn't talk to me. Gave orders, acted like I was gum on his shoe. Name was McLerie."

"Listen. Would you give a deposition about all this?"

"If I gotta." Anxiety entered Pacheco's voice. "What's it all about? That car wasn't contaminated in some way, was it?"

"Contaminated?"

"Like with radiation or something. I wondered if they were trying to cover up a lab accident."

"No. The car was evidence in a criminal case."

"Aw, shit."

"It's not your fault it's gone. But if I could get a deposition off you . . ."

"I'm not gonna have to drive up to Atocha, am I?"

"I'll put you up somewhere. But there's something you ought to know. Two witnesses have been murdered, and you oughta be careful."

There was a long silence. Then, "You shittin' me, man?"

"I wish I were."

"Oh, God damn. Dammit, anyway."

"I don't think anyone's gonna bother you. They wouldn't have any reason to anymore."

"No way I'm gonna give a deposition, man! Not if it's gonna get me shot!"

Loren glanced up to see Cipriano in the door. He waved the deputy in.

"I'll subpoena you if I have to," Loren said. "And if word gets out that I'm trying to talk to you, you'll get shot, anyway. Giving that deposition is your best protection."

"Chinga, man."

Cipriano was followed by Luis Figueracion and Manuel Maldonado, the chairman of the city council. Loren leaned back in his chair in surprise, then rose and shook hands with his visitors.

"Seriously, man," he said to Pacheco. "I don't think anyone's after you right now, but you be careful, okay? You see anyone hanging around, you let me know, right?"

"I don't know about this. This really pisses me off, you know? I mean, who are these guys?"

"I'll call you about that deposition. Once that's on file, nobody'll have any reason to harm you."

"Chite."

Loren hung up and looked at his guests. Luis had already sat down, and Manuel Maldonado was looking for a chair. He was a stocky, dark man who had fought with the Marines in Vietnam and retained the crop-headed short haircut for the rest of his life, serving the Figueracion family the same single-minded way he'd once served the Corps.

Loren settled into his chair. "To what do I owe the pleasure?" he said.

Luis leaned toward him. "Loren, we gotta talk." He glanced over his shoulder at Cipriano. "Close the door, will you?"

Loren looked at the three and grinned. "You won't *believe* what I've found out today. You know that pinhead Killeen at the Albuquerque F'bee office? I—"

"Loren," said Luis. He had a cigarette in his mouth and was lighting it with a kitchen match he'd struck on his thumbnail.

"You know that cache of explosives he couldn't find? I thought the whole thing was bullshit, but—"

"Loren," Luis said. "Shut *up* a minute, will you?"

Loren looked from one to the other, then nodded. Manuel and Luis were serious, and Cipriano, still standing by the door, looked as if he were suffering from a spastic colon.

"Okay, Luis. What do you need?"

"You got an ashtray?"

Loren opened a desk drawer, took out his ashtray, pushed it across the desk to Luis. Luis took it and propped it on one knee.

"Here's the thing, Loren. Trujillo's gonna put you on administrative leave, and we're going to let him."

Loren stared at him. He could feel heat flickering behind his eyeballs.

"With pay," Luis went on, "so don't worry about that."

"Hey," Loren said.

"Just till all these allegations get cleared up. That's all."

"Hey." Loren banged a big fist on his desk. *"What the fuck kind of crap are you handing me?"*

Luis glared at him through his thick spectacles. "Watch that temper of yours, Loren." His voice was sharp. "I don't know how many times I told you."

Loren bit down on his rage, forced himself to sit still. He could feel sweat popping out on his scalp. "Okay, Luis," he said. "Talk to me."

"We've had too much hassle about the police department," Luis said. "All these stories about you hitting people, about you yelling at the guy from the FBI, not giving cooperation when you need to."

"Who exactly is it that I haven't been cooperating with, Luis?"

"Things are a little too out of control. We gotta cool the town down for a while."

"Not cooperating with *who*, Luis?" Insistently.

"Arresting those ATL guys for carrying guns." Luis waved a finger at him. "It's their *job* to carry guns."

"Patience is trying to impede my investigation. He's hiding evidence, and he's ordered his company thugs to follow me around town. I thought I'd jerk their chain a little, show them they weren't invulnerable."

"Impede your investigation? Your investigation of what? Of who?" Aggravation grated in Luis's voice. He shrugged. "Some stranger gets killed, you want to make a federal case."

Superheated steam seemed to pour through Loren's frame. He felt it light a blaze in his bones. "If there's a gang of killers wandering around in my neighborhood," he said, "I got a right to be concerned."

"And those kids you beat up," Luis went on. "A.J. and the Bonniwell boy. That looks bad."

"A.J. was reaching for a gun! He coulda killed me!"

"A broken jaw. A broken nose." Stolidly. "And their fathers vote. You don't go beating up the children of voters. There must have been some other way to handle it."

"Shooting them dead, maybe."

"One other thing. Did you really give some of them thieves' money to Joaquín Fernandez?"

Loren blinked. "Yeah. To get his door fixed."

"That's tampering with evidence. That's what the D.A. tells me."

"I broke down the man's door. I figured I'd help him get it fixed."

Luis sighed. "Well. We can hide that one, I figure."

"Jobs," said Maldonado. It was the first word he'd spoken.

"Yeah," said Luis. He pushed hair back from his forehead.

"It's about jobs," Maldonado said.

"The thing is," Luis said, "this technology museum is gonna employ eight people. Full-time. Others part-time. And ATL has promised that local contractors are gonna be in charge of the remodeling project."

Loren looked from one to the other. "Luis, I don't believe I'm hearing this."

"That's money for the community, Loren."

"And all you have to do is get the cops to stop investigating a murder, right?"

"What I'm trying to do is to get the chief of police to stop making waves in the community."

Loren looked at him. "You're protecting murderers, Luis."

Luis's eyes were stone. "I don't know that," he said. "I don't think you do, either. What I'm doing is trying to keep this community alive after a disaster."

"Three people have died, Luis. Murdered."

Luis shrugged. "Who knew any of them? But eight people with jobs—" He waved his cigarette. "People with jobs pay their bills. And maybe the stores they owe don't go under. A community this small—*one* bankruptcy is disaster. We're gonna have more bankruptcies than that. Maybe we can save something if we play our cards right." He leaned toward Loren, his lined face appearing through a shroud of tobacco smoke. "We can *use* this, Loren. We can make these outsiders share. It means more than eight jobs in the long run."

Loren stared at Luis, his incredulous mind flashing on Luis's scenario. Luis was going to use the murders to put pressure on ATL to spend money in his community.

A part of his mind was compelled to wonder if Luis could get away with it.

"Listen," Loren said, "if you're going to cut deals with criminals, the drug dealers will pay you better."

"Shut up, Loren," said Manuel Maldonado. "We don't have to listen to this kind of bullshit insinuation."

Luis didn't seem concerned. He waved his cigarette loftily. "Everybody deals, Loren. Everybody. And Figueracion delivers."

"You're crazy. These people are like rabid dogs. You can't deal with them like this."

"I talk to the chairman," singsong, "I talk to the project head. Figueracion talks to everybody. They were gonna put their museum on their own land. Figueracion points out that they'll have security hassles, people wandering around where they shouldn't be . . ."

"Luis. Listen to me here. Don't go off into fantasyland here."

"Atocha's got buildings to spare. But there's this hassle. Your police chief, I'm told, he's arresting our people. And they're only doing their jobs." Luis pointed a tobacco-stained finger at Loren. "He's a loose cannon, they're telling me. And my own people are telling me the same thing. Beating up kids!"

"What was I supposed to do? Let A.J. Dunlop shoot me?"

Luis's voice was still dreamy. "So maybe the best thing is for the police chief to take a little vacation. Get away from it all, a hunting trip maybe, shoot some duck, shoot some elk. Get things in perspective." He smiled. "Nobody gets hurt. Deliveries get made. Jobs get created. People go to work, pay their bills. The town survives."

Loren couldn't sit still any longer. He stood up and waved his arms. *"Nobody gets hurt?"* he roared. *"Three people got killed!"*

Luis's look was benign. "Nobody we know, Loren. Nobody who votes. People die all the damn time."

Loren glared at him. "Not in my front hall, they don't!"

Luis waved his hand gracefully. "Strangers die. It's like it happened in Africa or someplace. Is Africa our fault?"

Bile rose hot in Loren's throat and he couldn't speak. He turned, kicked his chair out of his way, stomped to the window. Outside, the windblown sand was eroding the deco fronts of the buildings. The Rexall pharmacy sign swung on its cables. Loren's hands twisted in front of him as if they were holding Luis Figueracion's spine. He jammed them in his pockets, took a breath, fought for control.

"What if I find some evidence?" he said.

"Loren," said Luis, "I don't want any goddamn evidence. I want you to take it easy, go out someplace and shoot an elk, okay?"

"You're asking me to ignore what I know," Loren said.

"You know that Connie Duvauchelle runs a whorehouse, right? When was the last time you busted her?"

Loren swung back to him. "That's different," he snapped.

"The difference is," Luis said, "is that she gives back to the community. She's a *part* of the community. She does good things with her money."

"Paying us bribes, you mean?"

Maldonado and Cipriano winced, but Luis didn't so much as blink. "They ain't bribes, Loren. They're how things *are*. You wanna do business, you pay a price one way or another." He picked up the ashtray, put it on Loren's desk, rose from his chair. "I figure that's the end of the discussion, Loren. You're on leave. That's how things *are*." He must have liked the phrase, because he said it, a drifty smile on his face, for a third time. "How things *are*."

Maldonado stood. "I'll need your badge and gun."

Loren reached for the folder he carried in his shirt pocket—half had his police ID, and the other half, hanging out of the pocket, had the seven-pointed rayed star. "The badge you can have. I paid for the gun with my own money, and I'm keeping it."

Maldonado's lip quivered, as if he were going to bark out a command like a fantasy Marine D.I., but in the end he didn't add anything. Loren unclipped the badge—Star of Babylon, he thought; he hadn't realized the irony till this moment. He kept the ID—if they didn't ask for it, he thought, he didn't need to hand it over.

He looked at the star in his hand and decided that he didn't want to physically contact any of these people; he flipped the star through the air and Maldonado caught it out of the air with a quick businesslike snatch. The hardness in his eyes suggested he would not forget this piece of disrespect.

"Get some rest, man," Luis advised as he stepped out the door. "It's like a vacation, ése. Get out·and enjoy it."

Cipriano closed the door behind the two. Anxiety tugged at nerves in his face.

"Sorry, jefe," he said. "I didn't know this was coming till just now."

Loren stepped out into the middle of the room. He reached out a hand to touch his walnut desk. He leashed an impulse to touch everything, to make sure all was still there, still solid. His mind was filled with mist.

"What are you going to do about John Doe?" he asked.

Cipriano frowned. "I dunno, man. Hope somebody comes forward with information."

"Huh." He fought the shifting mist that was trying to occupy his skull, remembered his conversation with Pacheco.

With a surprise he remembered the Wahoo Mine and its rows of bombs and incendiaries. He'd forgotten about it.

Resentment clamped his jaw. He decided not to tell Cipriano about either one. He wasn't a peace officer anymore.

He could make use of it, maybe. Show everyone he was indispensable.

He'd have to think about it, anyway.

Cipriano was looking at him with a worried expression. "You okay, jefe?"

Loren gave a laugh he didn't feel. "How am I supposed to feel? Shot down for doing my job."

"It'll only be for a while, man. Till this museum thing gets settled."

Loren looked up at Cipriano. "It's forever, Cipriano. Don't you know that? What we've been told is *don't do your job forever.* That's what it means."

Cipriano looked away. "We always take orders from the politicians, right? So what's new?"

"The difference is that this community never built its economy on murder before."

Cipriano just shrugged. "We don't know that. We don't know what kind of deal the politicians made in the olden days. They were dealing with Bugsy Siegel and Mickey Cohen, for God's sake."

Loren took a breath, tried to clear his head. "I'm ten-seven outta here," he said.

And walked.

E I G H T E E N

He took the Fury home. He hadn't been told he couldn't use it anymore; once it was in his driveway, he doubted whether anyone would.

By the time Loren arrived at his house a vicious headache had filled his skull, soaking up the world's pain like a sponge. Debra's Taurus was in the driveway, but she wasn't home. Loren took off his gun, collapsed onto the sofa, closed his eyes. Anger shuddered through his body, alternating with a fierce despair like fever alternating with chills.

His thoughts rang with belated protest. He should have pointed out that tolerating a victimless crime like prostitution was significantly different from forgiving a series of murders.

He pictured the celebration in the mayor's office, Trujillo pouring the champagne. He'd got the hated Democrat establishment to do his dirty work for him, wouldn't have to face the consequences of his indiscretion with the baby-sitter.

Fuck 'em, he thought. Fuck 'em all. Then:

I live here.

Get busy on what's bothering everyone, he thought. Concentrate on blowing away the civil complaint from Dunlop and Bonniwell.

Funny that the thing that hanged him—or that had been used as the excuse to hang him—was the one thing in which his actions were perfectly justified.

A.J. and Len, he remembered, had been shooting cats. Maybe, he thought, one of the cats was a purebred that was worth money. Maybe the cats' owners could be talked into a collaborative suit against Dunlop and Bonniwell for the value of their cats, plus pain and suffering.

The Dunlops would drop their own lawsuit like a hot potato, Loren figured, when they realized it might cost them money. With Mack Bonniwell, he couldn't be sure. The man had conviction, and a grudge. But maybe he could talk to the judge about a parole hearing, threaten Len with lockup in juvie hall.

He got up and took some aspirin. Then he took the mobile phone and made some calls.

Someone had, in fact, made a note of the contents of the collar tags of any dead cats that had them, and these had been entered into evidence in the trial. The documents were no longer in the judge's office, having been sent out to a court reporter for transcription in her home office. Loren got the number of the court reporter, called, and got her out of the shower. Her tone told him she wasn't pleased by this, but read out the names, phone numbers, and addresses on the tags. He could hear her swiping water off the documents as she read.

Most of his phone calls went to empty homes. He got two children who promised they'd pass the message to their parents, and one elderly lady who said she'd think about it.

The headache was still beating at the inside of his head. He stretched out on the couch again, the portable phone by his hand, and closed his eyes. Pointless strategies floated through his mind. At some point he may have slept.

He came alert at the sound of the back door opening, followed by a woman's voice. The woman wasn't Debra; after a few words Loren recognized her as Madeleine Gribbin, the woman who lived in the house behind them. Debra's voice chimed in. He heard the sound of the refrigerator opening and something being taken from its shelves.

"I never know how he's going to feel about something," Debra said. "He's so touchy sometimes."

Loren's heart gave an illicit thump. They were talking about him. Maybe he'd better make his presence known.

"My brother's like that," Madeleine agreed. Something liquid splashed into glasses. "I know there are some things I just can't talk about. Like politics."

"I know what you mean."

"Well. Chief of police is a political office. But Elroy, he's a miner. And you can't talk to him about politics at all. He's such a yahoo. He thinks we should have nuked Russia for what they did in Armenia."

"Loren's not a yahoo," Debra said. "He's too individual for that." Loren's heart warmed. "But still, there are things I don't want to let him know about." Chairs in the dining nook scraped back. Loren heard the two women settling in.

"Katrina's abortion, for one thing," Debra said. "I really fought with myself over that one."

At the words Loren found himself somehow transformed, swimming in a translucent sea of absolute warm clarity. He was somewhere else, listening to two women who might be strangers, who might be suspects in some as-yet-undetermined crime. His mind hummed with perfect efficiency. He was surprised at the feeling of objectivity. It might as well be that he wasn't connected with this at all.

"He's against abortion, isn't he?" said Madeleine.

"Yes," Debra said. "But he's not a fanatic about it. He doesn't march or give money to the right-to-lifers or anything. He's just . . . well, he thinks people ought to face the consequences of their actions."

"That's the way a cop would think."

"I suppose. And of course his attitudes toward sex are pretty old-fashioned. He's talked about teenage bimbos trying to evade consequences."

That's not true, Loren thought. *I've never said that.* He found that he wasn't offended by Debra's words; his thought was still lucid and objective. Perhaps she was exaggerating for effect.

There was, he noticed, a cobweb on the white-painted particle-board ceiling. The web fluttered in some unfelt breeze.

"It's because he's spent his whole life here," Debra said. "Aside from his time in the Army. If he'd spent time in a city . . ." Her voice trailed away. "I dunno."

"Maybe he's never thought about it."

"I *know* he hasn't. And I finally decided that I didn't want him making up his mind when Katrina was pregnant."

"That was probably the smart thing to do."

"And who knows how he would have reacted toward Marty? You know what his temper is like."

Marty, Loren thought. Katrina's boyfriend from when she was thirteen to a little over a year ago. He'd always wondered why they broke up. He hadn't seen any signs of trouble.

And Katrina hadn't had a steady guy since, just a long, intricate tangle of hopeful suitors. No wonder.

Marty, he decided objectively, ought to have his knees broken.

Loren decided he didn't want to hear any more of this. One of the girls could come home at any time, discover him on the couch. He leaned back, tried to relax his body. Let the air out of his lungs.

He began, deliberately, to snore. Softly at first, not knowing how to make the sound convincing, but to him the snores seemed right enough, so he increased the volume.

A guilty silence loomed from the breakfast nook. Loren heard a chair scrape back and footsteps hesitantly move toward him. He moderated his snores, tried to relax his body. The pattern of light on his eyelids shifted; there was someone hovering over the couch. Loren blew his breath out through his lips, rolled on his side, tried to imitate coming slowly awake.

"Loren." Debra's voice. "I didn't know you were home."

"Taking a nap." Loren rolled upright, blinked his gummed eyes open. "I should have gone to bed."

Debra, he could tell, was thinking hard. Loren decided to let her. He picked up his gun from the coffee table, walked past her, and went into the bedroom.

His headache still beat at him, but he seemed somehow to have transcended it, put the pain in another realm. The exemplary efficiency of his mind continued unabated. He wondered if this was a migraine—he'd never had one to his knowledge, but this might be what happened. He hung his gun belt from the gun rack, stretched out on the bed, and lay straight with his hands at his sides, like a corpse waiting for the body bag.

So much for querencia.

Thoughts flickered through his mind, unwinding as if from a film reel. Perhaps he should move the explosives to another location, someplace where he could uncover it later, when he judged the time ripe to become a hero. The F'bee might not have got all the eco-terrs; the survivors might shift the stash somewhere else. He'd have to prevent that.

He could at least get the Dunlops out of the civil suit with his plan to mobilize the cat owners. The Bonniwells were another matter.

He'd have to just try the cat-owner plan and see. Mack had a lot weighing on his mind right now, his own joblessness high on the list. He might be too weary to hold his hatred for long.

Which left John Doe, William Patience, the wreck of the maglev.

His mind probed at what he knew, and the name of Joseph Dielh kept rising to the surface. Flying off the labs' private field in its private jet, the physicist had been in Washington since Sunday.

Maybe he was consulting his superiors. But it occurred to Loren that Dielh might have realized early on just how crazy Patience was and figured Washington was the best place to hide. If he could just get the man to return his phone calls, Loren might find out.

He could, he realized, fly to Washington. Nothing was stopping him. He could track Dielh down at the Department of Energy or Defense or wherever it was he was hiding.

He didn't have a job here anymore.

Hell, he could do anything he wanted. He was free. He had no responsibilities at all. With cold glee he realized that Luis Figueracion and Edward Trujillo had just given him all the freedom he needed to pursue any investigation he wanted.

Randal Dudenhof's blood splattered across his thoughts. Too much depended on whether Dudenhof and John Doe were the same person, whether there had been a miracle. His rummaging through Randal's coffin hadn't settled things, and Doe's disappearance had only confused matters.

How to find out?

Maybe it was for you. Rickey's words.

The man had called him by name. Called for help, and Loren could give none.

Betrayed. He had been betrayed. The unblinking realization rolled up from deep inside him, filled his skull, pressed outward. Pain crackled along the bone seams. His fit of abstraction had kept the feeling from him.

He had served Luis Figueracion all his career, and this had been his reward. Bounced out of his office, told to hunt elk while killers cleaned their guns and lined up the next target.

He had served his family with the same diligence that he had served Luis. And they had betrayed him as well.

What would he have done if he had been confronted with Katrina's need for an abortion? He thought about it and realized that he didn't know. Now, thanks to the silence in which he had so carefully been wrapped, he would never have the chance to know.

This seemed too large and important a concept for so small a room as the one he was lying in. He rose from the bed, walked to the door, and stood in the doorway. The scents of home, of querencia, came newly to his senses. He could still hear voices in the breakfast nook—hushed, self-conscious voices.

He walked down the hallway to Kelly's room and entered. Dirty laundry was ground into the carpet. Posters of male celebrities, bare-chested, long-haired, gazed from the wall with narrow-eyed, suspicious scowls that were, from one to the next, oddly similar. Loren drifted through the room, through the bathroom that smelled of baby powder, perfume, and hair spray. A pile of wet, dirty towels invited mold in a corner. The cowboys in the Wrangler ad on Katrina's door stared at him like members of a Hollywood posse.

Loren opened the door to the room he had built for his daughter and drifted in. Katrina was orderly compared to her sister. Books and tapes were filed neatly. There was room to walk here, and the only clothing in sight was her pajamas thrown over a chair, and the dress she'd worn to church that morning laid out on the bed. The computer she shared with Kelly sat under its plastic cover.

Two of the windows were open to the dusty wind, and a third—the one without a screen that she sometimes used as a door—was shut. Marty probably got in that way, Loren thought, and had very likely impregnated her on her own bed.

Loren decided not to think about that anymore. He stood in the room for a while, absorbing it, knowing that it seemed different now than it had before, not in detail, just in the way Loren was looking at it.

He realized that he was acting like a cop. He was looking for evidence, clues as to what was going on here. He didn't want to behave that way with his family.

He concluded that he needed an infusion of clarity. He went to his room, changed out of his uniform, put on Levi's and a jeans jacket. As he left via the front door he heard the conversation in the kitchen stop.

Once out the door he wondered whether he should have said goodbye.

He got in his Fury and drove at random around Rose Hill, past the Fortune house with the FBI seals on the doors, past the battered old Queen Anne where Roberts made his nightly consultations with his bottle and the Almighty. No prophet appeared; no miracle dazzled his eyes. He drove on, downtown, past the deco storefronts designed to speed into the future. He headed out beyond the city limits, past the turnoff to Connie Duvauchelle's, the hatchet-waving Indian of the Geronimo, and the speeding rocket of the Atom Lounge. The unnatural fenced-off flatness of the UFO field spread out on his left, and he slowed.

Weeds covered the field now, obscuring the pentagram that the patient, passive gang of saucerheads had assembled. The big metal-walled work shed where they'd slept and stored their tools was dripping rust from its galvanized roof. Loren turned into the field, bounced along old ruts, parked by the work shed.

Another millennium postponed. Joseph Smith and Samuel Catton had both announced the momentary end of the world in the impending cry of Gideon's trumpet; somehow the world had avoided its judgment and finale. Another apocalypse was to come in a rain of thermonuclear fire, again postponed indefinitely. The turn of the millennium was to feature the saucers, glowing vic formations rolling soundlessly across the midnight sky, bringing salvation and enlightenment to their sad, hopeful, hopefully sad worshippers.

The greenhouse was the world's nightmare now, glaciers calving, oceans rising, crops browning in the furrow-striped fields like waffles on the griddle. People like the eco-terrs, with their spiked trees and wrecked power lines, fought a rear guard against that future, a future already visible in the heat and drought that bleached this alkaline country.

That wouldn't be the end, either, though it would be bad enough.

Enough people would survive to imagine, perhaps realize, another, more ominous conclusion to their existence.

Loren got out of the car and walked through one of the gaps in the chain link fence that had been built to protect the mother ship from the violent frenzy of last-minute converts. The hot breeze burned the back of his neck. An ardis of the pentagram pointed mutely to Loren's boots. Concrete poured, straight as a die, into a carefully gouged rut, now crumbling, covered with dust. Loren chose a concrete line and walked along it.

Even over the wind he should have heard the howling from the Atocha pit, the trucks rolling out of the resonant cavity with their tons of ore. It was silent.

His world, Loren realized, the one that he had lived in all his life, had come to an end. The millennium had come, and he had only now noticed it.

Grouse exploded from beneath his feet, roaring up from a young juniper that had grown up here since the saucer-apocalypse had been postponed. He should have brought a shotgun, he thought, then realized that there was one in the Fury. He didn't like the Remington for hunting—it was too heavy, too awkward, not like the turn-of-the-century double-barreled Heym he normally used—but it was the gun that was here.

He went back to the car, got the gun, jacked out the rounds of buckshot he'd threatened to use on the poachers that afternoon, and loaded it with bird shot. He stalked carefully over the pentagram, feet stepping softly on the crumbling concrete, and brought down seven birds. The movement and shots were clean, precise. Nothing wasted. The powder smell was welcome in the hot wind. He picked up his spent shells to avoid leaving his sign on the land. Something, at least, was within the realm of his control.

Loren tossed the dead birds in the trunk of the car, reloaded the gun with buck, and walked up the drive to the metal-walled work shack. It had an old Master padlock, not worked in ages. He got in his car and backed out.

His headache seemed to have faded.

On his way through town he passed the parsonage, saw a parking place, and swooped into it. There was a little squeal of rubber as the car behind braked suddenly. Had he not been in a police cruiser, Loren knew, he probably would have earned a glare, a finger, a blast of the horn.

Rickey answered half a minute or so after Loren's knock. The parson was naked from the waist up and without his glasses. He blinked myopically and scratched the pale hairs on his sunken chest.

"You were taking a nap," Loren said. "I'll come back later."

"It's time I got up." Rickey turned around and walked away down the corridor. "You know the way to the study."

Loren seated himself opposite the dead computer terminal. Deco lightning bolts flashed at him from the back of the parson's chair. A carved plaster eye gazed at him from atop a pyramid. He heard Rickey bumbling around in the back, and then the parson appeared, his flannel shirttails out. Rickey sat opposite Loren and put his metal-rimmed spectacles on, perching them on his nose first and then placing the bows behind his ears, like a bookkeeper out of Dickens.

"I've been told what happened," Rickey said. "I'm sorry to hear about all that."

Loren frowned at him. "About all what?"

"About, ah, about your being laid off."

"Oh," Loren said. He waved his hand. "That's nothing. It's administrative leave with pay. It's a political tactic."

Rickey's eyelids battled with sleep. "Oh."

"I didn't agree with why it was done, but—" He fell silent, guilt's clawed finger stabbing at his throat.

Rickey's glance sharpened. "Why was it done? If you don't mind my asking."

"Because," Loren said, and stopped dead. He glanced at Rickey. "Public servants don't always agree with public policy, right?" he said.

Rickey grinned. "Nor do ministers with church doctrine."

Loren was surprised. "Really?"

"Of course. Think of the poor Pope! He has two thousand years of antiquated revelations, interpretation, and doctrine to deal with every time he opens his mouth." Rickey leaned back; the old chair creaked. "Even a radical American religion, formed by direct revelation in the nineteenth century, carries a lot of unnecessary doctrinal baggage with it. I'd just as soon dispose of most of it."

"I guess."

"That's why I like our doctrine of continuing revelation. We can renew or alter the church whenever it proves necessary. Keep the faith fresh."

"Good."

Loren saw he'd triggered another one of Rickey's unpredictable enthusiasms and resigned himself to a lengthy explication, but the parson, with a visible though genial effort of will, managed to drag himself back from the brink. He cocked his head and looked at Loren. "You were talking about public servants?"

"Yeah. How if you're a cop, you're not responsible for policy. You have to work within the system, and the system is imperfect. And you didn't *make* the system in the first place, you inherited it."

"Yes. I understand."

"And—" Loren restrained an impulse to rise and pace, to add visible motion to the impetus of his thoughts. "All I want," Loren said, letting his resigned hands rise from his lap, "is for my town to be a nice place. A *safe* place, okay?"

"I was in Uganda during the sigatoka famine," Rickey said.

"I guessed you had. From what you'd said earlier."

"The area had been hit hard by Amin, war, and revolution, and *then* by AIDS, and just as things were starting to look better, along came the plantain blight." He pronounced it *plahntain*. "Plantain and bananas are the staple of the poor people—you can raise enough plantain on a small plot to feed a family—" *Smahl plaht.* "—and the plantain and banana trees were being hit by black sigatoka faster than blight-resistant trees could mature. Well—" He shrugged his shoulders. "You know what happened from pictures on the TV. Refugees, unrest, revolt. Starvation." *Stah-urr-vation.* "I was supposed to help the farmers shift their production to wheat, but the American wheat I was given was unsuitable to Africa, and though an acre and a half sown with plantain will keep a family fed, you need a lot more land to feed that same family on wheat, and the land wasn't available. There's enough rainfall to raise wheat if the rain is distributed evenly, but in Uganda it doesn't come regularly, it comes in torrential cloudbursts followed by weeks of tropical heat."

Rickey shook his head. "I knew all of this, you understand, within a few weeks of my arrival. But my superiors in Washington insisted that I follow the program. Recommendations to the contrary were discouraged or ignored. And what could I do? I could do nothing and watch the Ugandans starve, or I could teach them to plant wheat and maybe save a few." He gave a long sigh.

"After a while I began to wonder if Washington really wanted to save anybody. I thought they were just after good P.R., they just wanted people to *believe* they were helping, but didn't care what actually happened."

"Good P.R.," Loren said. "I know what you mean."

"All the new wheat fields turned into eroded deserts. Worse than if we'd done nothing. The local people began to blame us, the Americans, for their problems. They identified us with the corrupt government that was getting rich off the relief effort. All the strife they'd had before had left a lot of modern weapons around. I got evacuated back to the States after some of the other Peace Corps people were shot or hacked up with pangas."

He leaned forward, looking into Loren's eyes. "All I wanted, Chief, was for Uganda to be a *nice place*. But it was not permitted for me to make it that way. Do you understand?"

Loren nodded, fully intending to thank Rickey for his little speech and leave, but guilt seized his heart and somehow he found himself talking on.

"That's not quite the way it is," Loren said. "It's more like, if you were in Uganda, and you had the food to give to the people, and your superiors told you not to."

Rickey's eyes flickered behind his spectacles. "You must feed the people, Loren."

"The thing is," Loren said, "they *say* it's because they can get more food later. But in the meantime, there's starvation."

"You cannot know what will come. You must feed the people while you can."

"I know who shot the man the other night," Loren said abruptly, "and I know who wrecked the train yesterday."

Loren saw surprise behind the glittering spectacles. "And you can't prove it?"

"I've been advised not to try. I've been put on leave so that I won't."

Rickey seemed genuinely surprised. He struggled with his thoughts for a long moment. "Your . . . superiors . . . are covering up a series of murders?"

"It's more like they don't want to *know* who did it. It doesn't matter to them. They've got other things on their minds."

"Like what, for God's sake?"

"Like saving the town. A bunch of strangers got killed, okay. They didn't have anything to do with it, they didn't know the people who died, it's nothing to them." He remembered Sondra Jernigan weeping in her car, Jernigan's head with its furious scowl. "Nothing to them," he repeated. "But they figure they can do a deal with . . . well, with some people connected to the people who did the crime. Get money and jobs for the town."

"Blood money." Rickey was appalled.

"I've been loyal to them," Loren said. "I've done stuff they wanted me to, even though I didn't like it. It's my town, you know? I had to take it the way I found it."

"I have heard, of course " Rickey chose his words carefully. "I have heard stories of corruption. Payoffs, that sort of thing."

"Some of them are probably true," Loren said.

Rickey said nothing, just looked at him.

"But it's not . . . it's not evil," Loren said. He felt sweat prickling his scalp. "It's just a way of life. It's almost neighborly, the way it happens. It's the way things have been here for over a century."

"It's still wrong."

"I accept that." He looked at the parson and the words grew dry in his mouth. "I live with it," he said. "It's not something I take pride in. But change it? I'd have to change everything."

"It will have to end sometime."

"I've been loyal to certain people." Insistently. "I've been loyal, and I've expected loyalty in return."

"You have reason to expect that."

"Damn right." Loren's fists clenched. "And they—I've been betrayed. My trust. I don't know . . ." His mind whirled.

"Render unto Caesar if you must," Rickey said, "but you must not conceal a great crime. You must arrest the killers. You must arrest them and put them away." The words *crime* and *arrest* were turned to fierce growls by his thick *r*'s.

"In order to arrest someone, I need evidence," Loren said. "I have to convince the district attorney's office that I have evidence enough to convict, and I don't have that. If I *had* it, I'd be able to arrest the perpetrators, sweat them until one of them agrees to cave in and testify against the others. That's the way it is. That's the way it works. But if the D.A. won't hold them, I can't do that, and if I told the D.A. what I know, he'd think I was crazy."

"But still you must—" Hesitation surfaced in the pastor's look. "The evidence you have—is it, ah, supernatural in origin?"

Loren gave a laugh. "My miracle, you mean? No, it's not even that good. It's circumstantial. Based on what I know of the people involved, their movements, and so on."

"I'm relieved." Rickey took a long breath. "I wonder what it is like, you know, to have a life on your conscience."

"I've thought about that myself. But I've never had to use my weapon. I've always found other ways of dealing with my neighbors. I'm proud of that." Defiance filled his mind. "Handling it informally. That's the best way, whatever the lawyers say."

Rickey seemed not to have paid attention. "That man who burned down my shelter," he said. "The arsonist. He probably knew the place had smoke detectors and alarms. How would he have known that twelve people would die? That he would kill children? That couldn't have been part of his plan."

"From what I've seen of criminals," Loren said, "they just don't give a damn what damage they do. It's not something that even fits into their calculations." He shrugged. "That's why we catch them, most times. Because they don't calculate at all."

"I'm sure that whoever did it is suffering," Rickey said. The pastor, Loren realized, hadn't heard a word Loren had said; he was locked into his own nightmare, his eyes focused a thousand miles away, on choking children and scarlet flames scarring the night. "How could such a man atone?" Rickey asked. "What service could he offer to society or to God?"

"A life busting rocks in Leavenworth wouldn't be out of line."

"A lifetime wouldn't be enough, surely." Rickey's eyes flicked to Loren's. "Murderers must be punished. Right must be done. If you know who . . ."

A hot bubble of frustration expanded within Loren, exploding in anger. "It's a goddamn game!" he said. "Right and wrong don't have anything to do with it! You've gotta dance a fucking waltz with lawyers and judges, dot every *i*, cross every *t*!"

"Dot them," Rickey said, his look intent. "Cross them."

"If this were the old days, a hundred years ago, I could just raise up a posse and find the perps and arrest them. Chances are I could count on the posse doing the judge's job for me, filling them with lead during the arrest or hanging them after." He shrugged. "But it's the twenty-first century. You don't do things that way, not even in Atocha. Things are run the old way here, but not that old a way. Not lynch law."

"You have seen a miracle." *Mirahcle.*

Loren's mind jolted onto Rickey's new track. He looked at the pastor in surprise. "Yes," he said. "I think I have."

"What did I say about miracles the other night? That they turn things upside down, that they change everything?"

"Yes."

"I want you to consider whether the miracle was intended for you, because you are meant to change everything."

Loren looked at Rickey bleakly. "Sword and arm of the Lord," he said.

"Yes."

"God's backing me into a corner. He wants something done and he's not giving me any choice."

"In a sense. Yes." Rickey's look was intense. "You are a public servant. You've lived in the world, among the fallen, but you are also a man of faith, because you sense a higher world. Perhaps you are being called to make Atocha a nice place. As you said."

Loren looked for a long time at the parson, then rose slowly from his chair. The sense of calling had not exhilarated him at all, just filled him with sick foreboding. His headache was coming back.

"I'll do what I can," he said.

"That is all anyone can expect."

He drove toward home beneath the overhanging elms of Estes Street in the darkness, and suddenly a car pulled away from the curb behind him, the headlights dazzling in his rearview mirror. The lights dimmed, then brightened again, then dimmed. He was being signaled.

His nerves hummed and his mouth turned dry. He was suddenly aware that he wasn't carrying a pistol.

He set the parking brake and drew the pump shotgun from its rest. The other car, a Saab, pulled around him and parked in front, in the spill of his headlights. He could see only a single passenger.

The man got out, a young man in a blue nylon jacket and work boots, with a neatly trimmed blond mustache. Loren turned the side spotlight on and shone it at the man, aiming it with the control stick inside the car. The man shaded his eyes with his hands—both hands. Loren wanted to see both the man's hands. He rolled down his window.

"Chief Hawn?"

"Yes."

"I'm Paul Rivers. We talked last night."

"Oh, yeah."

"I got the information you wanted. It's kind of weird."

The man reached into his jacket pocket. Loren tensed, his nerves screaming, and his grip tightened on the stock of the shotgun.

Rivers pulled out a piece of paper. "The same four guys were working all weekend. From Saturday morning on, no one else from our office was in the facility, aside from the gate guards."

Loren took the paper and looked at the names. Patience, Nazzarett, McLerie, Denardis.

"That's unusual, right?" Loren said.

"It's never happened before. And none of those guys have been on duty since first shift Monday. They're not on the roster, and I haven't seen any of them personally."

Whatever had happened, Loren thought, happened Friday night. And it had been so unusual that Patience had kept the same people on through the weekend, keeping the number of witnesses low, till he could get rid of the yellow Thunderbird on Monday morning and destroy the last of his evidence.

"I arrested Nazzarett on Tuesday afternoon," Loren said. "He was shadowing me in one of your Blazers."

Rivers shrugged. "He wasn't on the duty roster. I didn't think to check who'd signed out a vehicle."

"Okay. Thanks."

"I didn't want to call you. Patience can monitor any calls going in or out of the facility from his board, and—"

"Wait a minute." Loren stared at him. "Do the employees know this?"

"Some do, some don't. It's not a big secret, if that's what you're asking."

That was why Jernigan died. Because Patience had overheard his call to the lawyer on Tuesday morning.

"Anyway, Patience has other monitoring equipment. Phone taps and so on."

"They're illegal." Pointlessly.

Rivers only shrugged. "Things have been getting pretty tense. He's been pulling intruder drills, snap inspections. Being more hard-ass than usual. He's under some kind of pressure. Maybe he's tapping your line, maybe he isn't. Maybe he's tapping mine. I thought I ought to be careful."

"Okay." Loren looked at the list again. "Thanks." A thought struck him and he grinned. "If they're tapping my line, they're not getting anything but long hours of conversation between teenage girls. I almost feel sorry for them."

"You're not going to ask me for anything more, are you?"

"No." Looking at him. "I'm not."

Rivers seemed suspicious of this assurance, not relieved at all. He turned and headed back to his car.

Loren looked at the paper, then put it on the seat next to him. Just a few hours ago it would have meant something to him.

He drove home.

Debra was waiting on the couch as he walked through the door. The tube blared the theme song of a soap opera about a firm of lawyers who lived in a neon Hollywood spill of glamour, styled and hip and clever, a group who motored their midnight Ferraris over the throbbing night Los Angeles freeways to an endless synthesized disco snare beat, and who, if Loren was any judge, must have acquired their style and money from a swinging clan of drug-dealer clients that somehow never appeared in the television's frame . . .

Debra rose from the couch. Loren couldn't read her eyes.

"I'm sorry," she said.

Loren walked toward the kitchen. "About what?"

"About your job. Cipriano called and asked how you were doing, and I didn't know what he was talking about. So he told me."

"Yeah. Well. It'll work out." Loren got a glass from the cupboard and filled it from the water cooler.

"You look terrible. Are you okay?"

"I went hunting."

Debra watched him as he tilted back his head and gulped his glass of water. He put the glass in the sink and wiped his mouth with the gritty back of his dusty hand.

"People have been calling," she said. "Something about *cats*?"

"I'm going to take a shower," Loren said. Debra watched him go.

He stood under the hot water as the headache rolled in slow time through his skull. He wanted to stop thinking, just turn over and close his eyes and become the happy hick cop that William Patience thought he was.

Loren turned off the water, dried himself, and threw his clothes in the hamper. He put on his bathrobe and stepped out into the hallway, and immediately Kelly's door opened and she and Katrina came out. Kelly was dressed for bed, Katrina in her usual shirttails and jeans.

"We're sorry, Daddy," Katrina said. "We're really sorry."

"What can we do?" Kelly said. "Is there any way we can help?"

Loren looked at them for a long puzzled moment before he recollected what they were talking about.

"Don't worry about it," he said. "It's a political thing. As soon as the maneuvers are over, I'll be back in my office."

"Oh."

"That's good, then."

They both seemed a little disappointed—they had worked up to participation in a major crisis, and now it had faded.

"You're good kids," Loren found himself saying. "All we need to do is just stay out of trouble and things will work out."

They each gave him a hug and then started back down the hall toward Kelly's room. Katrina turned around in the doorway.

"Daddy?" Her voice was tentative. "Did you find out about Skywalker?"

"I called," he said, "but it was too early. I'll call again tomorrow."

She smiled faintly and closed the door. "I'm not interested in legalities!" someone shouted from the television. "This is a matter of right and wrong!"

Loren decided he didn't want to hear the rest of that conversation, so he went into his room and climbed into bed. He could hear the girls talking, sometimes laughing, in Kelly's room. Headache beat a melancholy drum behind his eyes.

He'd call all the cat owners tomorrow. Maybe even put an ad in the Friday paper. And talk to the judge about grounds for getting Dunlop's and Bonniwell's paroles revoked.

The door opened and Debra padded to the bed. "May I sit down?" she said. Her voice was tentative.

"Sure."

He moved over to allow her room. She sat on the bed and looked down at him, blond bangs hanging over her brows, her glasses sitting halfway down her nose. "I was wondering," she began.

"Yes?"

"We seem to have some sort of crisis here. How serious is it?"

"With my job?" Evading. He thought for a moment and restrained the impulse to shrug. "It's probably not very serious. I've decided . . ." He sorted through his feelings. "I've decided to do what I have to do," he said. "I think that'll get me back in the saddle pretty quick."

"It's really not very serious, then?"

"I don't think so."

"Good." Her eyes wandered. She seemed vague as to where to go from here. She took a breath.

"I was wondering . . ." She spoke rapidly, getting this over with. "Whether you heard my conversation with Madeleine this afternoon."

A cold caution crept into Loren's heart, a close approximation of the horrid objectivity he'd felt as he lay on the couch and listened to Debra's words. He looked at Debra narrowly and decided to let her sweat a bit.

"Not all of it," he said.

Debra glanced away. "We were talking about some things that I hope you haven't heard," she said.

"Like what?" He realized he was acting like a cop again, following the rules of interrogation: never let the suspect know how much you know. When his shock over this wore off, he realized, he would probably feel an abiding guilt about it.

But he didn't feel it now.

"About . . . family matters," Debra said.

"Important matters?" Loren asked.

"Yes." She glanced at him from under her lashes.

"If there's something happening," Loren said, "I need to know about it. I'm a part of this family, too."

Debra took in a long, shuddering breath, then let it out. "What we were talking about," she said, "it's something in the past. But yes, you're right. You should have been told then."

"If anything happens, I want to know."

"Yes." She reached out and took his hand, then squeezed it. "You'll know."

Sword and arm of the Lord, he thought. Rickey had given his blessing to whatever needed doing.

If only he could figure out what that was.

N I N E T E E N

Loren woke early, a little after two. The headache was gone. He stared at the shadowed ceiling, his mind humming with extreme efficiency, not racing, not wasting anything, just moving with quiet, unparalleled potency. His limbs felt relaxed, alert, ready for anything, ready to go six rounds with some heavyweight thug from the Santa Fe slams if he had to. He felt as if he wouldn't need to sleep for a hundred years.

He rose, put on some clothes and the smaller of his revolvers, and left the house. He didn't know if Debra came awake or not: her breathing didn't change. Perhaps she was spying on him the same way he found himself spying on her.

He drove the Taurus to the Circle K west of town on 81. The place had been closed for hours. There was a lock on the ice machine. One fluorescent light set over the gas pumps buzzed ferociously as if to warn off the swarms of insects that were batting themselves insensible against its glass cover.

Loren didn't think he'd been followed. He backed into a parking place near the store's two pay phones, just in case he needed to get away fast, and then got out of the car and plugged his phone company holocard into one of the telephones. He looked up a number in one of his notebooks and pressed the necessary buttons.

The phone rang four and one-half times before it answered. Sleepy, the physicist sounded a lot more Indian than he had awake.

"Amardas Singh."

"Doctor," Loren said, "I need some answers."

Twenty-four hours later the gunmetal Taurus rode a high trail under a bottomless dome of crisp bright stars. Loren had spent the evening in Socorro, talking to Singh, and he took the short route home, over the high land of the national forest, twisting hairpin turns with overhanging igneous crags on either side. The twisting road suited his mood; he felt he was himself navigating obscure mental pathways. His mind buzzed with a new vocabulary and he wondered how the hell he could phrase it all on an indictment.

His brain was still humming. He had not slept. Under the comforting glow of the Milky Way, he felt as if he had the universe in his hand.

Around him the forest burned, blood-orange flames reflecting off the walls of canyons, glowing in the sky, beneath the fleet of roaring choppers whose stabbing, hovering lights, floating below the night canopy, could make you believe the saucers had come at last.

When he came back from the Circle K he found the white recycled legal pad he had used to outline the John Doe case, and he sat in the living room under the dome light, almost until dawn, drawing diagrams in different-colored marker pens. He dozed then, head tilted over the back of the sofa, until a snarling dogfight in front of the house brought him bolt awake. He jumped to the door and saw that a Doberman the color of red clay was straddling a black Lab in the driveway and worrying at his throat.

Loren charged from out of the house and chased both dogs away. Neither, as they ran off in opposite directions, seemed seriously hurt.

He had forgotten about the dead birds in the Fury's trunk. The dogs had been fighting over something they could only smell.

Fourteen hours' delay wouldn't have hurt the birds; he'd heard of people hanging them up for a week. He took the grouse to the backyard, sat on his old weathered bench, and cleaned them. The Mexican wind, hot on his unshaven face, carried the down away. He bagged the entrails and feathers and dumped them in the trash, then put each cleaned bird in an individual freezer bag and placed them all in the big freezer on the back porch. By that time Debra was a-wake and cooking breakfast, and it was time to fetch Jerry from his trailer.

Jerry's topic of the day was ESP. He went on about Rhine cards and premonitions and how quantum physics showed that little atomic thingies—his exact terminology—could communicate at speeds faster than that of light. Presumably this demonstrated telepathy, though Jerry did not make this connection entirely clear. All this skimmed only the surface of Loren's attention: his mind stayed in its perfect hum.

Thursday's sin was envy. Rickey developed his thesis at great length, and with great exuberance, but it skimmed across Loren's mind like Jerry's talk of telepathy. Envy was not something he'd ever had much of a problem with. His concerns were more basic.

Singh either had classes or meetings till four o'clock that afternoon. It would take three hours or so to drive to Socorro. Loren was free till after lunch.

He made plans to shoot duck with Jerry the next day, took his family home, then drove the girls to school. He let them off in the high school parking lot under the HOME OF THE MINERS sign, then drove back to the City-County Building and parked in his reserved space. He saw Vincent Nazzarett parked across the street in a dark green Mustang and his mind began to hum at a higher pitch. The bastard was a murderer, and Loren was going to prove it.

He stopped for a short chat with Eloy at the front desk, then headed to Cipriano's office and knocked on the door. Cipriano was leaning back in his chair, boots on his desk, reading a battered thirdhand James Michener paperback.

"Qué paso, ése?" Loren asked.

"Just improving my mind."

Loren took a seat. "Much happening?"

Cipriano's shoulders twitched. "Drunks. Kids shooting up stop signs. The usual."

"Anything happened on the John Doe matter?"

Cipriano frowned, put the yellow carbon of a parking ticket in his book to mark his place, then put the thick paperback on his desk. "Nothing."

"I'm not surprised."

Cipriano was nettled. "Anything happens, I know what to do."

Loren looked at the Michener paperback. "My impression is that you got my job with the understanding that you wouldn't do any more about John Doe than was strictly necessary."

Heat flickered behind Cipriano's eyes. "I didn't ask for this situation," he said.

"I know."

"Anybody comes forward with information about John fucking Doe, I'll follow it up."

"I don't doubt that."

"But if the perps are good enough to steal a body *and* its goddamn internal organs from the M.I.'s office, *plus* his clothes and boots from the criminalistics lab—"

"Wait a minute—"

"—then they're better than anybody this office is gonna catch. You know what I'm saying, jefe?"

"*Hold on!*" Loren shouted. "Doe's clothes disappeared, too?"

"Yes. From a locked drawer in a locked building that had Albuquerque cops marching in and out all night. The only thing that was left was the plastic bags they put the stuff in."

Loren sat back in his chair, stunned. "Like the toe tag."

"The criminalistics boys didn't find out till this morning, and called this office first. That's how come I know about it and you don't. Now, what's this about a toe tag?"

Loren explained. Cipriano listened, tapping his fingers on the arms of his chair. Finally he just shrugged.

"This is too weird for me, jefe."

"I'm going to keep working on it," Loren said.

Cipriano's head gave an upward jerk. "You what?"

"I realized it this morning. I've got more freedom to pursue the Doe killing now that I'm on leave than I did when I was working here." Loren laughed. "When I was in the office, I had to deal with paperwork and hassle from the mayor and personnel problems and

God knows what else. Now you're stuck with all that, and I can work the killings full-time."

Cipriano's eyes narrowed. "This is just gonna get you in trouble."

"Not if I come up with indictments against the four scumbags who killed John Doe."

"Jefe!" Cipriano's tone was sharp. "Who the hell are you talking about?"

"William Patience. Vincent Nazzarett. Jim McLerie. And Carl Denardis."

"What evidence do you have?"

Loren told him about the revised work schedule for the four, that and the fact that none of them had been on duty all week despite Nazzarett's having been busted for carrying automatic weapons in his ATL Blazer.

"Who told you this?"

"Somebody."

Cipriano threw out his hands, "You gotta tell me, jefe. How can I evaluate this shit unless I know who it comes from?"

"I protect my informants," Loren said.

Cipriano leaned back in his chair, frowning, and tapped his fingers on the arms again. "Okay," he said, "but I have to be kept informed of your progress. I can't have you running around like a bull in a china shop."

"I'll be subtle. Honest."

This assertion seemed to make Cipriano skeptical. Loren considered telling him about the tow truck driver he'd found in El Paso, then decided against it. For all he knew somebody had bugged Cipriano's office.

"Look," Loren said, "I just came by to use the phone in my office. Is that okay?"

"I want to be kept informed, jefe."

The *jefe* lifted Loren's spirits. He rose, grinning. "You got it, pachuco."

Once in his office he called Howard Morton in the U.S. attorney's office. "I been expecting your call, hoss," Howard said.

"What's happening with my neighbors?"

"Tucked away nice and safe in the calabozo. Judge refused bond on account of they's terrorists."

"Even Skywalker?"

"Heh." A dry chuckle. "Skywalker Fortune. What kind of parents would name a kid something like that?"

"I guess we know what kind."

"Reckon we do. But don't worry—Skywalker's tucked in the county D-home. They might let her out if they can find a foster family in this jurisdiction—her lawyer's making enough stink about a minor being held on a terrorist charge."

"Who's her lawyer?"

"Heh-heh." A double-dry chuckle this time. "L. Roy Friedman."

Loren whistled. L. Roy Friedman was a coiffed blue-eyed world-class shark who picked his white and perfect dental implants with the bones of chewed-up district attorneys. His blonde ex-model wife probably shaved her legs on his cheekbones. He made gold-chained syndicate shysters like Axelrod look like bleary-eyed nighttime bail bondsmen.

"Friedman was waiting in the Federal Building when the caravan got here," Morton said. "Somebody back home must have called him. The Eco-Alliance had him on retainer and he flew in from San Francisco on his private jet."

"The trial's gonna be a circus."

"Three rings plus all the freaks in the sideshow. My boss is about pissing in his pants. I'm just glad I've got a full calendar and don't have to do anything on this one but watch. Jesus, it's gonna take Friedman three months just to pick the jury."

Loren laughed. "I wouldn't want to be Killeen right now."

"Heh. You got it, hoss. A hasty bust like that is just the thing Friedman'll need to spring half his clients on technicalities and make the rest of our indictments look like they were written by Larry, Moe, and Curly."

"Which they may well have, anyway."

"Shhh." There was amusement even in his shushing. "We don't *talk* 'bout that round here."

Loren and Morton conversed about hunting and the Miners football team for a while—the Miners hadn't scented a state championship since 1962, and their record seemed unlikely to change—and then Loren hung up. He called Debra, Jerry answered, and Loren relayed the information and the phone number of the

Albuquerque juvenile detention home. Katrina and Kelly could call their friend when they got home from school.

Businesslike, his mind continuing its efficient conduct, Loren next made his calls to cat owners. Every click and murmur of the phone system seemed loud as a cannon, pointing with steel-clawed fingers to wiretaps. The whole cat business seemed impossibly trivial by now, and he could picture Patience and his people listening to a disk recording and guffawing over what they were hearing, but the idea seemed to pan out. Several of the animal lovers agreed in principle to Loren's idea concerning a civil suit. A nice bludgeon, he thought, to hold over the head of Bonniwell, Dunlop, & Co.

He got up from his chair and went to the big walk-in safe and opened it. Stolen-and-recovered property and a generous supply of contraband sat next to plastic-wrapped UZIs taken from the ATL jeeps. Loren looked at the submachine guns and wondered how bad it was all going to get.

About as bad as I decide to make it, he concluded.

"I found out about the bedspread," Amardas Singh said.

A Rorschach sweatblot had imprinted itself on Loren's lower back after three hours in the Taurus. His hip and back ached. The highway's white center stripe seemed to have burned itself on his retinas as if by laser. He clutched his cold can of Coke and followed the physicist into his living room.

"The bedspread," he repeated. His mind was on other things.

"The bedspread in the motel?" Singh said. "That you said was Navajo but that I thought was Pakistani?"

"Oh. Yeah." Singh gestured toward a couch covered with a pattern of bluebonnets, and Loren gratefully sank into it.

"In the nineteenth century, the Anglos were trying to get the Indians to adopt weaving as a way of supporting themselves." Singh sat in an easy chair with a print of red and blue poppies. Apparently clashing floral patterns were an aspect of his oriental heritage he had not rejected.

Driving into Socorro, Loren had pulled into a Shell station and asked one of the locals for directions. The grease monkey cocked a wary eye at the Remington Loren had propped on the passenger seat, just in case, but had nevertheless directed him to Faculty Hill, a neighborhood of middle-class homes on a mild brown bluff above the New Mexico Tech campus. The door had been opened by a smiling blonde woman in her early twenties, Singh's wife, whom Loren immediately suspected, with no evidence at all, of having once been his student. The woman tossed her thin braids, offered Loren a Coke, called Singh from his study, and strolled into the back exuding an air of calm competence.

"The Navajos," Singh continued, "asked the whites what kinds of blankets and rugs they might be interested in buying, and the Anglo traders gave them Indian—East Indian, I mean—blankets and tapestries as examples. They were fashionable in the West at the time and there was a market for them. The Navajos started making copies. So what we now think of as traditional Navajo patterns actually originated thousands of miles from the Navajo homeland."

"Really," Loren said.

Singh looked at him and grinned. He'd just come back from teaching a class and he was dressed in tan corduroy slacks and a Black Watch-pattern flannel shirt with the sleeves rolled up, an outfit that made a more than usually odd contrast with the peaked turban and braided beard.

"I sense that this is not what you came here to talk about," Singh said.

"No. It's another mystery altogether."

"Your Mr. Doe."

"The very same."

"I'm at your disposal."

Loren took a drink of his Coke, then a long breath. "It's a long story," he said. "Can you hold tight awhile and listen?"

"I've got all night," Singh said.

"Good," said Loren. "We'll need it. Because I have to find out about the holes that electrons make when they move and how other things fill the holes and all that."

Singh's look was a little strange. Maybe Jerry hadn't got that part right.

Loren got the photocopies made from Jernigan's Panaboard out of his pocket, then started talking, anyway. His mind had laid it all out in advance, in perfect order.

Singh didn't have to interrupt at all.

Loren ate two pieces of bread with leftover meat loaf, the meal he'd missed last night, mashed between them, then started packing his Coleman cooler for the hot trip to Socorro. Grape soda—"all natural," it said on the can—another pair of sandwiches, a couple snack-sized bags of Fritos, all packed between slabs of Blue Ice. Debra hovered about, making thin conversation. He caught her looking at him sidelong from time to time, as if she were trying to figure out what was going on in his head.

There was a rapping at the back door and Loren was suddenly happy to have the weight of his gun pressing against his right kidney. He walked through the dining nook and twitched the yellow curtains back. The knocker was Paul Rivers. From his furtive, hunched look the man seemed to be crouching behind the fortress wall of his Ray-Bans. Loren let him in.

"I went through your back neighbor's yard," Rivers said. He slid the gold-rimmed shades off and hung them by one earpiece from the front pocket of his jacket. "I hope nobody calls the police."

"What's the problem?"

"Patience is the problem." There was a haunted gleam in the man's eye. "The man's raving."

Loren sat himself behind the flecked Formica surface of his dinette. "Have a sit," he said. "Tell me." He gave Debra a significant look, and Debra faded.

"I didn't dare come to the front door. He's watching you, I'm pretty sure."

"What happened?"

"He called a formation for eleven-thirty. Just an hour ago." Rivers breathed out, shook his head. "He does that from time to time. Makes us form ranks in the parking lot as if we were G.I.'s or something, then pulls an inspection. He gave this speech . . ." He looked over one shoulder as if he were worried someone would appear at the back door.

"Speech," Loren prompted.

"Yeah. He said things were coming down to the wire. Pressures were getting, like, intense. He wanted us to be alert for federal agents in town and around the facility."

"Feds?" Loren was surprised. "He's tight with the feds, isn't he? With Killeen, anyway."

"He said that information was getting out of the facility, that the leak was in his department."

"Leaking to the feds?"

Rivers wiped sweat from his forehead. "I'm the only leak I know about, bro. And you're the only guy I talked to."

"I haven't told anybody." Which was not exactly true; he just hadn't told anyone who would have told Patience. Unless—paranoia stabbed at him—Cipriano's office really was bugged.

"He said he looked upon the leaker as a traitor. And he wanted to know how many of us were ready to follow him, to do what was necessary. And then he took a piece of chalk out of his pocket and drew a line along the asphalt. Anyone, he said, who possessed faith and readiness—those were the words he used, I swear to God, faith and readiness—should walk across the line now."

Loren tried to picture all this in his mind, the well-dressed company muscle formed up like Texans at the Alamo, asked to their surprise to give themselves not to a cause, but to their commander's taut and raving will.

"What did you do?" he asked.

"What d'you think I did, man? I walked across the line. And so did everyone else."

"What do you think set him off?" Loren asked.

"Things were pretty normal earlier. So whatever happened, it's something that happened between the time I went on shift at eight and eleven-thirty, when I got instructions to report to noon formation." Rivers gave another haunted look over his shoulder. "So he told us to look for feds and men in black. Those were the words he used."

Men in black. The words gave an echo in Loren's mind, and then he remembered that the hoary old UFO myth had flashed through his mind when he heard of John Doe's vanishing act . . .

Suppose, he thought, Patience had been as surprised by Doe's disappearance as he had. Maybe it had taken him a few days to hear about it. And when he had, he'd gone apeshit.

"I'm on town patrol today," Rivers said. "I left my partner at Doc Holliday's eating a sandwich, so I can't stay." He rose from his chair and reached for his Ray-Bans. "The reason I came by is so that you'll know what happened if my body turns up in an arroyo."

"Thank you."

"I'm not doing you any favors," Rivers said, "I'm just covering my ass."

And Rivers was out the door, walking hunched over, his glance darting right and left, as if he were expecting the men in black to be crouched behind the neighbors' picnic table . . .

Loren, watching Rivers's retreat, couldn't help but keep an eye out himself. The scent of paranoia seemed honeysuckle-heavy in the air.

He'd take the Taurus, he planned, because if they'd put a beeper on one of his cars it would likely be the Fury. And once he got to the next town, he'd get a local mechanic to put the car up on the rack and he'd search every inch of its underside for transmitters.

In the event, he didn't find any, but by this point it was only the sensible thing to do.

"I can't do anything more than theorize." Singh raised his hands helplessly. The Panaboard copies flapped in his fingers. "All I can do is tell you a story. The story fits the facts, but that doesn't mean it's true."

Loren took his disk recorder from his belt. "Can I record this?"

Singh rose from his flowered chair and frowned at the opposite wall. "Let's go to my study," he said. "I've got a whiteboard we can mess with."

Singh's study looked a lot like Jernigan's, stacks of *Physical Review Letters*, file cabinets, a high-powered computer, a lot of marker-pen scrawls on the whiteboard. Instead of Einstein on a bicycle there was a photo of a man in a peaked Sikh turban carrying an AKM. Singh pressed a button and the whiteboard hummed, scrolling onto an empty space. Loren hit the Record button on the disk recorder.

"Let me try to reconstruct Tim's thinking," Singh said. "He was saying what on the phone?" He picked up a green marker. "The t-axis was symmetric in the equations?" He copied lines of Greek letters from the photocopies onto his own board.

"And t is time, right?" Loren said. "That's what had me thinking about time travel."

"I don't believe your time-travel theory." The green pen kept jotting. "It's contrary to too much of what we know." Loren's heart sank.

"But Jernigan was absolutely right about the t-axis. It *is* symmetric. Time can be either positive or negative. There's nothing in the physics or the math to prevent it. The world line extends both ways in time. You can read a Feynmann diagram backward or forward. It's symmetrical."

"So that *does* permit time travel?"

"Not really. All it is, is a way of *looking* at something, okay? And even if you have a scattering event large enough to drive a particle back in time, that doesn't mean you can do the same to a whole person, along with the automobile he's in." He frowned at the photocopies. "As an alternative to the Copenhagen Interpretation, Hugh Everett suggested a many-worlds hypothesis in which, instead of a wave function collapsing during each quantum event, an alternate reality is created instead. So that if you *could* somehow travel back in time, you could change the past, but only in a parallel world, not your own."

"And this means?"

Singh gave him an amused look. "It means that unless your Doe came from a world parallel to our own, in which he not only didn't die in a road accident but managed to stay young for the last twenty-odd years, your theory, uh, bites."

"Great."

Singh turned back to the board. "Delta E times Delta t is greater than or equal to slash aitch. That's what poor Tim had circled on his board. That's the uncertainty relation. Among other things it shows how a particle can jump over a barrier in potential. Quantum tunneling."

"So this doesn't have anything to do with time travel?"

"Not exactly. Let me think for a minute." Singh tapped the butt end of his pen against his upper teeth. He scrutinized the Panaboard copies again, then wrote more equations on the board. "I think I see what Tim was looking at. These other equations have to do with Kaluza-Klein theory."

"I've heard of him," Loren said. "Somebody at the labs—"

"Them. Kaluza and Klein were two different people."

"Oh."

Singh spat on his finger, wiped out a green Greek letter, replaced it with another. "Transcription error," he explained. "Tim's, not mine." He frowned at the board again. "What Kaluza pointed out in the 1920s was that general relativity was explained a lot more efficiently if you assumed five dimensions instead of four, because you could then unify gravity and electromagnetism." He turned to Loren. "I should be clearer. I'm sorry. Height, width, length are the three spacial dimensions we know about, okay?"

"And time is the fourth, right?" Loren said. "I had this explained to me the other day. And I've seen that old movie with that what's-his-name, that Rod Taylor."

"Time is another dimension, yes. Because you need to orient yourself in time as well as space in order to be certain of your location."

"So what's the fifth dimension called?"

Singh laughed. "It doesn't have a name yet, because we can't seem to find it except in the mathematics. But the point is that there seem to be rather more than five, because since Kaluza first published we've gone on to discover other forces in nature, like the strong and weak nuclear forces, and once you incorporate all those into the equations you get eleven dimensions total. Nine spacial, and two dimensions of time."

"Two time dimensions. Those two guys at the labs were talking about that. I didn't know whether they were putting me on or not."

"You're not alone—the *math* might be putting *all* of us on. But yes, there seem to be two time dimensions. And we really don't know what the other one does." Singh capped his pen, then changed his mind and uncapped it, holding it ready over the whiteboard. "But here's the catch: it's assumed that because we don't *see* the other seven dimensions, they've collapsed somehow into the other four, that the universe that we live in is incomplete. The most elegant version of the theory would seem to indicate that the eleven dimensions existed during the creation of the universe, but that seven of them could exist only in conditions of high energy, and that when the Bang cooled, they collapsed."

Loren stared at the poised pen as if it were about to put a period to the universe. He remembered the hologram of uncoiling energies in the ATL lab, the little spheres looping and boiling out of the bright flashing chaos, the imitation Bang, with the shining digits counting down the fragments of a second since the initiation of creation.

"So at high enough energies," Loren said, his mind picturing Randal Dudenhof racing his Thunderbird up the dirt road leading to his ranch, "the other dimensions come into being."

Singh's pen hovered, descended, and, to Loren's surprise, drew a little happy face.

A circle, two dots, and a smile.

Fires glowed on either side of the road, red beneath copper-colored smoke. Helicopter blades sliced at the night. The scene's vibes all screamed military action: napalm, aircraft, bright lights in the sky. The Taurus rose high, arching toward the stars.

Randal was heading for home, too, Loren thought. And after crossing the Rio Seco he made the turn off the main road onto his gravel ranch road, two miles or more from home. And the next thing he—Randal^2—knew it was twenty years later, and the ranch was gone, and the road was gone, and he was traveling over rough desert, and meanwhile twenty-some years down the t-axis, the other Randal, Randal^1, went on home with his belly full of bourbon and his cheek full of snuff and his latest case of clap to his ever-faithful, ever-hopeful Mormon wife, never knowing of his rendezvous with the sharp end of a steering column in the not-too-distant future. But Randal^2, outside of the cognizance of Randal^1, leaped into a new and slightly older world as if through the agency of some cosmic jump-cut, after which the T-bird plowed into something, a scrub oak or the sand barriers bulldozed over Randal's corroding driveway or a rock that had been shoved out of the way when they built the LINAC.

Patience's boys found him then, or he found them as he walked away from his broken axle in search of help and waved down Nazzarett and Denardis patrolling the perimeter from their Blazer. They'd phoned that they had discovered an intruder and then Patience had called an alert, pulled in the town patrol with Rivers to check the fence and see whether it had been breached. The guards who surrounded Randal exchanged their 9mm Tanfoglios for guns with .41 barrels and ammunition—probably just to confuse things, Loren thought, make it harder for outsiders to track what was happening. Patience had it all planned—Randal's murder was almost premeditated. Patience hadn't been waiting for Randal, but he'd been waiting for *someone*, some emergency that could help him realize his fantasies of power and control. Randal was moved to Security HQ, where Patience and McLerie were waiting, and Randal was locked in the detention room while Patience probably checked his driver's license and registration and noticed that they'd expired decades ago . . .

William Patience would have required more convincing than that. He would have been itching to exercise a few of his latent powers as proconsul of security, try out some of the skills implied by his various diplomas, skills having to do with imprisonment and interrogation . . . and all he would have learned thereby was that he had on his hands an angry, drunken, stubborn ole boy who would probably have insisted that he, Patience, was trespassing on his, Randal?'s, property.

By morning Randal apparently had Patience convinced, and the two head scientists, Jernigan and Dielh, had been called in to consult, to decipher a mechanism by which all this could have happened. Randal was kept in deepest lockup, fed sandwiches and coffee from the machines in the cafeteria, maybe dragged out as an exhibit for Jernigan and Dielh to mull over, evidence a good deal more solid, and more cantankerous, than spiraling tracks on graphs or rainbow projectiles hurtling through holographic simulations. Jernigan and Dielh called off their second run and their meeting with Singh; Patience jiggered the guards' schedules so that no one other than the original four—Patience, McLerie, Nazzarett, and Denardis—would have any contact with the prisoner.

Because what they had run into, apparently, was time travel, and travel in time, as Patience had doubtless portentously announced, had Serious National Security Implications . . .

"It's all so bizarre," Loren said. "It seems crazy almost."

Singh looked up at him. "Were you raised in any particular faith?" he asked.

"I'm an Apostle."

"That's a type of Christian, right?"

"Yeah."

"Okay. So as a Christian, you presumably believe in a young virgin conceiving by parthenogenesis, her son who healed the sick and raised the dead, who was executed by the Romans but who rose after spending three days retrieving some good folks who had been inexplicably misplaced in Hell, and who is now in Heaven but will in time return to Earth to rule as King." Singh cocked his head and looked at Loren. "That's the craziest thing I ever heard. Know what I mean?"

Cold resentment buzzed through Loren's brain. He could feel himself bristling. "I don't know about that," he said.

"My point is that although your beliefs may not be strictly rational, you seem pretty rational to me, and your beliefs are rational to other believers. You're not crazy."

"Thanks."

"Physics isn't crazy, either. It confounds common sense, but it's self-consistent and provable, and that means common sense is flawed, not science."

"Okay." Loren looked at the Greek letters rolling across the whiteboard. "But a man returned bodily from the dead—"

"Your religion already accepts that."

"As a miracle."

"Science has been known to produce a miracle from time to time."

The Greek letters swam before Loren's eyes. "It wasn't just Randal," he said. "It's happened before. There were those cows."

"Yes. Tim told me about the cows. We had a laugh over it."

"Probably it happened to other things, too. But nobody notices a clump of cactus or a new cholla or a piece of rock. And the security people shot the cows because they were an embarrassment."

And that's what they did to Randal, too, Loren thought suddenly, and his words dried unspoken on his tongue.

"Virtual cows. Virtual cholla. A virtual vintage Thunderbird." Singh's look was still abstracted; he wasn't amused by any of these apparitions.

"Holes in transistors," said Loren.

"Your brother got a few things confused," Singh said.

"More than a few," Loren said. "Believe me."

"I think he was getting virtual matter mixed up with Dirac's notion of the universe being filled up with undetectable electrons. But he was more or less right."

"Okay."

"Virtual matter is matter that is created out of nothing—well, out of the uncertainty relation."

"Heisenberg. That was his, right?"

Singh seemed surprised. "Yes."

"I asked people about your bumper sticker."

"The point is that regular matter—an electron, say—can borrow energy from the uncertainty relation to create, say, a photon, but it has to reabsorb the photon almost instantly, within a tiny fraction of a second, before the universe takes notice of the fact that energy conservation has been violated. And protons within an atomic nucleus have to be continually creating and exchanging pions in order to transmit the strong nuclear force that holds the nucleus together; but this likewise violates conservation, so the pions can't last long. Fortunately they don't have to." He put a dot on the whiteboard, then surrounded it with smaller dots. "You have to look at a particle as being surrounded by a cloud of virtual matter that we can't detect, but that leaps into existence momentarily only to disappear again, the whole thing happening skadzillions of times every second."

"Excuse me." Deciding to ignore the *skadzillions*. "The universe *notices?*"

Loren could almost see the shift in Singh's mind, as if he hit the Stop button of some internal recorder, rewound for a second, began again. Loren remembered Steffen's doing the same thing when replying to a question, and smiled. "The uncertainty relation holds only for very small things, for very short amounts of time. You *can* create something out of nothing, get a free lunch as it were, but it's a *very small* lunch, and you need a whole lot of specialized apparatus even to *see* it, and it doesn't last long, so even if you manage to eat it, it'll vanish from your stomach before digestion. That's what I find intriguing about your Mr. Doe." Singh tugged on his braided beard. "It's like a fluctuation about a zero-point energy. The way he vanished so completely, and the timing of his disappearance . . ."

As if he never existed. The M.I.'s words.

"A virtual human?" Singh said. "A virtual duplicate of someone who existed at another location on the *t*-axis. So strange . . ."

"But the universe noticed—well, *I* noticed—the duplication," Loren said. "When I opened the coffin."

"And the virtual being disappeared. Along with his organs, and his blood, and even his clothes, which were being held in another location. When your perception held both the original and the duplicate, the duplicate had to disappear."

A wave of inspiration rolled through Loren. "And other stuff, too, I bet! His wallet, his ID, things like that! Things Patience would have taken off him and kept!" He pictured Patience reviewing his evidence just that morning, looking for the driver's license and billfold and credit cards he'd taken off Randal, then discovering they'd all disappeared from wherever he'd locked them up, disappeared along with everything else, including the can of snuff taken from Randal's back pocket. It must have seemed clear that there were other players involved, some near-omnipotent investigators who could walk through walls and make things disappear. No wonder Patience was ranting about men in black and traitors in his office.

"There are any number of quantum actions that behave that way," Singh said. "Matter acts both as particles and as waves—they're particles when your experiment is designed to look for particles, waves when you're looking for waves, but what are they when you're not looking? According to the Copenhagen Interpretation they're both, simultaneously, and maybe other things, too, and only when you *look* does the waveform collapse and the particle become one thing or the other—and then once you *stop* looking, what does a particle become?" Singh raised his hand, palm down, and oscillated it, indicating a wide Californian range of uncertainty. "A metaphor maybe? Nobody knows. Observation seems necessary for some of these processes to work. If you don't see it, it doesn't happen. And if you hadn't opened up that coffin, John Doe might still be on his slab."

There was a gentle knock on the door frame. It was Singh's wife, gazing at Loren with her pleasant blue eyes.

"Will you be eating with us?" she asked.

"I brought a sandwich with me."

"If you don't mind barbecued ribs? We've got plenty."

Loren smiled. "I don't mind at all. Thank you." He had anticipated some horribly strange Pakistani dish, goat eyeballs cooked in rancid butter or something; ribs were something he could get behind.

"I just realized," he said, "I never got your name."

"Cynthia."

"Cynthia. Hi."

"Hi." She grinned. "I'll set another place."

Cynthia left and Loren turned back to Singh. He was staring at the equations with a little frown of concentration, had maybe been staring at them all through Cynthia's interruption. Singh stroked his bearded chin in time to his thoughts.

"Virtual matter lasts a tiny fraction of a second, then disappears," he said. "What I can't figure is why John Doe lasted a matter of days." He shook his head. "That second time dimension?"

Loren could think of nothing to add. Singh's fingers, stroking his chin, started to dig at his beard, picking long strands of hair out of his braids. "Weird shit," he concluded. "I think that second dimension has to be the explanation. The collider energy has just been vanishing, right? What Tim called the energy sump. Suppose it dumps into the second time dimension somehow, reconstitutes itself as virtual matter that duplicates something farther down the t-axis. Maybe virtual matter just lasts longer in the second time dimension."

He glanced at Loren, his eyes bright. "Tim wouldn't have known about Doe's disappearance, which is to me the event that suggests virtual matter. To him it would have really looked like time travel rather than a virtual re-creation of an earlier moment." He caught himself digging at his beard, looked at his hand with an irritated expression, then dropped the hand. He sighed. "I'll have to work at it. Mess with some figures. I'll call you?"

"Better not," Loren said. "I think they're listening to my phone. I'll call *you*."

"Fine."

"Dinner's ready!" Cynthia's voice carried to them from the dining room. Singh, still in his study, started for his door.

Loren put a hand on his arm. "Listen," he said. "Tim Jernigan *died* for this."

Singh's frown deepened only slightly. "So you tell me."

"I want you to be careful. Patience is crazy and a killer, and if he knows I've seen you, you and your wife are both in danger."

Singh shrugged. "The more people who know," he said, "the better. If I were you I'd just tell everyone. The more people that know what happened, the harder it'll be to cover the whole thing up."

"But. But." Loren hesitated for a moment. "*Does* this stuff have any applications? I mean, suppose time travel, even by a virtual human, turns out to actually be possible? Won't that have the kind of national security implications that Patience is worried about? I mean, Dielh's in Washington briefing *somebody*, right?"

Singh gave Loren a mild look. "This is all just an accident, okay? An unforeseen consequence of high-energy physics. Maybe the result of a superconductor not properly aligned, not properly crystallized. It's not even repeatable—the energy sump happens only in a fraction of the runs. We haven't controlled *any* of this, and I don't see a way to do it."

"Are you sure?"

"No." Singh gave a laugh. "I'll find out when I try to publish, won't I? Maybe I should try *Nature* first, something out of the country where the government'll have a hard time suppressing it. Or just send a lot of copies around by modem before I do anything. Once ideas get out, they can't be stopped."

Loren didn't know if he wanted ideas to get out or not. All he wanted was an end to Patience and his gang. Somehow he couldn't see himself, like Roberts the prophet, like the UFO devotees in their white robes, preaching his particular version of the truth up and down the length and breadth of his homeland. Standing on a stool at the Sunshine, holding forth to people like Len Armistead or Shorty Lazoya. *See, folks, there's this thing called virtual matter*. With Bob Sandoval and Mark Byrne calling out comments from the back. The only kind of converts he'd make would be the kind he didn't want, the kind who wouldn't understand how crazy it all was.

Numbly he followed Singh out of the living room, to the dining room, where Cynthia was tossing a salad. Singh stopped dead, then began to laugh.

"Poor Dielh!" he said. "He wanted a Nobel so badly, and now his entire results will be classified!" He turned to Loren, his brows lifting in amusement. "That is a kind of revenge, right?"

"There are better kinds," Loren said.

The ribs were very good.

Loren's foot slammed on the brakes as pale forms wandered into his headlights. Tires skidded, screeched; the horn blared. Loren fought for control, felt the front tires sliding on gravel. Startled mule deer leaped for the side of the road, pouring downslope off the asphalt like a smooth brown and silver waterfall.

The Taurus came to a halt in a rising cloud of startled dust. Loren's pulse hammered in his ears, louder than the throb of fire-fighting helicopters overhead. He took a deep breath and shifted into first. In time his scattered thoughts drew themselves together.

An hour or so after eating dinner, Loren thought, Randal[2] had had enough. The guards with their superiority and contempt were bad enough, but the two dispassionate physicists, examining him as if he were a urine specimen in a bottle, had probably been downright spooky. Whoever came for the empty dinner tray had got careless and Randal clocked him, skinning his knuckles in the process. He took off out the back, through the fire door. The man at the front desk would have seen it on his cameras and alerted the troops. Maybe Timothy Jernigan was getting in his car after a conference with Patience, maybe he'd just arrived to talk to Randal. Loren could picture Randal hauling Jernigan out of his car, diving in, tromping the accelerator just as two ATL security men burst out of the door behind him with guns in their hands. Shots caved in the BMW's windows, drilled through the door, bounced off Randal's ribs, and nicked his descending aorta.

Nazzarett was one of the shooters, Loren thought. His hand tested positive in the Shibano test.

So Randal had driven the stolen car out the gate . . . But no. There was a problem there. Because there would have been two uniformed guards at the gate, and these presumably would have noticed a bullet-riddled car roaring past them at ninety miles per hour. So either there were two more ATL people involved in this, or something else had happened.

Randal hadn't bothered with the gate, Loren realized. He'd just driven the car right through the chain link perimeter fence. The BMW's acceleration was doubtless superior to that of the guards' Blazers, and he wouldn't have given a shit for how many times he scraped his oil pan as he raced across the mesa.

Loren would have to ask Rivers whether he knew if any part of the perimeter fence had been repaired in the last few days . . .

The Taurus surged through a depression, swung into a rising switchback turn, headlights tracking across juniper scrub, and then red and blue lights swept across Loren's vision, and blazing halogen intensity burned his retinas . . . The Taurus slowed as Loren raised a hand to block the stabbing spotlight. A black state police car was drawn across the narrow road, the reflective shield on its side glowing gold.

Loren came to a full stop, the Taurus's engine idling. The array of colored lights rotated silently atop the black car, drawing blue and red across the junipers on either side of the road. Distant helicopters filled the air with their thrum. Loren couldn't see anything against the glare of the spotlight. He rolled down his window and heard the sound of feet on gravel.

"Don't move, sir." The voice was taut with tension and seemed to come out of nowhere. Loren recognized the tone and his heart gave a leap. He glanced at the shotgun lying propped on the next seat.

"Keep your hands on the wheel."

Loren did as he was told and felt sweat gather under his collar. Something loomed off to his left and he turned just in time to see the smooth black barrel of a gun, its muzzle silvered with use, slip into his window.

The cool gun barrel prodded Loren's forehead. Loren tried not to jump at the contact and give the man excuse to fire. It was a Thompson, Loren saw, the venerable submachine gun beloved of Al Capone . . . a heavy, solid, totally intimidating thing, unmistakably a gun that could really hurt you, especially when compared with the toy-department look of mini-UZIs and Mac-11s.

The man behind the gun was Spanish, dark-skinned and pale-eyed, in the black and silver uniform of the state police. He seemed very young. There was a pimple on his chin. His knuckles were white as he clutched the gun's foregrip. Loren thought wildly of Latin American death squads, Patience contracting murders with old Special Forces cronies from Salvador.

"Listen," Loren began. His tongue was dry.

"Get out of the car, sir, okay? Then put your hands on the car's roof."

The gun barrel eased out the window. Loren considered throwing the car into gear and running for it, or swinging the door open wildly, hoping to knock the barrel aside for just a few seconds.

The look at the kid's eyes told him these were very bad ideas.

Loren opened the door nice and easy and got out of the car. Warm wind burned his face. He put his hands on the cool roof of the car. Helicopters throbbed across the sky. Loren couldn't decide whether or not to tell the other man his name—the man could have been sent just to find him, and was reluctant to kill unless he had a positive ID.

"That your shotgun, sir?"

"Yeah." Hopelessly.

"Get down on your knees, okay? And lace your hands behind your neck."

Loren did as he was told.

"Put one ankle over the other."

Damn, Loren thought. The guy was going right by the book.

He crossed his ankles and then the state cop came up behind him, kneeling carefully with one shin across both Loren's ankles, controlling him. In order to handcuff someone you had to give up your weapon, and the kid was taking no chances. The Thompson jabbed Loren's right kidney and he jumped. Then Loren heard the jingle of handcuffs and a cold metal touch as his right wrist was cuffed. The kid hauled the right hand down to the small of the back, then the left hand, and then there was a rasp as he cuffed the other wrist.

The state trooper let out a long sigh. He stood Loren up, patted him down, then took his shoulder and spun him around.

"What are you doing with the shotgun, sir?"

"I'm supposed to have it. I'm—"

"You're supposed to have it? Is that it, sir?"

"I'm chief of police of the city of Atocha."

The other man's eyes flickered. He frowned, tilted his head. "You got ID?"

The terror poured out of Loren like out of a flooding sluice gate. The man hadn't been looking for him.

"In my hip pocket."

The state cop turned him around again, reached into the pocket, pulled out the little folder he normally wore in the breast pocket of his uniform. He took the card from its plastic window and looked at it in the glare of his spotlight.

"Where's your badge?"

"It's pinned to my uniform."

"Let me get you out of those cuffs."

Loren's nerves sang relief as his hands were released. He rubbed his wrists and turned to look at the man.

"Who'd you think I was?"

"Two men broke out of state prison. One's a double murderer. They were reported heading south on this road in a silver Taurus full of guns, just like yours."

Loren sagged against the car. "Jesus Christ," he said.

Cold nervous laughter bubbled from the state trooper. "No shit. I thought it was shoot-out time."

"You had the right goddamn weapon. How'd you get a Thompson, anyway?"

"It's my personal weapon. I gotta cover about eight hundred miles of road by myself, I want a friend with me."

"I gotta congratulate you on your restraint, man."

"You just didn't *look* like a killer."

Loren shook his head. "Some coincidence, huh?"

"I'm probably the only cop within thirty miles. I thought my goose was cooked."

Talking fast, babbling really, both of them happy to be alive.

It wasn't until later, heading south again, the car weaving along the blacktop through burned-out stands of pine, that Loren wondered who had given that description to the police, the description that so exactly matched his own. A telephone ghost, he wondered, with Patience's voice, floating down from a satellite relay to some state police switchboard in Santa Fe? Just on the off chance that some trigger-happy rookie would be patrolling a dark county two-lane and spot Loren heading home?

Too weird, Loren thought, too chancy. He'd drive himself crazy if he kept on thinking this kind of thing.

Virtual particles. Time dimensions. Ghosts given form, then not-form . . . It was reality itself that was crazy, that defied logic.

Loren wondered about his family, about how they moved in his orbit. He had thought their orbits fixed, but his recent observations had not confirmed this. What were they, he wondered, when he wasn't looking?

Dust and ash, carried by the high wind, swirled against the windshield. Black, dead trees cut the skyline. The Taurus, alone on a burned-over plateau, seemed to be moving in its own cloud of uncertainty, amid a constantly changing cast of ghosts, virtual beings that haunted the night, pressing their insubstantial presence against the windscreen . . . Randal Dudenhof, brought back from the dead, killed again, then proved not to exist; Jernigan and Vlasic, who died as if they were particles in one of their own experiments, accelerated and slammed head-on into a target; Patience and his crew of gun-toting villains, as sinister as any western gang of bank robbers; lost souls like Roberts the prophet or Jerry, unable, through some inexplicable absence of the proper energies, to fully materialize entirely as substantial beings; hosts of even more subtle, abstruse particles, particles from farther down the t-axis, the past that held the county in the grips of its unseen field—the Hohokam and Apaches, the miners delving for silver and copper, the unseen Anaconda, the Mormon polygamists and Spanish patróns, the upright Apostles singing psalms as they came on the train from Pennsylvania; and religions of faith and miracles, of a God closer than a neighbor, as all-encompassing and imminent as Dirac's sea of electrons . . .

TWENTY

Loren walked into his house to find Jerry snoring on the open convertible couch in the living room. A duck hunter's camouflage jacket and pants had been thrown over Loren's easy chair; Jerry's Iver Johnson shotgun sat atop them. One lamp was burning, and there was a smell of gin. Jerry had always seemed to find friends who would take him to the Line, get him drunk, then let him walk home. In this case it appeared that he'd only made it as far as Loren's house.

Jerry offered one last wrenching glottal spasm as Loren shut the front door, then opened his eyes and sat up. He seemed perfectly alert, unnaturally so. For him it was one of the effects of drinking. He was alert, he was convivial, he was chatty. Then he passed out.

"Howdy," he said. "What time is it?"

"Around three."

"Deb was nice enough to let me sleep here."

"So I see."

Loren leaned the shotgun in the corner. A spasm of pain rolled through his back. Jerry leaned forward with interest. "Get anything?"

"Solved three murders, I reckon."

"Good for you!" Brightly. "Are we still going to shoot some duck tomorrow? I mean today?"

Loren rubbed his back and thought about it. He knew how Randal

372

had died, but he couldn't prove a thing, and he wasn't a cop anymore in any case. "Might as well," he said. "We'll get started in a few hours."

"Aren't we going to church?"

Loren thought about that as well. "What sin is left?"

Jerry held up one hand and counted silently on his fingers. "Wrath."

Loren considered. Word would have got out about his being placed on leave; he didn't relish dealing with a whole crowd of people who would know about it. Loren looked at the shotgun propped in the corner.

"I figure I already know as much about wrath as I need to," he said.

"Sounds good to me." Jerry turned to the end table and picked up a slip of paper from under his wristwatch and ring. "You got a message. Cipriano called. He wants you to call back, whatever time you get in."

Loren started for the phone, then came to a stop. He sighed and turned around.

"Where you going?"

"I'll explain later."

Loren drove to Port Royal and Cipriano's home. The house was a southwestern design, flat-roofed, concrete cinder block plastered and painted brown to look like adobe. There was a wall around the property, similarly plastered, with a graceful southwestern arch above the gate. Loren let himself in and walked across the bare earth yard to the side of the house and Cipriano's window. A rusty swamp cooler stood on a platform below the window, slowly leaking moisture into a heavy patch of weed. Loren reached above the cooler to knock on the glass.

After a few seconds the curtains twitched and Cipriano's startled face peered out. He looked resentfully at Loren for a moment, then gestured toward the front door and vanished. Loren walked to the door and waited for it to open. A light turned on inside, then the door opened and Cipriano appeared, standing barefoot in the door wearing a threadbare terry bathrobe.

Loren grinned at him. "Yo, bubba."

"Shit, jefe. Don't you ever get tired?"

"Guess I'm just a night person."

Cipriano gestured for Loren to enter, then padded inside. Loren crossed an old Indian rug and sat on the brown simulated leather of the sofa. Cipriano rubbed his tousled hair and sat carefully in a spindly rocking chair he'd probably inherited from his great-grandfather.

"What the hell are you doing here? Why didn't you call?"

"Patience probably has our phones tapped."

Cipriano rolled his eyes. "Jesus."

"He's *got* tapping gear. I'm just being careful."

"Jesus," Cipriano repeated. He cleared his throat. "Where've you been? I've been calling for hours."

"I was checking around. I found out what happened with our John Doe. Who he was, what he was doing, who killed him, and why."

There was a long silence. Then, "Listen, jefe." Then another silence.

"I'm listening."

Cipriano's face was expressionless. "The report from the criminalistics lab came in. The two guns found in the train wreck were the ones used in the Doe killing. The firing pins had been changed, but not the barrels."

"Huh. Any record relating to their serial numbers?"

"Not yet. We're looking. But look, jefe. I'm gonna close the case, okay? Jernigan must have been the shooter. That's what the evidence says."

Heat danced through Loren's frame. "Two-Gun Tim? Are you serious?" He shook his head. "No way, ése. Listen to me. The thing with the firing pins makes sense. The two killers changed their barrels and firing pins after the shooting, then hid the barrels someplace and broke the pins. When they decided to frame Jernigan, they dug up the barrels, but they had to use the new firing pins because they broke the old ones."

"Jefe." Cipriano's voice was pained. "The damn case is *closed*. Don't you understand?"

Loren waved his hand in a calming gesture. "Let me talk to you tomorrow afternoon, after I get back from duck hunting. And I'll talk to Luis, too. I'll explain everything. Then you can decide." Loren leaned close. "You really want to spend the rest of your life living next to a bunch of killers?"

Cipriano gazed at him stonily. "I'll do whatever I have to do, jefe. But I'll listen to what you have to say, okay?"

"Fine." Loren stood. "I'll let you get back to bed."

Cipriano rose, studied Loren's face. "Loren? How long's it been since you got any sleep?"

"A couple days maybe."

"Will you get some rest, guy? You're beginning to worry me."

"I'll do that. When this shit is over."

"It's *already* over, jefe."

"I haven't heard the fat lady sing, pachuco."

Loren opened the door and stepped out into the deep morning. He heard Cipriano give another long sigh before the door thudded shut behind him.

When he got home, Jerry was snoring on the couch again. Jerry didn't wake up this time, and Loren padded quietly past him to the bedroom, closing the door behind him to shut out the snores. He took off his clothes and eased into bed.

"Loren?" Debra's voice, rising from the next pillow. She didn't sound sleepy at all; maybe she'd been lying awake.

"I'm back."

"Did you get what you needed?"

"Yeah. I know what happened."

Her hand reached out, took his. "Can you tell me?"

Loren took a breath, let it out. A cold grudge stood like a steel door in the way of his speech: he just didn't feel the proper level of intimacy anymore.

Still. There was no reason not to.

"I will," he said, "after I get some rest."

They fell silent. Loren stared sightlessly at the ceiling, his mind spinning. He couldn't tell whether Debra was asleep or not.

He didn't think he fell asleep himself. The darkness and silence seemed to intensify his concentration, heighten the way his mind moved along lengthy chains of thought and image.

He didn't have enough evidence even to bring in Patience and his men for an interrogation, let alone convict them. He would simply have to maneuver around them.

He would talk to Luis and convert him. Luis had an interest in keeping the county stable. He obviously had contacts within the ATL structure; he could use them. Luis could point out to Patience's superiors that one of their own employees was dangerously unstable. Patience had sabotaged one of ATL's own multimillion-dollar projects and killed two of the company's top men. ATL could launch its own internal investigation. Once they realized that there was no national security issue at stake, that ATL was not on the verge of developing a form of travel that could send commandos back into time to right history's wrongs, normal justice could take its course. Patience could be isolated from his followers, his followers from one another. Sooner or later one of them would talk.

They had held a stranger as prisoner, killed him, and tried to cover it up, killing two more people in the process. That was all that the investigators would allege, all they would need to prove—any speculation concerning the origins of the stranger were irrelevant to the crimes themselves. If the evidence was presented properly, if one of the guards turned state's evidence, if the judge was careful not to allow evidence concerning the more esoteric physics . . .

Loren could get a conviction. He could do it.

And after that he'd talk to Luis again. The mail would have to stop, and Luis would have to understand that. It was too embarrassing in this day and age, too unnecessary.

"Loren." Debra's voice. "You're grinding your teeth."

"Sorry."

He looked at the clock; it was nearly six. He slipped out of the bed and found his clothes where he'd left them.

"I didn't want to chase you out of bed," Debra said.

"You aren't. I wasn't sleeping, anyway."

He put on his clothes and went to the gun rack. He unlocked it with one of the keys on his belt, took the double-barreled Heym, a box of shells, and his cleaning kit, and left the room. Jerry, thank God, had stopped snoring. Loren picked up Jerry's Iver Johnson from atop his pile of clothing and went out to the back porch.

There was dust in the air, the persistent hot Mexican wind beating against the town for yet another day. Loren decided he didn't want the dust clinging to his gun and so he went back indoors, to the breakfast nook, and turned on a light. He cleaned and oiled the guns, regular methodical movements, a slow beat that paced out his thoughts.

In the quiet house he heard an alarm clock go off. He rose from his eat and made it to the other end of the house just in time to see Debra knocking on the door to Kelly's room. Debra turned to walk back down the hall.

"Jerry and I decided to go hunting early," Loren said. "I was just going to say that church is an option this morning."

Debra, without her glasses, squinted at him. "You're not kidding, are you?"

"You can go if you want. Or the girls."

"You're the religious one. Not me."

Loren looked at her with surprise. "I never made you go."

"You never hog-tied me and threw me in the car, no."

Annoyance warmed Loren's nerves. "Go back to bed, then. I'll get breakfast for me and Jerry."

Debra pushed lank blond hair back from her face. "I might as well do it. I'm awake."

Loren walked past Debra to Kelly's door and knocked, then entered. Kelly, dressed in a nightshirt and dusty white socks, brushed her hair as she stared blearily at a vanity mirror that rose from among an overwhelming pile of hair- and skin-care products. Loren could hear the sound of running water from the bathroom, and that meant Katrina was up as well.

"Jerry and I are going hunting," Loren said. "You don't have to go to church if you don't want."

Kelly looked at the brush in her hand and sighed. "Thanks, Daddy," she said, put down the brush, and climbed into bed.

Loren knocked on the bathroom door. "Did you hear?"

"I'm awake!" Katrina's voice. "I might as well get up and use the weight room at school."

Which meant she'd have maybe a sliver of dry toast for breakfast, work up an appetite, then gorge on junk food for lunch. Loren knew there was nothing he could do about it, so he turned and went to the living room.

Jerry slept on, oblivious. The automatic coffee machine threaded the air with the smell of hot coffee. Loren shook his older brother awake, then watched as Jerry stumbled off, hangover written across his unshaven face, to the bathroom. Loren went to clear his guns from the table.

By the time Jerry had his second cup of coffee he was in fine form, going on at the breakfast table about tunnels built under Moun Shasta by the same extraterrestrials who were buzzing about th atmosphere in UFOs.

"Anyone seen these tunnels?" Loren said.

"Sure. Lots of people."

"They take any videos?"

"Well." Jerry looked uncomfortable. "They couldn't have. The were traveling by astral projection."

"Ah." Loren picked up his cup of coffee and took a sip. "Someho I thought so."

"If they tried to go in person, they'd disappear. The governmen doesn't want that kind of information getting out."

"Uh-huh."

"Jer," Katrina said. She was nibbling, as Loren expected, on a thi piece of dry toast. "How come you didn't join the UFO people her in Atocha for the millennium?"

"Because Jerry didn't have any money to give them," Lorer said.

"Naw." Jerry was unoffended by this skepticism. "It's because the were *contactees*. People who say they get contacted in person by th saucers are obviously crazy or lying."

Loren looked at Jerry, finding this example of good sense suspicious. "Yeah? How so?"

"Because the only way to *really* contact UFOs is through telepathy."

"Oh." Loren thought about it for a moment, then grinned. "I thin you're very likely exactly right."

Jerry, pleased with himself, reached for another waffle. Debra came to the table with her own waffle, poured herself coffee.

"When we're out this morning," Loren told Jerry, "I'll tell you about my John Doe and who he was. I think you have just the type of mind to appreciate it."

"Thanks."

"Daddy!" Katrina said. "Tell us *now*. I wanna hear."

"Later. Tonight, after everybody's home."

"I have a *date* tonight. It's Friday."

"At dinner, then." He turned to Jerry. "Where'll we look for duck?"

Jerry's mouth was full of waffle. "We don't have any dogs with us. And I don't want to have to go swimming."

"La Ciénega, then."

"Good."

La Ciénega was a bit of flat ground where the Rio Frio, rushing from the mountains toward its junction with the Rio Seco, spread out and formed a bit of marsh. There was good cover amid the tangle of cottonwood, willows, and underbrush, and the water wasn't very deep. The water was unusable by human beings, contaminated by heavy metals washed down from nineteenth-century gold and silver diggings, but the ducks were plentiful.

"We'll take water bottles," Loren said.

"I'll have to wash mine out. I think it's still got some Coke in it from last year."

"We should get moving."

"Yeah."

Loren left the table and changed into his camouflage jacket, cap, and pants. When he opened the bedroom blinds, he could see the first touch of light in the eastern sky. It was time to get to La Ciénega before the ducks took flight. Loren got back to the living room in time to see Jerry, in his camos, carrying the two shotguns out the door. He could hear Debra moving in the kitchen. Katrina was crossing the room, sipping at a glass of the orange-flavored energy drink she used before working out.

Loren found himself watching this domestic scene with a surprising homely joy. Things could work out, he thought.

The screen door closed behind Jerry. Through the screen Loren could hear Jerry's boots on the sidewalk over the sound of a racing car engine.

The living room window exploded inward, the opaque white curtain dancing. Katrina gave a little scream, her orange drink spilling. The air was full of buzzing sounds. Things thwacked into the far wall.

Loren lurched forward, body-blocked his daughter, knocked her to the ground behind the sofa. He covered her body with his own. A picture on the wall crashed to the floor in an eruption of glass.

Guns like buzz saws ripped the night. Tumbling bullets made fierce hornet sounds. Family photos on the bookshelf splintered and shattered.

The guns fell silent. Glass kept tumbling off the bookshelf.

"What's going on?" Kelly's voice. Loren rolled over, saw her standing in the hallway, still in her nightshirt and stocking feet.

"Get down!" Loren's voice was a scream. He lunged for her across the floor, the rug folding up under him in waves, broken glass spilling on his head. He caught a stockinged foot and yanked. She tumbled down, landed on her tailbone, and yelled.

Tires squealed outside. Loren got to his hands and knees and moved like a crab across the floor to where he had the police pump shotgun propped in the corner. He snatched at it, peered out the torn screen door, and then gathered his legs under him and charged outside. His boots ground on gravel, on limbs of the front-yard ocotillo that had been severed from the tree.

Taillights glowed on the corner. A car made a shrieking turn.

One of the Taurus's wounded tires hissed as it slowly deflated. Jerry's body, hit maybe twenty times, was lying like a bloody sack in the driveway by the hammered rear end of the car.

Loren stared after the vanished auto as his pulse stammered in his ears. The gun in his hand, he realized, was useless. It was still loaded with bird shot from his hunting expedition a couple days ago.

Animal rage filled him like a blowtorch flame. He threw down the shotgun and screamed, screamed into the face of the hot dawn wind until his lungs ached and his brain reeled with lack of air.

Much, much too late, he heard the sound of sirens.

T W E N T Y · O N E

"We found the guns in the car," Cipriano said. "Two UZIs. Eloy's checking the numbers on the LAWSAT. The car was stolen—Keith Sands's Mercury—and we found it abandoned behind the Church of the Risen Savior out on Penny. No prints, but lots of casings. All nine-millimeter."

"Yeah," Loren said. "That's in the manual, right? You do a hit, you steal a car to do it in."

Cipriano was exasperated. "What manual? What are you talking about?" He spoke over the hard, echoing sound of hammering: some of Loren's neighbors were nailing sheets of plywood over the shattered front window.

"The book that Patience read. *Manual of Sudden Death*. Three volumes. It was on his bookshelf."

The skin was drawn taut over Cipriano's cheekbones. "Will you leave it the fuck alone?" he demanded. "You don't have any fucking evidence connecting Patience to this!"

Loren looked at him in amazement. "It's his M.O.," Loren said. "He stole a truck to wreck the maglev, remember? And who the hell else goes around town with UZIs?"

Cipriano looked as if he were going to say something, then he gave a quick glance at the other police officers, Buchinsky and Esposito, who were engaged in digging lead out of Loren's living room wall. Both of them were listening with frank curiosity. Cipriano closed his mouth.

"I dunno, jefe," he said.

"This investigation was buried," Loren said, "but it just got dug up. *You* know Patience did it, *I* know Patience did it, we *both* know that Jerry was mistaken for me, walking out into the dark with a couple guns on his arm . . ."

"We don't know anything of the fucking sort!" Cipriano shouted. He waved his arms in exasperation. "It could be those goddamn drug dealers after revenge! They pack a lot of firepower!"

"Do you believe that?"

"I'm gonna look at the evidence. Starting with where Jerry's been the last twenty-four hours."

"Look at where Patience has been. There's your answer."

The phone rang. Another round of hammering came from outside. Loren went to the receiver and picked it up.

"Hawn."

"Chief. This is Eloy." Eloy's voice was hesitant.

"What'd you find out?"

"Lemme just say how sorry I am about Jerry."

"Thank you."

"Everybody liked him. What happened was so pointless."

"Thanks." Loren took a breath. "Did you track those serial numbers?"

Eloy sighed. "They're ATL's guns."

"Good." Loren felt his mouth twist in a snarl of triumph. "That's just what I wanted to hear."

"But we had 'em last," Eloy said.

Loren's heart gave a lurch. "Say again?"

"Those four UZIs we took off those ATL guys earlier in the week—Jerry was shot by two of them."

Strength flooded out of Loren. He sagged against the wall. "Are the other two missing?"

"I haven't looked. I don't have the combination to the safe."

Loren hung up the phone. He stared at the plastic receiver for a moment, his mind working, and then he looked up at Cipriano. "Jerry was killed with two of the UZIs we confiscated from ATL earlier in the week. You didn't give 'em back to their owners, did you?"

Loren could see successive waves of paranoia twitch their way across Cipriano's taut face. "They're still in the safe, so far as I know," he said.

"Who's got the combination?"

"You and me, jefe. And Al Sanchez, since he's the sergeant."

Loren straightened. "I didn't give it to anyone. Did you? Did Al?"

Cipriano thought for a minute. "Yeah. I gave it to one of our men who called late at night. He needed to put something in the safe."

"Who?"

"I don't remember. It was years ago." He looked at the other two officers. "Was it either of you guys?"

Buchinsky and Esposito both shrugged. Cipriano turned to Loren.

"Jefe. How many years has it been since we changed that combination? A zillion people could have it by now. And that safe is old. A hundred years at least. Guys with crowbars could of—"

Loren took a breath, then another. He needed time to work all this out. "Nobody used crowbars," he said. "They opened it with the combination. Why don't you go and look at it? Maybe something else is missing."

"Okay. I'm ten-seven outta here."

"And *think* about what's happening, okay?"

"Sure, jefe."

"I'll talk to Al."

Loren watched Cipriano as he walked out through the wide-open screen.

He was following his own advice and thinking hard.

The morning was a wild chaos, flurries of frenzied activity interspersed with harrowing, throat-tearing moments of blind sorrow. Police interrogations, Kelly and Katrina in hysteria and tears, neighbors offering help and food, Debra trying to coordinate everything while Loren organized police response . . . He made himself watch while Jerry was photographed, while he was zipped into the white plastic bag and carried away. He wanted to record it himself, burn it into his mind.

Bystanders stood silently in the street or cruised slowly by in their cars. Soaking everything into community memory. Making a legend out of everything before the day was out.

They have struck at my family. The idea kept tumbling through the cold hollow emptiness of Loren's skull. He went to the bedroom and put on his gun belt. The familiar weight did not make him feel any better.

Rickey arrived immediately after his morning service. His eyes were wide at the devastation, at the smear of red that no one had got around to washing off the driveway. He huddled in the back with Debra and the girls, doing whatever it was that preachers do in such circumstances.

After Cipriano left, Loren stood for a long moment on the broken glass in his living room, working out his next moves. Then he talked to Al Sanchez, who didn't remember having given the safe combination to anyone, but who, in case he forgot it, had written the combination down on a piece of masking tape, which he'd then stuck on the inside door of his locker. Anyone with access to the locker room could have seen it anytime that Al had his locker open. "Small-time," Loren said. Disgust filled his heart. "This scene is so small-fucking-time."

The phone rang: Cipriano. All four UZIs were gone, along with the bag of grass they'd taken from Robbie Cisneros and his friends. "Those dealers," he said. "What'd I tell you?"

"Christ," Loren said. Loathing choked him. This wasn't even worth the argument. He dropped the phone onto its cradle without another word.

Two neighbors came through the front door, hammers in their hands. One of them was Archie Gribbin, the husband of Debra's back-door confidante Madeleine.

"We finished with the window," he said. "Anything else we can do?"

"Yeah." Loren glanced over his shoulder at the two officers still prying bullets out of particleboard. "Let me talk to you in the back for a second."

Gribbin was a foreman at the Riga Brothers power plant, a muscular shot-and-a-beer sort of guy who had helped Loren build the addition for Katrina's bedroom. Loren walked with him into the backyard, leaned close, and lowered his voice.

"I've got to get my family out of here," he said. "I can't concentrate on this unless I know they're safe."

Gribbin's reply was simple. "What d'you need?"

"Can you loan me your Jeep for a while? A few days maybe?"

"Natch. I'll bring it around."

Loren shook his head. "We're probably being watched. I'll bring them to your place, then they can get in the Jeep inside your garage so no one will see."

Gribbin took all this in stride. Maybe he watched a lot of cop shows on television and figured that police work was always like this. "I'll go get her ready," he said.

Loren found his family in Kelly's bedroom, surrounded by Kelly's usual perfumed chaos of schoolwork, grooming aids, and laundry-to-be. Rickey straddled a chair backward, hands clasped atop the chairback as if it were a pulpit. Kelly lay facedown on her bed clutching a pillow; her sister slumped, semi-reclined, on cushions piled against the bedstead. Debra was in another chair, staring hopelessly at the sky visible through the window. Crumpled tear-sodden tissues were scattered over everything.

"Excuse me," Loren said. Heads turned toward him. "I've decided that it would be safer to get you out of town till this is over."

Debra's reply was practical. "Where?"

Loren hesitated. "I'll show you later," he said. "But right now, I'd like you all to pack a few days' clothes. And schoolwork, books. Maybe some games. Whatever will pass the time."

Debra looked up. "Should I pack food?"

"There should be food there."

Loren's family rose at once, seemingly pleased with having something to do. Rickey rose from his chair. "Chief?" he said. "Can I talk to you for a bit?"

"Sure."

Rickey followed Loren out into the hallway, then into Loren's own room. Rickey turned and closed the door carefully behind them. Loren went to the gun rack, unlocked it, took out the Dragunov and a pair of magazines. He started loading with 7.62mm sabot rounds.

"Chief," Rickey said, peering up at Loren through his thick

spectacles, "I'd like to point out that the process of grieving is long and complicated."

"Yeah." Loading ammo. "I know."

"I suppose you would, in your line of work. My point is that I would like to see your family again. As often as possible in the next few days. In hopes of turning their grief in a constructive direction."

"After this is over," Loren said.

"With all respect—"

Heat gathered under Loren's collar. He tossed the rifle onto the bed. "With all respect, Pastor, my family isn't safe!" He realized his voice was louder than he intended, and he took a breath and tried to reduce his volume. "I have to hide them out somewhere till this is over."

"Hide them, by all means. But I would like to visit them. Or arrange for some other experienced counselor—"

"Later," Loren said.

"I—"

"They would follow you. Then my family would be dead or hostage, and you with them."

Rickey stared at him, blinking furiously. Then he straightened. "I see," he said.

"When the killers are dealt with, I'll bring my family back. Then you can see them all you need."

Rickey peered at him. "I should like to see you as well, Chief."

"After it's over."

"No." Rickey shook his head. "Before that. I want to reassure myself on a matter of conscience." He stepped close, looked up into Loren's face. "As soon as you come back from delivering your family. I need to know. I beg of you."

Loren wanted to burst into laughter at this preposterous piece of melodrama, but a knock on the door interrupted him. Buchinsky opened the door before Loren could respond. "Mr. Figueracion is here, Chief," he said.

"Let him in," Loren said. He looked down at Rickey. "I'll see you later today, then."

"Good." Rickey nodded. "Good. Thank you."

Luis was dressed in a blue suit and a red tie spotted with little gold zia symbols. Someone had combed his hair for him. He advanced into the room and clasped Loren's hand in both his own.

"I'm so damn sorry, Loren."

Loren withdrew his hand. "You should be." He walked around Luis and pushed the door shut, then swung toward the old man. "This is your goddamn fault."

Luis stiffened. His voice was dignified. "You're lucky you got an excuse for talking like that."

Loren stepped close. "Jerry was killed because somebody took him for me," he said. "And they wanted to kill me because I've solved three murders, okay?"

"I came here to say that I'm sorry about Jerry," Luis said. "If you're too upset to understand that—"

"Fuck you, Luis," Loren said. "You cut the fucking ground out from under me."

Loren could see the red crawling up from beneath Luis's collar. "Nobody talks to me like that!"

"You cut your deal with ATL!" Loren shouted. Spittle sprayed Luis's spectacles. "We get a museum, and they get an end to the investigation!"

"I don't haveta—"

White light flashed behind Loren's eyes. He straight-armed Luis with a smashing left palm to the chest. The old man stumbled back, arms windmilling. The disordered bed caught at the back of his knees and he would have gone over, but Loren snatched out a hand and grabbed Luis's tie, yanking him forward. Loren's gun, seemingly of its own volition, came somehow into his hand, rising smoothly out from the holster, the barrel jabbing just under Luis's chin.

"What if it was your brother, goddamn you!"

Luis's glasses and hair were awry and his face was red. He forced words out past the tie that was being drawn across his throat.

"Suéltame."

"What if it was your brother! What if some fucking jerkwater political boss took your job away and let a bunch of murderers think it was all right with *him* if you got wasted?" He thumbed the hammer back. Joy shrieked through his veins. Power and dominion flooded his mind like a drug. "I'm waiting for a fucking *answer*, here!" he demanded.

Luis's eyes were popping out of his head. His hands clutched uselessly at Loren's wrist. He forced more words out. "What d'you want?"

"I want my job back. I want it back by noon, okay?" He shook Luis like a dog. "I don't care how many IOUs you call in or whose balls you have to break. And I want you to call up your contact at ATL and tell him that your loyal and trusted police chief has found out that five of his own security force have killed two of his employees and one local townsman and that he'd better cut those assholes off at the fucking *knees*!"

Luis gave half a dozen rapid nods.

"I'm not done yet," Loren said. "I want your support. I want the whole town's support. Because I'm the sword and arm of the Lord, understand?"

Luis's nods turned frantic. Loren raised the pistol above Luis's head, fully intending to bring it slashing down across the old man's face. Luis cringed, closing his eyes. Power throbbed in Loren's heart. He hesitated for a moment, then let go of the red tie. Luis fell heavily to the bed on top of the Dragunov. Loren watched while the old man wheezed for breath. Loren eased the hammer and holstered his piece.

Luis ripped off his tie, opened his collar. "Enyerbado," he said. His voice was a thready whisper.

"Yeah," Loren said, "damn straight I'm crazy. Better keep that in mind."

"El mismo diablo."

"I'm a sight meaner'n that, Luis."

Luis straightened his glasses and looked up. "Last man to try that with me," he said, "got blown away with a shotgun."

Loren looked down at the rifle next to Luis on the bed. "I advise you not to try that." The Dragunov was unloaded, anyway.

"I wouldn't soil my hands with such a thing. But I know people." He pointed a finger at the ceiling. "*I* run this county! *I* run it! I don't take shit from nobody."

"You've been eating up ATL's shit with a spoon, Luis."

"Crap." Luis gestured grandly. "Figueracion's in charge. Figueracion's *always* been in charge."

"You're never gonna run anything as long as William Patience and his thugs are crawling around assassinating the citizens. They're running things exactly the way they want to."

Luis's chest pumped air like a bellows, but his look turned thoughtful. He cleared his throat and stood, then turned to pick up his tie from the bed. He stuffed the tie in a pocket.

"I'll make some calls."

"You do that, Luis." Loren opened the door.

"Tell Deb I came by."

"You can tell her yourself. She's right down the hall."

Luis hesitated for a moment, then nodded. "I'll do that. Thanks." He headed down the hall, knocked on Kelly's door.

Power and glory still sang in Loren's blood.

His mind turned over one plan after another.

It was as if God were whispering into his ear.

For the drive Loren wore his camouflage duck-hunting clothes with his flak jacket underneath. He jammed a green John Deere gimme cap on his head and carried the Dragunov over one arm, his Remington shotgun in the other. The family crossed to the Gribbins' yard crouched low so that they wouldn't appear above the four-foot cedar fence that guarded their property. Loren had removed some slats in the back fence to make a gap wide enough to shimmy through. A fire-fighting helicopter overhead gave the whole thing the air of a dismaying military evacuation, the ambassador and his family getting out before the rebels rolled over the wire.

Debra and the girls were wearing dark glasses, scarves, and dark colors in hope of seeming anonymous, but to Loren's mind they seemed the perfect picture of a family in mourning. Nothing, he figured, he could do about *that*. They piled their luggage and books in the back of Archie Gribbin's desert-colored beige Jeep, then climbed in. Its two bumper stickers said TRUST IN THE LORD and SUPPORT FIREARMS, both mottoes Loren was prepared to live by. Loren put the rifle and shotgun between the two front seats and told his family to duck down and keep their heads out of sight.

He kept to the side streets till he was out of town but had to get on

82 eventually. Once there he cranked the Jeep as fast as it would go, which turned out to be about sixty, with the transmission screaming louder than a fighter plane's afterburner. A little rent in the canvas top flogged in the wind and added to the noise. Loren made the turnoff onto 103 that led past the ATL facility and he reminded everyone to keep their heads well down.

He checked the rearview mirror continually. No one was following. He looked over his shoulder. The girls were lying side by side on the back seat, tight-lipped and pale. Scared to death, probably, hiding from some unknown assassins, their father in his flak jacket, guns lying propped up just in front of them. Somebody needed to talk to them.

"Long as you're here," Loren said, shouting over the howling of the transmission, "lemme tell you what's happening. Everything's got to do with that John Doe that died on Saturday."

And as the twelve-foot-high ATL chain link unscrolled on the left of the road, Loren told his story. The chronology might have been a bit muddled, and he probably garbled a lot of the physics, but he thought the central facts were clear. Randal Dudenhof had been duplicated, summoned from some unknown dimension by the colossal superconducting power of the LINAC; it was Randal[1] who had died at the Rio Seco bridge and Randal[2] that had been shot; ATL guards had done the shooting.

"And that's why your uncle Jerry got killed," Loren said. "They thought he was me."

He looked back over his shoulder. Katrina and Kelly glanced at each other, then at him.

"They were shooting at *you*?" Apparently this hadn't occurred to Kelly before.

"Of course," Katrina said. "Who would shoot Jerry?"

"It sounds like one of Jerry's stories," Debra said. Her voice was barely audible. She was slumped down in the front seat, staring at the sky through her shades. Loren couldn't read her expression.

"I know," Loren said. The El Pinto crossroads were coming up: he braked and clutched and the shrieking of the transmission fell away. "The thing is," he said, "if it *were* just one of Jerry's stories, nobody would have got shot."

"I suppose."

Loren accelerated through the intersection, the Jeep shuddering through the gear changes. This vehicle, he thought, was designed for masochists.

"I don't think you're in any real danger," he said. "Not as long as you lie low. Nobody's looking for you. I just want you out of the way so that I don't have to worry about you."

He took the turn to Joaquín Fernandez's bait shop—a sign out front said HUNTERS WELCOME—and, so he couldn't be seen from the road, drove up behind the building and parked behind Joaquín's old Ford pickup truck that was quietly rusting beside the L.P. gas storage tank. Loren found the old man asleep in front of a television soap opera.

Joaquín was happy to hide Loren's family in one of his cabins. Loren figured he had been disappointed in not being able to blast the robbers and drug dealers with his rifle when he had the chance: now, in the absence of other amusement, he was pleased to guard the womenfolks holed up in the fort.

Loren left Joaquín happily loading his .30-'06 and drove Debra and the kids past the trout pond, past pitted igneous rock and dying willows, past the pink frame building, with the new door still leaning on its little porch, where Robbie Cisneros and his friends had hidden out with their loot. To the last cabin in the canyon, a brown-stucco cottage framed by a pair of cottonwoods. A hideout worthy of John Dillinger.

Loren helped the family move its possessions into the two-bedroom cabin. It was immediately apparent that no one had stayed there in months, maybe years. Fastidious Katrina went in search of a broom and dustpan, discovering them in a closet stacked with cardboard boxes loaded with magazines that seemed to feature Joe McCarthy and the Korean War.

He looked at his family: Katrina sweeping, Debra looking for rags or paper towels to wipe the countertops, Kelly gazing through the bathroom door with an uncertain expression, apprehensive of the plumbing . . . Love and confusion thrashed in Loren's chest. Who were his family, he wondered, when he wasn't looking?

He didn't know. He didn't know their secrets any more than they knew his, knew the adultery and the violence and the payoffs, knew the secrets he was himself holding for other people, or knew and understood the strange and compelling fraternity of law enforcement . . . He had little more knowledge of these people than he had of Amardas Singh's particles, the tiny subatomic velocities which hid most of their lives in another seven dimensions, and which were something else when no one was paying attention . . .

Loren gave up trying to work it out. He might as well love them, he thought. They were all he had.

"Hugs," he said. Debra dropped the gray rag she'd found and stepped toward him. Her arms went around him, barely making it around the bulky flak jacket.

He made his rounds of the family, cherishing each contact. The hugs were wordless—this was a cop's family; they'd done all this before.

Then he was ten-seven outta there.

Loren parked the Jeep in the alley behind the parsonage, then went through the gate in the sagging wire fence, passing a pair of overflowing trash cans. Garbage pickup had been cut back along with everything else.

Loren knocked on the back door. Rickey, answering, expressed no surprise at seeing him sneaking in the back way. Rickey led him wordlessly to his study, with its ring of mystic symbols, and sat down in his accustomed place, before the dead computer screen. He was dressed in a flannel shirt and blue jeans. Loren sat down on his own lightning-backed chair.

"I hope this won't take too long," Loren said.

Rickey shook his head slowly. From Loren's perspective a pyramid, complete with eye, seemed balanced atop the parson's head.

"I hoped you could tell me," Rickey said, then fell silent a moment. He shook his head again. "No." Correcting himself. "I wanted you to *assure* me that your poor brother's death was not a result of my meddling the other day."

"Meddling." Loren's tongue explored the word.

"I urged you to action," Rickey said. "I assured you of the moral rightness of it. And now—I'm perplexed. I didn't foresee such a thing as this."

"Nobody did," Loren said.

"An innocent man. A bystander. Gunned down in such a planned way." Rickey looked at Loren. "They thought he was you, yes? I've been assuming that."

"I assume that, too."

"I can't understand it." Rickey licked his lips. "One sets out to do a thing, yes. A criminal thing, an awful thing. But the consequences are something other than what was anticipated." He looked up at Loren. The all-seeing eye on the wall behind him focused firmly on Rickey's bald spot. "How can the killers live with themselves? How can they—" Words failed for a moment. *"Is it my fault?"* Rickey asked finally. "I suppose that's what I want to know. Am I a part of this chain of consequence?"

"Jerry's death is the fault of whoever pulled the trigger," Loren said. "Nobody else."

"Yes." Unconsoled. "I suppose."

"And now I'll deal with it."

Rickey glanced up at him. "You have enough evidence to convict someone?"

Loren shook his head. "Not yet. But it doesn't matter. They're a menace to everyone in this town till they're dealt with. So I'll deal with them."

"How?"

"However it needs doing."

Rickey looked unhappy. Arab-sounding music thudded through the open window as a car passed by on Central.

"I've primed you for this," Rickey said. "I've filled you with righteousness and urged you to repair the wrongs of this community." His accent chewed on the r's, *primed, urged, righteous*. "It's a job I cannot do, nor anyone. And if you attempt it now, there will be consequences beyond what you can know."

"You're telling me not to do it? Not to protect my family?"

"I want no more innocents to die." Rickey's eyes were cold and brittle ice. "Jerry's killers hit the wrong man. If this becomes a vendetta, you don't know what—"

"I—"

"Loren." Firmly. "I've seen too much. All the deaths in Uganda, the children killed in fire . . ." After the word, pronounced *fye-urr*, his voice drifted away again. "The person who set the fire could not have known," he said. "Not have known that children would have died. It had to have been unplanned." He licked his lips. "If that man can atone, if he can find grace, then . . ." He shook his head.

Loren stared for a long, timeless moment into the eye-in-pyramid, his mind caught in a rising whirlwind of revelation . . . and then he rose deliberately and took Rickey by his collar and wrenched him up from his chair. The antique tipped and fell, clattering on the hardwood floor. The pastor gaped in wordless terror. Loren drove Rickey back against his desk, the computer monitor rocking for a precarious instant as Loren stared intently into the fluid, shifting depths of the pastor's spectacles.

"You set that fire, didn't you?" Loren's words seemed to come from a heart of flame.

"I—" Rickey's lips worked soundlessly. Loren could see yellow plaque between the parson's long horse teeth. Finally the man spoke.

"How did you know?"

"You've been confessing to me all week. Your speeches, your sermons. I just realized it." He tightened his grip on the man's collar, seeing the tartan flannel drawn tight over the veins at the side of the neck. Apparently it was his day for strangling people. Rickey reached back with one flailing arm, set the monitor to rocking again, grabbed the edge of the desk to support himself.

"I assure you." Rickey's voice rasped out past constricted vocal cords. "I thought the fire alarm worked. I never thought anyone would be hurt." His clouded eyes darted back and forth behind the distorting lenses. "But I couldn't take it anymore. The misery, the endlessness of it—I was fed up. But I was needed! I couldn't walk away."

"I *assure* you!" Loren mocked. He drove his right fist deep into Rickey's solar plexus. Rickey bent over, gasping, his face pale. "Made me work it out, right?" Loren's voice was loud as a trumpet in the small room. "Didn't have the guts to confess, you had to just hint around it till I caught on." He clubbed Rickey's temple with a hammer fist, dropped him to the floor. "How many other people have you played this game with?" he demanded.

Rickey whooped for air. "I—no one else could have guessed."

"You played it with everyone, didn't you? Gave you a thrill, right? Thought you were too smart for them."

Loren's rising foot thudded into Rickey's ribs, lifted him up off the floor, then dropped him back against his desk. The heavy desk lurched, the monitor rocking once again—and Loren drove the monitor off the desk with a furious backhand sweep of his arm. Glass shattered; the vacuum tube exploded. Fiery joy burned in Loren's heart, echoed in his roaring voice.

"I should make you eat the goddamn glass!"

"I would!" Tears poured down Rickey's face. "I would if it would do any good!"

Loren reached down, took the parson's shirt, hauled him to his feet again. Rickey gasped in pain, bent double, clutched his ribs.

"This way," Loren said. He swung Rickey toward the door.

"I've been trying to atone!" Rickey wept. "I've dedicated my life to service."

A shriek rose from Loren's lungs. "You wanted me to set the fucking world right for you! He shoved Rickey toward the door. "You wanted me to catch the killers so you could feel good!"

"Yes." Rickey reached out for the door frame, hauled himself through. His arms trembled like an old man's.

"A murderer." Loren's voice filled with bile. "You've killed children, damn you. And I was coming to you for advice."

"I have no right. I have no right."

"Shut the fuck up."

Loren seized the back of Rickey's collar and marched him out of the parsonage, down Central, across the plaza, and past the tarnished deco griffins into the headquarters of the police.

Eloy was behind the front desk, confusion dancing through his face. Loren flung the parson against the desk. Eloy peered down at him from over his foam collar. "Mr. Rickey," Loren said, "has a confession to make."

"Yes." The parson gasped for breath. "I killed some people."

Eloy looked at Rickey blankly, then turned to Loren. "He putting us on?" he asked.

"I killed some people," Rickey repeated.

Eloy's eyes widened. "Not Jerry . . . ?"

"Nobody you know," Loren said. "Read him his rights, get a disk recorder, take him to a room, and let him talk."

"Right, Chief."

"I'll do whatever you want," Rickey babbled. He adjusted his spectacles. "I must atone."

"Tell the truth first," Loren said. "Do your atoning later."

He turned away. Sickness and loathing clawed at his throat. He went back down the hallway to the front door.

"Chief?" Eloy's voice. "Aren't you gonna want to be a part of this?"

"I'm not a cop right now," Loren said. "I've heard all I need to, anyway."

He went out the doors and stood between the two griffins. The plaza glowed at him in the bright high desert sun. The flag on the Federal Building roof crackled in the high wind like a series of gunshots.

All this had been some kind of weird distraction, a hallucinatory interruption of Loren's day. He started across the plaza again, heading for the Jeep.

"Hey! Loren!"

It was Sheila, puffing from her daily run. She was in a ragged gray T-shirt and bright red satin shorts, and she wore one of those fashionable double-helix sweatbands that were probably good for any number of things, except absorbing any significant amount of sweat.

She jogged up beside him, blinking myopically without her glasses. "I'm sorry about your brother," she said.

Loren didn't shorten stride. "Thank you," he said.

"It's set things on fire in the office. The police are running around like idiots. Uh, no offense. And what the hell did you do to Luis Figueracion?"

Loren looked at her. "What do you mean?"

"Luis is trying to get the mayor to drop your suspension, and he got Maldonado to agree, and he went into Castrejon's office to talk him into joining them. The three are talking to Trujillo right now. But Luis keeps calling you a son of a bitch and swearing he's gonna have you killed."

Savage laughter echoed in Loren's head. "Yeah, that sounds like Luis."

"So what did you *do* to him?" She peered a little closer. "Or maybe the question should be, What have you got *on* him?"

Loren just shook his head.

"What's the story, Loren? C'mon."

"Luis is gonna use me to solve a little problem he's got," Loren said, "and after I've done that for him, he's gonna blame me for solving it and try to cut my nuts off."

"Can he do that? I mean, will he succeed?"

Loren shrugged. "Everybody who's anybody in this town has the goods on everybody else. It's like we've all got loaded guns pointed at each other's heads. So the first person to pull the trigger—who knows where that's gonna lead?" He found himself grinning. "I think Luis'll probably cool off before he does anything drastic. But if he doesn't—" He shrugged. "There'll be blood on the moon. Can't say as I care anymore. Whatever loyalty I had to Luis went away the day he sold me out."

Loren crossed Church Street. Sheila jogged silently along for a moment, then spoke. "Do you know who killed your brother?"

"Yeah. I know."

"Can you prove it?"

"No. Not that I much care."

"So what are you going to do, then? Once you get your job back."

He looked at her. "What any Atocha peace officer before me would have done."

"Oh, Jesus." Her face wrinkled in disgust. "Don't give me that peace officer crap. This isn't the Old West anymore."

Loren stopped dead in his tracks and looked at her in genuine surprise. "Whatever gave you that idea?"

She gave a little snort of annoyance. Loren started walking again, then turned down the alley leading to the Jeep. "The Old West is still here," he said. "It's just down the *t*-axis. The past hasn't gone away. It's—" He searched for a word he'd heard preachers use. "It's *imminent*."

"Don't give me metaphysics, Loren."

"Okay." Anger exploded through him. "I'll give you something real." He glared at her. "They shot a member of my family, Sheila. What in God's name do you want me to do?"

"Go to the police. You run the department, for Christ's sake. Or will in another hour or so, anyway."

"I can't. Someone on the force works for the other side."

"The FBI, then."

"The FBI works for the other side, too. And for all I know, the state police and the border patrol and everybody in this town and in the Democratic and Republican parties."

"That's crazy! That's paranoid!" Sheila's arm-waving was a bit inhibited, Loren noticed, without a pair of glasses in her hand.

Loren opened the door of the Jeep. "Miracles turn things upside down," he said. "That's what they're *for*. And even if it was a miracle that a scientist can explain, it's still a person that was killed, and that person had to be here for a reason. So God *wanted* him to be here, right?"

"You're not making any sense."

He got in the car and stared at the wheel between his hands. He felt strangely buoyant. "I guess I'm not," he said, and found that a smile was tugging at his lips. "I'm going to clean up the town. I'm going to do what God wants me to. He's backed me into a corner—I can't trust anybody. Not my family, the church, the government, the people who run the town . . ." He looked at Sheila. "That clear enough?"

"No."

"Be happy in your ignorance, Sheila." He started the Jeep, gunned the engine, put it in gear.

He thought of himself in the LINAC, accelerating down the long tunnel, gathering energy, gathering power.

Getting ready to collide.

The sun was nearing the horizon, winding down the day. All the dust and soot in the air had smeared red over the entire western sky, and turned the white mass of the City-County Building a watermelon-pink.

Loren used his key and slipped into the building the back way, up one of the patterned metal fire stairs. He went straight to his office and opened the big walk-in safe.

The odor of marijuana wafted out of the big steel box. Loren found the Ingram Mac-11 that he'd taken off the two Mexicans and dropped it into the satchel he'd just bought in the Hi-Lo store on Central.

There were five loaded magazines: he took those as well. His eyes scanned the shelves for anything else that might be useful, found nothing, and stepped out of the safe and closed it.

He took a pair of field glasses off the shelf and added them to his satchel.

He went to his telephone, pressed the intercom button, then Cipriano's number.

"Could I see you for a second?" he said. "I'm in my office."

"I didn't see you come by."

"You musta blinked."

Cipriano was looking restless as he came into Loren's office. Loren met him at the door. He put a finger to his lips, then led Cipriano down the metal staircase and out the back end of the building. By that time Cipriano was out of patience.

"What the hell's going on, jefe?"

"I think people may have bugged our offices, okay?"

Cipriano shaded his eyes against the red westering sun. "Well. Guess I got to take it seriously, since you're my boss again." He reached into his breast pocket and took out Loren's star, then handed it to him. "The mayor raised your suspension. But then I guess you heard."

"No, I hadn't. I was out of touch."

Loren got his ID out of his back pocket and pinned the seven-pointed star back in its place, then put the ID away.

"Where've you been all afternoon?"

"Let's go for a drive. Your car. Mine is full of bullets."

They walked around the building to West Plaza and got in Cipriano's Fury. Loren put the satchel on his lap. He told Cipriano to head east on 82, out toward the Line.

"I got called into Rickey's confession," Cipriano said. "That was something, wasn't it?"

"Yeah. The bastard."

"What did he do? Just up and confess to you?"

"He'd been playing games for a week. Just hinting around, being smug, confident I couldn't guess. But when I figured out what he was doing and confronted him, he popped."

"Jesus. Good work, man." Cipriano shook his head, then gave

Loren a nervous little smile. "I can't work it how you figure out this stuff."

The sun bounced red off the rearview mirror. Loren winced and ducked his head. Then he reached into the satchel and pulled out the Mac-11. The little gun looked like a toy in his big hands. Cipriano looked alarmed.

"Where'd you get that?"

"The safe. The way machine guns keep disappearing around here, I figured we better find someplace else to put this."

"Why not change the combination?"

"Till we change the combination, I mean. Turn left here."

"Have you slept today?"

"No."

"You look pretty strung out. Maybe you should get some pills or something, put you out for a while."

"I don't feel tired at all."

"This wind is driving everybody crazy. You know how many arrests we made last night?"

The Fury's tires sang as they bounced over the cattle guard, and the car swayed as it moved down the overgrown lane that led to the UFO landing field. Tumbleweed poured across the flat mesa like lumps in cream, piled high against the torn chain link fence. The hollows of the land were a corrugated contrast of cool deep violet and hot sunset-pink.

"Park around by the side here." Loren pointed at the metal-walled work shed.

Cipriano parked on the shady side and turned off the engine. Loren slapped a magazine into the butt of the Mac-11, worked the bolt. Annoyance edged Cipriano's words.

"Will you stop playing with that damn thing?"

"I want to talk first."

"About what?"

Loren pointed the gun at Cipriano. His nerves sang like violin strings. "About how you sold me out and set me up for a hit, asshole."

Cipriano froze for a long second, his jaw fluttering, pupils dilating. Then he summoned will from somewhere.

"Bullshit." His right hand clenched into a fist.

"Put both hands on the wheel." Cipriano's look was stubborn.

Loren felt a sad mental weariness. "Do I have to play a game with you here? After all these years?"

Cipriano put his hands on the wheel. "You damn well better. Pointing a gun at me like that."

"You were the only person who knew I had an informant in Patience's organization, and just a couple hours after I told you about him, Patience called out all his men and started a witch-hunt for a traitor. You've got the combination to the safe and could have walked right into the building and opened the safe and got the guns out. And you told me that stupid lie about giving the combination to someone you couldn't remember . . ."

"God damn it, Loren!" Loren watched the veins in Cipriano's forehead pulse with anger. "Anybody coulda opened that safe!"

Fury poured white-hot from Loren's heart. He could feel the gun tremble in his hand; he steadied it with the other and forced himself to order his thoughts, line them up in words, speak them.

"I told you, this morning, that I'd solved the murder of John Doe, and I named the five conspirators. I told you I'd make it all public after I got back from duck hunting. What the hell else could have got the killers outside my house before dawn this morning, ready to shoot down the first duck hunter to walk out my door?"

"Shit! Shit!" Cipriano beat fists on the wheel. Loren's nerves sang warning; his finger twitched on the trigger. Then Cipriano gave a long sigh, the air going out of him, and he sagged behind the wheel.

"I didn't think they'd kill anyone," he said. "I didn't think they'd kill Jerry."

A scream rose from Loren's lungs as anger flashed like white phosphorus in his mind, and he knew he had to do something before he just held down the trigger and emptied the magazine, so he started smashing the car seat with his left hand, smashed again and again while he roared. The car jumped with each impact. Cipriano hunched forward, hands white on the wheel.

The phosphorus burned low. Loren gasped for breath and clenched his numbed hand. "What did you think they were going to do?" he asked. "When they asked you to get the guns out of the safe?"

"Bury 'em, maybe." Cipriano gave a nervous shrug. "I didn't think they'd be crazy enough to kill someone." He snarled. "They knew what they were doing, the motherfuckers. The bastards made me an accessory."

"It take you this long to figure it out?"

"Shit." Disgustedly.

"Who else knows about this? Did Luis order you to work with Patience?"

Cipriano shook his head. "No. Patience called the other day. After you got suspended. He said he wanted to liaise."

"*Liaise.*" Bitterness curled Loren's tongue.

"He said he thought you were out of control. He just asked me to keep him informed about what you were up to. And—" Cipriano searched for words. "Shit, man. Luis made it clear enough. He didn't want us messing with ATL. And I didn't think you had a case against 'em, anyway. Dammit, jefe!" He beat the wheel again, then gave Loren a desperate look. "You *were* out of control! You're out of control *now*! All that wild shit you pulled, what you did to Robbie Cisneros!" He shook his head. "You were way the fuck out on the edge. I couldn't be a part of that. I had to look after myself."

Liquid nitrogen chilled Loren's heart. "You sold me out over *Robbie Cisneros*? To a bunch of killers?"

"I didn't think they'd ever killed anybody. I figured that was just another of your crazy ideas. And if you didn't get stopped somehow, you'd start phoning in more phony tips and trying to bust down doors at ATL. I could see you hauling Jernigan into the bathtub just like you did with Robbie. And I didn't want to be a part of that, jefe. No way."

"And you were having too much fun being chief of police, right? Trying out my boots for size?"

"You were on your way *out*, Loren!" Cipriano's eyes were imploring. "I tried, but I couldn't stop you from going down the tubes. What you pulled with that search warrant was too obvious. Once Robbie got a good lawyer, I figured the Wild West days were over."

"That's the second time somebody's told me that today. And it's not true, is it?"

Cipriano just stared at him.

"Some strangers with a lot of money and a lot of political muscle moved in and tried to take over," Loren said. "It happens over and over in this state. Except this time it's not over water or mineral resources or grazing rights. It's over human fucking life, right?"

"It's always been over human life!" Cipriano shouted. He banged his hands against the wheel again. "And we've always sold it!" He gave Loren a wild-eyed look. Sweat dotted his forehead. "People in this state have never been able to resist. Never! They're *happy* to sell their water or timber or whatever—sell their whole livelihood! Sell their communities, sell their neighbors . . . And if they resist, they just get killed—read your fucking history. How many people have died over land grants? How many people died over water rights? There used to be *farms* around here, a hundred years ago. My great-grandfather was *born* on one—I've seen the old photographs! But the farmers lost their livelihood because the mines wanted their water, and the county government was happy to give it. And now everybody drinks water shipped in from over the county line because of what the miners did to the water table. And who the fuck really cares, anyway?"

Cipriano leaned close. Loren could smell him. "Riga Brothers owned Atocha's ass for a hundred years, Loren—it's just been so long that you forget that you got sold out before you were ever fucking born. The only reason nobody in Atocha sold out to ATL was that ATL wasn't buying! But *now*—" He pointed a finger at the roof, waved it. "*Now* they see something here they want, and they're putting their cash down like everybody else! And now the only difference between those who have and those who don't is gonna be whether we had anything to sell!"

Loren lunged forward and drove his forearm into Cipriano's chest. He pinned the man against the far door and shoved the point of the Ingram into the softness of his belly.

"I don't care if you sell yourself," he hissed. "That's your own sorry affair. But you sold *Jerry*, and that's my business."

Cipriano looked into his eyes at close range. "Get Castrejon to give me immunity," he said, "and I'll testify to anything you want."

"I got a better idea." Loren moved back to his seat. He pointed the Mac-11 at the car's communication setup.

"Use the cellular phone hookup," Loren said. "Call Patience and give him a message."

Cipriano licked his lips. "What are you trying to do?"

"Tell Patience that the men in black have been to see you. Tell him you're scared, that you're calling from a secure phone, and you want to meet him here."

Cipriano stared at him. "The *men in black*? Are you serious?"

"Just do it."

Cipriano looked dubious, then shrugged. "You got the gun, jefe."

He picked up the mic, switched the commo rig from radio to the telephone channel, pushed buttons to make his connection.

He knew the number, Loren noticed. He'd been making that call a lot lately.

"Mr. Patience's office." The voice of Annette, Patience's secretary, came out of the commo unit's speaker.

"Mr. Patience, please. This is Chief Dominguez."

"Can you hold a minute while I locate him?"

"Yes, I can wait."

Canned music filled the car. Cipriano waited, the mic half raised.

"Patience here."

"Bill. I—"

"Where's Hawn?"

Cipriano licked his lips. Loren looked at Cipriano, mouthed the words "I don't know."

"I don't know."

"Who's he talking to?"

"Listen, Bill. I just had a visit from the men in black, and—"

"How many?"

Cipriano stared at the commo set in disbelief. Loren held up three fingers.

"Three," Cipriano said.

"What did they want?"

"I think we should talk," Cipriano said.

"Are you calling from a secure phone?"

"Yeah. Yes. A phone booth."

"Good."

"I know where we can meet. West of town, out on 82. You know the UFO landing field?"

"Yeah."

"There's a shack right by it. Nobody goes there."

"Right. We'll all be there in half an hour."

"Bye."

"Just hold tight. Don't move around. I don't want you exposing yourself."

"No shit," Cipriano muttered, giving a baleful glance to the Mac-11. He hung up the mic, then looked up at Loren.

"You got 'em coming to you, jefe. You gonna be waiting here with the force?"

Contempt drew an acid taste down Loren's tongue. "You haven't figured it out yet? They're coming to kill you."

Cipriano looked startled. His tongue flickered at his dry lips. "What d'you mean?"

"They're on the run from the men in black who stole John Doe's corpse. You're their vulnerability—the guy outside the circle who might crack. They've probably been planning on killing you all along. Plant a bag of pot on you maybe, the one they took from the safe, and make it look like you were dealing."

Cipriano stared out the car window for a moment, then pressed a hand to his solar plexus. "I feel sick," he said.

"Get out of the car," Loren said. "No, wait, give me your gun first. Hold it with two fingers, and toss it to me."

Cipriano blinked, then did as he was told. Loren put the gun on the floor of the car. "Get out," he repeated. Cipriano opened his door and climbed numbly out of the car. Loren got out his own door and walked around the car.

Cipriano was staring at the blood-tinged landscape. The hot southern wind ruffled his lank hair, banged a piece of tin on the shack roof. He turned to Loren. "I don't get it," he said. "Aren't you gonna call for backup?"

Loren looked at him. "No," he said. "I'm just going to take care of this myself."

He watched while Cipriano worked at this one. "You're not gonna arrest 'em?" he asked.

Loren just looked at him.

Comprehension flooded Cipriano's face. "Jesus!" he said. "You're crazy!"

"If I arrest them," Loren said, "there'll just be some deal made. We both know that. Luis'll try to play both sides against the middle. Before you know it, they'll all be claiming that Jerry threatened them with one of the shotguns he was carrying and they had to fire in self-defense. Maybe some of them will do time, but only ATL and Luis are gonna win."

Cipriano's look was wild. "I'll be an accessory!"

"It worked for them," Loren said. "Why not for me?" He gave Cipriano a deliberate smile, baring his teeth. His heart poured tingling readiness into his body. "Unless I got things wrong—unless you were getting ready to confess your role in all this to Castrejon?"

"You can't do this to me!"

"I'm going to put some cuffs on you and put you over in the arroyo," Loren said. He felt ready to go twelve rounds with the Champ. "All you gotta do is close your eyes, and in a while it'll be over. And the two of us—we'll conduct the investigation the way we want, won't we?"

"Chief! No!"

Loren smiled again. "Yes. I am the sword and arm of the Lord, and the town is given unto my hand."

"No! That's crazy!"

"It's the Day of Wrath, pachuco. Guess what Rickey preached on this morning."

Cipriano gave a cry and raised his right arm.

Then time seemed to give a little skip, popping from one point on the t-axis to another, and suddenly Loren's ears were ringing with the sound of shots and he was staring in shock at Cipriano, who had fallen next to the car with several bullets in him.

The recoil from the Mac-11 had numbed his hand. Loren looked down at it in surprise. He didn't even remember pulling the trigger.

He hadn't been ready to shoot Cipriano at all. Earlier, yes, but not now. He didn't think Cipriano would have . . .

His heart thrashed in his chest, echoed the shots in his ears. He tried to reconstruct what had happened. Cipriano must have made a move, he thought. Lunged at him, with his arm up. The shots were just reflex, defensive.

He knelt down by Cipriano just in time to see light die in the man's startled eyes. The strength went out of Loren and he sagged against the car.

Atonement, he knew, hadn't even started yet.

"I almost pissed at him myself. "I'd like to make it I mean to do you, but I'd listen to what was best to say," okay?"

TWENTY-TWO

Loren rose from his crouch by Cipriano's corpse and walked to the door of the utility shack. Hard soil crunched under his feet. Red oozed like spreading blood across the western horizon. His ears still rang with the sound of shots.

By his foot was the broken padlock he'd pried open earlier in the day. A gleaming new padlock sat in its place. Loren opened it with his shiny new key and entered the room.

The corrugated roof boomed in the wind. Loren could taste the thick dust that wafted through the air. The light switch didn't work; the power had long since been turned off.

In the dim light Loren could see the mounded tarps under which lay some of the explosives and incendiaries Loren had moved from the Wahoo Mine. He rearranged the explosives so as to free one of the tarps, then took it outside, spread it out next to Cipriano, rolled the body onto it, and dragged it into the shack. He pulled the body all the way to the dimly lit rear, then partly hid it with the tarpaulin.

The expression of stunned surprise remained fixed on Cipriano's shadowed face. Loren stared at it for a moment.

He had never pointed his gun at a neighbor. He'd been proud of that. He'd never shot anybody or shot at anybody.

Now who did he start with?

His heart flailed in his chest, trying to find the beat, some rhythm that made sense of everything.

Anger came to his rescue, anger that filled the whole of his being. *They* had made him do this. *They* had turned neighbor against neighbor.

He had only wanted his town to be nice.

He made his feet carry him to the door and looked back to make sure that the explosives were still under cover. He closed the door and the hasp and let the padlock hang open from the shackle. Then he picked up the Ingram from where he'd left it, scuffed some dirt over the spilled blood, took the satchel from the car, and walked across the mesa toward town.

Anger beat snare drums in his blood. He marched to its rhythm.

A hundred fifty yards from the shack a narrow arroyo barred his path, one of the dozens of twisting, eroded waterways that wound, in this case north, to the Rio Seco. Loren slid down the steep bank and walked along the tortured, tumbleweed-packed arroyo bottom till he came to an area where the earth wall had eroded and crumbled, forming a little ramp. In this little natural alcove he had stashed his gear wrapped in his camouflage hunter's jacket. The barrel and hollowed-out stock of the Dragunov stuck out of each end of the bundle. A child's stocking, purchased at Fernando's Hi-Lo store along with the padlock and the satchel, protected the muzzle from dust. He looked down at the weapon and felt a savage joy, the clean pure call of righteousness sounding in his veins.

Loren unwrapped the bundle and propped the Dragunov, the stocking still over the muzzle, against the arroyo wall. Loren put on a pair of gloves, his flak jacket, then his camouflage hunting jacket over it. He took a camouflage-pattern watch cap from his jacket pocket and put it on his head, pulling it down over the ears. He hung the field glasses around his neck, set the safety on the Mac-11, and put it in one of the big pockets of the jacket. It fit easily.

He wanted to make himself ready, perfect himself. He envied the Apaches their sweat lodges and their paint, the ability to purge the old self and create a new, angry identity with just streaks of natural pigment. If he'd had something to do it with, he would have striped his face.

The detonator for the explosives sat where he'd left it, a little plastic box, just big enough to hold a battery. There was one wire that he hadn't connected to the terminal. He reached into another jacket pocket and pulled out the detonator manual. Reading carefully, he twisted the last copper thread around the terminal, took off the cap that grounded the system against any static built up from the wires being rolled by the wind, made sure the switch was set to Off, and propped the detonator on the edge of the arroyo.

He took the sock off the end of the Dragunov and stuck it in another pocket. He climbed the eroded part of the arroyo wall, lay down on the brown soil with his body hidden below ground level, and looked at the landscape through the field glasses.

Huge tumbleweeds bounced across the plain. The shack and the line of chain link behind it glowed red in the setting sun. Yucca and ocotillo waved in the gusting wind. Tailings piles were mounded up on the far side of the invisible copper pit, a new mountain that obscured the real ones beyond.

It looked just like a UFO landing field was supposed to look. What else?

The setting sun was burning the back of his neck. He turned up the collar of the hunting jacket.

Cipriano was a traitor, he reminded himself. He bragged about how he sold out.

And he'd helped them kill Jerry.

Dead men flickered through his mind like images on a reel of film: Jernigan with his scowl, Vlasic dismembered, Randal[1] spitting blood, Randal[2] calling Loren's name.

Jerry lying crumpled next to the Taurus, red broken taillight glass scattered over him. Being zipped into the white plastic bag.

Loren's blood screamed for vengeance. He was doing the Lord's work.

Shadow covered the mesa, the tailings above glowing red, floating over the darkened land like clouds. A few lonely cars zoomed past on Highway 82, headlights already on. Loren spit dust from his mouth and wished he had thought to bring a canteen.

He heard gears grinding, then the roar of an engine. The sound was somewhere to his left, across the mesa. He looked that way, saw nothing from his little niche in the arroyo wall, then raised his head to get a better view.

Red firelight gleamed on silver farther down the arroyo. Loren narrowed his eyes and finally made out a whip antenna jouncing slowly down the arroyo.

Alarms shrieked in his heart. Patience had brought his own backup: that was one of his Blazers moving down the arroyo, moving toward Loren, only the antenna showing above the level of the ground. There was no way the driver in the Blazer could avoid seeing him as he passed by.

Loren dropped the Dragunov and clawed for the Mac-11 as he slid down the eroded arroyo wall. He yanked the gun out of his pocket, lost his grip on it, saw it fall. A desperate two-handed lunge managed to snatch the gun from the air. He juggled it for a moment, got his fist around the pistol grip, flicked off the safety, yanked the bolt back, and saw gleaming brass wink briefly as an already-chambered live round was pointlessly ejected . . .

The Blazer engine revved for a second, then died away. Loren froze, terror thundering in his veins. A door slammed shut.

Loren pointed the machine pistol down the arroyo and strained to hear footsteps over the fierce percussion of his own heart. He heard nothing but long gusts of wind.

A pair of vehicles passed on the highway, one-two, the hiss of the tires carried to him on the wind. Loren heard them downshift, one after the other, just after they passed his position, then heard the engines begin to labor. Turning off the highway, Loren figured, driving to the shack.

Loren's mouth was dry and full of dust. Sweat gathered under his watch cap. He didn't know how many people had been in that first Blazer, knew only that it had parked just a few yards away and that whoever had been in it was probably on an errand similar to his own.

He slowly lowered the pistol and turned back to the embankment. Little brown rivers of dust cascaded from his feet and knees as he slowly crawled up the crumbled arroyo wall. He cautiously lifted his head above the level of the ground, saw two chocolate-brown Blazers making their way to the equipment shack. The sun was well below the horizon; the mounded tailings were growing dark. Loren edged his eyes to the left and saw, less than ten yards away, the muzzle of a long rifle sticking out from behind the twisted trunk of a dead scrub oak.

Whoever was behind the rifle couldn't be seen because the oak had captured a dozen or so tumbleweeds that screened the shooter.

Loren slid his eyes back to the two Blazers in front of him. He slowly put the Mac-11 onto the ground, then reached for the Dragunov. His hands were sweating inside the gloves.

The two ATL vehicles came to a stop, one behind the other, a good twenty yards from the equipment shack. Doors opened and people stepped out onto the ground. Loren shouldered his rifle and put his eye to the soft rubber eyepiece of the 4x Fujinon telescopic sight.

It was too dark to distinguish one figure from another through the scope. Ironic regret passed through Loren that he'd bought more precise Japanese optics for hunting instead of keeping the Russian military sight that came standard with the gun and that featured infrared night capability.

Never mind. It would get light enough in a minute.

He took his eye away from the scope and stared through the increasing gloom at the ATL people. There were four of them: two had taken positions, lounging elaborately, behind the open doors of the rearmost vehicle, and another pair—dark, indistinguishable silhouettes against the bright tailings piles—were advancing toward the shack. There weren't any weapons in sight but Loren felt confident they were there. Probably the other two UZIs taken from the safe in his office, plus some Tanfoglios carefully fitted with new .41-caliber barrels.

Four of them, Loren thought. Patience, Nazzarett, McLerie, Denardis.

Who was the guy to his left? At least one other person was a part of this. And everyone's identity was hidden in a cloud of uncertainty.

Targets, he thought. And the rifle was like the LINAC, accelerating its bullets to terminal velocity.

One of the first pair waited by the door of the shack while another disappeared around behind, presumably to look at Cipriano's car. Loren hoped that darkness would hide the blood on the ground. If they were calling out or knocking on the door, Loren couldn't hear it over the sound of the wind.

Neither of them was in a position to see the detonator wire.

If only, he thought, Patience hadn't been so fucking arrogant. If he'd just told him the truth, that they'd arrested an unknown man, that the man had made a run for it in a stolen car, and that they'd shot him—if he'd only met Loren that far, Loren would have written his report and stuck it in a file cabinet, and the D.A. would have declined to file charges, and that would have been the end of it.

Damn him, Loren thought. *Damn* him for making me do this.

He reached his left hand for the detonator and flipped the switch to On. A red LED shone. His hands were trembling with anger. He took a firmer grip on the rifle with his right hand, pressed it against his shoulder to steady it, and held his left thumb over the detonator button.

The goon by the door opened it and gave the interior a careful look, most of his body covered by the door frame. His friend rejoined him, and the two slipped inside.

Find the body, Loren thought. Find the body and call to your buddies.

Instead there was a shout that Loren heard even over the blustering wind. The man standing by the driver's door of the second Blazer straightened, waving, obviously urging his comrades to run to the vehicles and get out of there.

Choirs of angels sang in Loren's brain. Day of Wrath, he thought, and pressed the button.

The explosion was immense and the shock wave tore the breath from Loren's lungs. He'd had no idea of the power of the plastique he'd used, and hadn't understood the complex math in the manuals; he'd just stuck a couple of the blocks together around a detonator. Sheets of blackened galvanized metal tumbled into the air like twisted pieces of cardboard. The incendiaries Loren had placed around the plastique scattered liquid fire in high streaming arcs. The two men by the rear Blazer were blown off their feet. The windows of the vehicles shattered into crystal shards.

It was bright as day. Loren brought the Dragunov to the firing position and put his eye to the sight. Lowering the conditions of uncertainty.

The man struggling to his feet in front of his vehicle was Vincent Nazzarett. Hatred boiled in Loren's veins. One of Randal's killers, probably one of Jerry's. Nazzarett was dragging at the pistol under his arm. His white shirt glowed in the light of the fire.

Loren centered the cross hairs on Nazzarett's chest and squeezed the trigger. The rifle punched Loren's shoulder; concussion bruised his ears. Through the scope he saw the impact clearly, the puff of dust or blood or whatever it was blown off the man by the force of the bullet, by the accelerated particle impacting its target . . . and then Loren was startled by the way the man fell, his limbs suddenly liquid as if the bones had been torn clean out of his body. The man wasn't knocked back like dead men were in movies; he just fell straight down like a sack of rocks.

Loren's nerves twisted at the sight, and then joyous heat flashed through his body, and he wanted to scream in triumph, a ululating Apache yell. He turned the gun on the other man, the one on the other side of the Blazer. He could feel his hands trembling with anticipation and he struggled to control them.

Sheets of galvanized metal were raining from the sky, scattering bursts of flame when they struck. The other target ran out around the front of his vehicle to look at Nazzarett's crumpled form. Loren could see an UZI in his hand.

Screaming hatred flashed through Loren's mind as he realized he was looking at Patience. He fired, pure reflex, and the bullet exploded a rearview mirror near Patience's hand. Patience ducked and began running around the front of the Blazer again. Loren pursued him with bullets. He didn't think he hit anything.

Earth fountained by Loren's position—once, twice, concussion heavy on Loren's ears—and then Loren ducked as terror flooded his veins. He'd forgotten about the man on his left.

He backed, sliding down into the arroyo as he reached for the Mac-11. He fumbled with the safety and flipped it off. The other man continued to fire, showering Loren with flying dust. Apparently he couldn't see Loren's position from behind the oak's twisted trunk and the screen of tumbleweed; he was just firing blindly toward the sound of Loren's own shots.

Loren flung off the little gun's safety and, out of pure nervous energy, worked the bolt again and dropped another gleaming bullet uselessly onto the sand. His heart thundered in his throat. Sweat was running down his face, pouring down his body. He stuck the gun out in front of him and started moving down the arroyo.

The gun blasts ceased. The clumps of brown grass at the rim of the arroyo were rimmed with reflected red and silver—the incendiaries had set the whole mesa ablaze. All the gunshots had set up a wailing in Loren's ears that wouldn't go away; he couldn't hear his own footsteps. He couldn't tell where anything was: everyone, all the particle-players, had vanished into an uncertainty relation.

The arroyo came to a turn and Loren pressed his back to the crumbling arroyo wall. Patience's sniper had to be right on the other side, maybe waiting for him.

Loren jumped at the blast of another shot. Something glittering dropped at his feet. Another pair of shots cracked out, and two more objects dropped to the ground. Loren recognized them as brass rifle casings, then felt panic skidder through him as he realized the sniper was standing right over his head, firing suppressive shots into Loren's old position.

Loren jumped out into the arroyo, spinning, raising the little gun, and found himself staring into the widened eyes of a total stranger crouched on the edge of the arroyo. There was a startled moment of mutual recognition while Loren froze, perceiving a humanity he had not expected, and then the man narrowed his eyes and started swinging the rifle in Loren's direction and Loren squeezed the trigger and turned the man into an object, a disgusting piece of hammered meat lying on his gun with one hand dangling over the brink of the arroyo . . . Loren held the trigger down till the bolt locked back and the magazine was empty, and then had to restrain himself from rushing forward and beating at the corpse with the empty gun.

Son of a *bitch*, Loren thought. He had read the look in his enemy's eyes. The man had tried to use Loren's moment of paralysis, the sudden wave of empathy, to kill him. Son of a *bitch*!

Loren remembered Patience, dropped the Mac-11, and ran for where he'd left the Dragunov. He grabbed the rifle, clambered back up the little slope, flopped on his belly.

There was an explosion as the gas tank of Cipriano's Fury went up. The wind tore at scudding flames, drew gray smoke out into a long flat plume. Loren had succeeded in starting a fair-sized range fire.

Loren blinked sweat from his eyes. Taillights flashed on the second Blazer, and then it was in motion. Patience was running. Loren shouldered the Dragunov, aimed at the passenger compartment, fired. The Blazer swerved off the road, passed behind the other vehicle. Loren fired three more times into the rear of his target and saw sparks fly as his fast-moving particles impacted their target. The rifle bolt locked back on an empty magazine and the Blazer didn't slow down.

Loren gave a scream of frustration and clawed for a spare magazine. The Blazer disappeared behind the shattered work shack, vanishing into the plume of range-fire smoke. Loren dropped the first magazine and slammed in the second, but his moment was gone.

Patience had vanished into the Figueracion Ranch, hidden behind smoke and darkness, the cloud of uncertainty. The Blazer was capable of traveling across country for as long as necessary. He could hope Patience would drive into an arroyo he didn't know was there, but he couldn't count on it. Most likely Patience would encounter a ranch road and follow it to a gate that led onto one of the county roads.

Loren rose to his feet, breathing hard, and tried to remember what it was he had planned to do at this point. He looked down and saw rifle casings gleam in the firelight. He fell to his knees and started snatching them up in his gloved hands.

The sound of a shot made his nerves leap. He looked wildly around. The shot was followed by another.

Ammunition, he realized, cooking off in the fire. Nothing to concern him.

He'd used sabot rounds in the Dragunov because the sabot blew away as soon as the bullet exited the barrel, and thus made it impossible to trace a bullet to a particular weapon. But ejector mechanisms could also leave traceable marks on rifle brass, and Loren intended to pick up his own.

He jammed brass into his pockets until he could find no more. There were probably more casings out there, but he couldn't see them in the dark. He straightened up again, looking for Patience and his Blazer, but he could see nothing on the mesa besides fire and wreckage.

The sound of a siren came gusting on the wind. It was time to leave. Loren dropped back into the arroyo and began moving along it. The weight of the flak jacket had him breathless and soaked with sweat. He picked up the Ingram where he'd dropped it, reloaded, put it in a pocket along with the jingling brass. Then he came upon the Blazer that the stranger had parked here. Its underside was clogged with tumbleweed that it had picked up as it scraped along the floor of the arroyo. Its door was ajar. He opened the door and saw the keys dangling in the lock.

Loren had parked Archie Gribbin's Jeep in the bed of the Rio Seco north of here, and had planned to walk to it along the arroyo, then drive to town along the riverbed. Now he wouldn't have to walk all that way.

He got in the Blazer and started the engine. It had already been shifted into four-wheel drive. As he revved it he looked down at the metal box that covered the machine pistols, grasped the latch, pulled it back. Two UZIs sat under their locked safety bar. He pressed 571, just as he had the other day, and the light went green. Triumph danced in his heart. He pulled the bar back and yanked one of the machine pistols free.

Patience wasn't the only one who hadn't got around to changing a combination.

A siren whooped by on the highway. Sheriff's office or Loren's own department, not the volunteer firemen yet. Their sirens didn't have the Yelp setting.

He drew the Mac-11 from his pocket, threw the gun out the window—he didn't need it anymore—and then he put the Blazer in reverse. He thumped carefully down the arroyo, tumbleweed grating beneath his floorboards.

"Cosmo, Cosmo." Patience's voice made Loren jump as it leaped from his radio. "Report your position. Over."

Loren put in the clutch and let the Blazer drift to a halt. His mind ticked over like the engine. Sweat dripped off his nose, patted on his jacket.

Cosmo. That would be Cosmo Vann, another of Patience's men who had been present on the night that Randal Dudenhof appeared. He hadn't been connected with anything else—Rivers hadn't reported that his schedule had been altered like the others—but apparently he'd been a part of this from the beginning.

Or maybe he was just a late convert. Carried away by enthusiasm as Patience drew his line on the pavement and reenacted the Alamo.

"Cosmo. Report your position. Over."

Loren tried to think like an Apache.

He reached for the microphone and took it in his hand. He

thumbed the Transmit button and tried to thin his voice, fill it with weariness and pain.

"I'm hurt," he said. "I need help."

What the hell. It seemed worth a try.

He waited. The radio's speaker hissed white noise for a long moment, and then Patience's voice returned.

"Bastard. You're a dead man, you bastard."

Loren found himself snarling at the sound. He thumbed the Transmit button. "You ran, cocksucker," he said. "You panicked and ran when the crunch came."

"I'm going to cut your fucking throat."

"Coward," Loren said. "You don't have the guts."

"I'm going to rip your nuts off."

"Listen to yourself, leader-of-men. You're a failure, a disgrace. Why don't you blow your fucking brains out?"

"*Come and get me!*" There was the start of a laugh, high-pitched and hysterical, pure adrenaline bursting past his throat, and then the transmission cut off.

More sirens whooped on the highway. Loren listened to them for a moment, then hung up the microphone.

Come and get him. Right.

"Hey." Another voice on the channel, female this time. "Was that you, boss?"

The woman's voice was disbelieving. Loren laughed—Patience had been threatening murder on a public channel.

There was no answer. Loren let out the clutch, began backing down the arroyo again.

"Mr. Patience, do you copy? Were you on this channel?"

The walls of the arroyo fell away and the Blazer jarred onto the dry gravel bed of the Rio Seco. Loren put the Blazer into first gear and spun the wheel.

"Mr. Patience, do you copy? Have you completed your exercise? Over."

There was still enough light to see fairly well in the steep-sided river bottom. Loren didn't bother with the headlights. The Blazer's four wheels clawed at the uncertain ground and the vehicle lurched forward as gravel rattled against its bottom.

"Mr. Vann? Did you request assistance? Over."

417

Gribbin's Jeep loomed ahead, parked against the north bank. Vann must have passed it going the other way; maybe he'd even scouted it out. Loren pulled the Blazer up next to the Jeep, killed the engine, got out, opened the Blazer's tailgate. Then he opened the back of the Jeep and started transferring the rest of the explosives and incendiaries he'd taken from the Wahoo Mine to the Blazer. Sweat and dust streaked his face.

"This channel is to be used for official communication only." Sententiously. "Unauthorized use is forbidden by federal protocols. Phony emergencies are subject to severe penalties."

Jesus, Loren thought. Patience really has them trained.

He put the last box, wine-bottle incendiaries, on the front passenger seat, then threw a tarp over the bombs in back. He'd return for the Jeep before dawn—no police search would go out this far before light. Any evidence around the burning shack would be thoroughly trampled by firemen.

Loren got in the Blazer and headed up the river again. Venus glowed softly above the horizon like a hovering UFO. Meditations on illegality flittered through Loren's mind like a flock of blackbirds. Everyone in this scenario, he thought, was held there by unbreakable strands of guilt.

Patience couldn't ask anyone for help, not without admitting what he'd done. Loren was in the same situation. And the Fortunes and the other eco-activists couldn't tell anyone about where the explosives had come from without admitting that the federal charges against them were true.

But Patience was under a deadline. Four of his men were lying dead on the edge of the UFO landing field. If he was going to head off questions, he'd have to work out some kind of explanation for what had happened, an explanation that would give him an alibi and also account for what had happened to people under his orders.

Unless, of course, Patience decided to roll up his pants legs and wade across the Rio Grande to Mexico. It was the most sensible thing to do, and therefore Loren assumed Patience wouldn't do it. Patience had never done the sensible thing, not once.

Meanwhile, all Loren had to do was assert his own innocence. He hadn't really left anything on the scene that could absolutely convict him; and he would be conducting the first part of the investigation himself, or sharing the task with Shorty. If the feds were drawn into it, he'd have a head start on cleaning up the evidence that would point toward him, and emphasizing what pointed toward Patience.

Where were you that afternoon and evening, Chief Hawn? I went hunting to clear my head, then I just drove around for a while. I went home and went to bed without listening to my messages, and I unplugged the phone. And by the way, if it's credence you want, I've got some freshly killed birds in my freezer that might confirm my story.

Loren laughed. This was glorious.

The Rio Seco embankments widened, revealing Atocha's lights gleaming on the bluffs on either side of the stream bed. Loren passed under the bridge and reached the point where Estes Street dipped into the river; he flicked the lights on and swung onto Estes going south. The engine roared as the Blazer climbed out of the riverbed, then swung onto Railroad Avenue heading east. Air pouring through the open window cooled the sweat on his face. He shifted out of four-wheel drive.

Heading for ATL. Loren and Patience, each from the other's point of view, had vanished into his own cloud of uncertainty, momentum and location unknown. Loren had to narrow the parameters of the experiment.

"Mr. Patience, please report." The female voice again. The message was repeated. Then: "We have received a call from the sheriff's office that one of our vehicles was involved in an explosion and fire. There are casualties. Mr. Patience, please respond. Over. Are you ten-seven?"

The message repeated several times, and then the voice ordered someone named Mr. Shrum to report to the fire site and see if any friendly personnel were there. Shrum reported that he was already there and about to contact local authorities.

ATL glowed on the horizon, the perimeter lights casting an icy halogen gleam on the wire-topped fence. Loren turned off the road before he reached the facility and took the gravel outside perimeter road.

The days of wind had piled thousands of tumbleweeds against the south side of the fence. Security cameras atop aluminum poles tracked slowly back and forth, the poles themselves swaying slightly in the warm gusts. Loren no doubt looked like one of ATL's own perimeter patrols.

Loren drove two miles along the road and made a U-turn, then started driving along the fence. He pressed in the dashboard lighter. When the cameras seemed to be pointing elsewhere, he lit the fuse atop one of the wine-bottle incendiaries and heaved it out the window. The pile of dry weed caught instantly. Loren continued his slow drive, flinging out one incendiary after another. Loren's heart leaped with every explosion, and he burst out in laughter as he heaved the bottles. Silver-bright jellied gasoline poured through the fence as orange flames towered high, reaching for the stars. Wind-whipped sparks flew high over the razor wire, landing among the dry vegetation on the other side.

It was just what the Apaches had done to Atocha in 1824, but a stranger wouldn't know that. ATL had blinded itself to local history, and history was about to have its revenge.

Come home, Mr. Patience, Loren thought. Your house is burning down.

Come to the apocalypse, Mr. Patience. Come to the Days of Atonement.

By the time Loren reached the highway, the landscape behind him was moving, a black-orange monster rolling across ATL's property. The Blazer rang with Loren's laughter. The woman on the radio was calling for available units to investigate and announced she'd called the volunteer fire department. Since they—having local priorities well in hand—were fighting the fire Loren had started on the Figueracion Ranch, Loren figured they would be a while. Loren headed north, past the railroad bridge and the main entrance, to the north perimeter of the facility. He shifted to four-wheel drive and headed cross-country, staying north of the perimeter road and out of sight of surveillance cameras.

Shrum's radio voice reported from the UFO field that he'd found Blazer No. 6 near the site of the explosion and that Vincent Nazzarett's body was next to it. It looked as if Vinnie had been shot.

There were at least two other bodies on the scene, though he couldn't identify them. The woman dispatcher announced that Nazzarett had been on a special exercise with Mr. Patience and that Patience hadn't answered his radio. She would contact Mr. Patton at Vista Linda and ask him to take charge.

The dispatcher probably had her hands full by now, and had other things to do than keep up the perimeter watch. Loren spun the wheel, pressed the accelerator, and launched the Blazer across the perimeter road at the shining silver fence.

The chain link shivered and buckled and gave way. Aluminum poles tore from the ground. Piled tumbleweed leaped like frightened jackrabbits. Razor wire screeched wickedly along the roof, raising Loren's nape hairs, then was left behind.

Loren continued his slalom across country, dodging chollo, yucca, and ocotillo. He could see very little ahead of him, neither the glow of illuminated buildings nor that of the fire he'd started, just the next bit of scrub. And then there was a black line ahead, something higher than the flat horizon, and he slowed and came to a halt.

There was an earthen mound stretching across his path, maybe ten feet high, stretching left and right as far as he could see. Stuck into it were things that seemed like traffic signs, round objects atop poles seen only in silhouette.

He left the Blazer idling, took the Dragunov, and climbed the mound. The climb left him breathless.

The mound was about twenty feet across. Lights twinkled distantly a couple miles away. Beyond was a crescent of flame, a wicked orange-red, its precise outline partly obscured by its own smoke. Loren laughed at the sight. For the first time he could smell fire. Behind him the woman dispatcher, her voice loud in the night, continued moving units around, continued asking Patience to check in.

Loren stepped up to the nearest of the poles. It *was* a traffic sign, or something similar, an aluminum pole ten feet high set into a thing like a Christmas-tree stand and held against the wind with guy wires. The round sign atop the pole bore only the number 33.

Loren looked left and right. The signs on either side were presumably 32 and 34.

Whatever it was, it was none of his business. He could get the Blazer over the mound without any trouble, and that was what he had come to check.

A helicopter roared out of the north, passed overhead at a low altitude and high speed. Forest Service, probably, come to check out the range fire.

As the Blazer topped the rise, it occurred to Loren that he was rolling over the LINAC. Long shotguns buried in the ground, he thought, barrel-to-barrel.

Maybe something more needed to go boom before Patience would show up. Maybe a range fire wasn't enough for him.

The more destruction, he thought, the wider the investigation. And Loren was just the person to make certain the investigation focused on Patience and his activities.

Maybe this would all end up making Cipriano a hero. Deputy Chief Dominguez, he thought (visualizing the news story), shot while attempting to arrest the perpetrators. The murderers subsequently blew themselves up trying to set off an explosion to cover their crime.

It was possible, he supposed, that the public was stupid enough to believe that. He doubted whether any investigators were—not unless their own superiors motivated them to drop the investigation.

Which could be arranged.

He came to a blacktop road and turned onto it, shifting the Blazer out of four-wheel drive. The lights of the main facility glowed ahead of him. He slowed the Blazer, downshifting, while he got his bearings. Another helicopter roared overhead.

The security office, he thought, was in a metal-walled building on the other side of the facility. He hit the accelerator, shifted into a higher gear, pulled the cowl of his watch cap down over his face. The faster and less recognizable he was, the better.

There were only a few cars parked by some of the office buildings—the area the employees called the Fairgrounds was otherwise empty. The strange jagged curves of *Discovered Symmetries* slid by on his right. He dodged between two buildings and saw Security HQ and its parking lot right ahead of him.

Six identical Blazers were lined up in the parking lot, all reversed in their parking spaces as if anticipating a fast getaway. There were also about a dozen civilian vehicles. Just, Loren thought, like horses tied up at the cavalry corral. The lot was well lit, but Loren couldn't see anyone in it. He drove into the lot and parked at the end of the row of Blazers.

The dispatcher was having trouble getting Mr. Patton, or indeed any of the off-duty people, to report. It was a Friday night; most were off somewhere having fun.

Loren stepped out of his vehicle, smashed the passenger-door window of the next Blazer with the butt of his UZI, and opened the door. He opened the gun compartment, pressed 571 with a gloved finger, and liberated another pair of machine pistols and several magazines. Helicopter blades throbbed through the air. There was a heavy smell of smoke. Loren put two of his three weapons back in his own vehicle, then stepped out the front of the line of Blazers, got on one knee, set the gun for full automatic, and opened fire.

Joy filled Loren's heart as bullets whanged off grilles. Headlights exploded. Blazers seemed to sink to their knees in submission as air gushed from punctured tires.

There was sudden silence as the magazine ran dry. Over the ringing in his ears Loren could hear pleasant summer-rain sounds as perforated radiators drained their contents onto the blacktop. Loren gave a long war whoop as he dropped the empty magazine, inserted another, and opened fire again, concentrating his fire on the vehicles that hadn't been sufficiently damaged the first time.

When that magazine was dry he inserted another. Let the apocalypse be general, he thought, delighted with his capacity to destroy, and he turned and hosed the civilian vehicles. He didn't want these people chasing him in *anything*—and any action that tended to the discredit of Patience was highly desired. He dropped the UZI onto the pavement, got in his Blazer, and backed out.

"Shots fired! Shots fired! Vicinity of Security HQ!"

Panic had entered the dispatcher's voice. Loren was surprised she'd heard the firing at all through the combined sonic interference of the roaring choppers and the steel walls of her building. Maybe one of his bullets had gone through the backstop of her wall. He accelerated, more war whoops passing his lips, and raced through the gate. Entering another cloud of uncertainty.

If this didn't get Patience to surface, Loren figured he'd just have to blow something up.

He headed north out of the Fairgrounds. POLICE OFFICER GOES BERSERK, he thought, DEMOLISHES RESEARCH FACILITY. The imagined headlines were very satisfactory.

If caught, he'd plead temporary insanity. He figured a good case could be made.

He switched to four-wheel drive and left the blacktop, bounced across the terrain till he decided he was a safe distance from any populated part of the facility. He killed his headlights and idled his engine, then got out of the Blazer to take a look around.

He wanted to scream and caper in triumph as he looked down at the ATL facility. The air was heavy with smoke, and the lights glowed red in the murk. Two helicopters churned back and forth in the distance, their undersides reflecting fire.

Exhilaration sang through Loren's mind. He took off the watch cap and let the wind cool the sweat that had plastered his hair to his head. He concluded that he'd won the first eleven rounds of the fight. The only way the challenger could win now was by a surprise knockout, and he doubted that was forthcoming. He had Patience on the ropes.

Righteousness ran through him like a river.

The woman dispatcher was replaced by a male voice who spoke with somewhat more authority, if not comprehension—presumably Mr. Patton, or someone like him, had at last arrived.

Loren heard the whooping of a siren on the wind and saw lights flashing, and he removed the caps from the eyepieces of his field glasses and scanned the horizon. Beneath the row of lights he saw one of the sheriff's department Broncos racing toward the facility from the main gate.

Loren grinned, imagining the blow to Patience's pride if he ever learned that outsiders had been called to help bail out his reeling security troopers, his own little carefully trained commando force that had been bushwhacked by a lone Apache.

Still, Loren would need to be more careful now that reinforcements had showed up. He looked at his watch.

At least nine hours till dawn. *Plenty* of time left before he'd have to withdraw. And of course he could always come back.

He wondered how long he could keep this up. Cochise, Geronimo, and Mangas Coloradas had lasted years.

Loren swept the field glasses over the facility. Another Bronco was rolling down the main road. This was going to be a long night for poor Shorty. A few employees' cars, unhip to any alarms, were cruising toward the exit, just late workers heading for home.

There was a needle-shaped jet parked by the hangar on the runway. Loren contemplated the satisfaction of blowing it to smithereens.

One low, windowless building, off to the east of the main group, had a number of cars parked in its little blacktop lot. It was, Loren realized, the LINAC.

Then, outlined clearly in the 10x power of the glasses, Loren saw an ATL Blazer with a shattered windshield and single remaining headlight.

A surge of glorious power took Loren's breath away. Acid joy burned at his heart. Patience had materialized, position known, a particle come within range of the detectors.

Round twelve, Loren thought. He jammed the watch cap back on his head, pulled the cowl down over his face, then ran to the back of the Blazer and started rummaging through the remaining explosives. He found one of the jellied gasoline bombs and held it in his hand.

That should do it, he figured.

Loren jumped in the Blazer and took off across country, a particle accelerating toward its target. He bounced into the LINAC parking lot and pulled up two slots away from Patience's Blazer.

He paused for a moment and let the surroundings soak into him. The air reeked with smoke; the whole southern horizon glowed red. Helicopters prowled restlessly through the air.

There was no one around to see him. He hung an UZI around his neck by the strap and took the firebomb in his hand, then got out of the car and approached Patience's Blazer. Silver-rimmed holes showed where his bullets had punched through the tailgate. He looked in through the shattered side windows and saw, to his joy and delight, that an UZI and a Tanfoglio had been laid carefully on the passenger seat. The two weapons that Patience had planned to commit murder with: the man probably didn't want anyone to see him with them. He had disarmed himself.

Loren, pure delight coursing through him, reached in through the broken window and pressed in the dashboard lighter. He waited for it to pop out, then used it to light the fuse on the firebomb. He backed into the parking lot and cocked his hand to throw.

One of the twin doors of the LINAC building slammed open and Patience walked out. He was with another man that, through some process of insight, Loren was willing to bet was Joseph Dielh. And from the earnest expression on Patience and the haunted, miserable look on Dielh, Loren could tell that Patience had spent the last hour or so explaining to Dielh how it wasn't his fault, how he really hadn't fucked up; and that Dielh was trying to figure out how to somehow extricate himself from this sorry affair without a desperate Patience putting a lot of bullets into him.

Loren screamed in rage and threw the firebomb at the both of them. It fell short and smashed open, covering the blacktop with a roaring sheet of fire. By then Patience and his companion were running.

Loren clawed for the UZI, snapped the safety off, and worked the bolt. His bullets chipped pieces from the LINAC's concrete walls as Patience followed his friend through the metal doors.

The doors were dragged shut by someone safely out of sight. Loren held the UZI against his chest and charged, circling to avoid the lake of flame he'd made. Loren held the gun in his right hand and yanked at door handles with his left. Both were locked. He backed up a step and pulled the trigger. Impressive, solid clanging sounds rang through the air as the gun punched a series of neat, silver-rimmed holes through both doors.

The gun's bolt locked back and Loren reached into his pocket for another clip. His breath was fire in his laboring lungs as he dragged air in through the woolen mask of the watch cap. He shook sweat from his eyes as his clumsy gloved fingers rummaged in his pocket amid spent brass.

The door boomed open and Patience came lunging out. Loren caught a glimpse of eye whites and bared teeth, heard a scream on the air, and then the shod heel of Patience's foot slammed into his solar plexus.

The blow was probably intended to take several ribs out, but the steel flak jacket absorbed most of the impact and Loren was only knocked back. Surprise clanged in his head. Patience lunged forward for another kick and Loren knew somehow to leap to one side, just as he'd done in his last boxing match, and unload a right cross over the other man's guard as Patience's lunge carried him forward and off balance.

Patience was faster than the con had been, or Loren had grown slower, because Patience turned his head and Loren's knuckles only grazed the side of his face. Patience whipped a back-knuckle punch into Loren's face by way of reply, but Loren tucked his chin into his chest and the knuckles bounced off his forehead. Loren's second right punch was better than the first, coming in low for Patience's left kidney, and the man grunted and turned pale. He spun away, arms shooting out as he tried to connect with blind spin punches, but Loren, weird joy caroling in his head, ducked under, bunched his fists, and came in.

A blinding pain in his right knee brought Loren to a staggering halt. The joint gave way. Asphalt scraped flesh from his knee as he went down. Agony jolted him and tears of pain sprang to his eyes. Patience pulled back the knife-edge kick he'd used against Loren's knee and aimed a second one at Loren's face.

Immobilize the opponent before using high kicks. Patience had even *told* him.

Loren brought up his right arm and managed to throw the kick over one shoulder. His left fist lunged out for Patience's groin, trying to take advantage of the fact that the man's legs were wide apart, but he grazed the thigh with his knuckles instead.

Patience tried another kick at Loren's head. Loren blocked it with both forearms, then grabbed the leg and pulled. Patience clawed at Loren for support as he fell, and his nails streaked Loren's cheeks with red. Loren smashed him in the face with a rising elbow as he came down.

Patience managed to twist away somehow, get behind Loren, and then Loren was brought up short as something cut across his windpipe. He clawed at it, found that it was the strap of the UZI. Patience had hold of the gun with both hands and was using the strap as a garrote.

Loren flailed, liquid terror bubbling through his brain as he tried to tear the gun out of Patience's hands. Pain tore through his skull as the strap under his chin yanked him off the asphalt.

Patience had got to his feet somehow. He'd turned away from Loren, the UZI strap over one shoulder, his back bent beneath Loren's back. Loren's entire weight was borne by the strap. His legs thrashed in the air.

The garrote was not fully effective—the angle was a little wrong, and Loren's raised collar made it less efficient—and Loren managed to gasp a little air into his lungs. He threw his weight left and right, trying to loosen Patience's grip, and accomplished nothing than letting the garrote get a better bite on him. The urge to vomit queased through his belly. He tried to kick Patience's legs out from under him but couldn't bring any force to bear. His own right leg wasn't working properly. Blackness pulsed on the edge of his vision.

He threw both hands over his head, hammering his doubled fists into the sides of Patience's head. Patience swayed a bit, but recovered his balance. Patience dug his chin deeper into his chest and evaded Loren's next smash. Loren tried again, hitting with palm heels to the temples and then clawing for Patience's eyes. His gloves made the clawing difficult, but he heard Patience give a grunt as the glove seams gouged flesh from lids and sockets. Loren reached back again and clawed once more. Somehow he got hold of both ears and twisted, pulling hard . . .

A hoarse scream grated on Loren's ears. Patience dumped him on the asphalt. Agony jolted through his knee. He dragged in the smoky air, feeling it draw blossoming fire through his chest.

His vision was completely black, but somehow, with the strange exhilarating intuition he remembered from his boxing days, he knew precisely where Patience was and how he was standing. He got his good leg under him and lunged upward, one rising uppercut connecting solidly with Patience's groin, a follow-up right hitting him in the side of the head. A third punch struck only empty air and swung him off balance, and Loren's bad knee gave out again. Asphalt bit at his arm. He tried to rise and fell again. Hot cinders filled the air. The flak jacket weighed a ton.

Loren's vision began to clear and he saw Patience getting to his feet only a few yards away. Loren planted his good left foot and rose, but

Patience staggered away, his shoulders hunched to protect his groin. The side of his face was a spiderweb of blood. He was heading for the door.

Loren lurched after him. At one point he realized he was holding Patience's left ear in his doubled right fist, and he opened the hand and let it fall.

Patience made it to the door ahead of him and tried to shut it in his face. Loren grabbed the door handle and the two men wrenched it back and forth for a frantic moment before Loren yanked it free and spilled backward, slamming breathless against the concrete wall but somehow managing to retain his grip on the door. Patience turned and ran, but he couldn't manage any speed and kept hitting the cork-covered walls, knocking free some of the papers that had been pinned there. Scientific articles tumbled in a blizzard of print.

Heaving poisonous smoky air into his lungs, Loren reached for the UZI, which was hanging down his back. He pulled it around and reached for a magazine. His movements were slow and deliberate, matching the speed of his jangled thought. He fit the magazine in, and the bolt automatically slammed the first round into the chamber. Loren blinked sweat from his eyes and pointed the gun down the corridor.

Patience was nowhere to be seen. He'd got away. Loren took a few more breaths, trying to clear his spinning head, then lumbered after. Pain shot through his right knee at every step.

Loren followed the trail of papers that Patience had knocked to the floor till the papers ran out, then took a good grip on the UZI and lunged through the next door.

Electronics breathed around him. He was on the balcony of the *Dr. Strangelove* war room, the control room of the LINAC, and the holographic projector was frozen in the middle of some explosion, little red and blue and green particles hovering perfectly and silently in the air. The thirty-inch high-definition monitors glowed with computer-generated images, graphs, silver columns of raw data.

A half dozen people were staring up at him. Apparently they were in the midst of conducting some line of research. Loren recognized Kurita and Steffens and the man Loren suspected was Joseph Dielh.

"Bill Patience!" Loren bellowed. "You seen him?" His voice sounded strange to his ears, gravelly and weak.

He doubted he was recognizable. The flak jacket bulked him up to several sizes larger than he normally was, and the watch cap covered most of his face. Strangulation had altered the quality of his voice.

He still held a wild hope he could get away with this kind of behavior.

"Bill Patience!" he repeated. "He needs medical attention. I've got to get to him."

The people on the lower level stared at each other, then back at Loren. Loren pointed the gun blindly and fired off a burst. Television monitors exploded. Glass rained. The people below scrabbled for cover. Legs and buttocks poked out from behind and beneath consoles.

"Don't fuck with the Cybercops, assholes!" Loren said, his voice loud in the sudden silence. "Dielh, get up here!"

There was no answer from Dielh, if that was indeed who it was—Loren could see him plainly crouching under a console, his buttocks raised high in the air as he covered his head in his hands. "Dielh!" Loren said. "I can *see* your sorry ass!" Loren fired another burst for the sheer joy of it. Glass showered onto the floor. Legs twitched and scrambled for cover.

"Virtual matter!" Loren said. "Kaluza-Klein! You got it all wrong, you fucking moron!"

He fired off the rest of the magazine. Sparks leaped, gushed fire. Electricity arced across violated consoles. "Think about it!" he yelled. Loren dropped the magazine and reached for another one. This unbalanced him and he went over, the bad knee giving way. Pain jolted through his spine as he landed on his tailbone. He slapped another magazine into the gun and hauled himself upright.

With a sudden burbling hiss, foam began to rain out of sprinkler heads set into the ceiling. An alarm began to clatter. Loren laughed and staggered out of the room. White foam drooled from his shoulders.

He stared down the corridor, then noticed that one of the bare concrete walls had a streak of blood. There was blood on the floor as well. Patience had been this way.

He followed floor tile marked by little droplets of blood, each a perfect sticky circle, until they ended at a heavy metal door that led to the room where the Cray, and allegedly Heisenberg, were kept. There was a bloody handprint on the door. Joy frolicked through Loren's heart.

He hit the door with his shoulder and lurched inward. Two strangers, a man and a woman, stared at him from beneath computer consoles. Someone had clearly told them to stay under cover. "Where is Mr. Patience?" Loren asked. His eyes searched the beige carpet for blood trails. "I've got a message for him."

No answer save the clanging bell. No blood trails, either. Loren moved farther into the room, his eyes flicking left and right.

The black Cray sat on his left beneath its transparent tetrahedron, humming merrily. The sign about Heisenberg was gone. Apparently he'd had the sense to disappear into his own uncertainty relationship before any of this trouble started. Banks of consoles and monitors gleamed on the far side. Several tall rows of disk-drive cabinets stood like high-tech bookshelves on the right.

"I don't believe I heard your answer," Loren prompted. "Where is Bill Patience?" He limped closer to the two strangers.

"Jesus," the man said. "Jesus oh God."

Loren fired at the Cray. Vaporized coolant jetted from the tetrahedron as if from a high-pressure steam hose, blasting against the ceiling. The air turned humid in an instant. Buzzing alarms filled the room. A rumbling noise layered itself onto the background as emergency pumps were triggered. Coolant began to cycle through the clear tubes that arched over the machine. Loren stared in delight at this display.

"Oh, God," said the man. The voice recalled Loren to his duty.

Loren pointed the UZI at him. "Where's Patience?" he said. "My message won't wait."

"Sir," the man said. "Sir."

"Tell me," Loren said.

"Sir," the man said, "the circuits in the Cray are gallium arsenide. When it melts, this whole room is going to fill up with poison gas."

"Is it?" Loren wondered if this was true. If so, the apocalypse was better than he'd anticipated. Magnanimously he decided to spare the company's aircraft from destruction.

He gestured toward the door with the gun. "Better clear out, then."

The man looked at him dumbly for a moment, then got to his feet and ran. The woman, coughing on the coolant that filled the air, waited long enough to see whether Loren was going to gun the first refugee down, saw he wasn't, then followed.

The jet of coolant lost energy. Fine precipitation was raining down through the room, and there was a ghastly smell. Loren could breathe well enough through the woolen screen of his mask. The emergency pumps seemed to be laboring.

Loren lurched back toward the door. "Bill," he called, his tone informative. "If we don't clear out, we're going to die."

The jet of coolant died away. The Cray began spitting out flaming pieces of itself, the clear tetrahedron shattering entirely. One of the chunks shot into the first rank of disk-drive cabinets, smashing the plastic cover. The emergency pumps groaned.

William Patience charged out from behind the tall row of disk drives, swinging a broomstick in both hands. Apparently he'd made a visit to the janitor's closet.

Loren ducked and threw up an arm. The broomstick cracked with stunning force on his underarm, pain rocketing all the way to Loren's toes. Loren took a step back, tried to make himself grab the broomstick, and failed.

Loren's ears rang. His left arm was paralyzed from the stick attack. He realized that without entirely deciding to, he'd just fired several bullets into his opponent.

Patience gaped at him. The man did not look well. The left ear was gone, his face was covered with drying blood, his eyes were swollen to narrow cracks. There were little cuts all over his face from flying glass. He was making an odd whistling noise. Blood began to drizzle on the soft beige carpet beneath his feet.

Patience lunged forward and swung the broomstick again. Loren dodged—the old reflexes were coming back—and fired more bullets. All of them seemed to strike home. At least one hit the disk-drive cabinet behind Patience, suggesting that it had passed through his body.

A piece of the Cray shattered a console monitor. White smoke was pouring from the shattered tetrahedron. Loren realized that the whistling noise that Patience was making was air sucking in and out of his chest wounds.

Incredibly, Patience swung again. He was getting easier to dodge, and Loren fired another few rounds. Patience went to his knees.

Patience raised the broomstick and began beating energetically at the carpet in front of him like a robot gone berserk. He lost his grip during one of the backswings and the broomstick clattered across the room, but this seemed to make no difference to his motion. His arms kept swinging up and down.

The air was burning Loren's lungs. He decided he'd had enough of this pistol-packing farce and emptied the magazine into Patience's body.

Loren staggered back into the corridor and shut the door behind him. Alarms were ringing through the corridor with unacceptable volume. There was an evil smell of smoke in the place. He dropped the empty magazine from the UZI and began searching his pockets for another. There was none to be found. He was out of bullets.

He dragged his bad leg down the white tile corridor. His body was soaked with sweat and the range fire glowed through the open door beyond. A sense of triumph rang distantly in his mind. He'd just gone twelve rounds with the champ and the fight was his by a knockout. If he had the energy he'd start screaming out war whoops again.

There was a clattering in the doorway and a man ran in, clutching an UZI in his white-knuckled fingers. The man stared in sudden and startled terror at the weird figure, bulky and masked and spattered in blood.

Paul Rivers, Loren saw. Time to surrender and plead insanity.

Time, he thought wearily, to atone.

If he weren't around to explain this, there was no way they'd ever figure it out.

He began to raise his hands. The empty machine pistol was in one of them.

Rivers, mistaking his movement, opened fire. The flak jacket was never meant to protect against such a torrent of bullets.

Loren was dead before he hit the floor.

T W E N T Y - T H R E E

Loren fell from the sky amid a rain of brown soil. Shock rattled his bones as he struck hard earth. Pain shrieked through one ankle. He sensed something falling and hunched. Whatever it was banged off his armored shoulders and back.

He lay stunned, crumpled onto his rifle. The light dazzled his eyes. He blinked and took a long breath.

Rage boiled in him. He knew precisely what had happened to him and knew he had been cheated. He jumped to his feet and screamed and kicked furiously at the ground around him. Pain jolted through his left ankle but he ignored it. He waved the Dragunov at the blue sky and white-hot sun and shouted pointless defiance.

His fury ebbed. Loren fell silent and stood, chest heaving, and stared at the world around him.

It was a bright New Mexico afternoon. Cumulus drifted silver in the sky. The mountains to the north, green and brown and gray, were familiar. He was still on ATL land.

He stood on a flat plain covered mostly with smooth green grass. A few yuccas stretched skyward here and there, along with scrubby trees.

Lying at his feet was an aluminum pole with a round sign on top. The sign had 33 written on it in large letters.

Idiots, he thought. They would look to see whether any of the signs had disappeared, vanished down the *t*-axis, and find that none of them had. Sign No. 33 would still stand atop the LINAC's mound.

None of them would figure out that it had been duplicated, along with Loren, sometime else.

Loren was covered with sweat, and the sun was hot. He tore the watch cap off his head, unzipped his camouflage jacket, and threw it to the ground. He unstrapped the flak jacket and let it fall at his feet. Sweat plastered his hair to his head.

He wondered when he was.

ATL did not exist now, that much was clear. They'd run an experiment in the LINAC, probably trying to duplicate Friday night's results, and Loren had been standing in the darkness, gazing at Sign No. 33, when the accelerator had fired and dimensions had uncoiled and . . .

And had made him here out of virtual matter. In midair, ten feet off the ground, standing atop a mound that did not exist in this time. He had fallen amid a shower of soil, simple dirt, a part of the mound that he'd been standing on, re-created here along with him.

He looked around him at the vegetation. The grass, green with the rains of summer, seemed different, in a not-quite-definable way, from what he was used to. It was thicker on the ground—lush for New Mexico, though Wisconsin would probably find it pretty bare. Possibly it had been a very wet summer; maybe it was a different kind of grass altogether.

Had there been a different kind of grass here once upon a time? Before white people came to graze their cattle? He strained his memory, but he simply didn't know the answer.

Or maybe he was in his own future, after the climate shift people were predicting. Maybe things had got wetter.

He took his field glasses and scanned the landscape. He couldn't tell what types of trees were cloaking the northern mountains, whether they were the same types he knew. To the south there was nothing but more plains, gradually more rugged. If Atocha existed at all, it was too distant to see.

If he was in the future, it was a future in which every trace of ATL had been carefully removed. He wasn't sure if he liked that idea or not.

His binoculars froze on a distant herd of antelope. They were moving lazily, grazing on the soft grass. Maybe it was hunting season.

He wondered if, somewhere down the *t*-axis, he had managed to get William Patience. He hoped he had.

At least he'd got the four coconspirators. He remembered that much.

He thought about his family and guilt stabbed at his heart. He'd made things safer for them. He thought.

But he had deserted them. Not voluntarily, but he had. He couldn't help them anymore.

He licked his dry lips and tasted salt. He was getting thirsty.

Pain throbbed through his left ankle.

Something glinted off in the sky, and Loren's heart leaped. He looked at it wildly. A plane? Sunlight off the white wing of a bird?

He didn't see it again.

Loren bent and looked at his belongings. He picked up the jacket, stuck the watch cap in one pocket, and tied the arms around his waist. The flak jacket was too heavy to carry for very long, so he decided to leave it. He picked up Sign No. 33 and stood it on its rest next to the body armor, just in case he needed to come back for it.

He picked up the Dragunov and began limping southeast. He'd hit the Rio Seco, then follow it. His ankle felt hot and swollen against his boot, but he was afraid to take the boot off to examine it. He might not be able to get the boot back on.

If there wasn't water in the river, he was probably going to be in trouble.

Weariness weighed him down. How many years had it been since he'd slept? He gave a little laugh at the thought.

Past or future? he wondered.

He tried to remember what Singh had told him about travel into the past. It was impossible, Singh thought, to change the past, because . . . because why?

Because you just couldn't.

Or if you did, Loren remembered, you created a whole other universe. That was what Kurita had wanted to do, create a whole universe.

Maybe Loren had just done it. Maybe he'd become God. Maybe that was why the vegetation was a little different here.

A weird giddiness floated through his mind. He couldn't really believe in any of this. His feet were moving on far too solid ground for it to have any relationship to this fantasy.

He hoped he was in the past, whether he was in another universe or not. He could survive well enough in the past. He had a state-of-the-art semiautomatic rifle with a 4x scope and spare ammunition. And he knew that there was a huge lode of silver in a bluff above the Wahoo Wash. Assuming there were any white people out here at all, he could do well. Maybe he could help build an Atocha in which the benign, styled, art-deco future was not a fantasy, in which it all came true . . .

If he was too early, if the whites hadn't come yet . . . well, he'd get along well enough with whoever was here. He could teach them things. He didn't know what, but he was sure there was something.

He wondered if he was in his future. That was where Randal had gone, and Singh had said you couldn't go into the past.

He wondered if he had anything to teach the future.

He realized, of course, that he might not have time. Virtual matter was supposedly short-lived. Randal had lasted only a few days. Loren might live for several days here and then dissolve into the nothingness from which he sprang.

But then Randal[2] had vanished because the universe had caught up with him, because Loren had opened Randal[1]'s coffin and provided a link between his present and future. Loren might have years, decades.

Thoughts of his wife and daughters rolled through him like a tide. Sorrow bit at his heart and his vision was dazzled by tears.

It was very hot, and Loren was very tired and very thirsty. The limp was slowing him down. He hadn't remembered to bring a canteen. He might well die of thirst before the universe had a chance to catch up with him and disperse him into nothing.

He hoped to hell there would be water in the stream bed.

There had once been, he remembered, a spring beneath Atocha plaza; and according to the Apaches there would be a spring there again.

He figured he had to take it on faith.

WALTER JON WILLIAMS

☐ ☐	55787-5	ANGEL STATION	$4.95 Canada $5.95
☐ ☐	55791-3	AMBASSADOR OF PROGRESS	$3.95 Canada $4.95
☐ ☐	55798-0	THE CROWN JEWELS	$3.50 Canada $4.50
☐ ☐	50181-0	FACETS	$3.95 Canada $4.95
☐ ☐	55796-4	HARDWIRED	$3.50 Canada $4.50
☐ ☐	55783-2	HOUSE OF SHARDS	$3.95 Canada $4.95
☐ ☐	51184-0	KNIGHT MOVES	$3.95 Canada $4.95
☐ ☐	55785-9	VOICE OF THE WHIRLWIND	$3.95 Canada $4.95

Buy them at your local bookstore or use this handy coupon:
Clip and mail this page with your order.

Publishers Book and Audio Mailing Service
P.O. Box 120159, Staten Island, NY 10312-0004

Please send me the book(s) I have checked above. I am enclosing $ _____
(please add $1.25 for the first book, and $.25 for each additional book to cover postage and handling.
Send check or money order only—no CODs).

Name _____
Address _____
City _____ State/Zip _____
Please allow six weeks for delivery. Prices subject to change without notice.